IN THE NIGHT OF THE HEAT

BLAIR UNDERWOOD PRESENTS

IN THE NIGHT OF THE HEAT

A Tennyson Hardwick Novel

TANANARIVE DUE AND STEVEN BARNES

ATRIA BOOKS
New York London Toronto Sydney

ATRIA BOOKS
A Division of Simon & Schuster, Inc.
1230 Avenue of the Americas
New York, NY 10020

First Atria Books hardcover edition September 2008

For information about special discounts for bulk purchases, please contact Simon & Schuster Special Sales at 1-800-456-6798 or business@simonandschuster.com.

Manufactured in the United States of America

10   9   8   7   6   5   4   3   2   1

Library of Congress Cataloging-in-Publication Data

Underwood, Blair.
In the night of the heat : a Tennyson Hardwick novel / Blair Underwood; by Tananarive Due and Steven Barnes.—1st Atria Books hardcover ed.
p.   cm.
At head of title: Blair Underwood presents
1. African American men—Fiction.   2. Actors—Fiction.   3. Private investigators—Fiction.   4. Hollywood (Los Angeles, Calif.)—Fiction.   I. Due, Tananarive, date.   II. Barnes, Steven, date.   III. Title.   IV. Title: Blair Underwood presents.

PS3621.N38315   2008
813'.6—dc22   2008030883

ISBN-13: 978-1-4165-6997-8
ISBN-10:   1-4165-6997-9

For the missing, the buried and the lost

I'm afraid you're a little late, Virgil.
We already got the guilty man.
—Sheriff Gillespie, *In the Heat of the Night*

Suggested MP3 Soundtrack

"Night Time Is the Right Time" (Aretha Franklin)
"Hollywood Swinging" (Kool & The Gang)
"Turn This Mutha Out" (MC Hammer)
"Stronger" (Kanye West)
"Superstition" (Stevie Wonder)
"Like You'll Never See Me Again" (Alicia Keys)
"(Don't Fear) The Reaper" (Blue Öyster Cult)
"Drown in My Own Tears" (Aretha Franklin)
"Theme from *Shaft*" (Isaac Hayes)
"Erotic City" (Prince)
"Closer" (Nine Inch Nails)
"All Blues" (Miles Davis)
"Groaning the Blues" (Eric Clapton)
"Let the Good Times Roll (Live)" (B.B. King)
"Cross Road Blues" (Robert Johnson)
"Hurt" (Johnny Cash)
"Oh, Mary Don't You Weep" (The Swan Silvertones)
"If I Was Your Woman/Walk on By" (Alicia Keys)
"Let's Stay Together" (Al Green)

IN THE NIGHT OF THE HEAT

ONE

My agent had just said the impossible—words any actor would kill to hear. But before I could be sure my ears weren't fooling me, I saw the gun.

It was noon, and Sunset's West Hollywood sidewalks swarmed with cell phone–symbiote lunch zombies. When Len Shemin called, I was scouting a handsome oak desk at a secondhand furniture store's curbside, killing time before I had to get back on set. The dark-stained wood was bolstered by iron struts at the legs and base. It squatted on the sidewalk like a massive pirate chest, something that might have graced Andrew Carnegie's office back in 1900. I was wondering how it would look in my den when my phone buzzed.

"Ten?" Len said. "Just heard from Lynda Jewell's office. She and Ron want to meet you tomorrow. Right across the street from where CAA used to be, at the Peninsula."

Impossible, I thought, as someone brushed against me. Two wiry, tattooed arms in front of me looked like green snakes, and one of them lunged for a low-hanging waistband. The jerky movement made me freeze and forget I'd just heard my fortune told.

"Ten?" my agent said in my ear. My killer was right in front of me, not a step away. I knew at least four ways to stop him before he drew the weapon, but reflexes don't work when your brain is locked in emotional carbonite. I couldn't breathe. I couldn't move. It was the best day of my life, and I was about to die.

A freckled hand emerged from the back of his pants, pointed in a mock pistol's L shape. The gunslinger was a pimple-splotched kid, about fifteen, grinning at me like a fool. "I know you!" the gunslinger said.

But even after I realized the weapon was only in my head, my gut and the knot of muscles at the small of my back tensed when he squeezed the invisible trigger. A year after some very serious professionals had tried to plant me in the desert, I still expected someone to put a hole in my head one day. History never dies.

I couldn't smile for the kid. I gave him a wave I hoped was polite.

"Did you hear me?" Len mosquito-whined in my ear.

I stepped beneath the awning's shade to lean against the shop's white-brick wall. My father used to stop and lean against a wrought-iron gate when we walked from the church parking lot to the sanctuary, when his heart didn't feel right. Sometimes you need to stop whatever you're doing to help your heart remember its job. The tattooed kid yammered to a Prius-load of college kids, pointing me out as evidence.

"Lynda Jewell?" I said. "Ron Jewell, too? Tomorrow?" Repeating the basic elements was like pinching myself to be sure I was awake. Anyone else? Stevie Spielberg would make it a Trifecta.

"A meet-and-greet at the bar. Five. What's your schedule?"

Meetings like that didn't happen to people like me. That kind of meeting was an anecdote an actor might recall on *Letterman*, or on *Oprah*. My schedule was wide fucking open.

"That's what I thought." Len's voice wavered. Len Shemin is glad when good things happen for me, which is more than most people can say about their blood relatives. "Her assistant's called twice already. We sent in your packet for *Lenox Avenue*, and that's her passion project. Ron's writing the screenplay, of course. Everyone's after it: Denzel. Will. Terence. Don." The Afrostocracy's single-name club. He didn't have to say Washington, Smith, Howard, or Cheadle.

I didn't know I had a "packet," but Len's agency was trying to brand me since I got cast on *Homeland*. All those years, I'd had it backward: I had to get the work *first*, and then I'd get my agent's attention. I got a guest spot on *Homeland* after the exec producer saw me kickboxing at Gold's. He didn't know I was an actor; he just thought I looked like an FBI agent.

A guest spot ballooned to a regular gig with occasional dialogue. I was just a desk jockey or scenery in the training hall, but with three or four lines or a little stunt in every episode, it was my steadiest work in a decade. And I was a celebrity in the twentysomething set after a series of five commercials running on Cartoon Network and Comedy Central, where I was the pleasant face of Progress. "The future looks bright!" the ladies purred. Laugh if you want, but those ads sell a lot of Smartphones.

Month by month, I had enough money to pay my bills, even the surprises, and I was stashing a few dollars in a new category called "Savings." I hadn't realized how good I had it at the time, but that's why they call it hindsight.

Now, Lynda Jewell was calling. In Hollywood, there are only two women with the power to greenlight a movie—to say *Make it happen*—and Lynda Jewell at FilmQuest Studios is one of them. Her husband, Ron, is a two-time Oscar-winning screenwriter, which only adds to the shine. Maybe she'd said *Hey, call that black guy from So-and-So,* and her staff called the wrong brother. I was sure it must have happened before.

"Why me?"

"Fuck *why*. Lynda Jewell is a *who*. Just be on time."

On time? Hell, I would be two hours early. I'd eat peanuts and bring my Kindle. No traffic jam or hailstorm or other act of God or man was going to get in the way of my meeting with Lynda Jewell.

The tattooed gunslinger passed me again, still grinning. "Hey . . . Future looks bright!" he said. Three teenage girls joined his side, all Gothed up with no house to haunt. I flashed them The Smile, and they grinned, making "Hail, Hail" bows in a row.

Didn't I tell you I was a god in the late-night twentysomething world?

I was the face of the future.

Rush hour was the major disadvantage to steady work. With the sunset glaring into my eyes, I spent thirty minutes snailing Hollywood Hills's narrow cliffside roads before I reached 5450 Gleason. I was home.

As I drove up, Marcela Ruiz was smiling as she climbed down my coral steps past the cactus garden. Her latest diet had stripped off twenty pounds. Newfound confidence made her walk with a swing in her hips as if she had shed twenty years, too. When I first met her at my father's nursing home, I thought Marcela was plain, almost homely. But smiles focused Marcela's round face, bringing out her cheekbones and eyes. All along, she had been a pretty woman hidden behind her worries. I hadn't seen a sign of those worries in months.

"*Buenas noches*, Ten," she said, kissing both of my cheeks. "Captain Hardwick bet you'd be late for dinner, and I'm glad I finally won. He waits, you know."

"He does understand that I'm on a series now?" I raised my voice, hoping that Dad might hear me through the open doorway.

"Just glad you made it," she said. She cast a fond glance toward the doorway. "He's doing so good." She blinked rapidly, as if beating back tears.

I squeezed her shoulders. "*Gracias a ti.*" Thanks to you.

Marcela shook her head and pointed skyward, blowing a kiss to God. I stared after her as she climbed into her white VW Rabbit and drove off after a last wave. I liked Marcela, but I still wasn't sure I trusted that smile.

Inside, Dad was in the kitchen. *Homeland* had paid for remodeling my counters: Now they were low enough for his wheelchair. When I was growing up, we were strictly a Banquet-chicken-and-macaroni-and-franks kind of house. Dad had always been good on the grill, but now he had a library of cookbooks, an elaborate spice rack, and nothing but time on his hands. In the months between the heart attack and the stroke, he'd taken up watching cooking shows on the Food Network.

By coincidence, the two Hardwick men knew our way around the kitchen more than most women do nowadays. If it weren't for cooking and the Raiders, I'm not sure if Dad and I would have had much to talk about. But it was still better than we'd done in years.

The muscles on Dad's forearm flexed when he pivoted his wheelchair toward me. I'd learned to see past Dad's chair to notice the things worth celebrating, like a sturdy muscle in motion. Dad was about to turn seventy-seven, but his face had filled out again, not caving in on itself. A year before, Captain Richard Hardwick (Ret.) had been practically paralyzed in his nursing-home bed, unable to sit up and feed himself, a slave to the bedpan. Now, Dad was wheeling himself through the house manually, insisting on the exercise. Rescued, as Marcela put it. Sometimes I wished Dad was living across the street instead of under my roof, but moving him in with me saved his life.

"Marcela in town for the holidays?" I said.

Dad's suspicious eyebrow shot up. "Whyyou ask?" He still hated the slight slur in his voice, but he could make himself understood when it mattered.

"Thinking about Thanksgiving."

Dad hacked at an onion with his knife. His hands were steadier than they'd been in a long time, but I still felt nervous when he picked up the cutlery. "You askin' her to work on Thanksgiving?"

"Just wondered if she'd be around."

I also wondered how long I was supposed to pretend Marcela was still only Dad's nurse, and how long she would call him "Captain Hardwick" around me instead of whatever pet names she used during their hours alone. If the secret was on my account, I wanted to tell him to forget it. My mother died when I was only ten months old, and I didn't feel any need to guard her place in his heart.

However, Dad being Dad, I occasionally struggled not to imagine their intimate time together. Too Much Information. I just hoped I wouldn't have to lie one day when Dad asked me what I thought about Marcela, who was twenty-six years his junior. In the nursing home's sea of piss and apathy, Marcela had seemed like a godsend— now, there was an uncharitable voice in my head that questioned the motivations of a younger woman apparently attracted to an elderly man. Dad didn't have many resources other than his pension and insurance policy. Could that be more attractive than his heart and mind?

Snakes hissed and coiled behind that mental door, along with a self-flagellating jealousy: *You just want him all to yourself.*

At least I'd been smart enough to say nothing. Dad and I were just getting to know each other, and there's no quicker way to kill a relationship than to question another's chosen. Percy Sledge had it right: *Turn his back on his best friend, if he put her down . . .*

Best friend, or son.

"Family in Florida, like April," Dad said finally. "She's goin' down south, too."

I recognized Dad's tactic: *You stay out of my business, I'll stay out of yours.* Dad had told me it would be fine with him if I flew out to Tallahassee with my girlfriend, April, to spend Thanksgiving with her family. He said April wanted me to invite myself along, and when I asked how he knew that, he insisted that anyone could see it.

April's name prompted me to check my phone. No voicemail. It was Thursday night, but that wasn't always a guarantee, not anymore. I felt anxious, and I didn't like the feeling.

"Thursday dinner," Dad said. "She'll be here."

To change the subject, I considered telling Dad about my Friday meeting with Lynda Jewell, but I was feeling superstitious. Could loose lips kill luck? Chances were high that this meeting wouldn't amount to anything, but sometimes an actor gets lucky.

"What are we making, Dad?" I said, picking up ingredients lined up military-style on the counter: Onions. Tomatoes. Peppers. Marcela was influencing his cooking, too.

"Salllllsa," Dad said. "Wash your hands."

"Yessir."

That word "sir" used to hang me up. Behind truancy, that word was probably most responsible for the ass-whippings of my youth. Dad had demanded "sir" from me the way his father had, but the word kept getting caught in my throat. Back then, I hadn't been man enough to show my father respect in a language he understood.

We went to work at the kitchen counter, side by side, our knives snapping against the cutting boards with clocklike precision. His, then mine, and his again. We still enjoyed each other most when we didn't talk, and maybe that would never change.

But that was all right. Words aren't big enough for every occasion.

April didn't use the doorbell anymore, not since I had given her a key. At ten after seven, she let herself in after two quick, shy knocks.

Who is *THAT*? I thought in the millisecond before I remembered she was my girl. April had changed her hairstyle, framing her face with chin-length braids in the front, elegantly styled into a shorter pageboy style in the back. Her haircut made a dramatic shift on her face, from cute and girlish to queenly. For a year solid, I hadn't touched anyone else. Monogamy was the last thing I'd expected in *this* lifetime.

My girl. My *girlfriend*. My life had a new vocabulary.

April undressed herself bit by bit as she crossed the room toward me; her jacket on the coat rack, her hat on the sofa. April's ivory sweater, stretched tautly across her bosom, made me wish we were on our way upstairs. April docked herself against me. "Sorry I'm late," she said. Her lips brushed too quickly across mine. "You won't believe . . ."

I interrupted her, holding her still for a kiss with a little flavor. Her lips relaxed, offering nectar. Then she pulled away shyly, as she always did when Dad was nearby. April was smiling, but she wasn't planning to stay. I could see it in her eyes.

"So get this: The brother's car blew up," April went on. "They chase him for nearly eight miles, and his Ferrari flips into a ditch. This poor old lady he broadsided on La Cienega might not wake up, but of course he walks away without a scratch."

April's stories from work made me feel tired. After staring down a gun barrel in the desert that day, I felt no *schadenfreude*. But April hadn't been with me in the desert. She was a police reporter, and death entertained her just fine.

"They're lucky nobody got killed," April went on. "These police chases are out of control. Yeah, he robbed a bank, but sometimes guilty people go free. Deal with it."

"Saw it on TV," Dad called from the kitchen.

Dad had hooked April up with police sources more than once, old buddies from his Hollywood division, many of whom had risen high on the ladder and were willing to speak off the record. Retired Captain Richard Allen Hardwick and April Forrest were becoming a formidable team.

"Where's Chela?" April asked me.

"Chess club, till eight thirty. She said not to wait."

April lowered her chin, skeptical. *"Chess?"*

"I bribed her into giving it a try."

"How much of a bribe?"

Dad wheeled himself into the dining room, a large plate of warm nachos on his lap. Suddenly, I was surrounded by observers.

"An iPhone," I said. "Let's eat."

"Plainfoolishness," Dad said, or something like it. With words at easy disposal, Dad would have been ranting. A nascent rant glimmered in his eyes. April sighed, too. Tag team.

The fact was, it was Chela's second chess club meeting in a month, which was more commitment than she had given the drama club.

Chela needed to buy into something new, and chess had a nice ring to it. Better, by far, than her alternative. Besides, Chela hadn't come around to liking April yet and wasn't sorry to miss Thursday dinner.

For now, separate corners worked best.

Dad mumbled grace too low to hear, the only time he spoke at length without self-consciousness. We couldn't quite make out the words, but the gratitude in his voice needed no translation. "Amen," he finished.

April's face lit up. "Oh, Ten, don't forget—the Tau fund-raiser is tomorrow night."

I searched my memory and came up dry.

"The scholarship fund, remember? You signed up for the celebrity booth. People come up and take pictures with you. The committee chair loves *Homeland*, and she was so excited when I said you'd come. Give me the dates for your episodes, and she'll have all our sorors TiVo you."

I'd forgotten all about the fund-raiser. When April's workweek ended, her community work began. Her exhausting schedule was one of the reasons we saw so little of each other.

"So you're tied up tomorrow night?" I said.

"But if you're there *with* me . . ." she said playfully, and grinned. Her dimples wrestled the disappointment right out of me.

"Okay." It was hard to say no to April, another growing problem.

I felt Dad beaming silently across the table. He must have thought he'd arrived in Heaven early. If police captains had the same powers as ship captains, he would have married me to April on the spot. Dad had just heard me commit my Friday night to a scholarship fund-raiser hosted by one of the country's most prestigious black fraternities, Tau Alpha Gamma. Dad was a Tau, too, but I had refused to pledge during my year in college, mainly because I knew how badly he wanted me to. Dad never left the house except to see his doctor, so I knew better than to invite him.

"Thanks, Ten." April draped an arm over me when she kissed my cheek, which gave me hope that she might come upstairs after dinner. "Guess who else committed today? T.D. Jackson." Her voice soured. "He must be on a goodwill tour before his trial. You *know* it must be for a good cause if I can stand to be in the same room with him. I'll have to meditate first."

T.D. Jackson. Fallen football and action star, accused of murdering his ex-wife and her fiancé. Despite a mountan of physical and circumstantial evidence, he'd been acquitted in the criminal trial six months before. No surprise there. The rich and famous rarely go to prison. Justice would have another crack at him, though: The civil trial would begin in a week.

Twenty years before that, T.D. Jackson lived in my dormitory suite for about three months while I was at Southern California State. He was a star from the moment he set foot on campus. What I remember most was the parade of girls to and from his door. Once, I ran into him in the bathroom as he flushed a condom away at six in the morning. The lazy sneer on his face said: *Most of you losers aren't even out of bed yet, and I've already been laid.*

T.D. Jackson made April crazy. The thought that he had gotten away·with abusing and finally killing an upstanding sister seemed to keep her awake at night, as if his very existence set back the progress of civilization. Her teeth were already grinding.

"Innocent until proven guilty," I reminded her.

Dad and April both made comments, but they kept them under their breath. The guilt or innocence of T.D. Jackson and what his case did or didn't say about the roles of race and gender in the criminal justice system had already brought too much arguing to dinner.

But I was glad I would run into T.D. again. I didn't expect him to remember me, but I looked forward to shaking his hand and staring into his eyes. Wondered what I would see there. If I was right, T.D.'s eyes would probably broadcast the same thing April had just told me herself: Sometimes guilty people go free. Shit happens.

Deal with it.

TWO

THE DOOR TO MY OLD BEDROOM was open—Chela's room now—so April and I stood in the doorway like fretful parents, spying on her in her absence.

Chela had left her TV on when she went to school, so Missy El-liot was busting sly, angular moves to an empty room. Three dirty cereal bowls at the foot of my California King marked Chela's breakfast spot. The floor was buried in the clothes I'd bought her, most of them dyed in brooding shades. A vague rankness suggested a fast-food bag concealed somewhere in the mess. I was happy about the stack of thick, shiny schoolbooks on Chela's desk, until I wondered why they had been left behind. *She SAYS she's at a chess club meeting, but how do you KNOW?*

I pulled the door closed to shut down my doubts. Chela was right: I had to learn trust.

"We can't all be neat-freaks," April said, trying to sound positive.

"I'm just glad to get her away from the TV. And her computer."

Especially the computer. The therapist had told me that Chela's sexual history might poison her current behavior, and she was right.

I'd had to cancel one of Chela's internet accounts eight months before, when I uncovered letters and photos she sent to some bastard she'd met online, three times her age if he was a day.

She's not my daughter, or my blood, period. But what Chela and I had been through makes family out of strangers. She was the little sister I'd never had. You don't want to see your little sister in pictures like that. Or read her saying things like that, regardless of how she'd made a living before we met. I wish I could wipe the whole thing out of my memory banks. That was over, but it had been a hard patch. I hadn't even told April, and I had promised not to keep secrets.

"It doesn't look right, Ten," April said. "You're a single guy. A sixteen-year-old girl living in your house . . ."

Officially, Chela was off the books. I had consulted a lawyer who said I might be able to qualify as a foster parent if I passed the rigorous screening, but as a bachelor, my chances of adopting Chela ranged from slim to none. Not to mention that April thought Chela had a crush on me. No part of it was an ideal situation. I knew that.

April was fishing for an argument, but I had other plans. I took April's hand and led her toward my new bedroom, the smaller room at the end of the hall.

"Lynda Jewell called Len," I said. "She set up a meeting with me tomorrow."

April's eyes grew bright. "Lynda *Jewell*?"

If I'd known the news would change her face so much, I would have said it sooner.

I moved closer to April. A slight pivot of her hip, and her delicious ass swung out of reach just when I was ready to rest my hands there. She sat on the chair across from the bed, a bad sign. Despite the grin on her face, April's legs were crossed.

"This is big, Ten. *Lenox Avenue*'s in preproduction. My book club loved it, and if she wants you for Troy, it's the chance of a lifetime." Since April's roommate was a producer, April followed *Variety* like an agent herself. L.A. is truly an industry town. "I just wonder *why*. What made her call you?"

If I hadn't been so baffled myself, her wrinkled nose might have offended me.

"The commercials," I said. "Oscar material."

April dismissed my sarcasm with a wave of her hand. "I told you Progress would do things for you. Didn't I say to give it up to God? If your meeting's tomorrow, you should prep. I'll break the book down for you."

I could see how the next few hours were going to play out, and not a minute involved me unhooking April's bra. Why weren't we bouncing on my mattress, with her congratulating me from my lap? I should have asked her right then and there: *What's going on?* Maybe Dad was right. Maybe it had something to do with Thanksgiving.

"I wasn't planning to work tonight," I said.

"Are you kidding? This meeting is . . ."

"I'm more interested in *this* meeting."

I squatted beside April and let my fingertips fall to her kneecap. If she wasn't going to spend the night, I wanted her to tell me straight out. I rubbed a lazy circle on her knee where the denim was thinnest, the place her body fought quietly to break the will of her clothes. "I can't make the lady happy if I don't know what she wants," I said.

"Try to guess what she wants."

"I shouldn't have to."

It dawned on April that I was talking about her. The excited glow left her eyes; they narrowed before darting away, as if my face no longer held her interest.

"I can't stay tonight, Ten." I'd expected the words, but they smarted more than a little, and it wasn't about sexual desire. I took

April's fingers between mine and held her hand. Gently, I kissed her knuckle, then massaged my chin with it. "Why not?"

"I've told you why."

Chela. April was convinced that overnight visits made Chela feel threatened, and I couldn't deny it. Dad wasn't much better: He gave me and April significant gazes when we appeared yawning and grinning first thing in the morning. I had offered both Chela and my father a home and a new start in life: Was I supposed to give up my life in the bargain?

"The dynamic is hard for me," April said.

Dynamic was a vague, alarming word. "What dynamic?"

"Me, you, and her. The fuzzy lines. Nothing is defined. You're not her father, and she acts like you're her man. I'm supposed to be your girlfriend, but . . ." The missing end of her sentence felt like the start of an ultimatum. I waited. The scent of jasmine on her skin made my heart race. "You feel like a secret," April said finally. "Nobody in my family knows you. Like we're sneaking around. Not just Chela. It's like hiding from everyone."

"I've never tried to hide," I said gently, and April had no answer for that.

I'd always known that if I let her hang around long enough, sooner or later April Forrest would see right down into the center of Tennyson Hardwick, where the light couldn't get in. She knew more about me than any woman since Alice. And we both knew that I wasn't the man April wanted to bring home to meet Dr. Forrest and the rest of her degree-laden family, who, when I imagined them, always looked like the Huxtables from *The Cosby Show*, except that her father didn't sell Jell-O or dance a lazy soft shoe. Besides, family dinners are the first stop on the way to the altar, and I wasn't ready to board that train.

I don't know much about relationships—April was my first girlfriend since high school—but as I watched April's troubled eyes pretending to study the colorful Jacob Lawrence print on my bedroom wall, I knew I was all wrong for her. April was smart: If I knew it, she knew it, too. I used to joke with April that I was an alley cat, and she was a hothouse flower. Her family groomed her for greatness—summers abroad, Jack and Jill, music tutors—while Dad could barely pull himself away from Hollywood division's desperation long enough to make sure I had clean clothes and food every day. He was a single father, and he was a cop. Bad combo for me.

April stood up, as if she'd made a sudden decision. She rested her arms across my shoulders, the way a buddy might at Boy Scout camp. Her breath smelled like sweet citrus. I wished our clothes weren't still on.

"Ten, listen . . ." she said. "Lynda Jewell is a huge deal. You can't expect to walk in there, smile, and dazzle her. You have to go ready to play. Show Lynda Jewell who Tennyson Hardwick is. Make her wonder why she took so long to call."

In the movie *Jerry Maguire*, Cuba Gooding Jr.'s football star has a no-nonsense wife who adores him and always has his back, played with gusto by Regina King. I'd wondered how it would feel to have a helpmate like that. Victorious Roman generals used to have a slave who would whisper *"Thou art mortal"* as the crowds roared and deified them. Most of us just need someone to whisper *"You can do it. It's not too late."*

And there she was, standing right in front of me. Almost close enough to touch.

"*Lenox Avenue* takes place in 1920s Harlem," April said. "Troy is a an ex-con poet who runs numbers. He meets this society woman, the mayor's wife . . ."

We fell into the story. Troy was a heroic, complicated dude, like a part written for Leonardo Di Caprio, the kind of role that doesn't come along every day for a brother. A man with a taste for danger who'd made mistakes and paid dearly, whose honor would drive him to his grave. While April told me about his adventures and heartaches, I imagined myself walking the sidewalks in a long trench coat while the Harlem Renaissance raged around me.

I recognized him. I could play that part. Maybe I could play the *hell* out of it.

April squeezed my hand. "Go get it, Ten."

My chest fluttered, and I wondered why. Maybe I thought it was the peppers in the salsa talking to me. I kissed her. It was our best kiss all night, and maybe for two weeks or longer. We let our tongues play. We closed our eyes to sharpen the taste of each other. April reclined beneath me, giving my skin a place to rest.

The knock on my door came with perversely perfect timing.

From the hall, Chela let out a shriek that made me leap to my feet. When I flung my door open, Chela rushed in breathing fast, as if she had been chased up the stairs. Chela and I had met in chaos, and chaos lay inside almost every interaction. Her face burned red beneath cream-and-coffee skin.

"What happened?" I said.

"Bernard Faison," she said.

I wanted to lay hands on whoever had made Chela look so upset, unsettling her ringlets of curly dark hair. So far, I'd avoided jail in my quest to give Chela a home and halfway-normal life—and I resisted some elaborate fantasies about how to dispose of Internet Guy—but maybe jail was my destiny. "Who?"

"Bernard Faison. From chess club. He's a nerd, but he's on the wrestling team, too. Nice butt." She gave me an evil grin. "Wears glasses most of the time, but in contacts you can see his eyes. They're green." Her shoulders went soft, and her face was just a bit wistful. "But his name is *Bernard*. On the *chess* team?"

My hands relaxed. Chela was in drama-queen mode. Bernard

Faison, whoever he was, would live another night. Chela flopped into my easy chair without acknowledging April, demanding the full might of my attention. I noticed that Chela smelled like cigarette smoke.

"You're in the chess club, too," I said.

"But I got *paid* to do it. He does it for *fun*, and he's actually on the team. His Alekhine's Gun is the bomb."

"His *what?*" April and I said at the same time.

Chela gave us the kind of smirk kids wear when they know something you don't. "Chess talk. You wouldn't be interested." She was looking at April when she said that. Meow.

"Anyway . . ." she chattered on. "He asked me to be his date to the homecoming dance. It's like a prom, with a *dress*. It's so *retarded*. What an asshole!"

As long as Bernard Faison wasn't a married forty-six-year-old musician living in Sherman Oaks like Chela's internet shitbag, he was an improvement already. Every thought about Mr. Music was a felony in waiting.

Hallelujah. Chela was buying into high school. She had a crush on a boy her own age, without the exchange of either money or body fluids.

April rubbed the top of my head with feathery fingernails. "Anyway, it's late," she said. "Early deadline, so I'm out. Hey, Chela. Glad you had fun at your meeting."

"Later," Chela said with a careless nod, turning on my TV with the remote.

The changing of the guard.

CNN flared on the screen, a habit I'd absorbed from April. Before Chela turned the channel, I saw the footage of a grinning T.D. Jackson striding out of the Los Angeles County Courthouse after his acquittal, and his iconic football toss into the cheering crowd. A long pass. A blogger covering the trial from Tokyo had caught the ball, waving it over his head.

"Killer," April muttered to the TV as I followed her out.

"Hater," Chela said.

"Homework," I told Chela with a snap of my fingers, like my father used to do.

In a few days, T.D. Jackson would be dead; the debate silenced at last.

THREE

At five o'clock, I was at the Club Bar at the Peninsula Hotel in Beverly Hills, and I was nervous. When the bar is also a Hollywood powerhouse meeting spot, there is more work than play despite the easy flow of drinks.

On my way in, I'd brushed past Kevin Bacon coming out, cursing at a lawyer or agent on his cell phone. *What chance do YOU have?* the evil voice in my head said, and that voice worked on me the whole time I waited for the Jewells. I left a foul stink in the men's room, but the guy who came in behind me didn't notice, too busy swimming in his own anxieties.

The Jewells were running late. Very late. Lynda Jewell's assistant, a curly-haired moppet who hardly looked a day over nineteen, kept me updated from her polite distance across the room while she waited for her cell phone to ring. Every fifteen minutes, she manufactured a new excuse.

Finishing a meeting. On a call. Managing a publicity crisis.

My face made Jewell's assistant stammer, so I grinned my most devastating grin at her every time she walked near. She was my staunch ally, buying me sparkling water and refilling it before I could ask. That assistant, aptly named Faith, kept me from cussing somebody out. Or running back to the men's room.

The Peninsula, like all of L.A.'s luxury hotels, is one I know well. There are several bars—one has cabanas and a gigantic swimming pool—but the Club Bar is the vortex. The bar has an intimacy the power brokers like, with dark-paneled walls of California birch, shining brass and sconces that make it look like a guest room in the White House. Or a museum: There are six marvelous paintings of scenes from historic Los Angeles and Beverly Hills. Faith had led me to an empty wing of the bar draped in light, colorful fabrics to give even more privacy to plush cushions arranged with mounds of mock Turkish pillows.

It was a pleasant place to wait, but waiting sucks. I hate waiting.

Because the invitation had been such a compliment, the delay felt like twice the insult. By the time the Jewells were an hour late and Faith was biting her lip with worry that our brief flirtation was about to end on a sour note, the Evil Voice in my head was a full-blown chorus: *You thought YOU were going to have a meeting with Lynda Jewell?*

I was so mad, I couldn't trust whatever might come out of my mouth. I had to walk out.

As I reached for my cell phone to tell Len the bad news, Faith flew to me again—this time, she was smiling. "Lynda just drove up," she chirped.

My heart somersaulted in a way that surprised me. My palms flared with the damp heat of nerves, the way they do before a demanding stage performance. Faith patted the small of my back like a mother saying *There, there, you'll do fine.* I gallantly kissed her hand, and her cheeks flushed; overripened strawberries.

BACK OUT NOW BEFORE YOU HUMILIATE YOUR-SELF, my Evil Voice screamed.

Suddenly, she was there.

Lynda Jewell was sparrow-boned and barely over five feet tall, so she upturned her face as I towered above her. Her face looked up at me like a full, bright moon. She was about fifty, although it took an expert eye to see it. Her tanned skin was taut enough from subtle plastic surgery, but she was standing so close that I could see the crow's-feet bordering her large, aquamarine eyes.

"Tennyson Hardwick." Her eyes twinkled like Aruba's ocean waves. "I'm a big fan."

It's dizzying to hear Lynda Jewell utter your name, much less proclaim that she's a fan. My heart leapt again, until I remembered that in Hollywood the phrase "I'm a big fan" translates to "My secretary's heard of you." Seriously.

"I'm flattered, Ms. Jewell," I said. I hoped my hand was steady when I squeezed her dry, cool palm inside of mine. "Coming from you, that means a lot."

Her gaze lingered, and her thin lips shifted in a way I couldn't read. She held my hand a long time before finally letting go. "Lynda," she said after she'd studied me. "Let's sit."

"Apple martini?" Faith asked her. She already had the drink waiting for her boss.

"Just one. Then we'll be fine here, Faith."

While we sat in a strangers' silence, Lynda Jewell's eyes were rapt on me. Intelligent banter is one of my specialties, but I was at a rare loss for chitchat. I quizzed myself on everything April had tried to teach me, but for a harrowing moment, I couldn't even remember the movie's name. I was lucky to remember her husband's.

"So . . . is Ron still coming?" I said finally.

"Not this time." She concentrated on draining her martini glass, her eyes closed. Just stress, or was she nervous, too?

Lenox Avenue, I remembered with a wave of relief. I tried on a confident pose, more like I imagined Troy: inclined comfortably, arm draped across the sofa back, leg crossed over my knee at the calf. Much more suave than I felt.

"I'm excited FilmQuest is doing *Lenox Avenue*," I said. "That story should be told."

Lynda agreed vaguely. "FilmQuest has a suite upstairs from a junket. Let's move our meeting up there."

The first alarm bell sounded in my mind. A one-on-one meeting at a public bar with a studio executive was one thing, but a hotel suite? I hoped Faith was up in the suite, too, but I doubted it. Besides, half the point of a meeting with Lynda Jewell at the Peninsula is to be *seen* having a meeting with Lynda Jewell at the Peninsula.

I could hear Len—my Good and Pragmatic Voice—talking to me this time: *Don't do it, Ten.* But Lynda Jewell was already on her feet, pulling on her oversized Mario Magro handbag. "I have a script up there," she said. "Ron's done a terrific take on the book."

The script was in her hotel suite. Oscar-winning screenwriter. Close enough to touch.

I gave Lynda Jewell a good, long look. I let her see I was mulling the pieces over.

"I'd love to see that script," I said, as if I was entitled to. I was acting already. I came to my feet and gestured her forward with a sweep of my arm. *Ladies first.* I'm an old-fashioned gentleman; some clients called me the black Errol Flynn.

Lynda Jewell smiled, appreciating my flourishes. "Then let's do that."

We were alone in the elevator, but as soon as the door closed, she took two steps over until she stood right in front of me. I could smell her Chanel shampoo, even without trying. When the elevator stopped abruptly at the third floor, her weight shifted backward slightly, and she brushed against me, buttocks grazing my thigh. It was so bold, it was almost plausible.

Shit, I thought. *I am so fucked.*

Instead of looking at her, I gazed at the mile-long, colorful carpeting that bespoke grandness, beckoning me out of the elevator car. I remembered that tantalizing script sitting atop a desktop only yards from where I stood. Another sweep of my arm: *Madame.*

While we walked together in silence, my mind raced: Okay, she was signaling big-time, but not everybody who flirts has the nerve to act out on it. If she'd just wanted to fuck me, she wouldn't have brought her assistant. Or called my agent. She would have done it another way. That's what I was telling myself as I followed her down the hall, toward a hotel suite I was almost sure must be empty.

For once, my Evil Voice was on my side: *What the hell? She'll show you the script. She might flirt a little, but that's just a game. Keep her focused on the script. This is yours.*

That was my plan. Finesse it somehow. I was good at that.

If I could pull off ten minutes of charm in the room—*hey, gotta race to an appointment in Culver City, a fund-raiser for college kids, dontcha know*—I could blast out of there, mission accomplished. She'd feel good, I'd have an important new friend. I'd exit smoothly, no ruffled feathers, a peck on the lips—and if she slipped me a little tongue at the door, that's nothing to take seriously in Hollywood. In some circles, a few inches of tongue are almost a courtesy. In Lynda Jewell's circles, no doubt.

PENINSULA SUITE, the door proclaimed. There I was.

Lynda Jewell had her keycard ready, and we were behind a closed door in a flash.

It wasn't my first visit to the Peninsula Suite, so it felt like returning to a rarely used room in my own house. The rug was the one I remembered, the same beautiful black baby grand piano nestled by the window. "I have a fond feeling for pianos; I still remember the three chords I learned in music class in junior high." At more than two thousand square feet, the airy suite was bigger than the house I'd grown up in.

I was relieved to see stacks of press materials and large cardboard cutouts of Colin Farrell and Matt Damon for the movie her studio was promoting, *Outside In*. The suite was like an office, and I felt myself relax. The actors' life-size images were vivid harbingers of better times to come. They had been in this room, only hours before. I could almost smell their success lingering in the upholstery where their asses had been planted for the parade of interviewers.

Lynda Jewell was at the bar. "Drink?"

I almost declined, but my Evil Voice insisted on sociability. "Red Bull and vodka?" At least I would be alert.

"Colin lives on those," she said. "Says he can stay up all night."

While she fixed my drink, I sat on the plush sofa and scanned the tables for the *Lenox Avenue* script. The sooner I had it in my hands, the better. No luck. *Shit.*

Lynda Jewell walked to me and handed me the drink, but she didn't sit. She stood over me, smiling with a secret. One by one, she kicked off her shoes.

"You mentioned a script . . ." I said.

"You don't remember me, do you?" She whispered the words.

No man wants to hear those words from any woman, much less Lynda Jewell. I could have kidded myself that we'd run into each other at Whole Foods and talked about life and the universe once, but the dance in her eyes told a different story.

My mouth went so dry, I couldn't feel my tongue. No glib answer for that, but I tried.

"I wouldn't forget meeting you."

She chuckled, a nearly masculine growl in her throat. "I'll give you a hint: I was wearing a wig. A horrible wig at that. I looked like Little Orphan Annie. And big Elizabeth Taylor sunglasses. They probably covered half my face."

"Are you sure it was me?"

"The Raffles L'Ermitage Hotel," she said. Specifics have terrible clarifying power.

I felt the world slip off kilter, and my fingers tightened across the sofa cushion. My old life and my new life almost never collided: I had made sure of that. Now, I could hear my agent's frustrated mantra from those days: *It'll catch up to you, Ten. Everything always does.*

As Lynda Jewell went on, I recognized what had spiced her smile when she first saw me: bemusement. "My friend Pauline put you up there. Paid every bill. Minibar. Room service. Massages. A month or more, wasn't it? You cost her five figures. And all you had to do when she slipped across the street from the studio was fuck her in the ass."

Suddenly, I remembered the woman in the ridiculous orange wig and sunglasses, a friend my client Pauline, another film exec, brought to watch us from across the room. She'd never said a word, too shy to join in. Apparently, Lynda Jewell had recovered from her shyness.

I would have stood up to leave if she hadn't suddenly swung one leg over to straddle me, nimble as a teenage gymnast. She weighed next to nothing on my lap. Her ample chest brushed beneath my chin. I hadn't noticed her chest before, and suddenly I could feel her implants. Her skin's scent, stark and new, filled my nose.

I'd underestimated Lynda Jewell, and I'd forgotten what and who I was. I was in trouble.

Lynda Jewell savored the battle she saw on my face.

"So . . . here's how it is," she said. "Right here. Right now. You walk out with a script, and I'll personally call any casting director in town to sing your praises."

Slowly, rhythmically, she slid herself back and forth across my lap. She exerted so much pressure that her bony hip hurt; I had to uncross my leg and shift position, which gave her even freer access to my private parts. Her warm groin against mine felt disloyal to April. When she touched my cheek, I flinched as if her fingers had sparked. My face burned.

It was hard to concentrate on what she was saying, but what I heard was enough. I wanted to clamp my palms to her tiny waist, lift her up, and deposit her away. But I didn't. A deeper instinct told me not to touch her. One person's gentle rebuke is another person's assault. Anything that happened in that room was Lynda Jewell's word against mine, and I didn't like the odds against me.

Besides, it wasn't a good idea to touch her at all. Touching would only make it worse.

"I wish I could," I said. Truer words have never been spoken. "Please get up."

Her smile glittered, and I knew she was going to try to make me suffer. Lynda Jewell was a tough negotiator, or she wouldn't be a kingmaker. "Really?"

She began unbuttoning her blouse, and the pang of fear in my chest felt as real and sickening as my day in the desert. As if I was about to die. Lynda Jewell was a bad dream I'd been having for years, replaying with my eyes wide open. I knew how this dream ended.

"Don't do that," I said, averting my eyes. I raised my hands as if she had a gun.

"Or what?" Her smile slipped past bemusement to something edgier, an implicit threat. Man or woman, anyone who claims not to enjoy power is lying.

She raced through the rest of her buttons and flung the blouse to the floor. Out of the corner of my eye, I saw a zebra pattern on her bra. I couldn't help peeking. Her chest was smooth and freckled, her breasts paler than the skin beneath her collarbone. Man-made mounds rising high. Her body looked just fine.

"You still like cash? There's five thousand in the drawer. Tax-free. I'll throw that in as a gratuity, assuming you earn it." Lynda and her friend Pauline were nothing alike. Pauline had been courtly and considerate, always calling ahead to make sure it was a "good time" to meet, never treating me like property with a price tag.

"I should leave now," I said.

"No ring, so you're not married. Girlfriend?"

I didn't answer. I didn't want to bring April's name into the room with us. But Lynda Jewell grinned, happy to have figured out the delay.

"I can't promise you Troy, understand." She twinkled at me. "Let me be clear about something now, so I don't get any pouting later. You're a hidden gem, lover, but you just don't have the recognition. But there are a dozen other parts waiting for your face, some of them very good. You'll have to audition if you want heavy lifting, but you're guaranteed a line or two no matter what."

Lynda Jewell was closing the deal. Her bra came off next, tossed away like a small animal scurrying for shelter. Her fingers were a claw as she pulled my hand toward her chest. "Pauline said you're a magician, and I need some magic today. Impress me."

I yielded to her hand's pressure, and my palm fell to her breast. Sank into her skin.

Whenever breasts make an appearance, my body assumes it's time to fuck. The discomfort in my groin was replaced by a sense of fullness, a remnant of the days when my erections punched a time clock. My heart drummed louder.

I'd done it a thousand times. The right touch here, carefully chosen words whispered there, and our contract was sealed. If you don't think a few good orgasms are worth a movie role, someone isn't taking care of business at home.

I felt a confusion that seemed like clarity: Maybe my past had been designed to lead me to this moment. Few men on this earth could have been better prepared to give Lynda Jewell what she wanted that day. The thought of tasting her made me feel sick to my stomach, but the call of her open legs across my lap—and the realization of how close to the Promised Land I had come—was arousing me. I was a pro, after all.

Lynda Jewell felt the mass growing beneath her. When you're as blessed as I am, there's nowhere to hide. "That's more like it," she said, rubbing against me. Massaging. "*Ten.*"

What the fuck? the Evil Voice said. *It's the only way in you've got.*

To this day, I'm not sure why it happened. Maybe I'd trained myself to fight my Evil Voice, so that last jab helped me wake up from the dream. I stood up abruptly, bucking my hips slightly, and Lynda Jewell let out a cry as she lost her balance and landed on the carpeted floor.

She sat there dumbfounded, crossing her arms across her chest as if I'd burst into her room and ripped off her blouse. Her face darkened two shades. "What the *fuck?*"

Ever the gentleman, I offered my hand to help her to her feet. She refused to take it, hoisting herself up against the sofa.

"I'm sorry, Mrs. Jewell," I said, torn between regret and rage. "That was an accident. But please don't ever waste my time, or my agent's, with this kind of bullshit again."

In the end, rage won. Troy himself couldn't have said it any better.

I've replayed that day over and over, trying to salvage the visit in my imagination, but it always ends the same way. Something that starts out that wrong can't be made right. And although April made the touch of other women feel foreign, I don't think I threw Lynda Jewell off of my lap because of April. I'd quit the sex-for-pay business five years before I ever met April.

I just couldn't pretend to go back to the person I'd been, even if it would have meant real work. Even if it would have remade my world.

Lynda Jewell's eyes boiled with rage and humiliation, and I recognized the poison lurking there: *All I have to do is scream and make up a story, and I can take your life away.*

"I truly am sorry. I had a reflexive—"

"You are the *picture* of nerve, you son of a bitch," she said, flinging her blouse on like a cape. "Why would I cast a nothing like you in *Lenox Avenue?*"

Lynda Jewell and my Evil Voice had apparently read the same script. Her words flayed me. Still, I was the only one in the room with my dignity intact, and I kept it by commencing my long walk toward her suite's door.

Lynda Jewell exaggerated a laugh behind me, following me step for step like a small terrier. "I wouldn't hire a talentless whore like you as an extra," she said. "If you don't get back over here and finish what we started, I'll make it my mission to drive you out of town. Do you hear me? Trust me, the future is *not* bright. Not for you, asshole."

At least she had seen my commercial.

I stepped out into the hallway. A door to my left clicked shut, probably closed by someone embarrassed for us.

"*God damn it! Get back in here and* fuck *me, you sonofabitch!*"

The hallway was empty. Barren.

I don't remember taking the elevator, or walking from the hotel. It took me four tries before I finally got my key in my car's ignition.

FOUR

THE TAU FUNDRAISER WAS A MISERY, all the more miserable for its frivolity. There are few chores worse than being the only one at the party in a bad mood.

Scratch that. It's worse if you're tied to a photo booth, smiling with strangers while flashing cameras stoke a monster headache. And worse still when your girlfriend's eyes are probing with unfinished questions, trying to take you back to an afternoon you'd rather forget.

It's not that men don't want to talk—we just like to choose our time. Lynda Jewell wasn't a story I was eager to tell.

The banquet hall of Culver City's Radisson Hotel was decorated in a carnival theme, filled with helium balloons in Tau crimson and white. Instead of the usual chicken breast banquet, they had food stands serving hot dogs, wings, and fresh popcorn. There were also poker tables, roulette wheels, and six celebrity photo booths. The last booth, awaiting the still-absent T.D. Jackson, charged one hundred dollars. Already, a dozen people waited in line.

I was in the second booth, with a twenty-dollar price, right next to dead cheapest, a guy with gold teeth who'd been a Hype man for Shareef back in the day. Since my episodes of *Homeland* hadn't even aired yet—and would it have mattered?—most people passed me without bothering to hide a sour pucker that said *Who the hell are you?*

Higher up the celebrity food chain at fifty bucks apiece were that light-skinned brother from *A Different World*, a sister from the UCLA women's basketball team, a *Playboy* Playmate wearing only a bikini, a Famous Hip-Hop Artist with three initials for a name (D.O.A., maybe? Chela would have known him), and Billy Dee Williams, who was still making young ladies swoon in his seventies.

Billy Dee was Troy back before there *was* a Troy. If I'd been in the mood for inspiration, I would have found it in Billy Dee. Instead, all I could think about was how unfair it was that Billy Dee was grinning and posing as if time had stood still for him alone, and back at home Dad needed help getting out of bed. A bad mood colors everything.

"Ooh, look at this luscious Hershey's Kiss over *here*," one huge woman said, eyeing me as if I were on a Mississippi auction block. "Honey, you should be charging more than twenty dollars to take a picture with *you*. Aren't you that phone guy?"

She grabbed my forearm with meaty fingers, so proprietary that my flesh crawled. My memories of Lynda Jewell were too fresh to tolerate a new woman's pawing. Gently, I slipped my arm away. She tried to hold on, but a final yank got me free. Her eyebrow arch told me, *That's okay, baby, I like 'em feisty.* I think I actually shivered.

The woman lumbered beside me into the booth.

"Stand up, baby," she said, holding up her red ticket. "Come to Mama."

She was my first taker in fifteen minutes, so I tried to look happy for the photographer. As the woman cinched her arm tightly around my waist, enfolding me within soft rolls of polyester-and-sequin-wrapped flesh, I cursed myself again for showing up. I could have

written the Taus a check for three times what I'd raised and spent my
night at home.

The camera went off, and my headache screamed.

Then, air crackled, almost as if lightning had struck in the
banquet-hall doorway.

Have you ever stood on a beach with water up to your ankles and
felt the tide recede? Even the grains of sand try to flee from between
your toes. It's a dizzying, startling sensation; a reminder of one's utter
insignificance in the face of nature's full force.

That's what happened when T.D. Jackson walked into the banquet hall.

"Oh, shit," said the woman standing beside me, and suddenly she
wasn't.

I've spent a career around the chronically charismatic, but T.D.
Jackson's presence was fuller than his six-foot-three frame could contain, stretching from one end of the hall to the other. All eyes and feet
gravitated toward him. He floated into the room on a wave of fierce
applause, as if he were Nelson Mandela freed after twenty-seven
years of hard labor.

T.D. and Billy Dee must have had similar genes, because the man
who strode through that door was only a slightly less bulky version of
the college sophomore I'd known back at SoCal State almost twenty
years before. He had always had an actor's face—a jutting chin, powerful cheekbones and oddly colored eyes that hypnotized females
when they flickered between golden brown and green—so I wasn't
surprised when T.D. transitioned to Hollywood in the middle of his
NFL career. Acting ability is secondary when you're a born star like
T.D. Jackson; his face and Super Bowl MVP memories won him forgiveness for his limited range.

Even at a stroll, he moved like a jaguar. It was easy to imagine his
famous leaps as he caught balls most players wouldn't dream of, land-

ing just within bounds with Baryshnikov's pointy-toed perfection. Some people argue that T.D. Jackson was the best wide receiver ever to play the game. My money's on Jerry Rice, or maybe Randy Moss, but the argument isn't dumb.

T.D. was flanked by five men who might have been linebackers, and I knew a couple of their faces from college, too. Classmates, friends, bodyguards. All of them, including T.D., were dressed in silk crimson suits, white shirts, narrow crimson ties, and sunglasses. The crowd in the room surged toward T.D., but no one dared block his direct path. T.D. Jackson was leading a moving train with no signs of slowing.

I forgot about the murders. Everyone did.

T.D. raised his arm over his head, a signal, and the hall's speakers blared to life. Tinny, inane carnival music was replaced by a deafening recorded shout and heavy percussion. M.C. Hammer's "Turn This Mutha Out" flooded the room.

T.D. Jackson and his crew fanned into a circle, facing us with wide-legged stances. On the beat, all six men thrust their groins forward in synchronization, their knees so low to the ground that they were bending backward. For several seconds, they froze in place, testing their impossible balance, their heads nearly touching. Onlookers squealed, shrieked and shouted. An excited chant swelled from the crowd, also in rhythm: "Go 'head! Go 'head!"

The step show had begun.

Step shows have been popularized in film recently, but they originated at historically black colleges in the 1960s. Black Greek organizations at mainstream universities like SoCal State have kept up the tradition, and that night T.D. Jackson took us all back to school.

T.D. Jackson was playing for his true home crowd.

Like the gears of a perfect machine, the men flung their sunglasses into the ecstatic crowd. The woman who had just posed for a picture with me nearly stampeded the poor young sister beside her as she snatched T.D.'s shades out of midflight.

Double time, leaping high while they jabbed their arms skyward with perfectly matched motion, the six men stalked to the waiting stage. To climb up, they leapfrogged in twos until all of them stood in a single line, moving like an optical illusion. They raised their knees high in synchronized clapping above and below their massive thighs. Their rhythmic stomping on the wooden stage sounded like thunder. I was sure the floorboards would snap beneath them.

T.D., the war chief, let out a shout. "When I say Tau, you say Heat. Tau!"

"*Heat!*" the men roared in unison, with perfectly timed stomps emphasizing the word.

"Tau!"

"*Heat!*"

All of the men dropped to the floor in a line, as if about to do push-ups. Each man except the last hooked his ankles on another man's shoulders, and they melded into a single unit. One by one, they raised themselves high, then back to the floor, a slowly undulating snake waving back and forth across the stage.

Women screamed. Every entrance to the banquet hall was crammed with hotel waiters, cooks, and housekeepers watching the marvel of giants moving with such uncanny fluidity. April sidled up beside me, in wide-eyed wonderment despite herself.

Another shout from T.D., and the men were on their feet. They danced in formation around each other, alternately thrusting their fists into the air and stomping out a pattern with their feet that sounded like angry drumming straight from the Motherland. The way they moved their torsos, elbows, and fists reminded me of karate *katas*. These were the warriors of our tribe, performing a mighty war dance. If T.D. Jackson and his crew had done their step show on the field before their bowl games, the other teams might have fled back to the locker room before the starting coin toss.

I'm in good shape—I work out, I can fight when it counts, and I can dance to anything from hip-hop to salsa—but on my best days, I couldn't will my body to move like *that*. T.D.'s crew carried their bulky frames with stupefying ease, capturing an odd combination of beauty and ferocity. Their shouts jittered up my spine. A premonition, maybe.

As the last of M.C. Hammer's music sounded, the other men heaved T.D. Jackson over their heads, holding him high as he lay in repose. They looked like pallbearers.

Once the show was over, April remembered her indignation. "You'd think he'd have the decency to keep a low profile until after the civil trial," she muttered to me over the room's raucous shouting and applause.

I chuckled. The phrase *low profile* had never been in T.D. Jackson's vocabulary.

April's eyes narrowed. "You think it's funny he got away with murder?" She said it loudly enough to elicit a gaze fit for blasphemers from a nearby older couple. I hoped April wouldn't be foolish enough to confront T.D. Jackson, but suddenly I wasn't sure. Women's mouths have earned their men a beat-down, or worse, since the dawn of so-called civilization.

"Chill, April," I said. "You knew he would be here."

April's eyes cut at me in a way I wasn't used to. Maybe there had been something in my voice she wasn't used to either. That was the way things were with us lately.

While the crowd swarmed T.D. Jackson at the other end of the room, I returned to my lonely booth to wait until April was ready to go. She was a member of the Taus' sister sorority, so the ladies were there to help keep the popcorn popping.

After the step show, the rest of us might as well have been invisible. The line for T.D. Jackson's photo booth was so long that organizers set up velvet ropes to keep order. The Bruin and the Bunny traded hair care advice while Billy Dee and the *Different World* dude exchanged business cards, talking politics.

"Now I have truly seen everything," a woman's voice said beside me.

Any number of unusual sights could have fit that description, so I followed her gaze: She was staring toward the flock around T.D. Jackson and his entourage at the other end of the room.

The woman was petite and smooth-skinned, dressed in an efficient gray pantsuit that told me she had come to the event straight from a job she probably didn't like. I didn't know her, but when she looked at me, I was sure I knew her eyes.

"Marilyn . . . Johnson?" I said. Her name came first.

She smiled. "That's impressive. I look . . ." Beat. ". . . different."

The long, embarrassed pause helped me remember her: She'd been the only other sister in my first college drama class. She'd had unfortunate acne and overprocessed hair, and I remember thinking that she would need to lose about sixty pounds if she wanted acting work. Apparently, she had. The weight was gone, shrunken to a healthy athletic frame that bespoke serious workouts. The acne hadn't left so much as a scar, and her hair had a raven sheen. Marilyn Johnson had gotten herself together.

I'm not the school-reunion type, but I was happy to see someone looking better instead of worse after twenty years, so I stood up to hug her. My hug surprised her, and I felt her body stiffen, so I pulled back sooner than I would have. I'd been careful to issue my Friendly hug—more upper body than lower—but Marilyn was skittish about contact.

Marilyn never met my eyes for more than a hot second, roiling with shyness that seemed misplaced. Despite her effective dusting of makeup to bring out her cheeks and large, almond-shaped eyes, in her mind's eye she was hideous.

"Hey, darlin'," I said. "You look terrific."

"Right back at ya," she said. "I've marked my calendar for your first episodes on *Homeland*. Love that show! I've been keeping up with you on the internet. I'll never forget turning on my TV and seeing you on *Malibu High* back in the day."

"*Way* back," I said, downplaying it. My entrée into television had been a minor part as a basketball coach on a *Beverly Hills 90210* knockoff.

Marilyn swatted my hand, just like April might. "Stop. Everyone didn't get triumphs like that to celebrate, Tennyson. Embrace your achievements."

It was the nicest thing anyone fully dressed had said to me all day.

The photographer had long since drifted away, but Marilyn waved him over. Then she opened her purse to find her twenty dollar photo fee. "You don't have to," I said.

She smiled. "I want to. A picture with you will wash away how the Taus just ruined my night." Her jaw could have cracked a walnut. Marilyn wasn't looking at T.D. Jackson anymore, but I realized she could see no one else.

"Not in the fan club?"

"He's guilty as hell," she said quietly. "And he knows it."

As the camera flashed, Marilyn posed by giving me a gentle kiss on the cheek. The kiss lingered, sweet and sad, as if she wanted to absorb some luck, or goodness, from me. I wished I had some to give. I expected the Let's-have-lunch riff, but none came. I could tell that she had abandoned her acting dreams long ago. Most people do.

"I'm disappointed with the Taus. They should know better,"

Marilyn said with the *My-people-My-people* shake of her head. "But it was good to see you, Ten."

Her expression was so fragile that I wanted to retrieve a memory to delight her. I tried to remember a single conversation with her from class, a friend or relative to inquire about, but I couldn't. Back in school, she had been invisible to me, and probably to almost everyone else. Watching her walk away beneath a veil of sadness, I wanted to reach back through time and invite her out for coffee after class. But all that was too little, twenty years too late.

I was ready to leave the Taus, too.

I'd lost sight of April, so I went looking. I found her at a Sno-Cone machine with three other women, deep in a huddle. Their fingers fumbled with cups and plastic jugs of rainbow-colored syrup. Even before I was close enough to hear, I could tell that the women were pressuring April about something, and I was paranoid enough to believe that they were talking about me. In a way, I guess they were.

". . . for you. You're the one who has to take control," one of the women was saying. "If you don't—" She clammed up when she saw me coming. She was as model-thin and as tall as I was, with hair dyed platinum in an ill-chosen contrast against her skin.

When April met my eyes, I thought I saw guilt tug at her mouth.

"Hey, Ten," April said absently, hooking her arm through mine. *Hey, old buddy.*

Four sets of eyes felt heavy on my face. "Is there a problem I can help with?" I said.

"No," April said quickly, before anyone else could answer. "It's nothing."

April didn't lie often—and maybe not at all since she'd been my girlfriend—but that lie made us even. On our way to the fund-raiser, April had asked me a half dozen times what was bothering me, and I'd relied on the same old line, too. Nothing. One bad lie deserved another.

"I'm ready to go," I said. "If you need to stay, I'm sure someone can give you a ride."

Around me, reflexive hands perched on hips. I felt unspoken refrains of *Oh-no-he-didn't*. April looked slightly embarrassed, but she gave me a gentle pull that made me think she was almost relieved to get away. "Maybe it's okay if I go. I'll ask Percy."

Whoever Percy was, I wanted to suggest some anatomically challenging acts he could perform on himself. Why was a stranger having a say with my lady? But I set my teeth and followed April toward the throng at the other end of the room.

"One of my sorority sisters found out she has lupus," April said as we crossed the room.

"Sorry to hear it."

"They want me to take over her project, but I'm not interested." April sighed. "A high school journalism class."

"You've always wanted to teach." April's father was a college professor, and she'd vowed to leave the newspaper for teaching one day.

She dropped the bomb. "It's in Soweto. Six months in South Africa. Classes start in three weeks, and I couldn't land there cold on day one. I'd have to take a leave from the paper, like, *now*. And sublet my room." April was no longer talking to me; she was thinking it through.

One night, after half a glass too much of wine, I had asked April to move in with me. That was probably when my feeling of unease began, if I had to choose a date on a calendar. Three months before. I'd seen surprise flare in her eyes, and I realized that maybe she'd misunderstood me. When I said it, I was mostly thinking what a pain it was that April couldn't spend the night more often—that was before she'd confessed that Chela made her uncomfortable. The way I saw it, why should she be spending six-fifty a month for a room in a two-bedroom apartment when she could live in my house for free? That was all. Convenience.

April had answered my offer with a laundry list of excuses: not enough notice for her roommate. Respect for her parents. The distance from her job. Her list of reasons, sounding a firm *no,* made me realize I'd been asking more than I thought. But this time, I already recognized the hungry ring of *yes* underneath her excuses. The challenges weren't a wall to hide behind; they were bricks to be torn down. April wanted to go to Soweto. She might not know how badly yet, but she would before long.

April pulled herself closer to me, reassurance. "I'm not interested," she said again.

"Yet." If April heard me, she didn't let on.

The man she was looking for, Tau chapter president Percy Duvall, also dressed in crimson, hovered near T.D. Jackson's booth to keep order along the velvet ropes. Duvall was below average height, with a Napoleon syndrome that kept his neck at full tilt. In proximity to T.D. and his crew, Duvall looked like a gnome.

T.D. was jocular and grinning as he posed for photos with admirers. Each newcomer, men and women alike, paid one hundred dollars for the privilege of giving T.D. Jackson prayers, hugs, and encouragement in his hour of need.

"Too blessed to be stressed, bro."

"Stay strong, brotherman."

"The truth will set you free, man."

"T.D., you're an inspiration to humanity." That quote is verbatim.

I had done my best to ignore the trial, since celebrity trials are a waste of taxpayer money. But anyone with ears knew the details: T.D.'s ex-wife, Chantelle, had been highly pedigreed. She hailed from a political family, and she was an entertainment lawyer well liked in the industry. While her two children were at their grandparents' house, she and her unlucky fiancé, Arturo Salvador, had been hogtied, gagged, and murdered in her garage. Having gained some painful experience with gags and hogties recently, I felt especially sorry for them. It's no way to die.

Even as murders go, this one was mean-spirited. Personal. The coroner had determined that the murderer killed the fiancé while T.D.'s ex was forced to watch, then she was shot execution-style in the back of the head. (In the end, was the killer unable to look at her face? That was my bet.) The killer's boot had left partial tread marks on his upper thigh. Injuries to the man's swollen groin suggested a bit of ill will. The murdered man had once been a probation officer, so T.D.'s defense had argued that the killings might have been retaliation for a job well-done.

But police records proved that T.D. had threatened and harassed his ex-wife in the year since she won half his fortune in their divorce. His blood was found on the scene, and threads from a type of fiber and weave identical with a jacket T.D. had had custom-made not nine months before . . . and what some considered a telling degree of mental confusion in the forty-eight hours following the crime—I thought the L.A. prosecutor's office might win a big one at last.

Nope. The justice system just isn't set up to penetrate a multimillion-dollar defense. Celebrity just makes it worse. The jury's failure to convict T.D. Jackson felt like a far cry from vindication, considering that half the jurors posed for pictures with T.D. after the trial.

To the Taus, T.D. Jackson was family, plain and simple. Ask any mother sheltering her fugitive child how difficult it is to give up on family. Still, that crowd's certainty of T.D.'s innocence—or, rather, their utter lack of imagination regarding the possibility of his guilt—made me wonder if they thought they could read the man's mind. I could understand T.D.'s classmates and relatives fawning without restraint or caution, but what about the people who'd never met him, and only knew him as a face on the screen?

Faces aren't windows. They're just masks made of skin.

Extraordinary talent or success implies a level of sanctification that can make wrongdoing seem impossible. Not to me. I've collected too many secrets of my own. There was every chance T.D. had killed those two people, despite his football records, hit movies, and boyish smile. I wasn't going to spit in his face like April would have liked to, but I wouldn't kiss his ass either.

I have too much respect for the dead.

Two blond twins with bodies like Playmate caricatures—overblown lips, concave bellies, and island-sized breasts—waited for T.D. in folding chairs just beyond the photo booth. They both sat with their legs crossed, their short dresses hiked up high enough to cast shadows between their thighs. They were hookers or porn stars, or maybe both, and they reeked of pheromones. Every sister in fifty feet tightened her grip on her man's arm.

T.D.'s crew hovered, too. They were former football players, but that night they were on protection detail. Hard, watchful eyes scanned everyone who came close. For an instant, April locked eyes with the biggest of them, who looked like a younger Jim Brown, and her face made him puff out his chest like a dare. *Don't start no shit, sister.* I hoped April had as much common sense as I thought.

April's shoulders rose as she steeled herself to approach the Tau president, which meant walking within ten yards of T.D. Jackson. She kept her eyes on Percy Duvall, never glancing at T.D. Truth be told, I think T.D. scared her more than his hulking friends. Smart girl.

"Percy? I was wondering . . ." she began.

"April, thank God," he interrupted. "Did you hear? We need you in South Africa . . ."

Suddenly, a hand was on my shoulder. A woman's featherlight touch. "I don't believe this! Tennyson Hardwick. Speak of the devil!"

I was trying to eavesdrop on April's conversation, and suddenly April wanted to listen to mine. April's eyes dashed away from Percy in time to see a woman rise to her tiptoes and kiss me lightly on the lips. I saw the delicate tip of an ear, long braids, a slender frame, and ochre-colored skin before the woman pulled back far enough for me to take in her face.

"Melanie Wilde," I said, recognizing her. Another classmate from SoCal State. I hadn't realized I had been in school long enough to make so many friends. Melanie's name hadn't crossed my mind in nearly twenty years, but her face was impossible to forget. She had a high forehead, button nose, and pronounced cheekbones, like a Senegalese princess. Exotic and beautiful. "Long time."

I was careful about my distance, opening a chasm between us. Melanie was T.D. Jackson's older cousin. We had met because she came in and out of the dorm, often carrying loads of T.D.'s laundry. I had asked her about the laundry once, and she only laughed. *Success is a family project*, she had said, her cousin's future dancing in her bright eyes. The Church of T.D. Jackson had opened its doors long before he won the Heisman or played in the NFL.

"Oh no, you don't understand," she said intensely, grabbing my hand. "This is uncanny. God is at work here, Tennyson. I was just speaking your name. Hey, Bumpy!"

She waved toward T.D. Jackson, and the sound of her voice made his head snap up. His offensive line stepped aside to make a path for her as she pulled me toward him by the hand. April's eyes burned a hole in the back of my head.

"Look who it is!" Melanie said when T.D. turned to face me. "This is the one. Tennyson Hardwick, remember?"

T.D.'s crew closed a circle around us, shielding T.D. from the waiting crowd. Anyone who was pissed about the interruption kept it to themselves.

When he saw me, T.D. Jackson's face lighted with a grin that no one could refuse to return. "How you been, man?" He leaned in for an embrace, patting my back. For an instant, my head swam. Maybe T.D. and I had been tight all along, like brothers, and I'd forgotten somehow.

"Who's this?" one of his friends said in a skeptical basso. He was square-jawed, with a deep cleft in his chin.

"Hardwick," Melanie said. "The bodyguard."

There were murmurs of recognition, and another pat on the back from T.D. The circle closed in more tightly. They checked me out, jock to jock. They'd seen movies, and knew a glance can't tell you anything about a man's skill with a gun, or behind the wheel of a car: two critical skills in the close-protection industry. And hand to hand? You just don't know. I work out with a skinny little guy who'll be sixty-five next birthday, one of the best real-world bodyguards there is. He won't play dojo games: You'll just wake up hurting, if you're lucky.

So about the only thing about me they could evaluate was my fitness. Not even that: They weren't going to ask me to run a hundred, bench my max, or hit the sled for them. And they weren't going to ask me what my ring record was, or number of red stripes on the black belt. They would take the instant, male-male snapshot appreciation, an automatic question most guys don't talk about much: *Can I kick his ass?*

Of course, there's a balancing question: *Can he kick my ass?*

You could divide men into categories based upon the instinctive choice of one of these questions. Whole families of life decisions and actions separate the worlds of the men who think of themselves as Thumpers and Thumpees. Neither is a better or worse human being. But trust me: They're two different guys.

T.D., these men, and I were all Thumpers. We all knew we'd bruise each other up. One level of reflexive male challenge done, and bonding begun. I wasn't afraid of them. I wasn't a monster, but my solid muscle was balanced, loose, bouncy. Watchful. They couldn't know how well trained it was, but they had to wonder why I wasn't intimidated. But if I was a leopard, they were lions. They figured they could kill me, even if they'd get scratched up doing it. *All right, you're okay buddy, you can watch my flank, and I'll watch yours.* We had sized each other up almost instantly, and the mutual answer was "yes."

I enjoyed being welcomed into the heart of that invincible tribe. I admit it. The rest of the banquet hall vanished.

All his career, the media had criticized T.D. for his arrogance and cockiness. But I watched the grin fade from his face, revealing what he kept from hidden from everyone except his closest friends and family: He was tired and scared. The smooth skin he'd had in college looked weathered, and his eyes were slightly red, even crazed. No telltale white residue on his nostrils, but his eyes looked like fried marbles.

Six men were talking to me at once.

"Since the verdict, it's crazy, man . . ."

". . . people done lost their damn minds . . ."

". . . can't even open his mail . . ."

Melanie raised her hand, and the men fell silent. She was the smallest of any of us, but Melanie Wilde was in charge. She surreptitiously showed me a grainy five-by-seven color photograph, and I nearly recoiled. That photo had run in the *Enquirer* after a police source leaked it to the tabloids: Chantelle Jackson bound to a chair, her lifeless head dangling to one side, taken inside the garage where she'd been killed. I was grateful the photo had been taken from behind, her face hidden from view. I'd already seen one dead woman too many.

"Where'd this come from?" I said.

Melanie leaned close to me. "Some coward slipped it on the table and walked away."

"Wish I'd seen the motherfucker," Basso growled, scanning the crowd. I scanned too: Nothing but well-dressed Taus patiently awaiting their turn to touch greatness. All smiles.

"T.D.'s getting threats," Melanie said, voice low. "Not just this. Ignorant people unfamiliar with our system of jurisprudence don't understand the words *Not Guilty*. Anyway, Dorothea Biggs teaches Sunday school with me at my church, and she talks about you all the time. Her son told her he's never seen a . . . what? Close-Protection Specialist? Quite like you. You pulled him out of a fire, during the Afrodite thing?"

She said it like she was trying to jog my memory. As if I could forget.

Serena "Afrodite" Johnson's death still infuriated me—I had nearly gone to jail myself after she'd been murdered, since I had spent a precious afternoon with her the day she died. Serena and I hadn't seen each other in five years until that day, and it had been like meeting for the first time. We might have started all over again, both of us born anew.

"He was a bodyguard for who?" said Skeptical Basso, looking me up and down. He had fifty pounds on me. I'm not small, but it was like an oak talking to a pine.

"Devon Biggs," Melanie told him. "And Afrodite."

"Well, shit, that didn't work out too good."

My eyes flashed fire. Knowing that I might have found a way to save Serena's life still sometimes made it hard to go to sleep at night. Linebacker or not, I wasn't going to tolerate taunting about Serena.

T.D. Jackson laughed, but without mirth. His glassy eyes shimmered. "You got heart, man. Don't let Carlyle fuck with you," T.D. told me, and shook my hand; almost holding it, really. "Melanie says you're the real thing, and my big cousin never steers me wrong. I need somebody I can trust, from way back in the day. The shit's gonna start all over with the civil trial. My boys got their own lives, you know? They can't keep babysitting my ass. That true about Devon Biggs and the fire? Six dudes shooting at you?"

"Three," I said. The memory of the trap set for me and Devon in retaliation for Serena's murder forced itself to the surface. I had shot and almost killed a man that day. I could still taste the soot and smell the gasoline. "The fire's true."

T.D. Jackson's face went slack with gratitude, the way he might have looked at a doctor who promised to cure a fatal illness. "*Yeah, man. That's what I need*, Tennyson. No bullshit."

In that instant, T.D. Jackson felt like an old friend I could invite home to crack open a six-pack and watch a ballgame. That's the ugly truth of it: People aren't all bad or all good. You can dig down to find the saint, or the monster, in anyone.

A business card slipped into my hand. I glanced down: *Melanie Wilde, Attorney at Law.* She worked at a downtown firm housed in a glass tower on Sunset.

"Let me know how to reach you," Melanie said. "We'll take you to lunch and talk details. We're not playing, so name your price."

A piercing gaze somehow has physical weight. April's eyes were bludgeoning the back of my head. Instinct made me want to call her over, and say, "Hey, guys, this is my girlfriend, April Forrest." But April didn't want an introduction. She wanted to know why the hell I was talking congenially with T.D. Jackson and a woman who looked like an East African postcard. I wondered, too.

I'd almost forgotten that I had a steady job, and that investigating Serena's murder had soured me on the bodyguard business. I'd almost forgotten my respect for the dead.

I made a show of trying to give Melanie's card back to her. She refused it.

"Wish I could help," I said, first to her, and then to T.D. "But I'm pushing the acting thing now. Might have seen me on the previews for next week's *Homeland*?"

T.D. blinked. No reaction at all.

"The Afrodite business was a onetime thing," I said. "Sorry."

"What?" T.D. said, genuinely puzzled. T.D. Jackson wasn't used to being refused. "You think I can't pay, man? I can pay."

"It's not that. I've got a gig, T.D. Sorry."

His eyes never wavered, but somewhere deep inside T.D. Jackson there was a seismic shift. For an instant I glimpsed a morsel of the rage his dead ex-wife might have known, whether or not he killed her. T.D. Jackson didn't have a Warm setting: He went from Cold to Hot. His eyes, which looked vaguely golden in that instant, were sharp as knives.

Melanie Wilde saw it, too. She moved toward T.D., standing between us, although her eyes never left mine. "Please keep my card," she said. "We could really use you, Ten. You can imagine what the stress is like. First the loss . . . then the trial . . ." Melanie had been making excuses for her baby cousin her whole life, and she was good at it.

Mostly for her sake, I opened my wallet and nestled her card inside—although I didn't offer her mine. Then I tipped an imaginary hat. If I didn't tend to April soon, I was the one who was going to need a ride home.

I met T.D. Jackson's eyes for the last time. They still glinted, sharp. "T.D.? Good luck with the security, man. If I think of anyone else, I'll let you know."

T.D. only shook his head with a scoffing, dismissive laugh. His eyes left mine, and I became invisible. He had exposed his heart to me, and beneath his armor he was sulking like a ten-year-old boy. "Triflin' motherfucker," he muttered, walking away. Melanie winced.

Just that quickly, I was out of the club.

I didn't know it at the time, but my tally rose that night. Serena wasn't alone anymore.

Now there were two lives I might have saved.

FIVE

I WAS SHOCKED when April announced she would spend the night with me after the fundraiser. I made a mental note to attend more meetings with her. Apparently, I'd explained my brush with T.D. Jackson well enough in the car to keep her in a good mood.

We got home late, so Dad was already asleep, and Chela was wrapped in the wall of loud music behind her closed door. I'd eaten dinner with Chela and Dad, so a knock at Chela's door and a "whassup" were all she needed for the night. I confirmed that she was where she was supposed to be. Chela, like me, was self-sufficient and couldn't stand crowding. Maybe that was why we worked so well.

I didn't tell Chela that April was with me, and Chela didn't ask.

I regretted that I had sacrificed my old room, the master bedroom, to give to Chela. The former guest room that had become my bedroom always looked overcrowded because I'd tried to stuff my kettlebells, heavy bag, and folding mats in, and there was hardly room for a queen-size bed. Chela's room, on the other hand, was the size of a generous studio apartment. If the room hadn't been upstairs, I would have offered it to Dad. But I figured that after living on the streets, with only a dead grandmother and a soulless madam as her caretakers, Chela needed a space of her own. I was probably spoiling her, but everything is relative.

I could tell that April felt cramped in my room, but she didn't complain. I turned off the light and pulled her close for the kiss I'd been craving far too long.

"Let's take a shower," I said. I wanted to wash myself, and I wanted April with me.

No small feat. The bathroom was across the hall. I pulled her hand into mine, unbuttoning my shirt with my other. But April's feet dragged behind me before we reached the doorway. "Ten, I want you to tell me what happened today. We spend all this time preparing for a meeting, and then you won't tell me anything? I didn't expect her to offer you the part on the spot, but still . . ."

"She never wanted to offer me a part," I said slowly. "She offered me a piece."

At first, April looked confused. Then she smiled, thinking it was a joke. But when she didn't see a return smile, hers evaporated. Her dark eyes flashed. "*What?*"

The shower would have to wait. Maybe for a long time.

I sat April on the bed and started from the beginning, garment by garment. It could have been worse: At least April already knew about my sex-for-pay past. She'd learned my history from a police lieutenant, a former student of her father's who had tried to keep her away from me. I told April about everything in the hotel suite, except for my arousal. Erections are involuntary, but I knew better. The story was tough enough for April. I saw that in her face.

"You went to a hotel room with her?" she said. Hurt cracked her voice in a way I had never heard from her. It felt like breaking a rare crystal artwork. "And let her put her hands on you? Why the hell would you do that, Ten? You thought that was business as usual?"

You shouldn't have told her, my Evil Voice said.

I put my arm around April to soften the way it sounded. "Baby, I didn't know. They'd used it for a press junket. In the back of my mind, I wondered, but . . . you've interviewed people in hotel rooms, April. You know most meetings don't include nudity. Be fair."

But you could have guessed, I heard her thinking, and she sat with that thought a while. I had culpability, too, and we both knew it. I could have left when Lynda Jewell first mentioned Pauline. I could have left when she unbuttoned her shirt.

"I was stupid," I said. "I won't put myself in that position again."

"I can't *believe* her!" April said finally, and I was glad her anger had found its rightful target. April's mouth moved like a fish fighting to breathe, speechless with rage.

That reminded me: I'd forgotten to feed the fish again.

April followed me downstairs. When she regained her voice, her mouth set loose a flurry of curses rhyming with "rich," and some that never leave my mouth but rhyme with "runt." My ears felt polluted to hear April's sweet voice wrapped around that language as we passed my father's closed door. It was almost as bad as hearing Chela curse.

"*Shhhh,*" I said. "You're gonna get us both kicked out of my own house."

"She called your agent for *that?*"

"It's over, April."

"Trust me, it's not. If she was as mad as you said, she won't let that go."

Len hadn't heard the full story yet. I'd managed to avoid his eager postmeeting calls because of the weekend, but he deserved a full disclosure by Monday. Len had always warned me my reputation was at risk. And if Lynda Jewell made good on her threat to bad-mouth me, my future in Hollywood was already my past. Hollywood is a small town.

Once the fish were safely fed, I led April back upstairs. Toward the shower.

By silent agreement, we were finished talking, or thinking, about Lynda Jewell.

The upstairs bathroom didn't have a double-headed shower like the one I'd given to Chela, but it was still a worthy meeting place. That night, it was sanctuary. Raising my finger to my lips, I locked the door behind us. Just in case Chela came looking.

To the untutored, sex in the shower can be a nightmare. It sounds great in theory, but too many passionate inspirations go awry against wet shower tiles. Luckily, I'd had great teachers.

While April undressed, I tested the water stream and temperature, keeping my eyes on my task. I knew April's body well by then—it was *mine*, as she liked telling me, and I loved to hear—but sometimes I denied myself the vision of April's nakedness as long as possible before lovemaking. I liked the surprise of her, new and fresh to my eyes.

"It's ready for you, miss," I said, like the perfect hotel porter.

"Thank you, sir," she said, and slipped past me in a blur of brown nakedness.

We were both playing the game of newness.

I peeled off the formfitting black shirt and black slacks I'd worn to the fund-raiser, my all-purpose L.A. Chic that saved me from the hassle of a suit and tie. Last, my black briefs. The small bathroom smelled like us immediately; a combination of perspiration, old cologne, and subtle body scents; some sour, some sweet. Already, the mirror was beginning to fog.

In the cabinet, I found two sea wool sponges I'd been saving for that occasion. I had been waiting to bring April back into my shower for a long time. Somehow, with the diminishing number of encounters, the shower rarely felt right. The bathroom was too close to Chela's space, and it always seemed safest to pen April's ardor in the bedroom rather than to risk snuffing it by opening the door.

I made a silent apology for the water I was about to waste. I have a Takagi on-demand water heater, so I was planning to take my time. Showers are designed for bathing, after all, and there's no better way to begin a journey of flesh. Grooming is primal.

I sidled in behind her and assessed my favorite view. I can close my eyes and still see exactly how April's ass looked that night: perfect proportions of roundness and firmness, with cascading streams gliding from its mighty shelf like a gentle waterfall. April was slender everywhere except where she burst forth in compensation. The weak wand I'd had in Lynda Jewell's hotel room couldn't compare to the club rising against my belly, a genie summoned by a rub from April's bare, wet ass. I could have stared at her ass all night. Hell, some nights I almost did. It looked good by the light of the moon, but damp and gleaming?

Art.

I soaped up my sponge and touched the small of her back.

She gasped, feigning surprise. "Who's that?" She only turned halfway, as if she couldn't see me. She crossed her arms high to cover her breasts.

"The wind," I whispered. I'm not sure she heard me over the beating water.

April was role-playing, but tight knots of muscles in her back showed me how tense she was. A sudden thought broke my concentration, almost as if it was hidden in the rushing water itself: *You're losing her.* My Evil Voice had followed me home.

No you're not, my hand with the sponge assured me. *Not tonight.*

I slid the sponge's coarse soapiness across April's shoulder blades. Up and down her spine. The sponge kissed the back of her neck. Her head nodded forward, and her face and hair were washed in the shower stream. April usually didn't like getting her braids wet, but she didn't seem to notice. I heard her moan gently, appreciating the sponge's path.

I savored her ass the way I would a rich dessert, and I almost lost myself there. My slow circles met her curves as her contours took me by the hand. The sponge sank into the dimpled valley of her flank and rose again to the summit. A little pressure, and the sponge teased between the two halves that made her whole. I slid the sponge down deep through her thighs, then scaled the twin peaks again.

I already ached to slip inside of her, and we were just getting started. I gave my body a taste, pressing against her for a quick visit with her hot skin. Warm soap oiled us, electrifying each pore. This time, I was the one who moaned.

But I stepped away, and April turned around to face me. Still pretending to be blind, she patted my cheeks and nose. Next, she soaped up her hands and ran them across my chest. Beneath her fingertips, my abdomen locked tight, too, but not from stress—from a desire for release. While I moved my sponge to April's shoulders, her hands descended to grasp the firmness rising tall between us. Both hands. Like I said, I'm blessed.

I pulsed in rhythm to her fingers' caresses. April's first strokes were a nest of butterflies, gentle and fluttering, and I felt myself pressing harder against her for a more lingering touch. Her hand's strokes tightened with urgency. Her thumb explored every ridge as her palm clamped across my taut skin with a rhythm so delicious it was almost agony. April's confidence as a lover had grown during our time together, but it was more than that: She touched me as if she might never again have the chance. I floated in the sweet chaos of April's touch and the bath of hot water. My toes curled against the shower tiles.

My guest shower is built with a narrow elevated shelf in the corner, probably designed as a shampoo caddy, but it has other uses as well. When April sat on the shelf, her face nestled my groin. Her tongue lapped at the beads of water that had washed away the soap. Any man knows that hot water makes testicles stretch and breathe, and April enjoyed having more skin to play with. Her hands roamed, and her mouth followed.

A slight adjustment of her face, coupled with my unconscious rising to my tiptoes, and I felt April's lips and tongue slide along my skin, then clamp tight. Gently, she sucked and caressed while wet fingers stroked above making spirals and counterspirals that made my breath catch. She was like someone new. After weeks of reserve, April had set herself free.

"Damn, girl . . ." I whispered, almost a plea. *Please stop. Please never stop.*

Instead of falling shut, my eyes fought to stay open, searching for hers.

When our gazes caught, electricity broiled from my groin up and down my spine. The vision of her petite sweetness nearly overwhelmed me. Beautiful. Whatever that word meant to me, April defined it. April was beautiful. *You could marry a girl like this,* a new voice said, before my thoughts were swallowed in the void of sensation. It wasn't my Evil Voice, this time. It was a voice I had never heard before.

Gently, I held April beneath her armpits and lifted. "Stand up, baby," I said. Following my guidance, April carefully stood up on the shelf, bracing herself against the wet shower walls. I held her waist tightly. "Don't worry," I said, desire hoarsened my voice. "I've got you."

Again, the shelf put us at the perfect height.

I don't mind unwashed skin—I can delight in a woman's 101 flavors. But freshly washed skin has its rewards, too, if only because women often worry that their taste won't be fresh enough. April's hips pivoted forward as she presented herself to me.

April never waxed, but she kept her pubic hair clipped low. Beneath my careful fingers, folds of dark brown gave way to the blood-fed pink hidden within. I explored her with the matching pink of my tongue, gently probing, lapping at the water in hopes of a taste of her. I lathered my hand with soap and reached behind her. While my tongue worked on April from the front, my slippery finger probed from behind.

April let out a gasp, shivering, and her arm fell from the shower wall, tightening around my neck. Her whole body went so tight that my index finger was held hostage inside of her.

"I've got you, baby," I said again, and she relaxed. Freed from the tight clamp, my finger wormed its way deeper. Even after years of marriage, most women's bodies are *terra incognita* to their men. The vagina gets most of the attention, but there are plenty of nerve endings in its backyard, too. In a shower, there's no excuse to leave any entry untended.

April hissed into my ear, clinging for balance as her knees trembled. "Oh, God . . . Ohhh . . ." To keep from crying out as an orgasm jittered throughout her frame, she bit into my shoulder.

Biting from April was something new. The flash of near pain sharpened my senses, and my need to be inside of her surged. Carefully, I turned April around and helped her ease down from her perch. With one arm wound around her waist to help her keep her balance, I lifted her leg, resting the crook of her knee across my forearm. My body sought its way to hers. Penetration is much easier from behind in a shower, but I held April facing me. I didn't want to lose sight of the joy and wonder in her face, even for a blink.

We had plenty of soap, but I wasn't tempted. Soap is an irritant to a woman, and there's no quicker way to spoil the moment. Water isn't the lubricant it appears to be, either. Instead, I trusted the juices my foreplay had stirred inside of April. Her scent, a fleshy undertone in the shower's downpour, told me she was ready.

"Guide me," I whispered, and April's hands groped for me again. She led my body's blind, rigid desire to the place where her heat reached its nexus. Suddenly, with a virgin's tremor, I realized I had slipped inside of her. She bore down with her mouth open wide as I filled her, and I was consumed by her endless, grasping embrace. I climbed as high as physics allowed. We rocked and moved together beneath the shower stream, whimpering in chorus.

For all we knew, water and pleasure washed us both clean away.

Later, without saying a word, April climbed nude beneath my sheets. I nestled beside her, spooning her as I enjoyed the treat of her company through the long night. The humiliation I'd felt with Lynda Jewell was nearly forgotten with her healing presence, as if April confirmed only the best parts of me. Like the first time she slept in my bed.

I had drifted off before I was awakened by April's wordless anxieties. She hadn't moved or made a sound, but I knew from her breathing that she wasn't asleep. I gazed toward her in the darkness until I saw a glimmer from her eyes.

Tears?

My heart caught. "Baby?" I said.

"I'm sorry I woke you up," she said in a tiny voice. Trying to hide the tears.

"What's wrong?"

It took her only seconds to answer, but the wait was years. Maybe I had lost her trust, which can't be replaced. I've rarely felt so helpless as I did waiting for her to tell me my fate.

April sighed a long, fractured sigh. I heard her nose bubble. "Ten . . . I'm just lying here thinking . . . and I might not ever have another chance like this. I have to go to South Africa."

I wondered why it had taken her so long to figure that out.

I wanted to try to talk her out of it, but that would have been self-ish. Most people travel less, not more, as they grow older. April was twenty-eight. It was her time.

"I know."

I thought about Alice, the actress who had left me my house in her will. She'd never had any children, and I was her favorite house-sitter, so she made the job permanent when she died. With April and Chela and Dad around, the house felt less like Alice's and more like mine, but within those walls Alice was rarely far from my mind. Alice was the closest thing I'd had to a relationship—and she was a client, not a true lover. I saw Alice very late into her life, until she was as old as Billy Dee. I was almost young enough to be her grandson.

Maybe if life had promised Alice more of a future, I would have wanted her in mine. I can't say; my thoughts had never dwelled there. But she was my longest-standing client, and my favorite. Every few months, she'd call and send me a ticket to join her in Calcutta, or To-kyo, or Johannesburg, and then she'd kiss me fondly good-bye at the airport, send me home, and vanish for a while. She had a "gentleman friend" the whole time I knew her. Sometimes Alice and I traveled together, and she introduced me as her nephew. Sometimes she left me behind to water her plants and feed her fish. In Alice's memory, I fought to keep those neons and tetras alive. All the original fish had died, but you replace one at a time, so the actual pet is the tank.

Her laugh was golden. I wish I had recorded her stories; she was the most fascinating person I have ever known. I missed her when she was gone. I still do. I remember sitting in Alice's empty house, stir-crazy while I waited for her to come home. Waiting is excruciat-

ing work. I told myself only a fool would agree to a long-distance relationship. Not me. Never.

That night, lying in bed beside the first woman who'd helped me
understand why a man would want to be married, I remembered my
vow: *Never.* I loved South Africa, but my drop-everything-and-leave
days were long behind me. I had a role in a series for the first time in a
decade. Responsibilities awaited me at home every day. *Never.*

"I'll wait for you," my mouth said, surprising me. "Only six
months, right?"

April nestled her face against my bare shoulder, exactly where
she'd gently bitten me, and I felt her shaking her head. "I'm not asking
you to wait, Ten. I can't. I won't."

The room was so pitch that I couldn't see her face. In the din of
our whispered voices, I suddenly understood our rediscovery in the
shower, and the clarity felt like an anvil straight to my gut. April's caresses hadn't meant she was loosening up, or letting me in.

She had just wished me good-bye.

SIX

MONDAY, OCTOBER 20

Dad was waiting for me when I came downstairs.

It was almost three weeks after my shower with April, our last night in my bed. She was gone so fast, it all seemed like a dream. Being barred at the security gate on Sunday while April walked toward a plane to the other side of the world felt like a sentence. We could hardly look each other in the eye, as if we'd had a blowout instead of merely divergent lives.

For days I'd been expecting bad news. Perhaps because when you hurt, it is hard to believe the rest of the world could possibly be in good order. I'd been cracking my father's door open at night to make sure I could hear his long, strained breaths in the dark. My stomach was hurting even before I saw the look on Dad's face, but his frown made the pain sharper.

"You hear?" Dad said.

"Chela?" I said, my first guess. It was almost 8 A.M. Chela was supposed to be up for school, but life doesn't happen the way it's supposed to. I steeled myself to hear that Chela was hurt, or had run away. Chela felt temporary, too.

Dad shook his head and motioned toward the living room. "TV," he said, truncating his sentence as usual. "T.D. Jackson."

Dad wheeled himself to the spot beside Marcela, who was planted on the sofa with a bowl of popcorn in her lap while she watched the wide-screen with fascinated eyes. I didn't have to hear the CNN announcer's voice to know what had happened. An aerial shot showed the facade of T.D. Jackson's gated Mediterranean house in Pacific Palisades surrounded by LAPD vehicles, the scene draped in telltale yellow tape.

BREAKING NEWS, the screen read. T.D. JACKSON FOUND DEAD.

A stentorian announcer filled in the rest: ". . . details emerging in the death of T.D. Jackson, who was found dead at his desk this morning after an apparent gunshot . . ."

"April get off okay?" Marcela asked me gently, realizing I was in the room.

I nodded, but I barely heard her. My encounter with T.D. Jackson made the news report so personal that it felt like watching my own house on TV. Between that and the mention of April's name, the pain in my stomach bloated into a boulder. I didn't know the man—and there was a good chance he'd killed those two people—but I felt a stab of grief.

I heard myself whisper, "Shit," before I ever realized I'd spoken.

I remembered T.D.'s manic, reddened eyes imploring mine while he grasped my hand, and that image morphed into April's stone-jawed profile as she turned away from me at LAX. *Your fault*, my Evil Voice said, and this time I couldn't disagree.

Dad glanced at me meaningfully. I'd told him about T.D.'s request. "Reap whatchu sow . . ." Dad said. His idea of comforting words.

The announcer went on: ". . . unnamed sources within the police department are speculating that Jackson, recently acquitted in the double murder of his ex-wife and her fiancé, might have shot *himself* at his desk, in a state of apparent depression about both financial and legal affairs . . ."

I remembered T.D.'s eyes. Financial problems? The strain of another trial, especially if money was a problem? No more movies or television . . . T.D. Jackson couldn't sustain his preferred lifestyle signing autographs, trust me. Sitting at his desk, playing with his gun . . .

Was it a revolver? How about a little Russian Roulette? Another line of coke, spin the wheel, thumb back the hammer, and . . .

Maybe. Hell, I could see it. How much ego damage could someone like T.D. take before he broke? What if the Tau event was the last hurrah before the hammer came down . . . ?

But something inside me couldn't believe it. Sociopathic monsters like T.D. Jackson don't kill themselves until they're cornered by SWAT. If police had found a gun on the scene, someone had planted it. T.D. Jackson had been murdered, just like he was afraid he would be.

"Man was *loco*," Marcela said. "Killing himself! He will go to Hell."

Dad made a *humphing* sound. Fifteen years as the commander of Hollywood division, and another fifteen on the police force, had taught him to wait and see. I sat on the sofa beside Marcela, and the newscaster recapped for me: T.D.'s body had been found by his housekeeper at six that morning, and she'd called police right away. There were no signs of forced entry.

"Messed up, right?" a voice said behind me, and I realized Chela was up. Late-start Monday meant she didn't to have to get to school until ten. My set call was late, too.

I felt my heart brighten. "Hey!" I said. I gave her arm a squeeze. As usual, Chela was dressed down in military-style drabness, hidden inside an oversized jacket and baggy jeans. "Yeah, pretty messed up."

"The media wouldn't leave T.D. alone," Chela said. "What did people expect?"

Chela dropped a heavy manila envelope to the sofa cushion beside me. "Just came," she said. "All those messenger dudes they send are total hotties. He didn't want to let me sign for you, but I said I was your daughter."

That pulled a smile out of me. Chela never referred to herself as my daughter, and nothing left Chela's mouth without a reason. She was telling me that even though she knew it hurt to let April go, I still had her. But Chela would never bring up April's name unless I did.

The new *Homeland* pages were in the package. I'd gotten a script on the set Wednesday, and there was a rewrite first thing on Monday. Another rewrite might be waiting for me on set today. Of course, I never had more than two or three lines, and I can learn that much in ten minutes. It didn't really matter much. I'd heard a rumor that my part might be expanded—I might actually get a story arc, be more than a line of dialogue, a drop-and-roll or a reaction shot—but it hadn't happened yet.

While the television droned on, and Marcela caught Chela up on the details of T.D. Jackson's death, I flipped through the script's yellow-colored pages to make sure my paltry lines were intact. That week's episode, entitled "Mole," was actually one of the better ones: An FBI agent who'd been a mole for a terrorist organization was discovered stealing computer files from a fellow agent, and the episode ended with a blazing firefight. It took some looking to find my lines, and but I noticed the changes right away. Huzzah! I no longer had three lines: I had four!

Sanford: "If I do this, what's in it for me?"

Sanford: "What's Kelsey's problem? My kid's ten, and
he's got better manners."

Sanford: "Just sit here, eyes on your book, mouth closed.
Your mom's on her way."

Sanford: "Watch out!"

Now there was a child character called Jalil in the script who
called Sanford "sir," hanging out with him while he waited for his
mother to pick him up from work. They'd cast a *son* for me? That was
major. That was huge. The writers were turning me into an actual human! Marcus Sanford, my character, was mostly fall guy, eye candy,
and comic relief to the gruff series regulars—never mind that I was
the only one in the cast who'd spent any time at an actual police academy. Hell, I'd come close to graduating. In a different life, I would
have been on the scene at T.D. Jackson's house instead of watching it
on TV. Almost wished I was.

When I saw Chela heading for the door with a bagel, I put the
script down. "Ready . . . for school?" Dad called to her before I could.
When I was a kid, Dad was so lost in thoughts and paperwork that he
barely noticed me. Call me childish, but Dad's attentiveness to Chela
irked me sometimes.

"We have a chem quiz, but it's not my thing," Chela shrugged.
"Hydrogen peroxide? Like I'm ever gonna need to know *that* in life."
Chela was casually brilliant, but I felt sorry for her teachers.

"What's up with that homecoming dance?" I said, remembering.
"When is it? Don't you need a dress?" I was no expert on homecoming dance fashion, but I was eager to support Chela's experiment with
childhood.

"Homecoming?" Marcela said with an intrigued grin. "What
memories, eh? *Terrifico!*"

Chela gave me a dirty look for bringing it up in front of witnesses. "No it's not *terrifico*. I'm not going."

"Why not?" I said. "You said this kid . . . what's his name? That chess guy asked you."

"Exactly. It's next Saturday, and I'm not going."

Marcela stirred as if to say something else, but I patted her knee. The full frontal assault never worked with Chela. I had more than a week.

"Nobody's gonna force you," I said.

"Got *that* right," Chela muttered.

A familiar woman's voice made me look back at the TV. Framed in the center of my screen stood T.D. Jackson's cousin, Melanie Wilde. I'll say this for Melanie: She knew how to pull herself together in a crisis. There was no mistaking the grief in her glassy eyes, but her businesslike clothes and hair were a perfect suit of armor. An interviewer asked the obligatory How-do-you-feel riff that April had confessed she hated most about her job, and Melanie snapped off answers like she was leading a press conference.

"Again, according to unnamed sources, drugs were found at the scene, and police are speculating . . ." the interviewer began, and Melanie cut her off.

"The *police* are way off base. The *police* never gave credence to T.D.'s safety concerns. The *police* have sympathized only with T.D.'s deceased ex-wife and her very influential family. So excuse me if I'm not too impressed with any bogus theory claiming my cousin shot himself. I've known T.D. since the day he was born, and of all the things he was ever accused of, suicide is the most unlikely. But don't you worry: The *police* were never able to apprehend the murderer of Chantelle Hankins Jackson—never made a serious effort because they were so busy hounding T.D.—but we *will* find out who killed my cousin. Bet on it."

Her eyes bored right into me. I imagined myself in the over-bright hallway of my old dormitory, Clayton Hall, opening the door for Melanie as she carried in a basket of T.D.'s laundry piled so high she could barely see over it. *Success is a family project.* Her face had always glowed at the mention of his name—now that glow had turned to fire.

I looked away. It's hard for me to watch a woman suffer.

"She'll come back to you again," Marcela said suddenly. "You'll see."

"What?" I said, startled to have my thoughts made public.

"April." Marcela said her name softly enough to make it sting. "She'll be back."

I blinked. Two whole minutes had gone by, and I hadn't thought about April once. My stomach remembered its ache right away, of course. But two minutes was a start.

Years ago, right after his heart attack, Dad told me a little about my mother's death. I think he was afraid he was going to die, and he didn't want to take all of his stories with him.

Mom had been undergoing radiation treatments, and he recalled taking her to the oncologist's office to hear her newest test results, where he saw blank face after blank face. The oncologist came into the room discussing options and plans, but he couldn't hide the truth in his eyes. That was how Dad knew. My mother had just had a baby boy six months before, right in time to die. *You'd think a cancer doctor would've learned how to give people bad news,* Dad said that day in his hospital room, shaking his head with the memory—all the while watching his doorway, terrified he would see That Look on his cardiologist's face when he finally came to call.

That was how I felt Monday morning when I arrived on the set of *Homeland*. Work was where I went to escape my troubles, but my troubles had beaten the traffic and were waiting there to greet me.

A soundstage looks like a warehouse, some of them as big as airplane hangars. The sets are nestled in corners brightened with lights and imagination, carved inside the gray drab of wires, cables, and industry. On *Homeland*, much like *24* and *NUM3ERS*, the conceit was to show field FBI agents coordinating with the egghead researchers back at the office to break up terrorist plots, with family interactions to give it heart. One of the show's consultants was a former FBI researcher, so the home-office set was elaborate—the commander's office, the rows of cubicles, the meeting rooms (with banks of big monitors meant to be visual for television, but definitely *nothing* like the true-life FBI), the break room (which is where I usually turned up at the coffee machine), and even a bathroom set, where agents had private conversations. There was a training hall with a gun range and a dojo, connected to the group showers.

Who knew there was so much hooking-up going on in the FBI? Realism was not our strong suit, but the show's ratings were great. We took single thematic threads and ran them through the home, the field, the office, and the judo mat. It worked.

There were almost two separate casts; the stars in the field, the rest of us at the office. I'd expected T.D. Jackson's murder to give us something to talk about in common, a bridge over the divide between the name actors and the rest of us who were still scrambling for an ounce of recognition and a paycheck, whose residuals alone weren't enough to pay for the mortgage, a cruise, and a time-share every month.

Instead of chatter, there was a hush. My senses told me it started as soon as I walked in. Quiet in a place the size of an airplane hangar looms large enough to become sinister. I could feel eyes from every corner, but whenever I turned to find a face, the eyes were suddenly gone.

Shit, I thought. I figured my lines had been cut that week, as they sometimes were, and nobody bothered to tell me before I hauled my ass all the way over to the Fox lot. In my head, I started to map out the rest of my day. Maybe I would drive by Len's office and tell him about my disastrous visit with Lynda Jewell. Plot out a defensive plan.

Then I saw a handsome black boy who looked about ten waiting in the wings with a woman I guessed was his mother, who had a face suited for the camera herself. Since the only other black cast member was the male captain, who was in his sixties, I knew that kid was mine. My lines hadn't been cut!

We were all grinning as I walked toward them. We needed each other to survive.

The boy stood up, straight and prim. Even from a distance, I could see that he'd curbed any childish tendencies toward twitching and playing in his quest to be an actor. He stepped before his mother, hand outstretched as if he'd just come from etiquette class.

"Pleased to meet you, Mr. Hardwick," the boy said, eager to let me know he had memorized my name. He gave me two firm pumps, adult-style. I noticed that the boy's complexion and facial structure *were* an eerie match for my own. Casting had done a good job.

He told me his name, Darnell, and dutifully ran through his credits: *House of Payne*, *Cold Case*, and even *Sesame Street* when he was three. His work had been steadier than mine. His mother beamed, but she kept a distance with a steady gaze that told me she would scratch my eyeballs out if I gave her a reason. I hoped a tigress for a mother would be enough to safeguard her son's passage to adulthood, but I know too many child actors who've grown up too fast and lost their way. I'm glad I didn't step in front of a camera until I was grown.

I had enough problems without jumping on the Hollywood Bullshit-Go-Round.

Elliot the Makeup Guy motioned over at me from the hall. Elliot looked like a teamster, in jeans and his trademark white sleeveless tees to show off his weight-room physique.

"Gotta go," I told Darnell. "See you in a few."

"I look forward to working with you, Mr. Hardwick!" Darnell piped with another perfect handshake. I hoped Darnell raised a little hell at home—at least a messy room. *Something.* Kids trained from diapers to be that eager to please everyone are in for a rude awakening.

The narrow makeup room was a wall of mirrors and three empty chairs. I glanced at my reflection in the mirror, dressed in a suit and tie just like Dad always wanted for me, and my imagination dared to dream. What if the kid became a semiregular? What if the writers created a home life for me—an honor reserved only for the leads? *What if . . . ?*

"Congratulate me," I told Elliot, easing into his chair. "I'm a dad. Wish I had a cigar."

Elliot made a clucking sound. Half his conversations were sound effects, not words. In that way, he reminded me of Dad.

"What's that mean?" I said.

Elliot made a two-toned humming sound, dusting my forehead with brown powder. "Kid or no kid, watch your ass today, Tin-Man." His nickname for me—as in heartless, since he considers my strict heterosexuality a sin against all gaykind.

You'd rather watch my ass for *me,* I thought. I'm comfortable around anybody, but Elliot's bold stares had taken some getting used to, especially since it was his job to put his hands on me every day. I checked Elliot's face in the mirror. His usual flirty smile wasn't in sight. The vanity lights gleamed across his bald-shaved scalp.

"What's up, man?" I said.

He pursed his lips. "A lot of mouths talking a lot of shit." Elliot's voice rumbled like a Brooklyn cabbie's.

"Man, just come out with it. I don't need melodrama today."

Elliot shrugged, his jaw flexed. "There's gonna be blood. Bang, bang." He motioned his head toward the countertop at the other end of the room. I saw a row of small crimson squibs lined up—plastic packs used to simulate gunshot wounds.

"Perry's out this week," I said. Not soon enough for me. The actor who played the mole, Kelsey—I'll call him Perry—was ending his guest-starring stint in a hail of FBI-issue "bullets." He was a former A-lister who'd starred in my favorite buddy cop movie when I was in high school, and I'd considered myself a true fan, not just the Hollywoodspeak kind. When I went up to him to introduce myself the first day he appeared on the set, he gave me a contemptuous look and asked for a decaf latte. Prick.

"Not just him," Elliot said.

"Nobody else eats lead in the script."

Elliot's throat burred. "Not yet. But after lunch? Who knows?" He whistled a long tone, a human teakettle. "I hear the writers were working all weekend. Tap, tap." Elliot also spoke in monosyllabic repetitions. "Like I said: Watch your ass."

At least I understood why it had been so quiet. Someone was going to be written out—maybe Darla, who complained incessantly about her salary. Or Vick, who had made it loudly known that he'd been offered a part in a Bruckenheimer movie. Then again, Elliot enjoyed his role as the ears to all, and sometimes he took his soothsayer bit too far.

My scenes were up first, so I had to get to work.

My exchange with Darnell was in a corner of the set fashioned to look like the break room, a few tables and vending machines. I saw Darnell walking in a circle in the corner, reciting his lines with a furrowed brow. The director, Avery, took us through the blocking, and Darnell sailed through, playing the kid like an angry wiseass. He reminded me of Chela. He was convincing, so I sparked off him. For those few minutes, he *was* my son—hell, he was *me*, déjà vu. When I snapped my lines, Dad's voice came out of my mouth.

Cut. Done. Darnell's mother clapped for us, full of praises for both. For the millionth time, I wondered how my life might have been different if I'd had a mother.

While catering set up the table with aromatic pasta salad, sandwiches, and fresh cookies, I felt a tap on my shoulder. "Rewrite," said Benny, the wide-bodied head writer, handing me a stack of blue pages. I only saw his broad back retreating as fast as it could.

Apparently, everyone else had gotten their scripts while I was shooting. Three or four sets of eyes dashed away like rabbits running for the bushes.

Elliot motioned for me again. He had the blue pages, too.

I sighed and headed for makeup. I wasn't going to read bad news in front of a crowd.

"Sorry," Elliot murmured.

I took my chair again. "Give me a minute. I haven't seen it yet."

Maybe I would only be injured. Maybe . . .

A TV script title page is like a production in itself, with the show's logo, the episode's title, and a list of personnel including the gaggle of producers, the director, and the writers. The first time I got a *Homeland* script with my name on a label, I kept it as proof that I was in control of my life again. I hoped this wouldn't be my last—not now.

Elliot read over my shoulder when I flipped open the pages, one of my pet peeves, but I was too worried to swat him away. He could probably hear my heart racing as I scanned deeper through the script, looking for my moment of glory. But the scene I remembered was gone. Over the weekend the writers had rewritten the entire third act. My eyes rushed over the jumble, trying to catch the gist: The mole, a guy named Kelsey, had shot someone.

Jalil had more lines, calling *Dad, Dad!* But where was Sanford? My stomachache came back with a kicking sensation as I fanned through the pages to see what I'd missed.

"There," Elliot said gently, pointing on page 39.

No dialogue, but I finally let myself see the stage direction: *Sanford reels backward, falling across his desk. Sanford holds his neck with bloodied fingers, twitching and gasping. CLOSE ON SANFORD'S FACE: He is dead. Agents whisk JALIL to safety behind a cubicle, ducking. JALIL cries.*

I had to blink once, then again. The squibs were for me. That's how it is in this business. No courtesy call over the weekend. No notifying my agent. No good-bye party. No *Hey, sorry.* Cold-ass motherfuckers.

"Sons of *bitches* . . ." I couldn't always find work, and I'd shot a couple of pilots that hadn't gone anywhere, but I'd never been fired from an acting job.

Elliot rested a brotherly hand on my shoulder. "Sorry, Tin-Man."

"If they're killing him off, why'd they hire this kid . . . ? "

Bam. I *got* it. It was just like in a horror movie: If a character mentions a fiancé or a kid, you can bet they're about to die. And it was worse than that: Horror and sci-fi movies became notorious for always killing the *brother* first. Traditionally in Hollywood horror or action films, killing a black man was a cheap death—a little pinch, but he wasn't quite a real person, a sort of inoculation against the *real* horror to come: threatening a pretty young white girl of child-bearing age. Of course, even better was if that black man died protecting that pretty white girl, so that the hero could screw her later.

The worst thing about *this* situation was introducing the kid just in time to leave another black boy without a father! It wasn't like me, but I was ready to call the NAACP and Al Sharpton.

"How'd you know?" I asked Elliot.

"I knew something was up, and your name was floating around. They're a bunch of bastards anyway, Ten. Fuck 'em."

It's hard to say *Fuck 'em* when you still remember being broke. Marcela cost three grand a month, and that wasn't counting Dad's physical therapist. That wasn't counting a whole lot. So much for my savings account. How long would the money last before my next job?

I wanted to call April, and I couldn't even do that. She hadn't sent me her number yet.

Instead, I tried to call Len Shemin, my agent. He was in a meeting. I left an urgent message, but it was a miracle to get Len on the phone before seven, his last call of the day. I couldn't bring myself to tell his assistant, Giovanni, what the problem was.

"What's next, Tin-Man?" The fond sadness in Elliot's voice made me feel more alone.

I wanted to go home, and in hindsight I wish I had. Fuck appearances. But I was a pro, and a pro does the job. I would stay to spite them, to show them what professionalism looked like. They could take notes and kiss my ass. That's what I thought.

"Put on the goddamn squibs," I said.

That day, there would be blood.

I deserved an award for my performance the rest of that day.

All afternoon, I ignored the flimsy, tight-lipped masks hastily slipped over my coworkers' curiosity. Suddenly, I was the bad luck nobody wanted to rub off on them.

I saw the head writer, Benny, picking over the sandwiches on the catering table, but he made sure I could only see his profile. Most writers are humble folk—an industrywide lack of respect knocks the asshole out of most people pretty quick—but Benny was an exception. He'd always been a pompous ass, and it seemed like the perfect moment to tell him so.

I also wanted to tell the director he had no imagination, the female lead that her hair extensions made her look like a Shetland pony, and remind the male lead that his name hadn't opened a movie since 1986, so maybe he could stop strutting around like Russell Crowe.

But I didn't. I did my job.

Television and movie gunshots are fake, usually without even blanks, but no production takes gun scenes lightly—especially since Bruce Lee's son, Brandon, died after being shot with a blank while filming *The Crow*. If there is a weapon on the set, everyone has to be present for the safety meeting—just in case. At the scene's start, Perry and other agents would fire guns with blanks so the gunfire would look and sound realistic. But for my close-up, Perry would switch guns and fire one *without* blanks against the side of my neck. The assistant director ran us through the motions with two black Glock 22s .40 caliber, standard-issue FBI. One empty, one loaded with blanks.

"Yeah, yeah. Are we done with the hand-holding?" Perry groused to his coffee, loudly enough to be heard. "I've done this a hundred times."

I glared at the wiry, white-haired actor whose performance had once delighted me—even inspired me. He was one or two words away from a plastic surgeon. Like I said, a prick.

"You got a problem?" I said.

Perry shrugged. "This is the biz, kid. You want steady? Get a law degree."

The director, Avery, gave Perry an irritated look, then he waved his hand over his head in his circular signal for *Let's get moving*. Finally. I was ready to shoot the scene and go home before I did something that would make the tabloids.

Avery motioned me to my cubicle on the set before my death scene. He knew I could have made his life hell that day, and he looked grateful I was still there.

"Wasn't my call," Avery said quietly, his obligation. He was olive-skinned and balding.

"Whatever. What do you need?"

Avery ran us through the scene: a quiet moment at the office interrupted by gunfire from Kelsey. Finally, with a sigh, Avery pointed to my character's desk, which was as spare as my undeveloped character. I noticed that someone from Props had added a framed photo of me and Darnell, expertly Photoshopped. Nice afterthought, but it was too little, too late.

"OK, Ten, so it's *bam-bam* to the chest . . ." Avery tapped the squibs strapped beneath my shirt, which would splatter after a radio signal coordinated with the gunshots. Low-rent productions use plastic baggies, but *Homeland* could afford better effects. "The squibs go off, bloodstains, yada yada, you fall down. Then Perry comes behind you—last *bam*, to the neck. Left side. Your hand slaps your neck with a squib, *splat*, you're dead. And that's it."

I could hear the relief in his voice at the idea.

Any other day I would have had a dozen thoughts on how to play the hell out of even a passive scene like that one, and maybe a few questions. Instead, I just nodded.

Considering how hard the rest of the day had been, my last scene was easy.

Sanford is typing on his computer at his desk. Kelsey shouts something. Commotion. Sanford looks up. I never had a chance to say anything, or reach for my gun.

I never heard gunshots, so I was startled to feel the squibs burst on my skin. Like sharp, shallow punches. It wasn't hard to look surprised and reel backward. No blanks sounded, but they could fix that in editing. I lost my balance when I stumbled back into my desk, which only added to the effect. I tried to imagine how a father would feel knowing he was leaving his son behind, and I fixed that horror on my face. I gasped for air, my last chance to *be*.

I dropped to the floor.

"Cut!" Avery said. "Where were my sparks?"

Gareth Priestly, the English propmaster who sported red hair and a beard to match, was already checking the gun's chamber. "Misfire," he said. "Blanks are there."

"Fuck it, we'll fix it in editing," Avery said. "Give him the empty. Let's finish."

I didn't move on the floor, waiting. I was just glad to avoid going back to makeup.

"Action!" Avery said.

On Avery's cue, the set became bedlam. More commotion. Shouting. This time, loud gunshots sounded behind me. I heard Perry's hurried footsteps behind me, his heels vibrating the set's floor. One step. Two.

Off camera, I nestled the last squib in my hand, ready to slap it to my neck.

I felt Perry's gun against my neck. *Good-bye, you assholes*, I thought.

Click. And—

My head exploded. The *world* exploded. I still don't know which was worse—the noise or the pain. A fiery lance stabbed through my ear and into my brain.

My shout wasn't in the script, but I would only find out about the shout later, because I didn't hear it. I opened my eyes, expecting to see only light, or utter darkness. With all sound gone, I was sure I was dead. My hand and shirt were covered with blood.

I saw Perry standing over me, his blood-specked face so pale he looked like a Japanese geisha lost in the prom scene from *Carrie*. Suddenly he was an old man—a stricken, confused old man. I was fascinated by the sight of his face shaking, the skin quivering from his jaw. Dad had looked that way in his hospital room.

BOOM-BOOM BOOM-BOOM BOOM-BOOM.

I thought the sensation shaking the floor was an earthquake, but it was my heart. My wondering eyes made the life snap back into Perry's haunted face, and his lips started moving. I couldn't hear him, but his lips mouthed in eerie slo mo, clear as day:

Somebody get a fucking doctor.

SEVEN

TUESDAY, OCTOBER 21

"Messed yourself up good this time, huh, Ten?"

I didn't need both ears to tell me what Reggie had said. Reggie, my doctor, has always been a smart-ass. He's my second cousin from a family intersection on my mother's side, and he used to treat me cheap. Now he was on staff at UCLA Medical School and working for the Lakers, so it's almost as hard to get a meeting with Reggie as it is with my agent. But this was an emergency, and Reggie is the only doctor I trust. Besides, he's family.

"Looks that way," I said.

Reggie leaned closer, shining his otoscope into my ear, and I sat rock steady. I didn't want Reggie to miss anything. Reggie's proximity made the roar of silence deafening.

Dad and Marcela watched from a corner of Reggie's office, and the worry in Dad's eyes was for me, for a change. I tried not to let myself see it. I was worried enough for all of us.

"How'd this happen?" Reggie's voice sounded like it was at the end of a long tunnel.

"Some asshole put blanks in a prop gun that was supposed to be empty. Got fired right up against my neck. That's where that burn's from. And now my head rings like hell, and I can't hear shit out of that ear."

I used to quiz myself when I was a kid—which would you rather lose, your hearing or your sight? That's a no-brainer. Hearing, hands down. Now that one of my ears had stopped working—and the other seemed anything but reliable—it felt like God had taken me up on my bargain.

I felt Reggie's sigh against my cheek. "Lucky you didn't get killed, man."

"You think I don't know?"

"(Schibhiwkh)."

I shook my head, and Reggie pulled the little cone-shaped black light out. Usually, I could hear at least faintly out of my right ear, but sometimes words were lost. Instead, there was only the ringing, like three loud bells tolling at once.

"There's ringing. And I couldn't make out the last thing you said."

"Hold still, Ten. Relax. You're gonna be fine."

"You hope," I corrected.

"Yeah. I hope." Unfortunately, I heard that part fine.

I wish Reggie had been older than two and out of diapers when my mother needed honesty from her doctor. Or that he'd been in the country when Dad had his heart attack. After Dad's stroke, Reggie got me through the worst moments by being willing to pick up his phone any time of the day or night. I never ran out of questions. Reggie is the finest doctor there is.

"Hold still," Reggie said again, gently. In my good ear, my right one.

Marcela said something encouraging, but I couldn't make it out.

I shared a house with a man in a wheelchair, so I knew that life goes on after a disability. As long as I could work, I could handle hearing loss. I could manage a lifelong struggle to enjoy music again— even though so far, my jazz, blues, and funk collection was only a painful exercise in frustration. It didn't sound the same. Too much was missing. Still, I'd be all right with that.

But I couldn't handle the ringing.

They say Beethoven heard ringing while he was going deaf. And an artist, Goya, whose paintings I saw when I visited the Prado museum in Madrid with Alice during one of our vacations together. They say that the ringing in their ears drove both of them crazy. The madness in Goya's work is hidden in plain sight—people shrieking and screaming and eating their young. I'd had the ringing for only a day, and I was halfway to bugnuts myself. Night was hell. Nothing but ringing, hissing, and roaring in my head, keeping me awake. How would I put up with one more night?

Reggie was my last stop before Panic.

"When's it gonna stop?" I asked Reggie when he straightened up, his exam done.

Dad wheeled himself closer to hear better himself, and Marcela hovered, too.

Reggie folded his arms behind his head and gazed down at me, his lips refusing to smile. "Don't know for sure, man. It probably will— it usually does—but it might not. I gotta be real with you: It might be gone tomorrow, or it might not be gone for a while. Weeks? Months?"

Marcela muttered in Spanish, shaking her head, maternal worry creasing her brow.

Reggie went on: "In the short term, there are things you can do: Avoid aspirin, caffeine, alcohol. Studies show that they make the ringing worse. And if it's bad at night, get a humidifier, an air purifier, something that makes low-level noise. That'll help mask it."

"*Mask it* my ass, Reggie. How do I get rid of it?"

That was when Reggie explained there was no known cure. And that the ringing might persist even after the hearing in my left ear returned—*if* my hearing returned, which was more and more doubtful after sixteen hours, and mine had been gone longer. And he explained that my mission now was to make sure the hearing loss didn't get worse. And recommended a good otolaryngologist, a specialist at UCLA Medical Center. Recommended some herbs and amino acids I could take.

In other words, there was nothing he could do. Just like the emergency-room doctor said.

Reggie's confirmation exhausted me. I would have lain down on the table, just let the weight of the knowledge sink down into my bones, except I didn't want to upset Dad. Or I didn't want to look weak to him, more likely.

"The gunshot and the ringing are related, but I'm gonna go ahead and look at them as two separate problems," Reggie said. "It's rare, but I've seen temporary hearing loss up to three or four days. I'm hoping you have what we call a Temporary Threshold Shift—as opposed to PTS, the permanent kind. We don't know if there's cell death unless the hearing doesn't come back, and that only becomes clearer with time. But if you look at your ear's function as computer hardware, the ringing is more like a software problem." He smiled as if pleased by the analogy. "It's a little more complicated. There's a bigger role that stress plays, for example."

"So it's in my head?" I said.

Reggie grinned slightly. "In more ways than one, yeah. So . . . take it easy for a few days. Chill out. Low stress."

That would be tough, with April, my job, and my left ear gone in a span of two days.

"(Twhig hie eeziiee), man," Reggie said with a smile, slugging my shoulder.

I nodded, but I hadn't heard him. Instead, I'd heard a sound like waves crashing over my brain. The noise wasn't always a ringing. Maybe I would have to get used to that, too.

When the gun went off, I'd just been relieved that all the blood on my shirt and hand wasn't really mine—it was only from the squibs. I was so grateful to be alive, I'd made jokes for Chela by the time she got home from school. (*"Your turn's coming, all that loud music."*)

But that had worn off. All I could think about now was the damage.

When I tried to ask Reggie to repeat what he'd said, I couldn't open my mouth.

"One ear's better'n none . . ." Dad said, turning on the TV. Pep talk over.

To Dad, a few words of hard, simple truth and an afternoon of Court TV were the answers to all of life's problems. Dad had learned how to appreciate what was left instead of fixating on what was gone. Me, I wasn't there yet.

"I know that." My teeth were gritted.

"Oughta sue 'em, though . . ." Dad said.

"Damn right I will."

Maiming and killing are against the law, so suing is the next best thing. I wanted to do great damage to the son of a bitch who had handed Perry a gun loaded with blanks. Gareth Priestly. He was the propmaster for *Homeland*, and that asshole's carelessness nearly got me killed.

Every hour on the hour, I had to talk myself out of driving to the set to talk to Priestly personally. Okay, I didn't want to talk to him—I wanted to hurt him. But I couldn't access the set anymore. I was fired. I was the reason every studio has a guarded gate. After Monday, I was the last person they would let in.

When someone knocked at my door, I let myself hope it was April. She'd changed her mind about South Africa. About me. I was desperate for a change of direction.

I opened the door to see Len Shemin, my agent, and I was almost as happy. My agent had never set foot in my house. If I had realized this was how to get Len Shemin's attention at one o'clock on a week-day, I would have blown out my eardrum a long time ago.

"Shit—hallucinations, too?" I said, meeting him in the doorway.

"Shut up, you. I was in the neighborhood. You gonna invite me in, or stand there gawking?" Then he hugged me. Another first. "Shitty week, man. *Shitty*. First the Lynda Jewell thing, now this."

Every once in a great while, an artist realizes his agent is also his friend. I probably should have guessed it sooner, but it was finally plain. Len Shemin is the biggest workaholic I know. I book lunch with him a month in advance. I could only guess what he'd rescheduled to make time to drive to my house.

"My dad's here," I told Len quietly, inviting him in. "We can't talk in front of him."

"Roger. But get us alone somewhere."

I needn't have worried about how to excuse myself from Dad and Marcela with so much T.D. Jackson news to digest on TV. They were hypnotized by the parade of ignorant analysts making guesses based on nothing. Dad mumbled a greeting at Len when I introduced him, but then Dad only fixed a disapproving scowl on the gel in Len's bleached-blond hair that made it stand up an inch. Between that and Len's red-framed Clark Kent glasses, Dad looked like he thought the circus had come to town. Sometimes I think Dad believed his age and infirmity made him invisible.

I whispered close to Dad's ear. "Weren't *you* the one who taught *me* not to stare?"

"You be sure to make this right, Mr. Shemin," Marcela called after us, as Len and I walked toward my home office, like Len was our plumber.

"I'll do that, ma'am," Len said. I almost believed him.

I'd moved my office into a corner of the screening room, which had once been the centerpiece of Alice's social life. She'd spent a fortune on it. My tiny corner desk, computer and printer faced opposite Alice's old nine-and-a-half-foot screen, two rows of seats, and a museum's worth of publicity photos in neat rows across the walls.

"Ten, this *house*! Jesus, all these years you're giving me this song and dance about no money, 'Get me work, Len' . . . This fucking house is bigger than mine. This room! I don't have a goddamn screening room. Who do you think you are—George Lucas?"

I powered up my computer. "Inheritance," I said. "Former client."

"You're kidding! Who?"

I shook my head. "You know I'm not going there, man."

Len admired Alice's photo collection on the wall, the record of her Hollywood friendships. Name someone, and their signatures and photos are up there. Name anyone.

"I'll look her up in the real estate records," Len said.

"Do what you gotta do."

With Len there, I almost forgot about my ear. Then my computer beeped as the screen came on. I barely heard the sound, as if I were in a fish tank filled with water.

Len was talking to me, and I had to concentrate to listen. Len, ever perceptive, noticed I was favoring one ear and shifted to my good side. ". . . times I tried to get you to walk away from that life, I should've been lining up clients, getting my ten percent."

I might have thought it was funny if it hadn't been so hard to hear.

"So you just came to say 'I told you so'?" I was surprised by the anger in my voice.

Len's face went sallow. "Hell no, Ten. I was just kidding. A joke."

Anger had hardened my face. I had to use my hands to knead my skin back to softness. The anger seemed to have boiled up out of nowhere, and that kind of anger is dangerous.

"Sorry, man," I said.

Len patted my shoulder and checked the closed door behind us. "Listen, Ten, in all seriousness: I'm sure Jewell got you fired off the show."

I'd had my suspicions, but if anyone would know, Len Shemin would.

"What makes you sure?"

"Your show-runner, Frank Lloyd, got his start at Dark Dream Productions, which was FilmQuest's television subsidiary, and he made them a fortune. I knew the Lloyds and Jewells play doubles at the Beverly Hills Tennis Club—that's why I sent her your packet. *Homeland* is his baby. All she had to do was pick up the phone, and you were gone."

Pick up the phone and say what? I wondered.

On my computer, I Googled my least favorite propmaster, Gareth Priestly. He got two hundred hits, including his MySpace page, where I saw a long list of credits. He'd started his career working on *Alien*, and he'd worked steady, high-profile projects ever since, most of them involving gunplay. He should have done a better job. Leaving blanks in a gun about to be fired against an actor's body was damn near as bad as filling it with bullets. There would be an incident review at the SAG Stunt Performer's Board. If his mistake was taken seriously enough, there might be charges.

Beside Gareth's name, I typed L-Y-N-D-A J-E-W-E-L-L. Searched them together. Call it a hunch.

There were forty hits. Most of the sites were movie listings, from three or four projects Gareth Priestly worked on that Lynda Jewell shepherded as an executive producer. That didn't count: They might never have even met.

But the last hit was a photo from *Variety*, which I could only access because of my subscription: Lynda Jewell and Gareth Priestly side by side at a FilmQuest premiere party, raising champagne glasses toward the photographer, their faces slightly ruddy from alcohol.

The blood in my veins cooled.

Not only had they met, but they looked cozy. Priestly was in his midfifties, but he was fit. Strong face. Maybe handsome. Where was her husband when that photo was taken?

Two clangs in my head reminded me that Len was talking to me.

". . . not much you can do except wait . . ." Len was saying. "So far, I haven't heard from Progress Smartphones, so that's good. Your contract runs through May . . ."

That bitch tried to hurt me.

The realization rang more loudly than the rest of the noises in my head.

The second time, I said it aloud.

"What?" Len said. He used that B-word plenty, but he'd never heard it from my lips.

"Lynda Jewell." I pointed out the photo on my screen.

"Who's that with her?"

"The asshole who gave Perry a gun loaded with blanks."

Len's eyes widened. He lowered his face so close to the screen that his nose nearly touched it. "No. That can't be right. You think . . . ? He'll probably get fired. What you're talking about is assault. That's . . . *prison.*"

"Or something. If I can prove it. Means and opportunity we have. Maybe motive, too."

Len looked at me with alarm. The tumult between my ears made me miss most of what he said, but I could tell how dismissive his words were by his body language. Don't jump to conclusions, he was saying. Give it a few days. Don't do anything rash. Len always gave good advice, but it's hard to hear him even with two good ears. For me, anyway.

I changed the expression on my face—admittedly, it must have been fearsome—and Len looked more at ease. Being an actor comes in handy every day. Before long, Len was looking at his watch, saying something about a meeting at Warner Brothers at three.

But first, he gave me another hug. "Next step, lawyer. If we make the case, you'll get a settlement. But your assault theory . . . remember what I said. Thin ice, Ten."

Whatever else he'd said didn't matter. "Yeah, yeah."

"Women," he said to my good ear. "If you find a sane one, bottle her."

Len hadn't said a nice word about women since his divorce. Once I told him to let all that anger go, or he'd drive himself crazy. If he was ever put on trial for any crime having to do with hating women, I'm not sure who'd be hotter to get me on the stand: the prosecution or the defense.

"It's not about women," I said. "I've known thousands of women, and most of them are saner than you. This one happens to be a sick and vindictive person."

My speech was intended more for me than for Len.

I suddenly understood why so many men were eager to join the Bitches-Ain't-Shit club. Ages ago, one of my clients told me I had contempt for women, since so many female sex workers have contempt for men. I'll admit that her theory messed with my head for a minute, but I eventually convinced her otherwise. I *love* women. Let me count the ways.

Lynda Jewell wants to rewire Tennyson Hardwick? Bring a lunch. But our time in her hotel suite was far from over. She'd been too sloppy.

Somehow—some way—someday—I was going to get her.

The rest was only details.

After I walked Len to the door, I returned to my computer to find out more about the connections between Lynda Jewell, Gareth Priestly, and Frank Lloyd.

But first, I checked my email. Finally, a note from BLESSED-GIRL was waiting for me. I hadn't heard from April since she'd left. I inhaled, and read the note before the breath left my lips: *Arrived safely! There's so much to talk about. I'll call you soon.*

And that was it.

My joy at seeing email from April was snuffed out by everything she hadn't said. She wasn't out in the bush: She'd told me they were checking her into a Holiday Inn. If she ever sent me her number, or called me, I would tell her what had happened Monday. If not, she didn't have time. Either way was fine. That was what I told myself.

I almost didn't recognize the next email's sender: SECUREG?

When I opened it, I saw the company's full name: SECUREGUARD.com It was a monitoring service I'd set up after my computer problem with Chela. They monitored keystrokes and kept track of email and websites. Pure invasion of privacy, but I owned the computer, I pay for the internet, and I don't care.

I'd almost forgotten I had the service. For months they'd been quiet, meaning that hopefully she'd been good. Now, for the first time in six months, I had a bulletin. SecureGuard could tell me if Chela tried to get back in touch with Internet Guy. I didn't spy on Chela's email more than once in a while, and lately only if I had a reason. SecureGuard had just given me one.

Chela wasn't home from school yet, so I went into her room to sign on to her computer. Knowing every keystroke also meant I knew her passwords.

In a way, we were in a war, Chela and I. She didn't know who she was messing with.

I signed on as Chela, using her password. Her only email was ten announcements from her high school, one a reminder for the homecoming dance. Chela, knowing I was spying, deleted almost all of her personal email immediately. But I knew how to check her Recycling Bin, and that was where I headed next.

That was where I saw a sender's name: DRUMZ62.

It was a new email address, but I knew who it was from: The guy in Sherman Oaks was a drummer with a Led Zeppelin tribute band called Stairway. I'd watched his show once, with plans for him in the parking lot. His first name was Zack. He was forty-six, born in 1962. Chela didn't realize it, but I knew everything about that prick except boxers or briefs. And hoped Chela couldn't fill that one in for me.

I'd wanted to break his legs once, and the feeling was back.

His email to Chela was dated the night I was at the hospital, another reason to be pissed. I could have been at home. That wouldn't have stopped his email, but at least she wouldn't have been without me when it came. I had made her promise to tell me if he ever again tried to get in touch with her. She said she'd seen the light: He was disgusting, and she never wanted to hear from him again.

Yeah, right.

I clicked DRUMZ62's message open, a single line:

I miss you. Where U been, beautiful?

My fists contracted. For ten seconds, I was so pissed I couldn't move my fingers. It was as if he'd snuck in through the cyberwindow. Into *my* house.

Heart pounding, I scanned the folder of SENT MAIL to see if Chela had answered.

She had, within a minute: *I told you not to write me here. Call me on our cell.*

Our cell? I'd bought her one, but obviously she knew I had access to the bill. That door was locked and barred, right? Hardly. Disposable or rechargeable cells are sold over the counter at every 7-Eleven. *Who paid for it, Chela—and how did you pay him back?*

Chela lied to me every day, and maybe always would. Lying was her nature. I was a fool to think I could stand in the way of a force that strong.

That was when the call came, when I was at my lowest.

Marcela knocked on my door. The knocking sounded so muted, I almost missed it. "Ten! Phone for you!"

My cell phone was in my back pocket, and no one called my house phone except political pollsters and bill collectors. I wasn't in the mood for the phone.

"Who is it?" I called back, not moving.

("Meghiehee Wiehe?")

"*FUCK*," I said, much louder than I intended. Rage was running loose in my throat, my muscles and everywhere else, and I couldn't rein it back. I didn't even want to.

I tried to ignore the startled look on Marcela's face when I flung the door open. Marcela's eyes looked too much like April's when she asked if I'd gone into a hotel room with Lynda Jewell, wondering why I'd let that woman sit on my lap. Hurt. Surprised. Emptied out.

"Who?" I said. "Jesus, Marcela, speak up. E-*nun*-ci-ate."

The phone in Marcela's hand trembled slightly. Her voice was uncertain.

"Melanie . . . Wilde? She said it's about T.D. Jackson."

EIGHT

I'D WARNED MELANIE that if she insisted on seeing me Tuesday, I wouldn't be at my best. But Melanie Wilde couldn't hear the word *no*, wheedling and cajoling nonstop on the phone. She talked me into letting her pick me up—only because getting out of the house seemed like a damn fine idea, and nobody else had offered me a ride. I didn't trust myself to drive yet. I also didn't trust having too much empty time left in the day. I was too pissed off in too many directions to have idle hands. Devil's workshop and all that.

I really wanted to drive to Sherman Oaks and commit a felony. Or to FilmQuest.

Instead, ten minutes later, Melanie showed up at my curb in a silver Volvo convertible, her braids loose in the wind. Driven music was playing on Melanie's speakers, but I couldn't follow it. She didn't smile, but she didn't have to. Grief chiseled her cheekbones. She was a sight, midnight skin wrapped in a sweater of spun gold. I had blocked Melanie's true beauty from my eyes at the fund-raiser, but that day my eyes missed nothing. Her beauty was hard, burnished, secure. She probably had known she was beautiful since she was a girl.

I stood beside her open passenger door. "You holding up okay?"

"Sorry about your ear," she said, ignoring my pity. "Let's take a drive."

Climbing into her car was easy. Melanie reminded me of what April might be like in a few years if she took off her brakes. Melanie could help me put off my talk with Chela after school. Nothing else I did the rest of the day was going to be harder than that talk, or more dangerous. So I thought.

The drive itself was easy, too. But climbing out of Melanie's car afterward wasn't.

We sat idling at the Jacksons' curb, in the shade of perfectly aligned jacaranda trees. The gated community of Hancock Park belied the turmoil I knew was caged inside the genteel, Tudor-style house on the corner lot. Len had fawned over my house, but Alice had never lived with the kind of opulence in Hancock Park, which has been home to black millionaires since Nat King Cole crossed the color line and bought his house there in the 1950s.

I realized, a bit late, that I'd fallen into the oldest trap known to man, or more specifically, to men: I wanted to get laid. Mind you, despite my history—or maybe because of it—I don't find myself casually attracted to random women. Maybe that's why it turned out to be so easy for me to be monogamous; I'd seen so many women, I lost the habit of looking. Sex always felt good, but it wasn't always worth the responsibility of new people.

But April was gone—she'd been gone two days and counting, and I still didn't know how to call her—and the more I missed April, the more I wanted to see Melanie without her clothes. Apparently, I'm one of those people who get horny during periods of pain: Who knew? I hoped Melanie Wilde was one of those people, too. Everything she did turned me on, even her harassment, because at least she was feeding my ego, and my ego was starving.

But what the hell would I have to say to T.D. Jackson's parents the day after their son's body was found? I wasn't even sure I was sorry about it. He probably deserved worse than he got.

"Give me one reason," I said. "Make it a good one. Or just take me back home."

Melanie took a long time to mull it over. "Do you know when Homicide considers a case cold?" Melanie said, staring at her steering wheel. Her voice dropped, whispering, but I never missed a word. "The point when they figure they have *zero* chance of solving it?"

"Forty-eight hours."

"That's right. And almost forty-eight hours after he died, instead of asking the public for tips, the LAPD jackass squad is still talking suicide. They're *glad* he's dead. I just want you to look into his parents' eyes. Hear them out."

"Assuming I *can* hear them, what will they want from me?"

"Right now, they just need to know somebody's willing to listen."

"There are plenty of licensed detectives."

"That's not the way my uncle and aunt want to go."

"Why not?"

Rare silence from her, a beat. "Judge Jackson likes to keep his options open."

Right. He wanted to hire someone off the radar. No license, no trail, no accountability. Alice had put me through the seventy-four-day ESI Personal Protection program in Colorado, and I'd actually used the training a half dozen times. And yes, I'd managed to survive—and solve—the entire sordid Serena Johnston affair. But a nagging suspicion that I might have discovered an unsuspected talent didn't necessarily lead me to that doorstep.

Besides, Judge Jackson might want more than a solved case and an arrest. He sounded like a pissed-off, grieving parent. I understood, but I had my own problem. I had plenty.

"I'm not the one, Mel," I said. "You're hurting. They're hurting. But I'm not the one."

She brought her hand to my knee and let it rest. Next, a glimpse of her pain-shattered eyes. Ugh. "Unless you *are* the one," she said. "How will you know unless you meet them?"

Part of me must enjoy doing what I know I shouldn't. Part of me always has. *I'd better at least get laid for this,* I thought, exactly as she knew I would.

"If I make even one phone call on this, they pay through the nose," I said.

"They wouldn't expect anything less."

"And you owe me a favor."

She arched her left eyebrow. Damn, she was cute. "All right."

"Then I guess one conversation never hurt anyone."

The gunshot must have blown away my memory, too.

I halfway expected a butler to answer the door, but instead it was Judge Emory Jackson. Judge Jackson was in his sixties and fit, with broad thick shoulders and a head of snowy hair. He was dressed in a dress shirt and tie even at home. He was four inches shorter and three shades darker than his son, but I immediately saw T.D. in his gait and gestures. T.D. Jackson had grown up to be just like Daddy, almost a carbon copy. In that way alone, their resemblance was eerie.

"Uncle Em, this is Tennyson Hardwick," Melanie said. "He was friends with Bumpy back at SoCal. They lived together at Clayton Hall."

Despite Melanie's exaggeration of my status in T.D.'s life, Judge Jackson didn't move to let me into his home. His dark eyes assessed me, then he glanced over my shoulder, probably to make sure no news vans were lurking, even with a guardhouse at the neighborhood's gate. The whites of his eyes were anything but, and his face was puffy beneath his eyelids. He looked embattled; he wasn't used to crying, but tears had forced him to submit for days.

"You kin to Captain Hardwick?"

"Yessir. My father. He's had some struggles, but he's doing fine."

Judge Jackson grunted. "Tennyson like the poet, huh? *Charge of the Light Brigade?*"

" 'Into the jaws of Death, into the mouth of Hell, Rode the six hundred.' But my mother preferred *Ulysses.*" More for Melanie's sake than Judge Jackson's, I recited lines I memorized in high school in my quest to know my mother: " 'We are not now that strength which in old days / Moved earth and heaven; that which we are, we are. / One equal temper of heroic hearts, / Made weak by time and fate, but strong in will / To strive, to seek, to find . . . and not to yield.' "

Melanie stirred beside me, a silent *Yes!* I hoped to hear that cry aloud later, in her bed. Poetry had been one of my popular extras as an escort. Judge Jackson looked at me with new eyes, intrigued. I'd passed his test. When he let me in, he came as close to a smile as he could.

The Jackson house was elegant and tranquil, a chapel of mourning. The house had high ceilings, and the winding marble staircase was too fine even for *Gone With the Wind*'s famed Tara. The living room brimmed with somber arrangements of roses and lilies, scenting the air with false spring, but the colonial-style furniture in the living room was a dour shade, probably like Judge Jackson's courtroom. I knew that the Aaron Douglas and Henry Ossawa Tanner original paintings on the wall had cost a fortune, but the décor was understated. I figured the Jacksons hadn't come into money in only one generation; they were comfortable with money. Steeped in it.

Judge Jackson led us past the tallest floral arrangement in the living room, where T.D. Jackson's face was framed by new flower buds.

BELOVED SON AND FATHER, a ribbon was inscribed. It was a high school photograph, senior year in cap and gown, acne and all. The unlucky parents who outlive their children always remember them most vividly from when they were young.

Three sets of soles echoed on the marble floor in the walkway. While the sound ricocheted in my head, Judge Jackson said something I didn't hear.

"You may have to speak up, Judge Jackson," I said. "Firearm incident. My ear."

Judge Jackson looked back at me, disturbed on my behalf.

"Don't worry, Uncle Em," Melanie said, shining a smile at me. "My firm's on it."

So, I had a lawyer now, and a good one, judging by the address I'd seen on her business card. I just hoped I could afford her—and dollars were the least of my worries. I guess that was my favor. I should have asked for two.

As we walked across the vast expanse of the house, we came to an open-air chef's kitchen, where a woman I guessed was T.D.'s mother sat on a tall barstool, staring into her teacup. It felt impolite to gaze at her for more than an instant; her agony was so pronounced on her thin face that she could have been naked. Her hair was hurriedly fixed into an unruly bun, with nearly half of her hair still loose. She wore a slightly frayed sweater that was clearly comfort clothing, designed for indoor use only. T.D. had had his mother's nose and long forehead.

Judge Jackson leaned close to her, gentle as a mouse. "Evangeline? This is Tennyson Hardwick. He knew T.D. He's come to help us."

She flinched, then she gave me the blankest stare I've ever seen— her brown eyes were a cavern. Tranquilizers, I guessed, and maybe a glass or two of wine. Bad combination. "All right," she said in a thin voice, sounding resigned.

Judge Jackson patted his wife's hand. "Richard Hardwick's son," he added.

A spark of light passed across her empty eyes, a flaming moth on a moonless night. "Richard Hardwick. The Beverly Hills–Hollywood NAACP branch. Such a good speaker! Got everyone so motivated. You look just like him . . ." Everywhere I went, I was reminded of how I resembled my father in appearance alone.

Her voice faded as the light in her eyes died. After another fond pat, Judge Jackson motioned for us to follow him.

"I pray to God she survives this," he said to Melanie. "I just don't know."

"Aunt Evie's just like Mom." Melanie linked their arms. "Like me. She'll survive."

"Hope you're right," he said.

At the other end of the house, double doors led to a large study with paneled wood worthy of the Peninsula. Melanie let us go in alone, waiting outside. She knew what Judge Jackson was going to say. Above the large oak desk, I saw the requisite array of certificates, diplomas, and degrees one would expect from a lawyer and judge, including one photo of Judge Jackson with Bill and Hillary Clinton; another with Barack Obama. Covering his bets.

The centerpiece was a glass-enclosed case that stretched the length of the room, the shrine to T.D. Jackson. "May I?" I said.

Judge Jackson nodded eagerly. Of course. He flipped a switch, and the display was bathed in light. It looked professionally mounted; part photo display, part trophy case, part collage of newspaper headlines. T.D. Jackson's gleaming bronze Heisman Trophy sat on a shelf, the old-school football warrior running with his arm thrust out. I'd never seen a Heisman up close, and I was surprised at its size. It looked like it weighed twenty-five pounds.

"T.D. gave me that the night he got it," Judge Jackson said, quickly wiping his eye. "Said it was mine by rights." No small honor: Few actors would let an Oscar or Emmy out of his sight, although Jimmy Stewart famously gave his Oscar to his father.

Judge Jackson looked up at me, his face suddenly full of pride. "You know what else? T.D. had his Super Bowl ring engraved to his mother and gave it to her. How about *that*? That's the kind of son T.D. was."

T.D. Jackson sounded like a hell of a guy.

The case wasn't entirely dedicated to T.D.'s career. On the far left side, the lacquered newspaper clippings were from the 1960s, before T.D.'s time. An older photograph showed a Southern California State squad in outdated uniforms, with four black men prominent in the center. Even with his helmet on, I spotted Emory Jackson's face, nearly fifty years younger.

"So you played, too?" I said.

"Not like T.D., but we thought we were doin' something."

The older team had done pretty well, I noticed: Beneath the photo was a single newspaper article, the headline reading SOCAL SPARTANS BOWL BOUND.

"I know T.D. went to you looking for protection," Judge Jackson said. He was standing closer behind me that I'd realized.

I had wondered if that would come up. "Yessir. I couldn't swing the schedule."

"Has your schedule changed?"

"Actually, it has."

"Tell me you give a damn what happened to T.D. Tell me you didn't forsake him for personal reasons." *Forsake* was a strong word, spoken from pursed, angry lips.

"Judge, I'd take the job if I could go back. I wish I could have prevented it. I never meant to forsake your son." I'd sounded genuinely sorry, and hadn't had to fake it.

Judge Jackson sighed. "All right," he said.

In the display case, he pointed out T.D.'s iconic jersey, Number 13, which lay beneath a poster-sized photo of T.D.'s Super Bowl reception for the San Francisco 49ers, the year he was dubbed "The Master of Disaster." (A tiny placard pointed out that it was the very jersey T.D. had worn that snowy day in Buffalo.) T-shirts, coffee mugs, and water bottles proclaimed his legend. On the far right side of the display, T.D.'s journey to Hollywood was chronicled in one-sheets and publicity shots. None of his movies ever fulfilled the promise of *Cody's Dawn*, T.D.'s first movie, where he played an injured Gulf War vet with surprising pathos and earned a Golden Globe nomination. But until a couple of years before his divorce—after a ridiculous direct-to-DVD mistake called *Space Bowl* made it hard to look at him with a straight face—T.D. Jackson had been an industry unto himself in Hollywood.

Judge Jackson toured me through his display case with more vigor than I could have mustered in his place, but his sigh deflated him. His shoulders shrank before my eyes.

"All this . . ." His breath clouded the glass until he dutifully wiped it clean. "A statue, paper, and memories . . ." He didn't finish, but he didn't have to. Death takes everything that counts, that's all.

Judge Jackson closed the study's doors so we would have privacy. I doubted that Evangeline Jackson could hear much of anything, but he took the precaution.

"This might seem strange to you, son, but I need to search you," the judge said.

I spread my legs and raised my arms. "I have a permit, but I don't carry a gun," I said.

"That's your own business, although you may want to start. I'm not worried about a gun." He patted me down as methodically as my father might have, with a special emphasis on pockets and creases.

He was looking for a tape recorder, I realized. Fireworks whistled in my head.

Judge Jackson gestured toward a leather recliner, and I sat. He sat across from me, atop his desk, facing me from several inches higher. Elevated, just like in court.

"You know I'm a sitting federal judge."

"Yessir."

"Mr. Hardwick, my son's killer is out there, and I want him found. Because the police don't give a damn, in the words of Malcolm, I'm left to do it by any means necessary. That's why this job calls for discretion. Delicacy. My niece believes we can trust you, but I want to hear it from your mouth."

"Trust me to . . . what, sir?"

"To keep what's my business *my* business."

Sounded safe enough. "I'm not the chatty type."

Judge Jackson studied me for a beat. Then he found a fat envelope on his desk and tossed it to me. It was heavy. "Ten thousand," Judge Jackson said. "Twenty percent up front. A solid lead gets you another ten. You provide me reasonable evidence that you've found the killer, the name makes fifty. Cash."

Impolite or not, I had to peek into the envelope just to see the neat stack of new bills, in hundreds and fifties. The scent from the envelope was strong and cloying. I liked that smell.

Reasonable evidence. That was a much looser standard than one he'd need in court, which, as he knew better than any of us, was *Beyond a reasonable doubt.*

"What's your definition of a 'solid lead'?" I said.

"I'll know it when I hear it."

"Does full payment hinge on a successful prosecution?"

"All I want is a name and evidence."

It almost sounded too good to be true. Granted, I didn't have a badge or a PI license, but that meant I had less to lose for trespassing or illegally taping a conversation. "I appreciate your faith, Judge Hardwick, but I'm way out in the cold. Do you have a lead?"

He picked up a sheaf of papers, dangling it like bait. "This is probably mostly a load of crap, but it's a start. It's a copy of the Robbery-Homicide murder book. You'd know what LAPD knows, as of 3:00 A.M. this morning. If this exchanges hands today and you get caught with it, you're on your own. And son, mention my name, and I'll bury you. You do not want to make an enemy of me."

My heart thudded. When Serena died, I would have sacrificed a digit to get my hands on the official LAPD murder book. Even with Dad's connections, the only way I'd gotten a simple incident report was through April. *She would be salivating if she saw this . . .*

But discretion was discretion. Even if she'd been here, I couldn't have told April. I couldn't tell Dad. I couldn't tell anyone.

"If I may be blunt . . ." I said. "You're taking a lot of risks, sir."

"Risk is a part of life," he said, looking annoyed. "Do you know how many of my fellow federal judges have been indicted in a decade? Accused of failing the bench? Four. Why do they do it? For money, usually. For power. For a blow job. For the risk itself. A friend of mine once told me, 'All you need is a reason.' Well, I have mine. And I'll sleep at night just fine."

"I hope you trust your LAPD connection."

"With my life," he said. "My source came to *me* and said LAPD was throwing the case. Sometimes, justice and the law are two separate and distinct entities, Mr. Hardwick."

We both knew the truth of that. When I nodded, he went on: "Internally, they call it murder—but to the outside world, it's a suicide. Without any pressure to find a killer, there's no incentive to clear up the confusion. That's where you come in." Judge Hardwick took a deep breath. "Do you think, Mr. Hardwick, that my son killed himself?" His eyes shimmered.

"Bullshit. Sir."

Judge Hardwick loosed a sour smile. "What can I get you to drink?"

"Surprise me."

Judge Hardwick busied himself with decanters and cut-crystal glasses and frosted ice cubes from a hidden minibar. He handed me a glass filled with tea-colored liquid, and poured himself an identical libation. I sipped. Damn. Good bourbon. I wanted to take a doggie bag home to Dad.

We sipped, sizing each other up. "So," he said. "Here's what you'll have: Certainty. A sense of purpose. The murder book. Access to the crime scene. And, if you want it, access to the body—but the funeral's on Sunday, so you need to make a decision fast."

I had already made my decision, I realized. Maybe I'd decided as soon as I saw Evangeline Jackson in her crippled haze at the kitchen counter. Or while I'd stared at two generations of glory captured inside that display case. Or sooner than that, when I'd seen T.D.'s high school graduation photo.

No matter what T.D. Jackson had or hadn't done, his parents deserved an answer. Any parents of a slain child deserved that small comfort.

I didn't ask what would happen to the accused if I gave Judge Jackson a name.

I didn't want to know.

NINE

WHEN WE GOT BACK TO HER CAR, Melanie paused before starting the engine. She settled back in her seat to say something important, her eyes unwavering. "I'm engaged."

"Congratulations," I said. It took me a second to remember why she'd even brought it up. The visit to Judge Jackson's house had erased my plans to see Melanie Wilde naked. As fine as she was, the fever had passed. Besides, we had just shared an experience much more intimate than sex. "Then I guess you'd better take me home."

All I could think about was Chela.

It was five thirty when I walked through the front door, and Chela had already been home for two hours. I barely greeted Dad in the living room, and Marcela had left for the day. *Chela might be on the phone with him right now,* I thought as I bounded up the stairs.

I flung Chela's door open, forgetting to knock.

She wasn't on her phone, or sitting at her computer. She was sitting cross-legged in the center of her bed, combing out her hair. Chela rarely wore her hair loose; I'd forgotten she had so much, with wiry spirals flowing toward her neck. She hid her hair most of the time, but it had been loose in her photos to Internet Guy. The memory made me feel sick to my stomach.

"Where's the phone?" I said to her startled, *who-me?* eyes.

"Jesus! It's called *knock*-ing." But my face told her to cease the shit flow, so she kept quiet. She knew what I wanted, but dug in her purse and handed me her iPhone.

"Not that one," I said. "Where's the phone he gave you? Put it in my hand *right now.*"

A pathetic desperation played across Chela's face. She knew it was useless to lie, but she couldn't think of an alternative. "What phone? What are you *talking* about—"

I went for her desk drawers first—the desk we'd chosen at Staples and I'd put together myself, piece by piece—throwing their contents to the floor. I saw gum wrappers, loose change, and a pack of Marlboro Lights, another broken promise. No surprise there. I had noticed the stink of cigarettes despite her gum and mints more than once, but I chose my battles. A slender flash drive fell out of the second drawer, and I stuck that in my back pocket.

Chela shrieked as if I'd struck her. "*Stop it!*" But she was frozen where she sat.

I yanked out her computer's power cords, and the screensaver photo of the two of us at Santa Monica pier vanished into blackness. "Where's the *phone*, Chela?" I said, lifting the monitor high. When she didn't answer—staring at me as if she couldn't quite place who I was—I surprised us both by throwing the monitor to the floor.

Even with carpeting, the screen cracked in two.

Chela jumped to her feet, as if she was afraid I would take better aim next time. She did a spin toward the door, but I blocked her and slammed it shut.

"*Stop it!*" she screamed. "I'm getting out of here—freak!"

"Oh, *I'm* a freak?" I said. The next words tumbled out of my mouth before I could think about what marks they might leave. "That's a joke, coming from a girl who sends dirty pictures to an old-ass man. Give me the fucking phone!"

I picked up the computer's brain next, the CPU, raising it above my head. Chela covered her head with her arms, hunching herself in a ball. I sure as hell would never throw any object at her, much less one that heavy—and I wasn't going to trash an eight-hundred-dollar computer—but maybe she didn't know that. Blood infused her face beneath her skin, splotchy and dark.

"M-my term paper's on there . . ." Chela whimpered.

I didn't know if she really gave a damn about her term paper or if she was only pretending to, but her sudden tears looked real enough. Chela's helplessness drained away my anger's volatility. Most of my rage wasn't for her. That realization flooded me with shame.

One of my ears heard Dad calling from downstairs, wondering what was going on.

I lowered the CPU to the floor and sighed. My voice grew whisper-soft: "The phone."

This time, Chela reached under her mattress and pulled out a small black cell phone I didn't recognize. When she gave it to me, she didn't meet my eyes. For only the second time since I'd known her, Chela sobbed. She fled across the room, finding the bathroom. She slammed the door, and I heard it lock.

Standing outside of that closed bathroom door, I remembered how tired I was. The racket in my head made it hard to sleep at night. All of April's warnings blended with the clanging in my head: *You're in over your head, Ten.*

I stood in front of the bathroom door, trying to think of magic words. None came.

"Did somebody used to hit you, Chela?"

"Until I learned how to change their mood." Her voice was muffled. She blew her nose.

"Who was it?"

"News flash: Who didn't? What do you care? You don't know shit about me!"

"So tell me."

After a while, Chela came out of the bathroom, and we both sat on the carpet, avoiding the bed. She'd come on to me once, at the very beginning, and I was always careful when I was in her room. Most of the time, I didn't enter her room at all.

Chela took a deep breath before she began, as if she were jumping into a pool:

"Nana was dead in her bed five days before anybody knew but me. She was the only one raising me, except she was dying, so she wasn't taking care of me—mostly, it was me taking care of her. She signed the checks, and I tried to make life less shitty for her at the end. Literally. Made sure she was clean and had enough to eat. We were a pretty damn good team. And she felt so bad, always talking about how she wished she could do more, telling me she couldn't believe how different my mom was after she started doing meth. She said it was like a demon came and took over my mom's body.

"So I try to remember my mom from Nana's stories about what she was like in school, and how she got accepted into college, but by then she was off track. After that. Mom was just the same fuckup I already knew, who hadn't come to visit us for two Christmases in a row. I try to feel sorry for her, but I spend most of my time hating her. It was bad enough to do that to your kid—but your dying mother? That's sick. My father might have died over some stupid gangsta drug shit, but at least he had an excuse for not being there to make sure Nana didn't die and leave me alone.

"But that's exactly what the fuck happened. I go to her room to make sure she's breathing . . . and she's not. She finally died. Finally. What did I do? I went to school. I wasn't dealing with it. That night was a lot of crying and hating life—*It's not fair! It's not fair!* All that shit—but I went to school again the next day. I got one hundred percent on a vocab test in my English class. And you say I can't concentrate on anything? No focus? My ass.

"So there I am, ten years old, eating SpaghettiOs and stale bread. Living with a dead lady. And now I'm thinking I'll be in trouble with the police for not saying anything sooner—I can just see myself on *Cops*, or in one of those interrogation rooms like on TV, with these cops standing over me with their arms folded, all like 'So, young lady, why didn't you report your grandmother's death sooner? Was there foul play?' This is what's going on in my head. I used to pick up the phone and consider leaving anonymous tips, but then I'd think how stupid that was. They would know it was from me! And I even turned the heat off because . . . you know . . . I'm only ten, but I understand you can't leave a dead body lying out when it's hot. And this is Minneapolis, so let me tell you, house without heat gets pretty damn cold.

"But I wasn't ready to say, 'Hey, okay, I give up my whole world now.' Nana's house was always too cold, and smelled like piss and vomit, but it was the only home I had. I liked my room. My school. My friends. I had this crazy fantasy that Mom would show up out of the blue, and suddenly she'd be off the meth, just in time to solve all my problems. That is definitely the way it would happen in a movie, so I even wasted time going through Nana's pile of telephone numbers for Mom, Last Known Number kind of thing, trying to see if I could find her. I'm making all these calls, waking people up all times of day and night, but trying to act all casual, like, "Hey, is Sherry around?," and some people were like "Sherry Who?" but most people said, "I didn't know Sherry had a kid." I couldn't make myself say her mother was dead, or I was alone. I couldn't say it to strangers, and they didn't know shit anyway. I thought I had a lead, but it only went to a pay phone. I cried over that shit for about six hours.

"To be honest, I would have held out much longer than five days—I was thinking of long-term plans, maybe burying her in the backyard. But then the gas man came. I saw the truck drive up, and I run outside to make sure he isn't from a SWAT team or something. And he's walking around the house over to Nana's window to read the meter. The meter's right below Nana's curtains. And I know I closed her curtain, but in my mind there's just enough gap for him to see something's not right: 'Whoa—there's a dead body in there.'

"Or maybe he just seemed like a nice guy, somebody's dad, and while he was standing next to that window, I thought about how sad he would feel for me if he knew. And, man, the floodgates just started. 'My gramma's dead! My gramma's dead!' I almost gave the poor guy a heart attack. He probably still sees my face in bad dreams. It made the news and everything—CHILD LEFT FOR DAYS WITH DEAD GRAND-MOTHER. I think it was even on national news, someone told me that, but I had other fish to fry.

"The child authorities, not knowing my mom like I did, were sure all the publicity would make her come flying in like Wonder Woman. So it wasn't awful in the beginning—I was at this low-stress group home, and I thought of it like this summer camp I went to once, except with nicer beds. I cried a lot, but nobody gave me shit about it, and the caseworkers were really on top of my situation because it was in the news.

"Six months go by. Nothing. Suddenly they're talking about a foster family, and this couple comes and takes me home with them. They already had six other foster kids there, so it's not like they were bad people, it was just an unhappy place to be. Not yelling, but too much noise. So I ran away—for the first time.

"The funny part is, that was the best place I would be for a long time. I just didn't know it yet. I wish I'd known. I would have stuck around.

"But I was the Runaway Queen. Any shit I didn't like, I was gone. I don't like the way foster dad's looking at me, I'm gone. Somebody tries to pull the my-thing-or-the-highway routine on me too hard-core, I'm taking the highway every time. Whatever. That's me. I knew from jump that nobody could take care of me except M-E. A dead body under your roof will teach you that whole lesson about being alone in the world pretty damn quick. So one day I just said, "Fuck it!" and jumped in this guy's Ford pickup, and by some mira-cle he didn't murder me somewhere on the drive between Minneapo-lis and California. What he wanted in return for the ride didn't seem like that big a deal."

I hated to even wonder.

"How old were you?" I asked.

"Old enough to eat corn bread without choking. Freak that he was, at least he was a freak who kept his word, and as soon as we crossed the California state line, I was like, "Okay, I gotta go." And that was it, we parted ways. I figured that wasn't my shining moment in terms of decisions, but I'd figure it out later. I didn't know how far Los Angeles was from where I'd gotten out, so I was hungry that same day. Dumb luck, if you can call it that: I got caught stealing from a gas station right from the beginning. I think that guy was keeping his eye on me the whole time—I must have looked like I didn't have shit, which I didn't. He made me blow him, then called the cops anyway, and I got sent to juvie. I didn't tell them my real name. I never said I was from Minneapolis. Nobody could get my story.

"So they lost interest and flushed me into the system. First place they sent me, I said something smart to the guy's wife, and he smacked me across the head. And he was a prison guard for a living, for real. Six months was like six hundred years.

"Then my caseworker sent me to a group home, I got popped for trying to steal an iPod with this friend of mine—shit, everybody had iPods but us—and I spent six months in juvie. Let's just say that I now understand what people mean when they say they'd rather die than go to prison. You don't mean shit. You're a number. You have no rights. Somebody's telling you when to sleep, when to eat, when to turn the lights off. I lost fifteen pounds in six months, and I never weighed that much to begin with. I thought it was just the shitty food—Oh, I didn't even mention how shitty the food is—but really I think I was on a hunger strike and didn't know it. I threw up a lot.

"I told God if he ever got me out of there alive, I would never go to juvie again. And that is one promise I definitely intend to keep. I was in another group home for a while, and I really tried to make that work, but one day I met Mother, and that was that."

Mother was Chela's madam. *Our* madam.

Mother had brought Chela into my life. Mother was worried about one of her prize breadwinners after Chela disappeared with a celebrity client—and I like to think Mother was genuinely worried about her, too, even if it's best not to ascribe normal human emotion to her. Mother had asked me to find Chela; I did, but just never brought Chela back. I couldn't.

I started working for Mother when I was twenty-five, back when I was even more hardheaded when it came to seeing a mistake in plain sight. But Chela had been only thirteen when Mother found her. I'd figured out that much. Mother always said she didn't send Chela out with clients until a year after taking her in, but you're a fool to believe Mother at her word.

"Where'd you meet her?" I said.

Chela sighed. "This isn't about her. She saw I was miserable, that's all."

"Where?"

"She didn't get me into the business, if that's what you're wondering. Three other girls and I were splitting a room. I'd been in The Life for months. I found out about a big party at a hotel on the Strip, and talked my way in. Made serious money that night, and one of the other girls threw me a bone—an even bigger party up in the Hills. I didn't realize it, but she was a scout, and that was an audition. I spent my entire roll to get better clothes, and spent all day on my makeup and hair. Walked into that party like I owned the place. My contact"—she looked at me shrewdly—"no, I'm not going to tell you her name, liked the way I handled myself, and sent me to meet Mother. At a place called 'Mrs. Winston's.' "

"Green Grocery? Best salad bar in L.A.?"

She nodded. "That's the place."

Century City's best "hidden" restaurant. So Mother had chosen a public, healthy, casual spot for her seduction.

"The whole all-u-can-eat salad bar still blows my mind. She told me all these awesome war stories about Kosovo. She was like me—a survivor."

My stomach was an icy knot. "And you went with her?"

"You didn't see where I was living."

I was surprised it wasn't under a bench in the park. Chela was a survivor. And she'd recognized a better berth when it was dangled in front of her.

"Anyway . . . it worked out," she said.

"It worked out how?" I tried to wash the judgment and rage from my voice.

"It was the best place I ever lived. She treated me nicer than anyone. I had my own room, I had spending money. After I started going out, I had thousands of dollars in the bank. And she didn't treat me like a kid. She gave me credit for having a brain."

"You don't see anything wrong with what she did?"

"All I'm saying is, I don't *care* what people think. If I wanted to go back there, I could've done that already. But that doesn't mean I don't appreciate her giving me a life."

I rubbed my forehead, trying to quell the raucous pain between my ears. I wasn't used to headaches with a sound track. If I'd seen someone like Chela at Mother's when I first met her, I would have known to turn right around. I wouldn't have associated with a madam who profited from child prostitution. I still hated to believe it. It made my time with Mother feel even more sordid.

"How many other girls are there? Young ones?"

"What—you think I'm about to rat out Mother?" Chela said. "Forget it. Number one, I don't know. I never asked, and I was the only one who lived with her. Number two, I wouldn't tell you. Or maybe you didn't hear a word I just said."

"Oh, I heard you."

"Then get off your high horse," Chela said. "You had a police captain to keep you safe. A house to sleep in. We're not even on the same planet."

"Then how did I end up at Mother's, too?"

"Fast cash. Easy work. Just like everybody else."

I'd never told her the story. Maybe I'd finally found the right time. "When I was thirteen, one of my teachers invited me to swim at her house. Things went on between us that shouldn't have, and it went on for a long time. The vibe was all wrong. I didn't see it that way— hell, what boy past puberty would?—but a kid has a kid's appetites. Suddenly sex was the only thing on my mind, and getting laid was my number one preoccupation. I've hung out with dozens of sex workers, and every one of them started having sex young. People don't just wake up at eighteen and say, 'Hey, I'm gonna go shoot some porn,' or 'Hey, I'm gonna go sell my ass.' The more I heard their stories, one day I realized, 'Hey, when I was a kid, I swam in those waters, too.'"

"There you go, always making it negative. Like sex is evil."

"No, it's not evil," I said. "But it's powerful, Chela. It's *powerful*. It's like fire. It can cook your eggs or burn your damned house down. The results are unpredictable. Like the way you can't keep away from this guy, even though I think you really want to."

She hid her eyes from mine. I'd broadsided her by bringing up Internet Stud. For a while, we'd allowed ourselves to forget about him.

"I haven't had sex with him," she said.

"Would you tell me if you had?"

A half smile. "No. But I hate lying to you, so it's my lucky day."

I was too tired for ultimatums. Do-what-I-say-or-else. Her childhood story had just told me she would bolt if I came on too strong.

"Chela, you're gonna get me sent to jail. Do you understand that?"

She sighed but didn't answer.

"Do you love this guy?" I said, petrified to hear the answer. If she loved him, there was nothing I could say. Nothing.

"Hell, no. He's married. We're just friends."

"What about the pictures?"

"We don't do that anymore." She said it like it was nothing. It was all right now.

"Chela, in your world, you think adults and kids can hang out like that. His attraction flatters you, you like teasing him, you're having fun. He told you what you think is his life story. To you, he's a great guy, misunderstood by everyone but you. But look at what he is to me: To me, he's the turd in my punch bowl. His very existence hurts you, and that makes me want to hurt him back."

"All we do is talk on the phone. Not even sex stuff. We started over."

"You think he doesn't want a shot at you? Get real."

"I told him it's just talking," she said.

"For now."

"Now is all there is, Ten. I don't worry about later."

I didn't know how to reach her, until I heard the muffled sound of my father's voice beyond the door. Suddenly, I had a brainstorm: My father was Chela's hero. He reminded her of her dead grandmother, the symbol of all that was right and good.

"What would my dad have done if he'd known about my teacher and her pool?"

"Captain Hardwick?" Chela laughed. "Put her ass in jail, probably."

"What would have been the *right* thing?"

Chela's face darkened. "Jail is bullshit. But he would have made you stop going over there, gotten her ass fired from the school. For sure." I was relieved she had a moral compass still working somewhere. After a pause, Chela said. "Don't tell him about me and Mother."

"I won't tell if you won't."

We smiled. But my smile disappeared.

"I will hurt this man," I said. "I might do worse than hurt him."

"Yeah, you'd probably kill him," Chela said. She had met me under a crazy spell, when I was waving a gun.

"Bet on it."

Chela shrugged. "I can't do that to a friend, so it's over. Promise." She tried to sound detached, but I heard how much it hurt her to let him go. She didn't have many friends.

"There won't be any warning next time," I said. "I hope you know I'm not playing."

That seemed like the right note, so I left.

When I emerged from Chela's room with the CPU and both cell phones, Dad was waiting for me at the foot of the stairs. His wheelchair lay on its side, empty. Dad sat on the bottom step with his hand on the railing, perspiration gleaming from his brow. He'd been trying to climb up.

For a moment, feeling horror for him, I stood up high without moving. If I'd ever seen that angry, humiliated shadow across his face when I was a kid, I would have soiled my pants.

"Boy, get your ass down here," Dad said. He didn't have any trouble speaking, and I didn't have any trouble hearing. We were a medical miracle.

Both of us were perspiring by the time I'd helped Dad back into his chair. Dad was too pissed off to be embarrassed by his limbs' jerky motions. He was glad to lean on me so he could get as close as possible to eye level. His open palm was shaking; he wanted to slap me.

"Dintchu hear me calling?" he said.

"I had a problem with Chela."

Jaw locked like a trap, Dad propellered his arms across his wheels to send his chair speeding across the floor, toward his room. "Comewithme," he said.

"Long day, Dad. Let me catch my breath."

He ignored me, rolling like Speed Racer. I had to follow.

Over time, Dad's room had become less a glorified medicine cabinet—slash—rehab room and more a living space. My downstairs guest room had a bathroom and a fair amount of square footage, so we'd brought in the old antique oak rolltop desk he'd put in storage after he got sick, the one where he'd spent most of his late nights studying case files and crime-scene photos when he was a detective, then payroll records and memos after he got promoted. That desk was like his office, and we both liked having it around.

Marcela had also launched a project to preserve his awards and certificates, so in its own way, Dad's room didn't look so different than Judge Jackson's study—except without any sign of his son. I noticed Judge Jackson's name on an appreciation certificate to Dad from the Beverly Hills–Hollywood NAACP. Small world, and getting smaller.

The only photos of individuals were snapshots of my parents together, my mother alone, and one of all three of us, when I was six weeks old. Apparently, that was when Dad had stopped taking pictures. The delicate-boned woman who gave birth to me looked like she had a dancer's frame, with a bulb nose and skin that matched mine perfectly. She was sitting at the bench of the old black piano that had sat in our home until Dad got sick and we finally sold it. I wish I'd kept the piano, but I never really learned to play it. Here's what I can tell about my mother from her photos: She liked to laugh, she knew she was pretty, and she thought my father walked on air. Her photo with her baby is the only one where she isn't smiling, just tired. No more laughter. In nine months, she would be dead.

I try not to take it personally.

I almost overlooked a new photograph on Dad's desk in a small ceramic frame: Marcela standing in the kitchen chopping celery, her face glowing.

"Don't . . . you . . . ever . . . dis-re-spect . . . Marcela . . . again," my father said. I couldn't pretend I didn't know what he was talking about. Dad was overreacting, but I'd been rude to Marcela when she told me about Melanie's call. I knew better.

"She's . . . 'fraid . . . you . . . lost . . . your . . . mind."

"I'll call her and apologize." I would have reminded him that my life was in a free fall, but pity wasn't his strong suit. "Tonight. Before it gets late."

"What about . . . Chela?" Dad said. He folded his hands, ready to hear.

My allegiances felt torn, but not for long. I needed allies. "There's a guy on the internet she was in touch with a few months ago, and he showed up again. I squashed it."

Dad grunted. I had never told him outright that Chela had been a prostitute, but he knew she was a runaway, and he knew their world. Dad had dedicated the last ten years of his career to Hollywood's teenagers.

"She . . . staying?" Dad said.

"We'll see by morning. I'm not gonna chain her down."

Silence. I always felt itchy in Dad's room, but there was nowhere to divert my gaze, except to photographs of the dead woman who haunted both of us. I thought about Chela's anger toward her mother and let myself feel how much I was pissed at mine, too. You can't get sick and die when you have a kid. You find a way to fight.

"Her gramma was dead . . . five days . . . 'fore any help came," Dad said.

"She just told me." I couldn't be jealous Chela told Dad first; I was just glad she'd had someone else to talk to. Sometimes I worked fourteen-hour days on the set. Used to, anyway.

"Helluva life . . ."

"Yeah." I sighed, still itching to go. "But she listens to me. I've got some insights."

"Howso?" Dad shifted in his chair, leaning on his elbow, settling in to talk.

I am not about to have this conversation, I told myself.

"There was a teacher who used to invite me over after school. First it was swimming, then it was more. For a while I was hanging out there almost every day."

I watched Dad's face, but it didn't change. Either his stroke had wiped nuance from his expression, or my words had had no impact at all. I didn't know what I'd expected him to say, but his silence was pissing me off.

"How . . . old?" Dad said finally.

"Thirteen."

Dad's head snapped back. He sucked in his breath. He didn't ask me which teacher. He didn't say he wished he had known, or what he would have done if he had. He held the information in his head for a while. "Too . . . young," he said.

I shrugged. I still felt ready to bolt his room, but not as much.

"I went to Judge Jackson's house today," I said.

"Whafforr?"

I told him about almost everything except the murder book. I trust my father well enough, but a promise means something to me. Although I didn't mention Judge Jackson's suspicion of an LAPD cover-up, Dad nodded as if he knew the whole story. Nothing could surprise him. Same old, same old. I could almost hear his thoughts.

"You . . . taking . . . the case?" he said.

I'd brought the money home, but if Dad helped me change my mind, I could always return it. "Thinking about it."

"Don't . . . break the law."

I nodded, but I didn't make a verbal promise. And Dad didn't call me on it. "Anyway, there's probably no chance in hell of figuring this one out," I said.

"Not just one," Dad said. "Two."

"Two what?"

"Not just T.D. The . . . wife. Good chance . . . they're . . . re-lated."

I hadn't thought about it that way, but he was right. I would have a much better chance of solving T.D. Jackson's murder if I could learn the truth about the death of his ex-wife. I needed to drive back to Judge Jackson's first thing in the morning and give him his money back. I must have been out of my mind to take it, I thought. Who in the hell could sort through this mess?

"If anybody could . . ." Dad said. ". . . you could."

If anybody could, you could? Was he reading my damned mind?

I was sure my ears were messing with me. My father never gave me compliments. Never.

Once, after I'd only been escorting Alice about a month, on our first trip to Morocco, she said "I love you" while she stroked my stomach in our bed. Or, that's what I heard. Or thought I did. I didn't know what to say, and she never said it again.

Just like with Alice, the night Dad said the nicest thing about me I could remember, I was too startled to say a word.

TEN

IT WAS EARLY WHEN I GOT TO MY ROOM, not even ten o'clock, but I was ready for sleep. Unfortunately, sleep wasn't ready for me.

LAPD's murder book sat in my nightstand drawer, waiting. Between the racket in my head and the mystery of what lay within the police accounts of the death of Thomas Dorsey Jackson, I couldn't keep my eyes closed. I wished I'd taken Reggie's advice and bought a humidifier to mask the ringing in my ears, but I didn't feel like going back out that night.

Instead, I turned on my brass banker's lamp.

I'd seen murder books from Dad's days on the force, so I knew they were usually bound. This one wasn't. I pulled out a loose stack of about one hundred pages from the manila envelope Judge Jackson had given me. I'd had manners enough not to peek while I was in the car with Melanie. She hadn't asked to see it, so I hadn't offered, sliding it under my seat.

With only quick glances, I fanned through the pages of crime-scene photos, documents, reports, and handwritten notes from detectives' slim notebook pages. Flipping through, I noticed that some page numbers on the documents were missing; apparently, some of the two-sided reports had never been flipped over, or whoever made the copies had skipped pages, accidentally or deliberately. The records had been copied by someone close to the case, because no one else would have had access to it long enough to copy it. Despite the access, they had definitely been in a hurry. More than a few pages were crooked, or marked by dark shadows signifying that the lid of the copier had been opened too early. Impatient.

Still, it was a treasure trove. And I realized how foolish it would be to try to translate the jargon alone. I would have to let Dad see the murder book. I would need his help on this one.

That night, I tried to take from it what I could.

The very first page was a photocopied picture of T.D. Jackson's corpse lolling back in a plush office chair facing away from his desk. His face was so dark that his features were shadowed. Just as well, I thought. I found an empty spiral reporter's notebook April had left behind and started making notes.

I could see the exit wound just below the right temple, so he'd shot himself with his left hand. He was notoriously ambidextrous on the field, but . . . his very best catches, in the biggest games, were made with his right hand. Under pressure, he was a Righty. Odd.

Did suicidal depression qualify as pressure?

Other photos revealed other details: T.D.'s right hand limp on the armrest. A light metal .38 automatic on the floor to his left, below his dangling arm.

To me, T.D. looked posed. Had he posed himself, or had someone else done the posing?

The blood toxicology wasn't included in the coroner's report, which would tell me if he'd had any drugs in his bloodstream—those always took forever—but the coroner provided badly needed details. T.D. had been shot squarely in the left temple, the slug causing massive trauma before exiting the right side of his head. It had been found in a bookshelf, wedged in the binder of a leather-bound edition of *Think and Grow Rich*. I doubt he would have appreciated the irony.

"You had some balls, brother," I muttered, just in case it was suicide.

According to the report, there was GSR—gunshot residue—on T.D.'s left hand, which fueled the suicide speculation. A lazy cop's wet dream.

The copies of the autopsy photos were very dark and hard to see, but I'm neither a necrophiliac or a forensic ME, so I'm no expert on corpses—even if I saw every *Faces of Death* movie. One close-up showed T.D. on his stomach, from the waist down, mostly his buttocks. I puzzled over the significance until I noticed a dark marking on one flank, the left: a symbol. An "H" keloid scar the size of a silver dollar. That must have been what the photo was trying to capture, I realized. I didn't have a magnifying glass for a better look, but I made a note to ask his family whether they knew anything about a tattoo.

I scoured the police reports next, and two names jumped out at me: Arnaz and O'Keefe. They were the homicide detectives from Hollywood division who'd knocked on my door to tell me that Serena was dead, all the while scanning my living room for clues in the murder. Since I'd spent a beautiful afternoon with Serena only hours before she died, I was a ready-made suspect. I'd even left my DNA behind in a condom.

Apparently, their dead-wrong instincts about Serena's murderer hadn't kept them from getting promoted to Robbery-Homicide, LAPD's most prestigious assignment, except for SWAT. They were both apparently in RHD's Homicide Special Section, which meant high-profile cases and serial killers. I chuckled, shaking my head. Figured. Lieutenant Nelson, who had been in charge of Serena's case, must have woven a tapestry of bullshit to arrest the real killer without admitting that I'd done LAPD's job instead, and those two detectives had been rewarded for making him look good. Or for keeping their mouths shut.

Had Arnaz or O'Keefe photocopied the murder book for Judge Jackson? It didn't seem likely. But either way, I wasn't going to give them a call. If Lieutenant Nelson caught a whiff that I was working the Jackson case, he'd find an excuse to lock me up. Period. The brother was my father's protégé, but during our run-in he hadn't struck me as the sentimental type.

Those officers' names resurrected bad memories, so I moved on to the report's red meat. The investigators had dotted every i and crossed all of the t's, at least on paper. The typed sections were impeccable, and even the handwriting was neat. The only thing missing was a shiny red ribbon. The report was as spiffy as if it had been written for posterity.

Since he died on a Sunday, T.D. Jackson had spent his last day with his children. According to the initial investigation, T.D. had attended a 10 A.M. church service at Faith Central Bible Church at the L.A. Forum on Manchester with his parents and two children. (T.D.'s thirteen-year-old daughter, Maya, and eight-year-old son, Thomas Jr., lived with his ex-wife's parents. The Hankinses, apparently, did not attend the morning service with them.)

Afterward, T.D. and his kids—as well as a small entourage including his lawyer and his friend Carlyle, whom I'd met at the fund-raiser—had spent an afternoon at Universal CityWalk, the domain of tourists and divorced dads looking for a way to substitute Fun for Family. At 6 P.M., T.D. had dropped the children back at his parents' house—the designated neutral ground for the two families— then joined another set of friends for drinks at the Mondrian Hotel. I didn't recognize the other names, but Carlyle was at the Mondrian, too. Apparently, he and T.D. were attached at the hip. A waitress at the bar reported that T.D. looked intoxicated, and he "might have had" cocaine residue on his nose. She also said T.D. was there with two blond twins who seemed like "hookers."

The waitress had been an observant witness. I made a note about the twins: *Mother?* And put a checkmark beside Mother's name. If T.D. Jackson had a taste for prostitutes, he would have been in touch with Mother. Mother specialized in a celebrity clientele.

Despite reports of partying, T.D. Jackson was home early for the night—and, as far as police could determine, he'd been alone. Carlyle had driven T.D. home. The last he'd seen of T.D. was a wave from the front door at 9:45 P.M. ("I always watched him until he was through the door," Carlyle told investigators. "He was living under siege.") Carlyle had a roomful of witnesses to corroborate his whereabouts afterward, since he'd been at his girlfriend's house.

T.D. disarmed his ADT alarm two minutes later and wouldn't reactivate it for more than an hour. Plenty of time for an intruder to get inside.

Phone records showed T.D. made six calls in the next hour. First he checked his home voicemail. Next, he called his father, his probable bookie, his driver, his lawyer, a promoter in Tokyo, a girlfriend in San Francisco, and his lawyer for a second time. With the civil trial coming up, T.D. needed a lot of hand-holding.

Then, T.D.'s phone fell silent. He armed his alarm at 10:53 P.M. Since there was no video surveillance inside the house, the rest of the night was pure supposition. The bathroom showed signs that he took a shower, and possibly shaved. Odd. Then, by all appearances, he went to bed.

T.D. was wearing a faded SoCal Spartans T-shirt and 49ers gym shorts when he died, clothes his parents confirmed were his pajamas. *One last shout-out to the fans at the end,* I thought. All of the football players I know were affected by their experience on the field in a way similar to combat veterans. Maybe it's because the game of football is so much like war. It's hard to imagine anyone breaking his spine playing baseball.

T.D. Jackson had been killed by a single shot to the temple by a Smith & Wesson automatic. Only three bullets remained in the clip; there was room for eight. No one heard the gunshot. It was a big house.

I knew the rest from the news: His body had been discovered by his housekeeper at 6:00 A.M. She had a key, so she routinely let herself in. She also knew the code to disable the alarm, and she noticed that it was already disarmed when she arrived. That was why she assumed T.D. was home but busy somewhere, since he rarely armed it when he was there, especially during daylight hours.

The housekeeper, a Dominican woman named Rosaria San Martin, was not considered a suspect or a person of interest. She had been asleep beside her husband at the time T.D. died, and she had worked for T.D. for almost a decade. The housekeeper was also so distraught by his death that the video of her wailing was playing in a loop on the cable news shows. I was sure I'd seen Dad watching her being interviewed on *Larry King Live*, and she'd been crying then, too.

I stayed up two hours reading the murder book. By the time I finished, I wondered if Judge Jackson had wasted his money looking for a killer. The image of T.D. Jackson shooting himself in the head was appealing, and there was certainly no evidence of anything else. As unlikely as suicide was, it was possible. T.D. might have been hated by Chantelle's family, and her fiancé's family—and the murder book included a long list of people who had made threats against him, from outright kooks to a woman in the prosecutor's office who had a nervous breakdown—but the evidence in the reports cleanly added up to suicide. Maybe *too* cleanly.

Every actor has his own technique for getting into a role. I have my own way, cobbled together from every acting class and seminar I've ever attended, along with my own mental quirks. I visualize the scene. See it as an audience would, then switch to see it from the position of each actor, in turn.

It's what I call my "Stage."

I walk from the wings onto the Stage, as I have a thousand times before. Blank. Intimidating. I dressed it: a desk, wall plaques, a plush chair. A minimalist office. I watched T.D. Jackson walk to the chair, and sit. Take a gun from a desk drawer . . .

I am the director now: "Wardrobe? Does he have to be wearing pajamas . . . ?"

So, what . . . ? He dressed for bed, then decided to kill himself? He was in bed, and had a guilty dream and decided to blow it out of his head?

How about this: He is in bed, and the front doorbell rings. He disarms the alarm, because he knows the person on the other side of the spyhole.

The lights went down. The stage disappeared. I was back in my room again. It could all be suicide. But if it was murder . . . he knew his killer.

My stomach cramped, and I knew why. All night, without realizing it, I'd been running a conversation with April in my head: *Can you believe these guys got promoted to Robbery-Homicide? Can you imagine what Nelson would say if he knew I had this book? What does your gut tell you about what happened to T.D.?* I had a hundred questions for her. A hundred things to say. April was another part of my mind—another part of me—and she was gone. The silence in my head was the only thing worse than the ringing.

She hadn't called me. That wasn't an accident, and it made my stomach hurt.

My digital clock told me it was eleven thirty, which made it eight thirty in the morning in Johannesburg. I called four different Holiday Inns in Jo'burg before I found a room registered in April's name. By the third ring, I was ready to leave a message.

"Hello?" April sounded breathless.

The connection was flawless. She might have been sitting next to me on the bed.

"It's me."

"Ten?"

She knew my voice, so there was no use repeating my name. It was still her turn to talk. She needed to explain her silence, so I waited. Ten seconds might have passed. The longer I waited, the sorrier I was I'd called. I suddenly imagined the vivid image of a naked man lounging next to her, and my gut clenched like a fist.

"I've been a real jerk not to call," she said, finally.

"You've been busy."

She sighed. "It's not just that, Ten. I mean, yes, I am busy . . . *crazy* busy . . . I can't believe you caught me in my room, because it seems like I'm never here . . . but I guess I'm just upset with myself because we could have had this conversation in person, but I didn't let myself see what I needed to see . . . and now it doesn't feel right on the phone."

"That doesn't sound good."

Another sigh. "Ten, I only have five minutes. My ride will be knocking on the door any second, and I have to get to the school."

"Then talk to me."

"I just don't want you to think I'm a horrible person. I really didn't plan it so I'd swoop off like this. This South Africa thing came up without any warning. But once I got here . . ." Her voice sounded very young to me suddenly, as if I'd never heard it before. I didn't try to coax her along this time. She had to do this on her own. "Ten, I am so lucky to know you. L.A. is a city of special people, and you're at the very top. Everything with us felt right before, and then . . . it didn't. I don't know why. It must be me."

I couldn't help it. I chuckled, almost a laugh.

"Please don't be mad," April said. "That's what kept me from calling. I didn't want to lose everything with you just because . . ."

"Because you've moved on." A lonely voice in my head screamed *Tell me what to do, and I'll do it. Tell me what to change, and I'll change it.* Maybe that was what April needed from me, but there's nothing we can do about our past. Nothing we can change.

"I wouldn't say . . . 'moved on,'" April said, choosing her words as carefully as a presidential candidate. "I'll be gone six months. Maybe the bigger world will help me feel something—a different kind of courage—by the time I come back. I really want to. My priorities need to change. That's the closest thing I have to a plan, Ten."

"You could have been clearer about that before you left."

"I said not to wait for me." Almost a whine.

"Giving me permission to fuck isn't the same as telling me the truth." I could almost see tears well into her eyes, but I pressed on, my tone purely analytical. "And since you knew you hadn't been clear, you should have called sooner. Or clarified yourself in your email."

"I'm sorry. I just kept wanting . . ."

"To grow up?" I finished, unable to catch all of the sarcasm in time. It surprised me how much I wanted to say something hurtful to her.

"Yes," she said. "I've been trying to grow up."

"How's that going?"

"Slow."

"Have you met someone?"

"No, Ten. I swear. And I wouldn't lie about that."

The naked man in April's room vanished. My bubble of anger

popped. I missed her so much it felt as if there were a vacuum where my heart used to be.

"Ten, my ride is here, but this isn't the last time we'll talk about this. I'm really sorry I didn't call before. I can call you back tonight. I owe you that. Like . . . seven my time?"

I didn't want a mercy call. "There's no rush. You know my number."

"Am I a terrible person?" she said.

I wanted to kiss every inch of her face. Sift through her hair with my fingertips. "No."

"Well, you're the most incredible person I know. That hasn't changed."

"Something has."

I heard April's nostrils bubble. Evidence that she was crying helped a little, but not nearly enough. "I wish I knew what," she said.

I knew.

"Lynda Jewell was the first big mistake I've made in a long time. I'm sorry, April. Nothing even close will ever happen again." *And Lynda Jewell will be sorry it happened at all,* I finished to myself.

"Ten, it wasn't that."

But April was lying to herself. It was *exactly* that. Lynda Jewell had not only climbed onto my lap and pulled my hand to her chest; she had once watched her friend pay to have sex with me. Lynda Jewell was my past, still living and breathing, and there were women like her all over Los Angeles. April and I couldn't pretend it away.

I wanted to tell April that I would climb back through time and remake myself inch by inch, starting with my seventh-grade teacher's pool. Nothing had ever cost me so much.

My life was barely ordered chaos. April deserved better, and we both knew it.

"It's okay," I heard myself telling April. "It really is. I understand, baby. We're okay."

I sounded so good, I almost believed it.

ELEVEN

WEDNESDAY, OCTOBER 22

Melanie Wilde had taken the week off from work, her receptionist told me the next morning, so I tried her cell phone. When I told Melanie I wanted to talk about T.D., she invited me to her Santa Monica condo. I can't say I was disappointed.

We were both in mourning. I brought Melanie a small potted white lily plant. I've never cared for bouquets; they die too soon. At least an uncut plant has roots and a fighting chance.

Far from her traditional office attire, Melanie was wearing flowing, loose-fitting purple-and-lilac pants and a matching tunic, perhaps West African. It's the world's oldest cliché to tell a woman she looks like a princess, but the words almost slipped out when I saw her. Her unadorned skin was a shade of dark brown I doubted makeup manufacturers could imitate. Melanie's skin spoke best for itself. Sunlight from the doorway gleamed on the bulb of her nose.

Again, she didn't bother smiling. "Thoughtful," she said, taking the plant. "Thanks."

Thoughtful wasn't the right word. The plant was a prop. I'd dressed in my white turtleneck and brown leather bomber jacket to see her. I was in full stalk mode; if Melanie had a fiancé, that was between her and her conscience. I'd prepared a list of questions for her, but I expected more than conversation. Experience had taught me that I only had to find a way to ask. If there was any part of her that wanted me, I was going to find it.

"Wish I could do something more," I said.

Melanie's lips pressed together, inching slightly upward. Her sad attempt at a smile made me sorry for being at her front door.

"Uncle Emory called me this morning, and it's like night and day. You've given them hope, Tennyson. And I know you'll do more than that. Let's talk."

Inside, I smelled incense. Not jasmine, thank God. Something with spice, a reminder that I was in a new place. Melanie's condo was neat but free-spirited, with bean-bag chairs, stained-wood crate shelving, and a large futon instead of a furniture-store version of a living room. The open-air space was almost a loft. Her walls were covered in colorful, beaded masks that looked South African, a lovely Dogon door intricately carved with stylized rows of women, and marketplace paintings I recognized as Haitian. Most of the living room's shelves were empty. Boxes sat in orderly stacks against the dining-room wall. There was no table.

Melanie's living room had a large picture window, so the room was bathed in light. Outside, there was a partial view of the ocean three blocks west. Not bad. Aretha was singing from speakers at a volume so low that my ears couldn't make out the song, but it was earthy and sad. Nothing could soothe the loss of a beloved family member, but Melanie's condo was doing its best. I glanced toward an open doorway and saw the foot of her bed, covers turned back.

Melanie brought me a mug of coffee on a small tray with creamer and sugar on the side. SOCAL STATE SPARTANS FOOTBALL, the mug read, emblazoned with the sword-wielding mascot.

"Nice place," I said.

"Won't have it long. I'm pretty much living at Simon's house. We're getting married in June." Melanie was trying her best to shut me down. She'd seen where my eyes had drifted.

"Simon," I said, trying on the name. "A brother?"

Pow. I'd hit her so fast, she hadn't seen me coming. Melanie's eyes flitted away, defensive. "No . . . he's English. From Sussex."

"Hey, that's cool. Great town, Sussex."

So. Miss Afrocentricity 1992 was marrying a white boy, and even if she hadn't felt a nibble of guilt or self-doubt, I could give her one last chance to redeem her Negritude points. I might be the last black man she ever touched. Ruminating on my luck, I took off my jacket and folded it over my crossed knee. I could barely fight off my smile.

"How's your ear?" Melanie said.

"If you want me to hear you, better sit on the right." She started to sit in a chair across from me, but I patted the spot beside me on the futon. "Closer is better."

"Did you hear me mention I was getting married in June?"

"Lovely ring." Her white gold and diamond engagement ring had cost plenty.

"I would appreciate it if you would bear that in mind."

"I'm sure."

Melanie locked eyes with me; the same gaze I'd given Lynda Jewell. She knew, and I knew. The only question was which of us would get our way. When Melanie sat beside me, I could feel her body heat right through her clothes. "Tell me what you need to do your job."

"You weren't with T.D. on Sunday," I said. "Why not?"

"You get to work fast," Melanie said, eyebrow arched. Part admiration, part irritation.

"Some things I do fast. Others, slow."

"I won't pretend I'm in church every week, because Lord knows I'm not. But I had a Black Lawyers meeting in New York last weekend. Just curious, or are you looking for an alibi?"

I shrugged, remembering my coffee. It was fine black, so I left it alone.

Melanie sighed. "You're right. I wasn't in church with T.D. on Sunday, and I wish I could change that. I have a hundred regrets. Anything else on that subject?"

"No, darlin'. But I've been meaning to ask you . . . Why did you call him Bumpy?"

Melanie almost smiled at a memory. "He's three years younger, so he was always just little Bumpy. A big fat face, fat legs, and always running into the furniture. Born running." She kept smiling even when her tears came.

Then Melanie got tired of reminiscing. "This is where you're supposed to ask me if I think I know who did it," she said.

"Yes, ma'am," I said. I pulled out April's notebook. "I'm sure you have some ideas."

"Too many to count," she said. "So I'll start with the most obvious: Look very closely at the Hankins family. I might be able to kiss their asses and get you a meeting today or tomorrow. Chantelle's father has come apart since her death. Chantelle was their only child. But LAPD treats Donald Hankins like he's made of glass. Unfortunately for Uncle Emory, Hankins trumps a federal judge."

When I gave her a blank look, she went on. "Two-term state senator, Ten. Plays golf with the mayor and police chief. Backed a huge law-enforcement initiative to pour money into LAPD's coffers. More cars. More officers on the street. He's planning to run for governor, and he polls very high. He's hoping for an Obama Effect."

I scribbled fast. I remembered that Chantelle's father was a politician, but I hadn't remembered the details. A war between these two families would be a clash of titans.

"Murder is risky for a man with that much to lose."

Melanie shook her head. "For someone that unhinged, risk doesn't matter. Look, I'm not saying he did it: I'm saying I think he could have made the call. Start with him and feel him out for yourself. I have very strong instincts about it."

"Who would he have called?"

"That's where the detective part comes in," Melanie said grimly. "You tell us."

I gave her a look: *So it's like that?* "Just asking, sister. Anything else?"

"Chantelle was engaged." Melanie paused but kept some thoughts to herself. "Her fiancé was Arturo Salvador, a former probation officer who quit the grind to go to law school. He seemed like a good guy. Great with the kids. Most of his family is in Mexico, but he has a brother, Miguel, who was convinced T.D. had killed him. He lives in Pomona. Miguel threatened T.D. He said if the police didn't put him away, he'd 'take care of it' himself."

"At the trial?"

"No. Before the trial, he wrote T.D. a letter I found in his mail. You should have it in the police records. I told them to keep it."

"There was an interview. Salvador had an alibi." An officer's handwritten note had described Miguel Salvador as "grinning from ear to ear" when they brought up T.D.'s death, but his wife insisted he had been in bed with her in a San Francisco hotel room when T.D. died. I made a note of his name. He would have been smarter to try to contain his glee during his police interview, at least. My gut told me that the killer would have known better, but maybe not.

"What about T.D.'s buddies? Those guys at the fund-raiser?"

"I'll vouch for every one of them," Melanie said. "Most of them played with him on the Spartans. They were all Taus, and three of them were a team within a team: They called themselves the Four Horseman of Heat."

"Heat?" I wrote that down. I remembered the scar from the autopsy photo. "Does T.D.'s H-shaped scar have anything to do with that?"

"Yes."

"It looked like a heat scar."

"They took their little club very seriously. Too seriously, I think."

"Seriously enough to get matching brands . . ." I mused.

"How did you know about the H?"

I paused. "Autopsy photo."

Melanie blanched slightly, her lips tight. But she went on. "That fool Bumpy couldn't sit for a week. Carlyle and T.D. did crazy shit once in a while, but they had sworn to watch out for each other, and all those Heat guys always did. But Carlyle knew him longest. He was T.D.'s best friend since junior high."

"All that matters is access. Could he have gotten into the house? Or the rest of them?"

"I'll give you their names and anything else you need. But it's a dead end, Tennyson."

"Where can I find Carlyle?"

Melanie paused, uncomfortable. "I saw him . . . the day we heard. Monday. But I haven't seen him since. He hasn't returned my calls since Monday, after I told him."

Now it was my turn to raise my eyebrows. "Not even to find out about the funeral?"

Melanie shook her head. "He's broken up over it. *Broken* up. They were like brothers. T.D., I'm getting worried about Carlyle. His girlfriend said he hasn't been coming by."

"Ten, you mean."

"What?"

"You just called me T.D.," I said gently.

Melanie looked at me, startled. "I did?"

I nodded, and her eyes overflowed. I patted her knee; still stalking, even then. I almost went in for a consoling embrace, but I have a heart. And I'm patient. Besides, I had more questions.

Melanie shifted her knee away from my touch. "I can give you a dozen more names."

I wrote Carlyle's name down, and a checkmark. "I've got time."

Melanie named everyone from disgruntled former business partners to ex-girlfriends, and I noticed that most of the names she mentioned had been absent from the police reports. She even mentioned a former barber of T.D.'s who had trash-talked him on television after T.D. started getting his hair cut somewhere else. Said he'd confessed to the pedicurist. Last, a celebrity stalker who had been released from a mental institution six weeks before.

T.D.'s charisma had attracted the bad as well as the good, and Melanie had been keeping her eye on every one of them.

By the time she finished, she was weary. Primed for The Question of the Day.

"Mel, did T.D. kill Chantelle and her fiancé?"

Melanie sat up as straight as a rod. Everything about her bristled. "If I thought my cousin was a killer," she said, "I would have told you."

"He never said anything? No moment of remorse after a few drinks? Or a few lines?"

"No," she said, ice in her voice. She didn't appreciate the reference to T.D.'s cocaine use, but she didn't bother denying it.

"Would he have told you if he had?"

The ice thawed, only slightly. "I doubt it."

"So it's a possibility. You know that."

Instead of answering, Melanie stood up and gathered up our empty coffee mugs. She walked to the kitchen and back before she answered me. "I know he had a temper. He might have hit her, but that only happened once. She was seeing Arturo while she was still married—no one wants to talk about that. And T.D. found out about it. A lot of guys would lose their composure in that situation."

"So she was cheating, but he wasn't?"

Melanie winced. "T.D. wasn't a perfect person, Ten. I know it and you know it. He drank. He did coke. Yes, he was running around. Please—he was T.D. Jackson. Chantelle was a big girl: She knew T.D.'s lifestyle. Those guys live in a world unto themselves, starting in school. But he couldn't handle it when she started seeing Arturo. She didn't try to keep it quiet like he did. She tried to provoke him, make him jealous. He got mad, he hit her, she got a restraining order. That all happened three years ago. T.D. and Chantelle put the divorce behind them to raise Maya and Tommy. Those kids were the center of their universe. After Chantelle was killed, did I have doubts? Of course. I know how it looked. But I won't believe he could do that to the mother of his children. Not T.D." She wrenched out the words, her voice coarse.

"And his blood in her garage?"

"It was his garage once, too. The blood evidence wasn't conclusive. Ask the jury."

That was all I was going to get out of Melanie on that subject. Her body was rigid, arms and legs crossed. If I wasn't careful, she was about to ask me to leave.

"I have calls to make . . ." she said, a beat behind my thoughts.

I closed my notebook and laid it down. Then I leaned against the back of the futon for a better view of her, my palms locked behind my neck. Her tough-girl act was wearing thin on her face. "You were T.D.'s rock. Now you're your uncle's. Who's yours?"

"You're wasting your time, Ten." Her words were resistant, but not her eyes.

"Why are you staying at your condo instead of Simon's place?"

The mention of her fiancé's name made Melanie frown. "Because I wanted to be here. Simon's in London for a couple of days. He'll be back before the funeral."

She didn't have to tell me that. She shouldn't have.

"Busy man," I said.

"An IT conference. He was booked a year ago, and he couldn't miss it. He hated to go."

I could hear her disappointment even as she defended him. Usually, I would have taken it slow, drawn out the chase. I tried to talk myself down, but I couldn't.

"My girlfriend broke up with me last night. Long-distance."

She was the first person I'd told.

"Then it's a bad week for you, too."

"Not like yours, Mel."

We sat with our misery for a moment. I ventured another hand to Melanie's knee. After a pause, she brushed it away; but that pause told me what I needed to know.

I stood abruptly. "Excuse me a second."

I headed straight for her bedroom. I closed the door behind me.

"My guest bath is out here!" Melanie called after me.

I didn't answer. I wasn't interested in her master bathroom.

The bedroom was more cluttered than the living room, the last room packed. The walls were the color of red Georgia clay. There were framed photos of her with T.D. all over the walls, at every phase of life. Just as I thought, Melanie had always been beautiful. She and T.D. seemed more like brother and sister than cousins, I noted. Both of them were only children, and their parents lived locally, so the bond had been forged early.

On her nightstand, I saw a photo of Melanie with a tall, mousy white man I assumed was her fiancé. He had a weak chin and thinning light brown hair, about fifty. Not much to look at, but he was probably a decent guy. Smart. Successful. He'd had the nerve to make his move; he hadn't backed away from her. Maybe that was all she'd wanted. I felt sorry for the other guys of all hues who'd missed out on their chance with Melanie. But I had mine.

I turned the photo with Simon so that it was facing the wall. Then I yanked Melanie's rumpled bedspread, straightening it. I smoothed out the creases. It's not polite to lie on someone's bare sheets in street clothes.

I slid out of my shoes. Then I lay down across the center of her bed, my head propped on my elbow. The direct approach was risky, but it was my best chance.

She knocked on her bedroom door. When I didn't answer, she opened it tentatively.

Melanie stared at me like a mirage. "You must be out of your damn mind," she said.

I patted the mattress. "Come sit."

"Fuck you. You definitely have T.D.'s ego. Get off of my bed."

"Can we hold each other?"

Either she would walk out of the room, or she wouldn't. Clean and simple.

Melanie stayed in the doorway, watching me with a combination of incredulity and anger. Maybe no one had ever tried the direct approach on her. She intimidated the hell out of the men she met; I was certain of that. Most of my clients had been just like her.

"Who's holding you, Mel?" I said. "Who's your rock? Come. Sit."

It was no longer a suggestion; it was a command. Melanie's eyes narrowed. Then, like a woman sleepwalking, she took halting steps toward the bed. *That's right. Come on, girl. Come to Papa.* She sat at the edge of the mattress, out of my reach. But close enough.

"I'm engaged, Tennyson," she said. "He's number two. I want this one to work."

"I'm not trying to change your future. I wish you bliss. You just look like you need to be nestled up against somebody right now. And I know I do."

Honesty is always the most effective pitch. It's hard to argue against the truth.

"Get thee behind me, Satan," she muttered. "You look different in your pictures."

"Shhhh." I held out my hand to her. "Let me do for you what Simon would, if he was here. Please."

Slowly, with a shudder that might have been a muffled sob, Melanie lay beside me. She kept her arms folded across her chest as I slid mine across her waist, cradling her from behind. My chest settled against her back. My nostrils lay at the nape of her neck. I closed my eyes and inhaled the smell of her—African black soap and ripe cherries. My arm drew closer around her.

"I can't do this," she said.

"You're not doing anything."

We lay still for a while, our hot cheeks resting together. Her cheek was damp. Her body relaxed against mine, and her next sob came free. Melanie Wilde was out of her mind with grief; I knew that, and yet I held her in her bed. I touched her hair and skin while she cried.

"There's no way around it except through it," I whispered. When I kissed her neck, I felt her skin tremble beneath my lips.

"Why am I doing this?" She sounded confused. Lost.

"To forget," I said, and slipped my hand inside her colorful tunic. No bra. With such a heavy fabric, she didn't need one. My fingertips scurried, finding her breast. It was a hefty mound, natural and full. Her nipple rose to meet my touch.

"I can't . . ." she began, a plea. But there was no mercy in me. Not an ounce.

"Shhhhh." I squeezed her nipple gently, and she sucked at the air through her teeth. Women's nipples betray them as much as penises betray men. Melanie's eyes screwed tightly shut. I had her.

Melanie was moaning when I burrowed my head beneath her hot tunic and rubbed my face against her chest. Her nipple slipped into my mouth with a slight taste of baby powder. I licked, then my lips clamped gently and pulled. Only slightly. Melanie writhed. Her hands cradled the back of my head, but she didn't push me away. She held me in place.

Still sucking and teasing her breasts, I yanked the string of her drawstring pants, slowly pulling them down, freeing her long legs.

My face was perspiring when I pulled my head out of Melanie's tunic, back to fresh air. I liberated Melanie from the rest of her clothes. Her body was slightly thin for my tastes, her ribs and collarbone showing in a way April's did not, but she was magnificent. My hands traveled over her shoulders, her chest, her waist. Her belly jumped beneath my touch. My tongue darted into her navel while my hands explored her thighs. Melanie moaned.

I rubbed our faces together, but I didn't try to kiss her. I also didn't remove my own clothes, despite the urgent tug in my jeans. Neither of us was craving kisses. Only escape.

Tie me, Melanie whispered. My ears missed it, but I read her lips fine.

"*Shhhhh*," I said, forcefully; my arm around her waist became a vise. She didn't want her sexual healing sweet—she wanted it rough. Simon might not like bondage games; maybe they felt too politically incorrect. His loss. I was in the perfect mood.

Melanie was breathing faster already within my grip. I felt her chest rising and falling.

I unbuckled my braided black leather belt.

"Don't say another damn word," I told her. Melanie gasped, anticipating. Gratitude shone within the grief in her eyes.

I'd retired my bondage kit, which had been elaborate and imaginative, but I was a master with a belt. I twined the leather strap tightly around Melanie's wrists, pulling her closer to the coffee-colored wooden rail of her bedpost. I had just enough leather left to secure the belt to the rail, leaving my hands free. She tugged her binds, testing.

This way, she wouldn't feel responsible.

When she realized she couldn't move, she smiled through her tears. But nervousness fluttered across her face. There's always nervousness with a playmate. Bondage games mean different things to different people. Usually I ask women to give me a "danger word" to let me know when the games have veered from pleasure to pain. From fun to fear. But I didn't want to break the fantasy with Melanie, so I watched her eyes instead.

Her eyes would tell me what she wanted, and how she wanted it.

Our game began.

I knelt between Melanie's spread legs and lifted her torso, hooking her knees across my shoulders. My belt buckle clanked against the wall. I lifted her high to heighten her feeling of helplessness, and she gasped her approval. Her pubic hair was closely clipped, a dusting growing out of an old bikini wax. My tongue roamed the fleshy ridges. She tasted like tears.

When Melanie bucked, my grip across her hips tightened. This time, I held her in place. My tongue circled her damp clitoris, and Melanie thrashed and shouted. The belt clanked again.

"Shit . . ." she whispered. "Oh, shuh-shit . . ."

"I told you to be *quiet.*" The irritation in my voice was almost real. I waited for obedient silence until my mouth dived in again. I didn't penalize her for whimpering; most women have never experienced oral arts the way I practice them. Her juices flooded my face. A growl rumbled in Melanie's throat as she tried not to scream.

I could have left it at that. I almost wanted to. *Enough,* a voice inside me said. But my juices were surging too. I reached into my wallet and pulled out one of three condoms I always carry. Still fully clothed except for my open fly, I rolled the condom across my taut, ready skin.

Sorry, Simon, I thought. *You should have stayed home.* That's the dirty secret. That's what people in relationships don't want to admit. Anyone can stray. Anyone.

Melanie's knees were still wrapped around my shoulder, and I hoisted her higher so our bodies could meet. I know I'm large, so I'm careful about penetration. I took it slow. I saw her eyes widen, surprised, and I watched them for any sign of *Stop.* When none came, I tested a deeper thrust. She gritted her teeth, but her eyes never faltered. I pulled back slightly to gather moisture, and thrust again, harder. Her eyes were steady until they slowly melted away, lost in sensation. Pain was gone. Grief was gone.

I wasn't gentle. I wasn't tender. I pounded.

From habit, I'm always preoccupied with my partner's needs first. I studied her pleasure for a long time before I allowed myself to feel my own. Slowly, I let go. Melanie was tight, and her muscles massaged me with each stroke, much more practiced than April. I felt her clenching me, hoarding me. I ventured deep, until our pelvises bumped. The cords in Melanie's neck strained as she felt me fill her up. Not every woman can tolerate my full length inside of them, but if Melanie was suffering, she kept it to herself. Or maybe she needed the pain.

I stared at her bound hands. Her violently jiggling breasts. Those snapshots fed my fever. I thrust harder, and my next thrust *clanked* the belt when her headboard bumped the wall. I was sweating as my heart raced, driving me. My body controlled us.

Melanie's eyes flew open when my palm clamped around her throat. I held on tightly enough to get her attention, but not enough to cut off the flow of blood or air. She tested her ability to swallow, and I felt her rigid body relax when she realized I wasn't choking her.

Her eyes stayed steady on mine. She flung herself against me, mouthing ecstatic gibberish. So I held on.

I'm often quiet when I climax, but I wasn't that day. I howled, too, as a shock wave rode all the way from my balls to my eyebrows, frying everything in between. My body kept thrusting even after I was sure I had collapsed against her, my muscles sapped of strength. I forgot who I was, where I was. What I was.

When I saw her face again, fresh tears were streaming down Melanie's cheeks. For some women, remorse kicks in immediately. I looked away. Like I said, that was between her and her conscience. She was a grown-ass woman.

Maybe Simon's a nice guy, Melanie. Guess what? I'm not.

I lay beside her, catching my breath as I stuffed myself back into my clothes. I wanted to go, but I wasn't finished yet.

I rubbed her Melanie's arms, toward the belt that held her. "I'll ask you one more time," I said, my voice still in character. "In all these years, you never saw any behavior in T.D. that made you think he could have killed Chantelle?"

Melanie sighed, heavy and fractured. She was withholding something.

"Tell me," I said, more gently. I played with the belt, but didn't unhook it. I didn't say so, but she knew I wouldn't untie her until she spoke up.

"In college," Melanie said in a husk of a voice. "I . . . walked into his room, and . . . one of his girls was there. Naked. She was looking for her clothes while T.D. was in the bathroom. She said . . ."

"She said what?"

"She said T.D. had hurt her."

"Hurt her how?"

Melanie shook her head, closing her eyes. "I don't know. She said, 'That fucker tried to kill me,' but she didn't stop when I asked her what she was talking about. She pushed past me and left. In a hurry. She was a football groupie. No one I knew."

"Did she have marks? Bruises?"

"Her face was bright red. Puffy lips, maybe. I don't know. I just . . ."

"You just what, Melanie?"

More tears. "I didn't want to believe it."

"Did you ask T.D. about it?"

Sniffing, Melanie nodded. "He said . . . it was nothing. And I let it go." Melanie's next sob was from a deeper place, shredding her throat. "Oh, God. I let it go."

With the terrible sound of her crying in my ear, I rushed to unhook the belt that bound her. As I pulled Melanie's arms free, she hardly moved. Wherever she was, she had left her body far behind. Melanie Wilde's pain was back, too. I pulled her tunic back on, covering her to her thighs, and held her close. I hushed her, rocking her. Like me, she couldn't carry any more weight on her conscience.

"I'm sorry," I whispered.

This time, we had nowhere to hide.

TWELVE

THERE'S A USEFUL AXIOM IN LIFE: Don't shit where you sleep. I should have remembered that before I drove to Melanie Wilde's condo to take her to bed. There were a dozen other ways she could be useful to me—especially in getting me an audience with Chantelle's parents—but suddenly we weren't in the mood for each other's company.

I cursed myself as I started my drive with nowhere to go. I was fooling myself if I thought I was going to solve T.D. Jackson's murder, or Chantelle's. I couldn't solve my own life. The eastbound 10 was already clogged just because. There's tough competition in L.A., but the 10 may be my least favorite freeway.

Out of one ear, I heard a cell phone ring. Not mine. Chela's. The ring tone was a song I didn't know. I glanced at both of her phones, which lay on my passenger seat. My hands had the steering wheel in a death grip until I realized that her iPhone was glowing, not the one she'd gotten from Internet Guy. I saw the lighted Caller ID: FAISON, BERNARD.

I knew that name, so I picked it up. "Hello?"

"Uh . . ." The sound of my voice threw him. He and puberty

were having an argument, with no clear winner. "I must have the wrong . . ."

"This is Chela's number," I said. "She left her phone at home. Is there a message?"

"Never mind," he said, ready to flee.

"Wait," I said. "Are you the guy from the chess club? You asked her to the formal?"

"Uh . . . yeah."

"Great," I said. "I know she's really looking forward to it."

"Really? Wow. That's awesome! But . . . surprising. She never actually agreed to . . ."

"She'll be there. Arrive at the house a half hour early to pick her up, and bring a corsage. You and Chela are just getting to know each other, so don't take this the wrong way, but girls remember these formals the rest of their lives. This matters, and I want you to make it special. Do you have our address?"

Stammering, Bernard asked me to wait while he grabbed a pen. After he wrote down the address, his voice became more confident. "Whoa. Thanks," he said. "I wasn't sure what to think. Chela's kinda . . . I mean, she's *great*, but she's . . ."

"Don't worry. She'll be ready to go. And I expect you to be a gentleman that night—hear me?"

All confidence was suddenly gone. "Uh . . . yeah . . . I'm not . . . a lech or anything."

"Chela's had a tough life, Bernard. Try to be one of the bright spots."

"Cool!" Bernard said. "I can definitely do that. If she'll let me. Hey, thanks."

He sounded sincere and aware, even mature. I liked him. Now I just had to convince Chela to go to that dance. But I had more than a week left, and a date was half the battle.

When I hung up the phone, I finally had something to feel good about.

All of L.A. was spread before me from the 10, with arteries that could take me toward every possibility in my search for T.D. Jackson's killer.

But I knew the best place to start. I drove straight home.

The living room's television set was playing for an empty sofa when I arrived with Asian chicken salad from The Good Earth. Chela was at school, and Dad's door was closed.

When I knocked on Dad's door, Marcela called out instead. "I'm giving Captain Hardwick his bath!"

Too Much Information. Trying to block unwanted images from my head, I sat at the table to wait. I'd seen Chela leave for school, and she hadn't had a duffel bag full of clothes with her. That was a start. Now she just had to make it home. School was out at three, so I might know by four. If she was still in a bad mood, she would enjoy making me worry.

On CNN, file footage showed Melanie Wilde in a business suit as she demanded answers on T.D.'s death at a press conference Monday. The same clip I'd seen. I tried not to contrast her fiery composure on the screen with the shattered woman I'd just bedded, but there was no running away from the memory of her nakedness. As a rule, I don't feel guilty about sex. Ever. But the rules in my life were changing. I was grateful when the clip was over.

From the television studio, Lieutenant Rodrick Nelson himself, Dad's former protégé, coolly answered the commentator's questions about whether LAPD was mishandling the case, even venturing a pitying smile. He was my age, but with an authoritative face. He always reminded me of Richard Roundtree in his prime, down to the mustache.

"We're hearing from everyone from conspiracy theorists to astrologers." Nelson's baritone could have won him a newsman's job if he'd wanted it. I remembered that voice from Nelson's questioning after Serena's death, and it does what it's supposed to do in an interrogation. "Public reaction to this case has been strong. Naturally, who can fault a family member for her grief? But the evidence of suicide is overwhelming, and we follow the evidence. That said, if any sign of foul play emerges, we'll pursue it. Absolutely."

"Mmmm! Chinese chicken," Marcela said, peeking into the takeout bags on the table. She had appeared from Dad's room while I was captivated by the screen.

I remembered my manners and gave Marcela a hug. I had never called her to apologize the way I'd promised my father, and I was sure it was the first thing Dad asked her when she arrived that morning. Her skin felt warm and flushed. She smelled freshly bathed, too. I used to flirt with Marcela back when Dad was in the nursing home, but that had stopped long ago.

"Sorry I was an asshole yesterday."

She patted my shoulder. "We all have bad days, *chico*. How's your ear?"

I shook my head. "Same. The hearing loss is permanent."

She pinched my earlobe gently. "Not so fast, Ten. Hearing loss can last for weeks, even months. I'm lighting candles for you. Maybe God will restore what doctors can't."

I nodded, but I didn't hold out hope of divine intervention. I wasn't exactly one of God's regulars. Still, I never turned down a prayer. Eternal optimism was part of Marcela's charm.

When Dad wheeled himself into the room, he shot me an evil look.

"He apologized, Captain," Marcela said. "And he brought food."

We ate at the table together, but neither Dad nor I had much to say. Marcela made up for the lack of chatter, as she usually did, with stories of the elaborate Christmas pig she always prepared for her family. From time to time, Marcela reached over to help Dad cut something, or to wipe food from his chin. Dad was still a clumsy eater. I waited for one of them to mention that we might be spending Thanksgiving together, but neither of them brought it up. When Marcela asked how April was doing, I only said, "Fine." Barely looking up.

But it was enough for Marcela to understand. Her features flattened; she looked genuinely grieved, almost ill. Then she changed the subject. *Thank you,* I thought.

I gave myself the entire fifteen minutes we were at the table to talk myself out of my plan, but I never managed to. It had always been hard for me to ask for my father's help, but this time I would be betraying a client's confidence. My codes of honor might not impress most people, but they keep me inside the lines. I wouldn't want to know myself without rules. But this was a special circumstance.

While Marcela cleared the table, I brought down my manila envelope.

"I need you to take a look at this, Dad."

Dad eyed the envelope in my hands, tantalized but already wary.

We went to his room, and I laid out a few pages on his desk. I waited patiently while Dad fumbled to reach his reading glasses on his bureau. I tried not to offer help unless he asked for it, which was almost never. Marcela could wait on him hand and foot, but not I.

Dad only glanced at the papers before he whipped his glasses off again, as if he wanted to erase what he'd just seen. His hand was so unsteady, his glasses dropped to the floor. This time, I reached down to pick them up. They were out of his reach.

"Where . . . ? " Dad said, his shorthand for Where *did you get this?* His face was ashen.

"Judge Jackson." I'd thought about omitting his name, but Dad would have figured it out. He probably knew before he asked. The stroke had devastated his body, but not his mind.

Dad sighed, shaking his head. I knew that look on his face: He was overrun with things he wanted to say, but he knew his mouth couldn't keep up. He reached for his yellow legal pad on his desk and found a black Sharpie. My childhood home had been littered with Dad's legal pads, and now those pads were the best window into the workings of my father's mind.

Over time, with practice, Dad's handwriting with his left hand had improved. His right hand wasn't paralyzed, but his right side had never fully recovered from the stroke. Handwriting was better with his left hand now. For clarity, he always wrote with block letters. His lines were rigidly straight, like a schoolmarm's.

YOU SAID YOU WOULDN'T BREAK THE LAW.

When my only answer was an impassive stare, Dad sighed and started writing again.

THE INVESTIGATION HAS BEEN BREACHED. THIS IS AN ACTIVE CASE FILE. YOU'RE IMPLICATED IN EVIDENCE TAMPERING.

"Only if anyone finds out," I said.

Dad laid down his pen. "No one . . . else . . . knows?"

Melanie knew, but I didn't dare say so. "Judge Jackson doesn't want it public. And I'm not stupid."

"You . . . sure . . . about that?"

"Most days."

"Better be."

He was right. Evidence tampering with the intent to help a criminal evade justice could put you behind bars for years. What I was doing . . . well, it was in a gray zone. Whoever had gotten it for the judge was in more trouble than I. If the law came after me I'd stonewall and probably be up for an obstruction charge. Not fun, but I probably wouldn't end up at Guantánamo either.

"I get it, Dad," I said. "I'm not taking it lightly. You're the only one I trust with this."

Dad sighed again, running his left hand across his scalp, which shone through patches of white. He sometimes ignored his right hand and right side, entirely, as if the stroke had made part of him invisible to himself. Gazing at him, I realized that not long ago, I never would have believed that I would be discussing an LAPD case file with my father at his old rolltop desk. Two years ago, I had bought his plot at Hollywood Cemetery. I was still making monthly payments.

"Jackson's . . . gone . . . crazy," Dad said, and I remembered that he knew Judge Jackson.

"His son is dead. He wants to know why. Maybe that's enough to make him crazy."

ENOUGH TO BE IMPEACHED, Dad wrote. WHAT'S YOUR EXCUSE?

Dad waved me away, exasperated by my silence on the questions that mattered to him. I thought I'd blown it, until I realized he wanted to be left alone to look at the pages. He didn't like what I'd done, but he was intrigued. Once a badge, always a badge.

I had reinforcements.

While Dad read the murder book, I went to the screening room to fire up my computer. A call came from Len on my cell phone while I waited to boot up, but I left the call to voicemail. I needed to focus. I wasn't an actor anymore, at least for now. And although I was pissed off about Lynda Jewell and her buddy in props, I had probably just lost my lawyer, too.

Managing my life was too much work, so I wanted to lose myself in the case. I Googled the names from my notes: *Miguel Salvador. Carlyle Simms. Donald Hankins.*

Salvador's name came up frequently in articles about the murders of his brother and Chantelle Jackson; he was obsessed with his quest to see T.D. on death row. I didn't see any threats against T.D. attributed to him, but the letter Melanie mentioned was enough. I hoped I could get my hands on it—Dad's contacts inside LAPD might be able to help with that if Dad would agree. According to one article, Miguel Salvador had a rotisserie chicken restaurant in Pomona called Mama Cluckers. I wrote down the address.

Next, Carlyle Simms. He had played for the Spartans offensive line with T.D. back in the early nineties, later gone pro. He retired from the Miami Dolphins after only three seasons because of multiple concussions. After Chantelle's murder, when T.D. was so distraught that he'd holed himself up in his house, Carlyle was the one who had talked him into unlocking his bathroom to face police. T.D. had a bottle of sleeping pills in his hand, according to some reports—another indication that he might have had suicidal tendencies.

Carlyle had also been T.D.'s primary alibi in court, claiming they'd been at Carlyle's house watching *Monday Night Football* when the murders took place. Carlyle's testimony was part of what had saved T.D.'s ass. Money and celebrity had done the rest.

Could Carlyle's conscience have gotten the best of him after the acquittal? Had they argued? Carlyle's protectiveness of T.D. at the fund-raiser didn't fit the portrait of his future murderer, but Serena's case had taught me not to trust anyone.

Last, Senator Donald Hankins. Google produced a slew of hits for the law-enforcement initiative Melanie had mentioned—worth millions to LAPD alone—but the articles that caught my eye were ten years old, from when he was still a Los Angeles city councilman. A political rival's aide accused him of threatening to make him "disappear" when they clashed over a proposed building project. They both sued and countersued for defamation. Hankins denied the story, and both cases were dropped, but I printed out a copy of the article.

The aide's name was Kevin Wong. I found him listed as a Washington lobbyist, if it was the same Kevin Wong. Last-known contact information was a firm in D.C. I noted it.

Marcela stuck her head inside my door. "Ten? I knocked."

I hadn't heard a knock. Hearing loss in one ear wasn't going to be a small problem, I realized. It was hearing loss, period. I felt like I had a bucket on my head, muffling everything. Maybe people got used to it, but I didn't see how.

Marcela grinned, walking up to me. She spoke more loudly. "Captain Hardwick wants to see you. What are you two plotting?"

I slid my arm around Marcela's shoulder and steered her away from my computer screen, toward the doorway. My voice hid my frustration. "Sorry, darlin'. Can't talk about it."

"Whatever it is, keep it up. It's good for him to engage, *comprende*? He needs to feel invested in the world outside. You're a good son, Tennyson."

"Wish I could claim I'm doing it for him," I said. "It's strictly selfish. My last resort."

Marcela laughed and wagged her finger at me. She thought I was joking. "A good son. Admit it, just once."

I winked scandalously. "There's nothing good about me, Marcela."

In Dad's room, I saw that a few of the pages I'd given him had fallen to the floor, scattered beneath his desk. One page had flown as far as his bathroom doorway. As I picked it up, I tried not to notice the smell of pissy clothes hanging in Dad's bathroom. He might have wet himself overnight and tried to wash out his clothes in the sink; I'd done that at camp when I was eight, afraid the counselors and other campers would learn my secret.

I gathered the pages without comment and pulled up a chair beside him.

"How's it look?" I said.

"Padded." The word sounded gummy, so I didn't understand. He tried another: "Thin."

"Thin how?"

Dad consulted his yellow legal pad. I saw several lines of handwriting, but he didn't show me his notes. "Nothing . . . on . . . Hankins. No . . . inter-view."

Dad thought Donald Hankins could be a suspect, too.

"What do you know about him?" I said.

"Gets . . . what he wants."

"Except a conviction in his daughter's murder," I said. "How dirty is he?"

"More'n . . . most."

Then he ripped the page out of his notebook and handed it to me. He'd written a virtual report himself, one painstaking line at a time:

1999: HANKINS ACCUSED OF RIGGING A CAR ACCIDENT. NO FORMAL CHARGES, NOTHING IN THE NEWS. HEARD THROUGH THE LAPD GRAPEVINE. BUT SOMEONE SAID HE TAMPERED WITH BRAKES. A FATALITY.

"There was a lawsuit around 1999," I said. "Kevin Wong?"

Dad shook his head. "Diff'rent . . . case." He motioned for me to read on.

HANKINS HAS BEEN ACCUSED OF STRONG-ARM POLITICS. HE DOESN'T FORGET HIS ENEMIES AND HE KNOWS WHERE THE BODIES ARE BURIED. THAT'S HOW HE BUILT UP HIS COALITION FOR THE GOVERNOR'S RUN. HE'S TIGHT WITH CHIEF RANDALL, AND

HE TAKES CARE OF LAPD. T.D. JACKSON WAS SUP-
POSED TO BE DELIVERED GIFT-WRAPPED TO HIM AF-
TER CHANTELLE. DIDN'T HAPPEN. NOW THEY HAVE
ANOTHER CHANCE TO MAKE HIM HAPPY.

"Could it have been a police hit?" I said.

Dad's face soured. He thought about it, but he shook his head.
"Don't . . . think so."

"But it's possible."

Dad shrugged. Then, reluctantly, he nodded.

"What about Dolinski?" I said.

Hal Dolinski was a cop my father had known for years, still on the
job but holding his breath until retirement. If not for Dolinski's help
on the inside, I would have faced worse than prison after Serena was
murdered—I would have died. Dolinski had warned me that I was a
target for dirty cops. Two cops who had kidnapped and almost executed me in the desert were still out working the streets. From time to
time, I still dreamed about them.

Dad held out his hand for his pad, Sharpie ready.

FORGET DOLINSKI. THIS IS DYNAMITE. I DON'T
WANT HIM IMPLICATED.

"We don't have to say why we're asking," I said. "But he
might know something about the investigation. Isn't he Robbery-
Homicide?"

With an annoyed sigh, Dad underlined the words FORGET
DOLINSKI. I understood. Dad was protecting his friend. We were
the ones who owed Dolinski, not the other way around.

"There's no one on the inside we can go to?"

Firmly, Dad shook his head. "Find out . . . what hap-pened . . .
in '99."

"You said it never made the news. No police report. Where would
you start?"

"A . . . reporter," Dad said. "*Times*. Made . . . calls. Ask . . . April."

Somehow, Dad always knew the one thing I didn't want to do.

Melanie was waiting at the curb, leaning on the hood of her silver Volvo. She'd shed her at-home clothes, back to pinstripes. Her skirt wasn't long enough to hide her bare legs; I peeked even when I knew I shouldn't. Melanie's eyes wrestled mine away. Her tears were gone, iced over. She walked toward the house, her arms crossed as if she were walking into a wind.

I followed her, keeping pace. I wanted to say something, but I wasn't as good at reality as I was at role-playing. My stalking clothes smelled like her bedroom, so I had changed into my suit. "Melanie . . ."

"Proud of yourself?"

"Not even a little."

She shot me a glare over her shoulder. "Imagine how it feels on this end."

"I probably have no idea."

She climbed the Jacksons' porch steps, her walk brisk. "Lucky you."

I could feel a physical force field radiating from her, prickling my skin. The same day I had touched and tasted her, the sensation was like a blow. I'm sure I was thinking about April, but it hurt. I never want to make a woman unhappy, much less one I've made love to. Melanie and I had broken up, and we'd never dated.

"I'll bring the money back," I said. "I don't want to cause you problems. I mean that."

She opened the door. "Don't flatter yourself. Just get your head on your fucking job."

Don't shit where you sleep.

The Jackson living room was bursting with even more flower arrangements, some of them already wilting. Melanie led me past the living room toward the long kitchen with its gleaming black floor, where the granite countertop was stacked with wrapped foods, offerings from well-wishers. The stool where T.D.'s mother had sat for my first visit was empty. Judge Jackson's study was dark through the closed glass double doors.

Melanie pointed toward sunlight from an adjacent room, the family room. "Wait in the back garden," she said. "Judge Jackson will be right down."

She didn't even want me in the house. Melanie peeled off, her heels rapidly retreating against the floor. In the dimly lighted family room, the back door was half-open, waiting.

I let myself out. The courtyard behind the Jacksons' house had an aged coral fountain at its center, atop a patio of coral stones speckled brown. The fountain's water dribbled from an overflowing stone chalice, a soothing sound. Beyond the fountain, there was a rain forest of palm trees, bougainvilleas, and rosebushes. A stone path led to the backyard's tall fencing, with a latched wooden gate door. Long ago, I mused, that had been the service entrance.

When no one came outside right away, I drifted away to explore the quiet. It could have been a Japanese meditation garden. The neighborhood outside of the fence might as well not exist. I thought I heard a water spigot go on nearby, and I assumed it was a gardener. Out of curiosity, I drifted around the corner, which had hidden the more traditional garden's rows of sprouting vegetables in raised wooden beds.

At first, all I saw was a broad straw cowboy hat from someone kneeling close to the house wall, filling a bucket with water from a bursting spigot.

Evangeline Jackson gasped, turning around. I was quiet, but she must have sensed me standing behind her. Some people have a sixth sense. The sun was setting, so she was half in shadow, half in golden light. Her face registered no recognition. She looked literally petrified.

I stepped back to appear more nonthreatening. "I'm sorry, Mrs. Jackson. It's me—Captain Hardwick's son. Melanie asked me to wait outside. I didn't mean to startle you."

She nodded, but her expression barely changed. A small scare in her back garden was probably a respite from the rest of her day. She turned off the gushing water flow. The smell of peat was strong from the garden.

"I'm mulching for spring," she said. "Not enough rain. I thought it would rain more."

"Yes, ma'am."

"Last year, it rained more." She sounded like the lack of rainfall would make her cry. As she picked up her bucket, I saw the trembling of her gloved hands. Water spilled. Evangeline Jackson's face looked no older than her early sixties, but her body behaved as if she were twenty years older. She looked too frail to stand.

"Let me," I said, walking toward her to take the bucket. "Just show me what to do."

After taking off her muddied gardening gloves, Mrs. Jackson led me to the neat rows of raised beds, jabbing her hoe to show me where she wanted more water.

"Not too much," she said. "Don't drown them. They'll . . ." *They'll die*, she wanted to say. She couldn't bring herself to utter the word. ". . . They won't grow."

"Yes, ma'am."

She stumbled on a stone, and I instinctively held her arm to steady her. Just as instinctively, she pulled her arm free. "Thank you, I'm fine," she said curtly. I would have to handle her with care, gaining her trust. She didn't like to be touched.

"Cauliflower?" I said. I recognized the sprouts from Alice's garden, which had died soon after she did. I tried to keep her fish alive, at least, but I wasn't a gardener.

"And broccoli. You know about gardens?"

"I've had a little fertilizer under my nails."

"I'm surprised. Young people don't have the patience. My grandmother lived in Georgia, and every vegetable we ate at her table was out of that garden. She spent so much time out there tending those plants! Now I understand her better."

"In what way, ma'am?"

"You can control it," she said, her voice shaky. "Some things are out of your hands—the rain, the cold. But if you mulch . . . if you enrich the soil . . . you feed them . . . if you do what you're supposed to do, they come out all right. They come out just fine." She was whispering.

"Not always," I said. "Like you said—some things are out of your hands."

Mrs. Jackson gave me a baleful gaze. She didn't seem to mind my thinly veiled therapy, but she wanted me to know she had seen through it.

"You know why my father's hair was gray by the time he was thirty-five?" I said.

Mrs. Jackson curled her lips, glad to think about Dad. "Emory called him Cap'n Snow."

"My fault. I ran him crazy. There was nothing he could do. He's still trying."

Mrs. Jackson cast her eyes down. For a moment, we let the water in the fountain talk for a while, a soothing gurgle.

"Do you know the Hankins family?" Mrs. Jackson said finally.

"No, ma'am. Haven't had the pleasure yet."

"Well, I know them *well*, or I used to. We shared fifteen years as family. Donald and Loretta are like a brother and sister. And after Chantelle . . ." She paused, her hands shaking again. "It's all they think about now: the hunt; the answer; the trial. Day by day, minute by minute. I swore I would never be like that. Some things don't have answers, and never will. Some things trials don't fix. Might as well let the police handle it and go on somehow. Emory can't have T.D. back. I wish you'd tell him that."

She pointed toward the mulch again with an unsteady hand, and I flung out some water. Not too much.

"I'll make you a promise, Mrs. Jackson," I said. "I won't look forever, but I have to look. If I don't find anything—if I think there's nowhere else to go—I'll sit your husband down and tell him exactly that. Case closed."

Mrs. Jackson nodded. "I just don't want him consumed. And T.D. wouldn't want it. I don't know Don and Retta anymore. They're strangers."

The question came to my lips, and I couldn't think of a reason not to ask. But I had to ask just right: My voice dipped, almost a verbal caress. I chose my words carefully.

"Do you think . . . T.D. ended his own life?"

Her face was suddenly caught in a ray of dying sunlight, just when I needed to see it. She made a sudden motion, and her voice left my ear. Whatever she'd said, I didn't think she would want to repeat it. But I had to ask.

"Excuse me? Ma'am, this ear is bad." I leaned toward her.

"He may have had reason to," Mrs. Jackson said slowly. "He may have had reason."

Judge Jackson called to me from the back door.

"He hates to hear a word against T.D.," Mrs. Jackson said quickly to my good ear. "You may learn things that will break Emory's heart. Please don't tell him anything he doesn't need to know. Don't destroy him. T.D.'s memory is all he has left."

Judge Jackson called for me again, sounding impatient.

"At the vegetable garden!" I called back, just as he rounded the corner.

Judge Jackson seemed startled by the sight of me carrying his wife's watering bucket. He walked in a gingerly way on the damp soil, lifting his pant legs, careful with his shoes. Melanie trailed him, but she stopped short of the damp soil in her heels.

"Is he bothering you, Auntie?" Melanie said.

"Not at all," she said. "Mr. Hardwick is very helpfully watering my mulch."

Melanie's eyes skimmed me. "A man of a thousand talents."

Judge Jackson beckoned, and I set the bucket down where Mrs. Jackson asked me to. A little helpfulness had gone a long way. T.D.'s own mother thought he might have had a conscience guilty enough to drive him to suicide. *Mother knows best*, I thought.

Judge Jackson took me to a small round patio table at the corner of the garden, beneath the shade of an awning sagging with dead leaves from the jacaranda trees beyond the tall fence. I sat first, and he sat across from me. Melanie stayed behind him, at a distance. I tried not to look at her, but I could feel her eyes.

Judge Jackson held a smaller manila envelope this time, and dumped the contents on the clean glass table. Two keys on a SoCal State key ring jangled to the tabletop.

"There's no LAPD seal on T.D.'s side door," he said. "I don't mean the back door—I mean the sunroom on the north side. This key gets you in. If you go in any other door, they'll know someone was there. Melanie can show you. Turn on only the lights that are necessary. I don't expect any police, but the neighbors are on a hair trigger."

I made a note: I had to interview the closest neighbors. The police had already questioned them, of course, but no one had even heard the gunshot. With temperatures dipping at night, no windows were left open after dark. Still, I might get lucky.

"What about the alarm?" I said.

"We canceled the account," he said. "There's no alarm now. One other thing: Don't leave fingerprints."

"Of course." The last thing I needed was for my fingerprints to turn up at T.D. Jackson's house. Lieutenant Nelson wouldn't need Viagra for a month.

Judge Jackson's eyes settled into mine. "I hope I don't have to tell you not to take anything from the house. Nothing better show up on eBay."

"He won't take anything," Melanie said.

Still, I didn't look at her. Her eyes were wearying.

"Are you sure you don't want to come with us?" I asked Judge Jackson.

He shook his head. "Not yet. They let me in to get his suit for the funeral, but that was enough for now." He said it matter-of-factly.

"I understand. When do I get to meet the Hankins family?"

"I'm working on that," Melanie said. "You'll know."

I had to meet her eyes. "You don't have to tell them I'm investigating T.D.'s death. I'm an actor. I can be whoever you need me to be."

"I'll remember that."

I braced myself. "Have they ever met your fiancé?"

"Is that supposed to be funny?" she snapped, a dagger in her voice. "No, they haven't met him, but Maya and Tommy know him very well."

Judge Jackson nodded. "Just pick up the kids tomorrow. Take Hardwick with you. Evangeline can call, smooth it over. She and

Retta still get on all right. Two mothers. Retta wouldn't refuse her a chance to see the kids."

"I don't want Maya and Tommy involved," Melanie said.

"It's a crime they haven't been here yet. Or with you." Judge Jackson's voice was suddenly drenched with resentment. "You have every right to get them. Tommy's been calling."

He sounded so adamant that Melanie didn't argue.

"It's almost dark," Melanie said. "It's been a long day. Let's get to T.D.'s house."

THIRTEEN

AT THE CURB, my car was parked behind Melanie's, almost kissing her rear bumper.

Melanie's car beeped when she pushed her remote, the locks clicking. "Follow me. If we get separated, you have the address."

"Be sure to park around the corner," I said. "Not in front."

"Do you think I'm an idiot?"

I almost let Melanie and her bad mood have the last word. It wasn't like I hadn't earned it. Don't shit where you sleep: I knew that. But I had to set the ground rules.

"Melanie, I meant it when I said I'd quit for your sake," I began, "but if we're working together, you need to remember you didn't hire me for my manners. I found a killer the police couldn't. Period. So are you ready for the truth or not?"

Melanie didn't answer, but I knew how much she wanted to know the truth, even the parts she was afraid of. She might be more ready for the truth than Judge Jackson. I softened my voice. "I know you are brilliant. But under emotional duress, even people as smart as Melanie Wilde and Tennyson Hardwick make mistakes, and we can't afford any more mistakes. I need help at T.D.'s house, and you're the only one who can handle it. Let's get this done. Okay?"

After a short sigh, Melanie nodded.

I opened my car door. "Like I said, be sure to park around the corner."

With Melanie's eyes heavy on me, I climbed into my car.

I had lost Melanie, so my navigator took me to T.D. Jackson's street. After his divorce, T.D. had bought himself a $6 million mansion in Pacific Palisades. His neighborhood was the opposite of mine— instead of houses stacked on top of each other, each estate was spread out over two or three acres. No wonder none of the neighbors had heard a gunshot.

There was also no curb for parking, so I drove back two blocks and ended up leaving my car near a drainage culvert, where I hoped it wouldn't be too conspicuous. Luckily, it wasn't quite dark, so I didn't look as suspicious as I might have. I carried my notebook in plain sight; at least I would look like I was working. I was in my *Homeland* suit and tie, so I was a ringer for a cop.

I called Melanie's cell phone. "Where are you?" I asked her. "I'm here."

"Had to get gas. Fifteen minutes."

I told her where I was so she could park near me. Walking together, we would look like a well-dressed couple on a stroll. Alone, I was still a Black Man at Night. With the last brown-gray glow of the sun, I ambled up the street, dodging headlights as a small stream of residents came home from work. There were no sidewalks, so I walked at the edge of the road. On news reports Monday and Tuesday, the whole street had been roped off. I was glad it no longer was.

T.D.'s house was set back so far that it couldn't be seen from the street—only a tall mechanized gate. Police tape littered the driveway, which was made of crushed shells.

Across the street from T.D.'s gated house, I saw three teenage boys working under the raised hood of a vintage Mustang. Two girls sat in the grass nearby; watching, but mostly talking. One was too thin, one too chubby. I wondered if they had been questioned by police.

"You guys live around here?" I said.

Their conversation stopped, and five startled pairs of eyes looked at me.

I raised my notebook. "I'm a Realtor. Just checking out the neighborhood."

The biggest of the boys, wearing only surfer shorts despite the chill, was the first to decide to trust me. "My dad's place," he said. "I hang out on weekends mostly. Came home early."

"He goes to USC," the bigger girl said. "Thinks he's hot shit."

I made a face. "USC? Across the street from T.D. Jackson?"

Their faces froze again, not sure what I meant. I laughed. "He played for SoCal. Big rivals. Just a joke."

"T.D. Jackson used to play for SoCal?" the thin, dark-haired girl said, and I cringed on behalf of T.D.'s father. History is lost as soon as it happens.

"Yeah, like he only won a Heisman," surfer boy said. He might be a football player too; he had the build for it.

I knew my Mustangs pretty well. The car was white, with a thick black stripe painted down the hood. "Sixty-seven?" I said.

"Sixty-eight," said surfer boy. "Bought it from the original owner."

"Sweet—428 Cobra Jet?" I noticed a bright red bong against the passenger seat inside the car, so it was time to shed my "cop" look. I slipped my notebook into my back pocket and nodded toward the bong. "All right! I remember college."

They all laughed, the girls louder than anyone. They sounded like they'd already had a few visits with the bong.

"*Busted,* Ry," the chubbier girl said.

Surfer boy studied my grin and decided I was all right. Still, he changed the subject. "So, check it: Jackson died right over there. Pretty crazy. I could barely get out of here to drive back to school Monday. This street was nothing but news vans."

"Were you guys around Sunday when it happened?" I said.

"That's the weird thing," surfer boy said. His face grew earnest. "I think I *was.* I mean, like right here." He patted the car's raised hood.

"You mind?" said a wiry boy working under the hood. He was slightly older, and his hair was dyed jet-black, hanging over his eyes. "That's my ear." I could empathize.

My heart stirred in my chest. I was only fishing, but I might have caught something. I didn't remember a police interview with a teenage neighbor. "You heard a gunshot?"

Surfer boy nodded. "See, I was heading out . . ."

"What time? Like eleven?"

"Something like that. I've got Nine Inch Nails playing, the top down, and I hear a car backfire. But muffled. I think it's in somebody's garage, right? No-brainer—no pun intended. But now I'm thinking maybe I heard it happen."

"So you heard a *pow*?" I said. "Like a popping sound?"

Suddenly, surfer boy's face turned red. "Okay, the truth? I was smoking a bowl."

His friends laughed.

Surfer boy went on. "Can't smoke in Dad's house, can't smoke while I'm driving . . ."

"Who says?" the too-thin girl said, and they all laughed again.

"So I was parked out here, I dunno, like ten minutes. Maybe longer. And I heard this sound, *pow*, like you said. Then I heard it again, right before I left. *Pow.* Or I thought I did."

My heart pounded. *Two* gunshots? I kept my face neutral, only mildly interested, but I was excited. I was sure there had been nothing about two gunshots in the police report. One shot had killed T.D. Jackson just fine.

"How long . . . between the bangs?" I asked him.

He shrugged. "Man, like I said, I was smoking, so you know how time slows down. But it was at least ten minutes. Maybe fifteen. Twenty tops."

"You're a dumb-ass stoner," said the boy still working under the hood. "What was the first one, a practice shot? He's making sure the gun worked?"

"Hey, I dunno," surfer boy shrugged, uncertain. "I just heard it."

I noted the name on the vine-covered mailbox: *Rasmussen*. I could track the kid down later, if I needed him. "Did you tell the cops? Or the reporters?"

Surfer boy grinned. "Dad says they all came by Monday and Tuesday, but I was back at school. What am I gonna do, announce I was in my car smoking when T.D. Jackson killed himself? My dad thought I was gone already. Screw that. It's just weird, you know?"

I laughed. "True, true. One for the grandkids."

I changed the subject, shooting the shit with him about his car, how much it cost, the Cobra versus the Super Cobra. Then I said good-bye and walked back toward my car, trying to hide the bounce in my step. Two gunshots! There might have been someone else at the house. LAPD was so in love with the suicide theory that evidence of a confrontation might have been overlooked.

One thing that T.D. Jackson conspiracy buffs tended to misremember is that the police loved T.D. They dug his action movies, especially when he played a heroic cop in *Thin Line*. They remembered his football victories and partied at his house. When his ex-wife was murdered, they gave him every courtesy imaginable, unable to believe that their buddy was anything but a victim. When the evidence finally overwhelmed their good will, their sense of betrayal was palpable. But had they been pissed enough to kill him, or cover up his murder?

Maybe it was a stoner's imagination—sound effects from Nine Inch Nails amplified by THC—but now I knew what I would be looking for at T.D.'s house.

Bullet holes aren't easy to hide.

Melanie had parked, waiting for me. She was sitting inside her car with her elbow resting across her open driver's window, her head bent down low as she spoke on her cell phone. I walked close enough to hear the gentle vulnerability in her voice. *Definitely not a business call*, I thought, right before I heard her say, "I love you, too." When she looked up to see me standing over her, shame swamped her face.

Melanie stammered a good-bye and hung up, looking ill. Her drawn mouth gave me a glimpse of what she would look like as an old woman. Melanie got out of her car without a word, and I followed her, walking at a careful distance.

I didn't want to approach T.D.'s house from same side because those kids had looked comfortable, so I was glad when Melanie took a much longer way around. Our walk was silent.

I decided not to mention the kid's story about a second gunshot. It wouldn't be fair to stir Melanie's hopes over something I couldn't prove yet. She probably had no idea how much she wanted to believe T.D. was murdered—she could forgive him for being murdered. She thought murder would make her feel better about his death. But she was wrong.

We reached a gate on the far side of T.D.'s property, nowhere near the front driveway, and Melanie pulled out her key. I noted that there was room for parking by that gate, a neatly mown swath of grass, but it was just as well we'd parked as far away as we had.

I pulled out my flashlight and swept the ground for tread marks. Too grassy, maybe.

"We look like burglars," Melanie said.

Good point. I switched the flashlight off. There wasn't as much traffic on the side road, but I could come back to examine the ground in daylight. If I were a killer, this was where I would park. Neat entrance to the house, not as much chance of being seen. It was a tidy hiding place in a neighborhood of fortresses that didn't offer many.

Melanie unlocked the gate, and it swung open with a sigh.

The pool area looked like a party in progress. The pool was lighted bright, several glasses were scattered on the patio table and on the patio's Mexican tiles, and towels were slung across two beach chairs. The pool must have been heated, because swimming weather had been over for a month, or longer. The bright pool's impossibly blue water winked in the light. Beautiful.

"He loved this pool," Melanie said, her voice stripped raw. "He'd never had one."

Instinct made me want to put my arm around her, but I had lost the right. I never had the right. "You okay to do this, Mel?"

She sniffed and nodded, quickly wiping her nose with her wrist. "Sunroom's this way."

As we walked, I quickly scanned the pool area and pool-house walls for anything that might be a bullet hole. Nothing. *But the gun wasn't fired outside. It would have been too loud.*

We neared an inconspicuous white door beside a huge picture

window shuttered with white blinds. "You probably already know this . . ." I began. ". . . but once we walk into that house, we've contaminated the crime scene. Even if we find something, we decrease our chances of a conviction. A good lawyer . . ."

Melanie nodded. "He knows that."

I reached into my fanny pack and brought out two new pairs of plastic gloves. She took a pair without objection or question, sliding them over little fingers. Then she unlocked the door.

Inside T.D. Jackson's house, it was pitch-dark.

"Give me a minute," Melanie said, slipping away. Soon, a light came on from a nearby hallway. I was in a sunroom with a pool table and a wet bar. The shelves above the bar were crammed with liquor bottles as well worn as a bartender's. In the corner, the white-tiled floor was stacked with a tower of pizza boxes.

"One big bachelor party," Melanie muttered. She motioned for me to follow.

Apparently, the sunroom was the only room the housekeeper didn't straighten. The rest of T.D.'s downstairs was immaculate, from the living room to the kitchen. There were two dirty glasses on the counter, but my reports said they had already been dusted for prints— and the only prints were T.D.'s.

There was evidence of everydayness all around: a hastily scrawled emergency contact list on the fridge, the open Yellow Pages on the kitchen counter (R for restaurants), junk mail on the table, an *L.A. Times* still in its plastic bag on the sofa.

"I'll show you the way to the den," Melanie said. "Where he was."

"Not yet. Let me see the rest of the house first. Get a feel for it."

Melanie let me take the lead while I wandered from corner to corner of T.D. Jackson's house, turning on just the necessary lights. Except for the sunroom, where we'd come in, T.D.'s décor looked like it was straight from a hired decorator's imagination, like so many celebrities with square footage on their hands. The living room was earth tones and masks that looked more Asian than African, with Japanese screens for aesthetics. It could have been a hotel suite.

"How often did you see T.D. here?"

"Once or twice a week. Sometimes I brought the kids for their weekend visitation, sometimes Aunt Evie brought them. T.D. didn't like to drive. And we all liked the pool."

Police tape strung in the adjacent hall showed the way to the den, but I veered upstairs.

The first two bedrooms were the children's, with a jack-and-jill connecting bathroom. There were bunk beds in each room with slides and ladders, and they were both stuffed with toys that looked new, some of them still in their boxes. Clearly, T.D. had done his best to spoil them into feeling at home, but there were no books, no home-work pages on the desks, and only church clothes in the closet. For his children, T.D.'s house had been far from home.

T.D.'s bedroom retreat, down the hall, was decorated in basic black, from the bedspread to the black marble fireplace to the faux black marble dresser and nightstands to a huge silk-screen wall hang-ing above the bed. Most of the bedroom was dedicated to T.D.'s wall-sized entertainment center. A huge plasma TV was attached to a movie theater's worth of hardware. Photographs were conspicuously absent.

It felt like a place to sleep, that was all. Obviously, it had taken a long time for T.D.'s new house to feel like home.

T.D.'s walk-in closet was the size of a small room, ordered with mil-itary precision; rows of color-coordinated suits, shirts, and T-shirts. A line of sneakers sat on the shelves above, with another row of shoes still in their boxes. A striped tie had fallen to the closet floor, probably while T.D. was dressing for church the day he died. I peeked into the black wicker clothes hamper, which was half-full of dirty socks and underwear and smelled like none of my business. But I was wearing gloves, so I rifled through. If someone else had been there, they might have left blood. People in a panic do stupid things.

Melanie's eyes were watchful while I examined the clothes. I couldn't blame her: T.D. Jackson's dirty underwear would be a hit on eBay. Especially if it sported . . . how can I say this delicately? Genetic material, perhaps.

In the bedroom, I opened T.D.'s bottom bureau drawer first. Bingo. I found his porno collection—DVD covers picturing classic porn-star blondes with Double-D's, and a few all-black compilations with names like *Brown Sugar* and *Chocolate Anal Party*. Aside from one DVD featuring midget women, entitled *Li'l' Fuckers,* and one with a three-hundred-pounder called *Bad Mamma Jamma,* it was pretty standard. The drawer above it was dedicated to his sex toys: lubricants, flavored condoms, and lots of leather.

When Melanie realized what I'd uncovered, she left the room to wait in the hall. She was probably making a note to confiscate the collection and destroy it at her first chance. One last favor for her cousin.

The sight of a leather gag with a red ball brought back memories of the desert; I'd worn an almost identical gag while two cops with guns were ready to execute me. Not my first time in a gag, but definitely my last. The rest of the drawer was crammed with leather straps, shackles, and a bullwhip that looked like it could draw blood.

I didn't see blood on the whip, or on any of the accessories, so I closed the drawer. I would have to see Mother soon to find out if she knew anything about T.D.'s tastes and histories. She might even know the two blondes. I couldn't keep putting it off.

"Did he have a lot of women here?" I called to Melanie.

When she saw that my sex tour was finished, she ventured back into the room. "Of course he did. He was a single man after fifteen years of marriage. Those two blondes at the fund-raiser were his favorites, but I doubt that their real names are Luscious and Lovely, so I haven't been able to track them down."

"What about his girlfriend? Is she the jealous type?"

"Girlfriend? Please. Chantelle was the first woman he invited me to dinner with, so I knew he was going to marry her right then. For T.D., women were a sport just like football."

"Carlyle would know more about T.D.'s women."

"No doubt. I hear they were quite a tag-team." Her voice was laced with disgust.

The longer Carlyle was missing, the more his absence bothered me. Donald Hankins or Miguel Salvador might be more obvious suspects on principle, but they hadn't gone AWOL. I'd left a message for Carlyle on the cell phone number Melanie gave me, reminding him that we'd met at the fund-raiser, but I wasn't holding out much hope that he would call a stranger.

"Can you try him later?" I said. "He's more likely to call you than me."

"I'll try now," Melanie said, and whipped out her cell.

In T.D.'s master bedroom, a towel slung across the toilet was evidence of the shower he'd taken the night he died. I tried the bathroom drawers, where I found rolling papers and a roach clip next to the toothpaste tubes and razors, but no other drugs. The police report had mentioned several grams of cocaine under the seat of his car; apparently, T.D. liked his drugs mobile.

I heard Melanie's voice pleading with Carlyle's voicemail: ". . . I know you're broken up, C., but you better pull yourself up out of whatever bottle you crawled into and call me. You need to man up, C. Just let me know you're okay. I don't need to be worried about you, too . . ."

His disappearance might be suspicious behavior, or it might be a tough guy falling hard. When I was a kid, a cop friend of my father's told me that men could put a shell around their hearts, but if something ever got caught in the soft tissue, it was hard as hell to cope. In retrospect, I think he was trying to explain Dad's daily grief over my mother's death. Tough guys weren't used to grappling with something they couldn't master. Maybe love turned inside out had driven Carlyle to kill his best friend, just as T.D. might have been driven to kill Chantelle.

"I know he's checking his messages," Melanie said after she hung up.

"How do you know?"

"The mailbox would have filled up by now. He must be getting a million calls."

Smart lady, I thought. She was probably right.

"Ready for the den?" I said.

"I was ready to go there first. I'm still ready."

In the den, Melanie flicked on the overhead light, and a ceiling fan whirred a lazy twirl. I heard her sigh, and I could see why. The den was where T.D. had really lived.

"He called this The Jungle," Melanie said. "He had a room like it at his old house. He modeled it so it's almost identical. This one's just bigger."

The crime-scene photos hadn't done the room justice.

The den was the size of a studio apartment, with a thirteen-foot ceiling and rafters overhead artificially aged to look like relics from a medieval church. Near the doorway, tall potted palms sat between old-school pinball machines and arcade games I used to play when I was younger, Galaga and Pac-Man. They looked like museum pieces. Galaga's space fighters dipped and fired, and the Pac-Man chomped on, waiting for someone in a playful mood. The whole setup took me back a long way.

The television in the den was bigger than the one in the bedroom, mounted on the wall like a movie screen. Speakers hung on the walls no doubt added plenty of sound. A less-than-new cream-colored leather sofa hugged the wall in front of the television set. One half of the room was strictly entertainment, and the other side was home to T.D.'s corner desk, leather office chair, and file cabinet.

On the office side, I finally saw evidence of whose house I had entered: T.D.'s SoCal State and '49ers jerseys were framed on the wall above his desk. Above them, too high to see clearly, hung a panorama-style team photo from SoCal State taken at Spartans Stadium. Still, there was nothing like the shrine I'd seen in his father's study.

The office chair where T.D. had shot himself was pulled out from the desk, farther than it had been in the crime-scene photo. It was also facing a different direction, away from the desk and corner wall, toward the television side of the room. I ran my gloved hand across the chair, carefully avoiding the dried bloodstains I was sorry Melanie was there to see.

There had been plenty of blood from the side of T.D.'s head. The bullet's exit wound had been much bigger than the entrance, as would be expected. I tried not to imagine what it would feel like to see a chair stained in the blood of someone I loved.

"Do you mind?" I asked Melanie quietly. "I'd like to move this back where it was."

She nodded. "Just leave everything the way you found it."

Working from memory, I pushed the chair two yards closer to the desk. It rolled nearly silently across a bamboo floor mat. I turned the chair until Melanie was behind me. There.

"I'm going to sit," I said. Melanie didn't answer, but she didn't object.

Slowly, I sank down into T.D. Jackson's plush chair cushion, keeping well clear of the bloodstains. The leather hissed beneath me. Instead of facing the desk, the chair faced a wall with a leather recliner, a reading lamp, and a palm tree in need of water and light.

As I sat there, I looked at the den through T.D.'s eyes. Gun in my hand, contemplating my last sights. My eyes traveled upward, and I saw a large framed portrait of Tommy and Maya on the wall above the recliner. The photo might have been taken at about the time their mother was killed; two to three years ago. Their bright faces and eyes shone from the frame. His children were lovely, and their faces were a revelation.

No way, I thought. *He couldn't shoot himself staring at them.*

My eyes traveled back down to the empty recliner. Had someone else been sitting there? It was about six feet from his chair, but not too far for conversation. Clearly, that was why the chair was there in the first place, since it was on the wrong side of the room for a view of the television set. A reading chair. *A guest chair.*

Carlyle had told police that T.D. kept his gun in his far right desk drawer—which was equally distant between T.D.'s chair and the guest chair. Both T.D. or a guest might have reached it. But how many guests knew it was there?

"Wait," Melanie said suddenly.

I was ready to stand, thinking she didn't want me in T.D.'s chair after all. But Melanie's eyes were gazing up high on the wall above T.D.'s desk, at the SoCal State team photo. She squinted, walking closer to his desk. She stood directly over me. She'd forgotten the blood.

"That's not right," she said.

"What?"

"His team photo. It shouldn't be that high. All of them are too high. The jerseys, too."

"Maybe he moved them?"

Melanie wrapped her arms around herself; she looked like she'd felt a chill. "He was so obsessed with getting it right, just like they were at Chantelle's house. He asked me a million times, 'How's it look? How's it look?' I can still hear him . . ." Her voice withered.

"How much higher?"

"Two feet, maybe."

Two feet was a big difference. My hunch wasn't yet fully formed, but I knew something was there. My heart began pounding as I re-played the stoner kid's voice in my memory: *And I heard this sound, pow, like you said. Then I heard it again, right before I left. Pow.*

Carefully, I took off my shoes. "I'm gonna stand on the desk, take a closer look."

"Be careful," she said. "Don't knock anything over."

T.D.'s desktop was mostly bare, but I had to navigate around his computer monitor and a large office caddy bursting with pens, high-lighters, and used Post-its I would rifle through later. I felt oddly off-balance, so I braced myself against the wall. The unsteady feeling probably had to do with my ear, I realized. Hearing was related to bal-ance. *Fuck.*

Once I caught myself against the wall, I reached for the jersey. SOCAL STATE SPARTANS—13, white with purple numerals and trim. Up close, the jersey gave me a charge. Anyone who liked college football had seen T.D. Jackson play in that jersey. I'd taken my father to the bowl game where SoCal beat USC. I heard the deafening sound of a crowd's roar; an eerie sensation, until I remembered that it was only my ear. *Fuck fuck fuck.*

Gingerly, I gripped the frame from the bottom and lifted it toward me, only two inches. It swayed, but it didn't fall from its hook. Even without my flashlight, I could clearly see the small holes in the wall where it had originally been hung. They were directly at my eye-level. Since it had been moved up, the frame covered the holes from sight. T.D. hadn't lived in the house long enough for the wall to show discoloration.

"You're right," I said. "I see where it was."

"Why would he move it?" Melanie said.

By now, I thought I knew why. But I didn't say anything. I wanted to be sure.

I had to stand on my tip-toes to reach the team photo high above the jerseys. I was slightly off-balance when I grabbed it, so a tug brought its full weight unexpectedly into my hands as it fell. *Nineteen-Ninety-Two Spartans*, said the inscription that fell against my nose. I was lucky not to drop it; it was much heavier than it looked.

"*Shit*," Melanie said. "I said to be—" Mid-sentence, she gasped. "What's that?"

Once I'd steadied myself and the photo enough to glance up at the wall, I knew right away. A hole from a bullet is much larger than a hole from a nail.

T.D. Jackson might have fired his own gun twice, but why would he bother to hide the hole? I tried to think of a gentle way to tell Melanie that we had found exactly what she thought she wanted: evidence that T.D. probably hadn't been alone the night he died. Evidence of a confrontation. Melanie figured it out without my help.

"Those motherfuckers!" Melanie screamed, startling me from below. "Those sorry, lazy-ass *motherfuckers*. They're supposed to be the police—how did they miss that?"

A kind of rapture crossed her face, and then a pain that looked physical. "I knew it . . ." she finally whispered in a ghost's voice. "I knew it . . . I knew it . . . I knew it . . ." Her legs folded beneath her, and she was on her knees.

I hurried down to her. Melanie sank against me when I wrapped her in my arms.

We spent two hours at T.D.'s house. I checked drawers, garbage cans, and closets. I checked the garage. I filled half my notebook with notes and tidbits, unmarked phone numbers, and details about what was where in case it mattered later. But the only notes I cared about were written in block letters and underlined twice: FIND CARLYLE. MOTHER.

I had taken two hundred digital photos inside the house. But the one I kept flicking back to my camera's screen was the bullet hole, conspicuous even at miniature size.

"This is proof," Melanie said, looking over my shoulder.

"Not proof," I corrected her. "But it's evidence. It paints a picture. Definitely a reason not to rush into a suicide theory."

"Why would LAPD cover it up?"

I shrugged. "Maybe they didn't. They missed it. They didn't know his den like you did. Didn't realize the picture had been moved. T.D. had gunshot residue on his hand, they saw what looked like a suicide. He's about to go to trial again, he's high. He's stressed out. Or, they figure he has a guilty conscience. Human nature does the work of conspiracies just fine."

Melanie didn't look convinced. "Conspiracy or not, this is now a murder. No doubts."

"I'll need alibis from everyone in his family," I said. "Judge Jackson, too."

"Fine," she said. She didn't blink.

"I need to see Senator Hankins."

"Tomorrow. Come hell or high water," Melanie said.

"And tracking down Carlyle just became my top priority. He was the last person we know of to see T.D. alive, Mel."

Melanie looked newly stricken. "I don't understand Carlyle being gone. It feels so wrong. Like I don't know him."

"Maybe you don't, Mel. But there's no proof he had anything to do with this. Not yet."

"Right now, nothing would surprise me."

Good thing for that, I thought. For Melanie, the surprises were just beginning.

I caught a late dinner, so the house was quiet and sleeping when I got home. Before I went upstairs, I cracked open Dad's door, holding my breath to listen for his.

An impossibly long interval passed, and I heard only buzzing. My ear again. Finally, I heard Dad's gentle snore, and my mood improved.

Next, Chela's room. I'd asked her to turn off the TV at midnight, a new rule, so her room was quiet. And dark. I peeked inside, and saw her sleeping where she was supposed to be.

My family was fine. For me, it was a good night.

FOURTEEN

While I drove to Brentwood the next morning, I dialed the telephone numbers I'd found at T.D.'s house, searching for Carlyle Simms. I thought about Chela trying to find her mother after her grandmother died, and I wished I was driving somewhere else. I concentrated on my calls, hoping for a last-minute reprieve.

"Hey, whassup, is C around?"

Same greeting every time. Either they would know him or they wouldn't; they would talk or they wouldn't. Most of the numbers were businesses, so I got nowhere even with his full name. One woman told me she hadn't seen C in a couple of weeks, but she hung up on me before I could explain why I was calling. When I called back, no one picked up the phone. I gave the number a checkmark and dialed the next one.

My phone beeped in the midst of an unanswered call. SOUTH AFRICA, the screen said.

"April?"

"Hey, Ten." Her tone was sober, as if one of us had died.

"Don't sound so down," I told her. "I'm doing all right."

"Really?"

No.

"I said 'all right.' Not great, not fine, but I'm all right. How about you?"

"I'm all right sometimes."

"Well, I know a lot of people who would settle for sometimes." There was so much to tell her, but I didn't have time, or even the inclination. April had been more than my girlfriend, and I needed help. "April, I'm working another investigation. Freelancing."

"What about your job?" she said. After Serena's case, I had used phrases like *Never again.*

"It's not an issue."

She paused, but she didn't press. "T.D. Jackson?"

I was surprised at her guess, until I remembered she'd seen Melanie try to hire me once already. "Yes. But that's confidential."

"That whole suicide thing . . ." April began, skeptical. I could feel her sudden hunger to be back at home at her newspaper desk. Our investigation of Serena's death had given her career a huge boost—she'd broken the story first. "Got anything interesting?"

I gave her a nibble. "The police missed some evidence." I didn't have to tell April it was off the record. Everything between us was off the record—until it wasn't.

"Homicide?"

"Looking more like it."

"What do you need from me?" I heard girlish excitement in her voice.

I wished I could hold her. Instead, I quickly summarized Donald Hankins's alleged involvement with threats and violence against political opponents. I told her that my father remembered an *L.A. Times* reporter calling about the claims.

"That has to be Casey Burnside," April said. "He's been the senior political reporter forever, and he loves that stuff. He'd know. Mention you're a friend of mine."

The word *friend* stung, but I was glad to be a team again. I took his email address and the number for the newsroom, which would get me past the menus for subscribers and advertisers. The newspaper was a labyrinth. It was essential to have a name.

"Who will you talk to when it's ready to break?" April said.

"It may never break. It's a private case. No police involvement. But if it does . . . you know I won't talk to anyone else."

I could see her dimpled smile. "God, it would be so hard to work it from here!"

"You'll find a way."

That brought the conversation to a halt. We both remembered what we were losing.

And I had arrived at the house in Brentwood sooner than I expected.

I coasted to the curb about twenty yards from the house, feeling a part of me fold up as soon as I saw the familiar row of orange trees lining the driveway. I wasn't used to guilt, but it could be persistent; and I felt something else bound inside it. I couldn't stand bringing April so close to Mother.

"I have to go," I said.

"Me too. I just didn't want our last conversation to be . . ."

"Our last conversation," I finished. "And this one isn't either. Promise."

"Good, Ten, because I couldn't stand that."

"Like I told you, I'm all right. Thanks for the tip on Burnside."

I love you. The unspoken phrase hung in the silence before we said good-bye.

I noticed that I felt worse after talking to April, just like last time. I hoped that would go away, or it would be hard to work up enthusiasm for future conversations.

The suburban two-story house with a double garage was painted a bland beige, Mother's cloak of anonymity. Her house was far from the nicest on her street, worth well under a million dollars, but Mother owned a castle in Europe and real estate worldwide. She might well be one of the richest madams in the country. Two newspapers piled by her driveway mailbox gave the house a careless air, when nothing could be further from the truth.

It was only ten in the morning, so I figured Mother would be at home. I'd never visited her house without calling first, but I needed all the leverage I could get. I had to let her know I wasn't the same Tennyson she was used to. I was someone new. Someone unpredictable.

But Mother doesn't like surprises.

As soon as I rang the doorbell, I saw a blur of white fur as her two large attack dogs charged from the backyard, running at me like I was the mechanical rabbit at the track. They charged in disciplined silence. Even if I hadn't been cornered on the porch, there was nowhere I could have outrun them. Their growls sent tremors to my hindbrain. They were standard-size poodles shaved with ridiculous puffs on their legs and tails, but trust me—I noticed their teeth, not their bows.

Moving slowly and steadily, I doffed my jacket and wound it around my arm, creating a target for their jaws. Once a canine has locked on, I had two choices: kick him in the throat, or roll him over backward, breaking his neck.

I hoped neither would be necessary.

They bracketed me, growling. "Don't make me kill your dogs,"

I said to the wireless video camera hidden in the floodlight mounted above Mother's door.

A loud whistle came from the intercom speaker, and the dogs drew back, teeth gone from sight. One of the monsters had the nerve to start wagging her tail at me, as if to say, *Just doing my job. We cool?*

Mother said something in Serbian, and the dogs took off running for the back again.

I hate those dogs.

"I remember when your manners were legendary," Mother's voice crackled over the speaker. I had never heard her sound so angry. Her accent nearly overwhelmed her words.

"Let me in, Mother. We need to talk."

The door stayed closed. "Is it about our friend?" the speaker said again.

"You'll find out what it's about when you open this door."

"If you have brought strangers, Tennyson, I will never forget this."

Cops, she meant. Mother was cagey, with good reason. "I'm alone," I said.

The door opened. Mother rushed away before I could get a good look at her, slipping toward the back hall. She moved so quickly that she lurched.

"You didn't have to set your dogs on me," I said.

"You will sit and wait," she called, not looking back. Her voice was phlegmy. "This is a great disrespect to me."

"I won't inconvenience you long."

If I knew Mother, she already had her elegant little .22, which had its own colorful biography of ways it had saved her life in Kosovo. Mother knew how to kill people, and I never forgot that. At the moment, I suspected that she wasn't quite as angry as she seemed: It was just another way of exercising control.

Even with one bad ear, I didn't mistake the sound of nails scrabbling against Mother's tiles as the dogs ran back into the house. Dunja and Dragona sat at their posts, one panting at each end of the living room, bodyguards in pink bows, as deceptive in appearance as their master. While we waited, the dogs and I locked eyes.

Mother's house looked and smelled like any grandmother's house, awash with bric-a-brac and delicacies. One large mirrored display case was dedicated to a large collection of crystal figurines, mostly angelic children. My teeth ground as I thought about Chela living under Mother's roof as her surrogate daughter while Mother primed her as an earner.

I'd let myself be charmed by Mother, too; at one time, I'd been foolish enough to consider us friends. Mother preyed on naïveté.

When she finally came out twenty minutes later, she gave me a look that probably had been the last sight of more than one man before me. Mother wasn't wearing her trademark red wig, the first time I'd seen her without it. But she was wearing a dress instead of a robe, she'd rubbed rouge on her cheeks, and her hair was hidden beneath a scarf. The white hair I saw at her scalp line looked thin and fragile. Her face looked fuller, too. I realized she hadn't had her dentures on when she came to the door. No wonder she was so mad. I didn't know anyone who had ever seen her without them.

"So, speak," she said. "What is so urgent that you forget all manners?"

"Aren't you going to ask about her?"

"I hear nothing in all this time. Why do I expect to hear anything now?"

"She's fine. She's in school."

"Here, she was in school, too." Mother's eyes mocked me. I saw her hand listing comfortably at her waist, within easy reach of her hidden gun.

I decided to sit down, too. Mother might be getting nervous in her old age, and I didn't want to end up dead because she thought I made a sudden move. "I need a favor from you, Mother. Information. Then I'd be happy never to see you again."

Mother chortled. "A favor? You are deluded. Why would I do this?"

"To feel good about yourself."

Mother laughed again, this time more freely. "You are still a delight, Tennyson. You say very amusing things. You have that face, yes, but you are so much more. I know a woman from Colombia who would pay you six figures for one weekend. But, ah . . ." Mother waved her hand in a magician's flourish. "You are selling telephones now. Your face, it seems, has many uses."

I smiled. Yes, she wanted me angry, off my game. Mother loves to put people off-balance.

"T.D. Jackson," I said. "He and his friend Carlyle Simms liked to pay for sex. On the night he died, T.D. was with blond twins. They call themselves Luscious and Lovely."

Mother laughed again.

"Mother, there's this odd thing about memory. If yours gets too fuzzy, mine might snap into focus."

Mother's laughter stopped, and her green eyes blazed at me. "Why are you here, Tennyson? The truth."

"I've come to offer you a trade," I said, in the most soothing tone I could summon.

"And I get what from this trade?" The phlegm in her throat rumbled.

"You get to sleep at night. You get to know that nothing about our friend will ever come out. You took a girl headed for the gutter, and gave her . . ." I almost choked on it. "A better life. Not everyone would understand."

Her eyelashes fluttered. I could not read her expression at all. "You think I do not sleep?"

"I'm sure you could sleep better."

Her lip quivered, ready to unleash something unkind. But she didn't. Either she had a conscience after all, or she wanted me to think she did.

But Mother kept her lips pressed tight, her wrinkles' folds trapping her young-woman eyes. Mother was almost eighty, and looked it. Eighteen months had trampled her. Mother's eyes held the secrets of impending death.

"This subject must never come up again," Mother said.

"It won't."

Mother inclined her head: *You've made your point.* Her imitation of a smile quickly soured. "The twins are not mine," she said. "But those two men . . . I may know them."

"And?"

"I never discuss my clients," Mother said. "I taught you this much, I hope."

"You taught me plenty." I suddenly remembered my first visit to her house, feeling lucky and special. Mother could fling bullshit around like pixie dust. She had a gift.

"His friend had a great love of American television," Mother said.

She'd hardly said anything, but Mother had told me everything I needed. She wouldn't say another word about it.

I stood up. "Chela's in the chess club. Her homecoming dance is next week. Saturday."

Mother only stared at me, her face as frozen as glass. As if she didn't recall the name.

But deep in her eyes, I saw a flicker of light.

✦   ✦   ✦

I'll call her Jeanine. You know her by another name.

She wanted to meet at Mel's Diner in Hollywood, which sur-prised me—most actresses would avoid such a public place without hours of makeup and wardrobe at home. But then again, Jeanine had left acting long ago. She said she'd just gotten out of her Pilates class, so she asked to meet in a half hour, at twelve thirty.

I walked past Jeanine twice before I realized she was the silver-haired woman in a black turtleneck and beat-up denim jacket with her hair cut down to a fuzz, wearing funky red horn-rimmed glasses. Jeanine had been a blonde icon when I was in high school and col-lege; she was unrecognizable without her long tresses.

But she looked good. So healthy I couldn't help staring.

"I know. Different," she said. "Sit down, Ten."

She'd had some plastic surgery. I didn't see the looser folds at her neck I'd spotted the last time I saw her, and her eyes looked a little se-vere. But Jeanine hadn't overdone it. Her hair color alone told me that she wasn't the same desperate woman I had taken to Mother's.

"I had chemo," Jeanine said, too cheerfully. "The hair fell out, so what the hell? This is my hair now. Richard Gere is sexy with gray hair, and women can be, too. Fuck Hollywood."

I hadn't heard she had cancer. "Are you . . . ? "

"Six months in remission, so we think I'm good," Jeanine said, knocking on the tabletop. She didn't elaborate, squeezing my hand across the table. "I'm so glad you called."

The last time I'd seen Jeanine, she was in Mother's living room—about to jet off to sell her body to a sheik in Bahrain, even in her early fifties. A lifetime ago, in the seventies and early eighties, Jeanine was a television star with top billing on a top show. After cancellation and a popularity slide made her panic, she asked me to introduce her to Mother. She asked *me*, I always told myself. Since then, Jeanine's name had taken her further under Mother's care than anyone else's.

But one glance told me Jeanine wasn't doing business with Mother anymore. Like me, she'd finally broken away. She wore her freedom like a glow.

"They do breakfast all day," Jeanine said. "My treat."

Since my only breakfast had been a piece of toast, I opened my menu. I never get tired of steak and eggs. Mel's was bustling, of course, but the lunch rush was perfect cover. In a restaurant where you might run into Johnny Depp, nobody pays attention to the nobodies.

"Sounded like you've got a lot on your mind, darlin'," I said, trying to draw her out.

Suddenly nervous, Jeanine poured herself tea from her small metal decanter. "What are you after, Tennyson? Working for the scumsuckers now? The bottom-feeders?"

"You know me better than that."

Tabloids. Years ago, while she was on her series, Jeanine had been a tabloid regular; diva blowups on the set, and a messy cliffhanger of a divorce involving her ex's affair with a major actress. But Jeanine sued the *Enquirer* and was awarded a large wad of cash because of a story claiming she was a drug addict, and after that the tabloids left her alone. I've seen Jeanine snort plenty of white powder, but addiction must be hard to prove in court.

Jeanine didn't look coked up now. She looked as sober as a nun.

"Well, you're not working for the police," Jeanine said.

"Got that right."

"Who, then?"

"Can't say. I'm doing a favor for a friend."

"Then what happens?"

"That's up to my friend."

Jeanine frowned, dissatisfied. "I don't know. I have things I want to say . . . but I don't want to air it out for nothing. I want it to mean something."

"It will."

"You promise me that?" she said. "And you'll keep me out? Completely?"

"When have I ever betrayed your confidence, Jeanine?"

"Never, thank God." Her eyes got a pained, faraway look. Remembering. I wanted to tell her she was wasting her time. We can't go backward.

"You remember that day?" she said. "When I saw you at her house?"

Her was Mother, of course. In public, you never referred to Mother by name—or even by nickname. Mother trained us all well.

"I remember."

Jeanine fidgeted. "That look on your face . . ."

I'd been mortified to see Jeanine at Mother's, but I'd tried to hide it. "What look?"

"You know what look—'She's still doing *that?*' An actor can't fool another actor."

Busted. "Sorry if I . . ."

"You really pissed me off, Tennyson. You made me feel like shit, as if you were so damn superior. But it was a wake-up call. That day, I swore to myself that the next time I ran into you, I would say, 'By the way, I haven't done business with her in a long time.' And now that day is here. It's been almost eighteen months."

The waiter brought our food fast. We paused just long enough for him to scurry away.

"Congratulations," I said finally. "But you know I can't judge."

"You were smart. You got out."

"It took me some time, too, darlin'. It's hard to walk away."

"Too hard," Jeanine said quietly. I didn't doubt it: Jeanine would have been irresistible to men with memories of teenage lust. I'd had Jeanine's poster on my locker, too. Even dressed to be anonymous, she drew stares from men as they passed. Jeanine emitted vibrations.

"So . . . that look I gave you did it?"

"You were more like the second-to-last nail in the coffin."

"What was the last?"

"Carlyle."

I swallowed too fast, almost choking on my first bite of beef. "What about him?"

Jeanine leaned across her folded arms and lowered her voice so much that I had to point my good ear her way. Even so, it was hard to hear her above the restaurant's clamor.

"Two years ago. He called me."

I forgot my food and started taking notes, keeping my pad in my lap so I wouldn't draw attention to us. "Around the time T.D.'s wife got killed?"

"The same night, Ten."

My ear roared with my heart's burst of excitement. "What happened?"

Jeanine blinked. Her blue-gray eyes were an open door. "It was late, two in the morning. Money wasn't always involved with C, not after the first few times. Once in a while, he invited himself over. But it wasn't like him to call so late. And he had a rough side, but that night he practically threw me on the bed and power-fucked me. I was still sore the next day. In the middle of sex, he suddenly stopped and looked at me with an expression I'll never forget . . ."

"Like what?"

"He was all wide-eyed, keyed up on coke. He looked down at me and said, 'There's no bigger turn-on than shooting someone in the head.' "

All other sound in the diner vanished. I could hear only Jeanine. "You're sure?"

"How can I forget it? I hear his voice in my sleep. When the news came the next morning about Chantelle Jackson and Arturo Salvador, I almost had a heart attack."

"Who'd you tell?"

"No one. Not even her." Mother, she meant. "But she knew something happened. She knew something about Carlyle made me quit. If she'd asked, I would have told her."

Mother's credo was the paragon of simplicity: Never discuss clients. Period.

Jeanine might have heard Carlyle Simms confess to killing T.D. Jackson's ex-wife, and she hadn't gone to the police. If she had, her prostitution history would have likely become public. Witnesses have plenty of reasons not to talk.

"What else did Carlyle say?"

"I don't remember everything. He was rambling, and it was late. He kept saying *we*, though. 'Guess we'll see now.' 'Guess we won't be worried about that shit.' I didn't understand until the next morning. On the news. I was sure he killed them." Jeanine's voice rose with so much indignation that I shushed her, flashing a plastic smile to an older couple walking past us.

"Was Carlyle with you when the news came out?"

Jeanine shook her head. "He was only there about an hour. Maybe ninety minutes."

The time of the killings had been estimated at 9 P.M., when both men had claimed to be at Carlyle's house watching *Monday Night Football*. Plenty of time for Carlyle to make it to Jeanine's house by two. Murder was a heavy cross for a friendship to bear.

"When's the last time you saw him?"

"That night. Two years ago."

"Do you have a number for him? An address?" I might always have missed one.

She shook her head. "He called me. That was our arrangement."

"Anything else?"

She shook her head. Her eyes looked unburdened, but they pleaded with me. "I was too afraid to speak up. Too selfish. Do something with it, Ten. Make it matter."

"It already matters."

Across the table, I held Jeanine's delicate hand and squeezed, both apology and solace. I wished I had never introduced her to Mother. I wished we had both known better. Jeanine clasped my hand inside both of hers, almost a prayer position.

"I'm reading scripts again, but I'm afraid to audition," she said softly. "Or to call an agent, even. I haven't had real representation in a decade. I'm afraid . . . everyone knows."

"Some of them will know," I said. "Audition anyway. Call anyway."

Jeanine nodded, holding my hand so tightly that she might have been clinging for her life.

FIFTEEN

DRIVING AWAY FROM MEL'S DINER, I decided to take my own advice to Jeanine. Nobody, no matter how powerful, was going to force me out of Hollywood. I finally called Len and left a message for him to file a sexual harassment complaint against Lynda Jewell, and to pursue a SAG inquiry into my accident on the set of *Homeland*. I left him Melanie's name and number as my attorney. If Lynda Jewell wanted a fight, she had better gear up.

Round two.

Len's assistant, Giovanni, dutifully took my message, but I could hear him wincing at every other word. "Uhm . . . Lynda *Jewell*? I'm sure Len will want to, uh . . . talk to you about . . ."

"There's nothing to talk about," I said. "Just tell him I want it done."

If my prostitution history became public, it was meant to be. Dad was strong enough to handle it—but was Lynda Jewell? She might take me down, but I could take her down, too. All I had to do was find the evidence to prove my case, and I was pretty damned good at that.

There's no bigger turn-on than shooting someone in the head. Jeanine's words sapped away my celebratory buzz after my decision to go to war. People like Carlyle Simms don't understand the line between fantasy and reality, between rage and madness. There's a huge difference between wishing we could kill or hurt someone—and acting on it. Carlyle and T.D. had most likely crossed that line once. Had Carlyle crossed it again?

I pulled over at a meter to go through my notes and plan my next move. Ordinarily, I would have called Melanie by then—she hadn't called all morning—but I wanted to bring Melanie real news, not a story she would be eager to dismiss. To Melanie, Jeanine would just be a hooker; far from a reliable source about a man Melanie had known as a brother.

The list of Carlyle Simms's favorite hangouts I had collected from Melanie was long: sports bars, restaurants, and hotels from Palm Springs to Vegas. He had no permanent address of his own, so the man could be anywhere. I decided to start at Ground Zero, his girlfriend's house. Luck had been on my side so far.

Of course, finding Carlyle might not be all that lucky. As I drove toward the address near Leimert Park in the Crenshaw district, I wished I had my gun. Prudence told me to drive home and get it, but home was too far out of the way. So I'd play it cool, I decided. No heroics, no theatrics. Just a few questions. If I could, I would check the place out and see if I could slip in a sound-activated tape recorder on a future visit.

Don't break the law, I heard my father's voice cautioning me. I didn't want to go down like Anthony Pellicano, the Hollywood private detective convicted for racketeering and a pile of other charges for snooping on celebrities for powerful clients, but I was pretty sure T.D. Jackson's case could take me past the line. I just couldn't let myself get comfortable with the idea.

The neighborhood was occupied by working folks; most of the

driveways were empty. The house where Carlyle reportedly spent most of his time wasn't remarkable on the exterior; a white cement-block house on a street of fairly identical homes except for paint color and level of care. The layout was odd, jutting into the backyard, so I was sure it was larger than the exterior made it look. It had neatly tended rosebushes and a full yard of mown grass, but it was nothing fancy. No wonder Carlyle preferred the Hotel Bel-Air or the Bellagio in Vegas.

I sat at the curb within view of the house for at least a half hour, watching to see if anyone would enter or leave. A single car sat in the driveway, a fairly new rose-colored Toyota Celica that struck me as a woman's car. A bumper sticker on the rear proclaimed the driver's pride at having an honor student at Hyde Park Elementary School. A UPS truck ambled past, driving slowly, but the street was quiet at one thirty in the afternoon. Most people were at work, and the kids weren't yet home from school.

The front door finally opened, and a curvy woman came rushing out with her keys ready. She was in a hurry. If she hadn't been carrying a fussy boy who looked three on one arm, pausing to strap him into his car seat, I wouldn't have made it to her before she drove off. I practically had to leap out of my car and jog across the street.

"Excuse me . . ." I said, and she looked startled. "Sorry. Is Carlyle around?"

I didn't call him by his nickname; she'd never seen me before, so it was pointless to pretend I was a friend. She slammed the rear car door quickly on the wailing toddler, as if to protect him from me. She might have been a fair-skinned black, or a Latina, or both. She looked about thirty, but she dressed from the Juniors section in low-cut Lycra and tight jeans with studded legs. Naturally, she was gorgeous.

Her green-brown eyes sparked at me, but her face seemed to sink inward. "It's not enough his best friend just died? Ya'll gotta harass him too? Damn. *No*, he's not around. Just like he wasn't around yesterday. Just like he wasn't around this morning."

I was wearing a black T-shirt and jeans, but she'd pegged me as a cop. At least the police hadn't forgotten about Carlyle after his initial statement on Monday. Maybe they were trying harder than they seemed to be.

Melanie had told me that Carlyle's girlfriend was named Alma Grays. Alma wasn't happy about Carlyle's disappearance either. Her face was painted with too much green eye shadow to hide raw and puffy eyelids. She had been crying.

"Miss, I'm sorry . . ." I said, adhering to the rule never to call a woman under forty *ma'am*. "But I'm not police. I'm a friend of Melanie's. She wants to make sure he knows about T.D.'s funeral on Sunday."

Her face softened, and I glanced inside the well-kept car at the toddler. He had a very fair complexion and wispy hair; probably not Carlyle's son, at a glance anyway. Too bad. It was one thing to ditch your girlfriend—another thing to ditch your child.

"I feel for Mel, but she's just as bad," Alma said. "I don't *know* where he's at. Tell her it's a real bitch for me, too. Three days, and he hasn't called to say if he's dead or alive or what."

"I'd sure like to help you find him, if you'd let me. She's really worried, too."

Alma peered at me, trying to discern my intentions. My face was all gentle sincerity.

"Look, I'm in a hurry," she said. "I was on my way out . . ."

"Sure, yeah," I said, rushing to open her driver's side door for her. "I won't keep you. You must feel like the world's come crashing down."

"Welcome to my life," she muttered, climbing into the car.

"Does Carlyle take off like this a lot?" It was a risky question, but I was out of time.

"Only lately," she said. "Everything's . . . too much. Ever since T.D.'s problem, it's just one hassle after another. And after all that—it ends like *this*?" She shook her head, newly stunned by T.D.'s death. "Yeah, no wonder he's freaked out. C and all the rest of them are probably out drinking themselves to death. Their hero's gone." She gave a heavy sigh.

I took another chance: "T.D. was a great ballplayer, and God rest his soul—but the brother was high-maintenance."

Alma laughed ruefully. "That's the damn truth. When it's just me and C and my kids . . . it's perfect. But if T.D. . . . ." she paused, ". . . *when* T.D. *was* in the mix . . . nothing but drama. Truly. The phone would ring, and C would be out the door. 'See you Monday,' and next thing I know, he's in Vegas or New York or somewhere, like they're all still kids. God bless T.D., like you said, but I won't miss the drama. Maybe this is the last time. Maybe C just has to get over it." She sounded so hopeful, I felt sorry for her.

I could hardly bite back the words: *Was Carlyle really here with you the night T.D. died?* "I guess he was out late with T.D. Sunday . . ." I ventured instead.

Alma's eyes glazed over. Dead end. The wailing toddler was suddenly muted as she slammed her car door shut.

I tapped on her window. "Will you ask him to call Mel if you hear from him?"

After a baleful look, Alma slid the key into the ignition and cranked her car to life. Her window slid down. "Carlyle's a grown-ass man," she said. "He'll call her when he's ready."

Alma didn't pull out right away. She sat there idling, and I realized she didn't want me snooping at her house. She was waiting for me to leave first. So, I walked down the street to my car. She still waited, so I pulled away first, too. I gave her a honk and a wave as I drove past.

Alma Grays didn't wave back. In my rearview mirror, I never saw her pull away.

I had learned something important about Alma Grays: She might or might not be telling the truth about Carlyle's alibi on Sunday, but she would lie for him. Her eyes had told me.

So, I waited around the corner, hoping I would see her drive past. After thirty seconds, she did. My hands tightened on the steering wheel; instinct told me to follow her. Instead, I drove back to the house, where the driveway was empty. I stared at the tempting house, scoping up and down the street. The longer I sat, the faster my heart raced. I recognized the signs: I might be about to do something dangerous. Or outright stupid. I was itching to let myself in.

When my cell phone rang, I drove off with a squeal of rubber. Saved by the bell.

I picked up without checking caller ID, expecting Len or Melanie. Instead, it was a nasal male voice I didn't know. "I'm looking for . . . Tennyson Hardwick?"

"You got him."

"I just got an email from April Forrest." He said that as if it identified him. When I didn't answer, he went on: "Casey Burnside? I write for the *Times*. She said you have some questions about Donald Hankins . . . ? "

Even an ocean away, April had my back. I had left a voicemail for Casey Burnside as soon as I got off the phone with April, but apparently he'd checked his email first.

I took a breath, trying to clear my head. My heart was still pumping from the idea of breaking into Alma Grays's house. My thoughts were so full of Carlyle Simms, I could hardly remember what I'd wanted to ask about Donald Hankins. I almost ran the light on Crenshaw.

"If you have a few minutes later, maybe I can drive by," I said.

"I'm in D.C., and I have five minutes," he said. "Right now. On the phone."

As it turned out, that was plenty. In more ways than one, his call came right on time.

Burnside asked me polite questions to make sure I wasn't a competing journalist. When I told him I was just doing a favor for a friend, he seemed amused, but it got him talking. I parked at a gas station and took notes, my fingers racing to keep up with him.

"I was new on staff when the allegations came up in '99, and I've never been happy about walking away from that story. My editors said I needed more sourcing, since there were no police records to back up the allegations. There was something to it—I just didn't have the contacts yet to bring it home. Once Hankins announces his governor's run, it might start bubbling up again. These stories usually do. That's politics.

"So here's the way I remember it: There was a real estate deal, a zoning thing. Hankins is hot to push it through, probably a sweetheart deal, but there's opposition from one of these neighborhood groups. Not a bunch of housewives, mind you—most of these people were lawyers. Very savvy. Hankins is used to bulldozing the council, and he's frustrated. I have the minutes from one of the meetings, and Hankins basically called one of these guys an asshole, just not in so many words. A real temper. Anybody could see he was losing his composure.

"Then one of these opposing lawyers ends up at Forest Lawn after his car drives off a ravine out in Hollywood Hills. That takes all the wind out of the opposition's sails, and the zoning goes through a month later, hardly a peep. Then I get a call from the dead guy's wife. She's been looking into the accident, and she claims she's got a guy who can prove there was tampering with the brakes. She'd also been doing some digging on Hankins, and she pulled together a good little case. Circumstantial, but a case. As it turns out, Hankins and the developer's CEO had done business before. Campaign contributions, consulting fees, the whole nine. Different company, five years before, so there were no ethics violations screaming. Still . . . it doesn't take a leap to see the potential for financial benefits to Hankins after the zoning change went through."

"There's a big difference between being a crook and being a killer," I said. "What else did the dead guy's wife have to go on?"

Burnside sounded slightly annoyed. "Don't get ahead of me: I didn't say Hankins got under the car and messed with the brakes himself. But the wife claimed there was a strong-arm guy who paid her husband a visit two weeks before he died, in the parking lot of his office. He told his wife about it, and she remembered after the accident. An African-American."

"Aren't they always?" I was surprised to hear myself say it aloud. I thought I'd kept that sarcastic thought in my head.

"Hey, I'm just telling you what he told me. The guy was built like a house, she said. It only resonated with me because there'd been a big guy arrested on a trespassing charge two years before that—I think his name was Ronald. Roland. I can't say off the top of my head. A cop told me, and I wrote it down. It was another one of these contentious situations with Hankins, a property dispute in Hollywood, and the other party thought Ronald or Roland had been sent by Hankins to intimidate him. The charges were dropped, so there was nothing in the police files. Believe me, I checked. But I got the feeling there was something to it."

"Why?"

He sighed. "The cop I called seemed to know more than he let on. He wanted to talk, but he asked his supervisor first, and I never heard from him again." I wondered if that supervisor had been my father. Internal politics might have forced Dad to silence his officer.

"Who's the officer?" I said.

"Sorry. No can do. A source is a source. But I'll say this: Donald Hankins, being nobody's fool, got real cozy with LAPD after that traffic fatality. The wife said she got stonewalled. LAPD wouldn't touch the case. It was just a car that drove off the road."

A beep on my phone told me I had a text message, but I ignored it. "Did anyone ever bring Ronald-slash-Roland in for questioning?" I said.

"Nope. I've got nothing on him. Guy was a ghost. His name's in my notes, but I won't be back in town until next week. Even then . . . we're talking about a story that's almost ten years old. I can't promise I could find the notes. I can't even promise I'll look."

At least he was honest.

"What about the wife?"

"Her, I'll talk about. Name was . . . Laura Ebersole. With a B. She called me every day for six months, then she dropped out of sight. No contact. I found out she'd moved to Canada. Toronto. The forwarding number had already gone bad."

"Retired?"

"She was in her thirties. Felt more like . . . she was scared off. It was sudden. She just dropped everything."

Grief drove people to drastic changes, but I agreed with Burnside. Seemed sudden.

"You think Hankins's thug got to her?" I said.

"No proof, but sure, it's possible. I got a heavy breather once myself. Someone called, and a gruff guy's voice said, 'Let it alone.' Southern accent. Click, he's gone. I didn't have a clue what he was talking about at the time . . . but who knows? Could've been Ronald. Roland. Whatever."

Interesting but thin. Nothing like the tip about Carlyle Simms that Jeanine had dropped on me that morning. Still, sketchy as the details were, I wrote them down.

"Guess what?" Burnside said. "Your five minutes are up. I've got an interview."

"Hey, man, thanks. If you find the mystery thug's name, let me know."

Burnside laughed. "Don't hold your breath. Hey, tell April we'll miss her. She'll be Mandela's press secretary before you know it."

God, I hoped not.

As soon as I'd hung up, I checked my text message. It was from Melanie.

WE'RE IN—HANKINS AT 7—CALL ME.

Like I said, Burnside's call came right on time. You never want to underestimate the man you're about to interview face-to-face.

I was about to meet Chantelle Jackson's parents, the same day I might have learned exactly how their daughter died.

SIXTEEN

"I HEAR YOU'RE CHECKING UP ON ME," Melanie said.

She was waiting at our designated meeting place—the Jackson's curb, beneath the jacarandas. The previous day's anger had vanished from Melanie's cheekbones. They don't call dusk the Golden Hour for nothing: The setting sun ignited a quality in Melanie's face that fooled my eyes into thinking I was seeing her for the first time. The sight of her made my memory sluggish.

"New York?" she prompted.

Right. The day before, I'd put in a call to the Black Lawyers' League in New York to check Melanie's alibi. I'd found her name on the event program on the internet, but I wanted to make sure she'd been there. Second nature, after what happened to Serena. Melanie's story checked out. At the time the coroner said T.D. died, Melanie was at a late-night mixer at Trump Tower. The guard's log confirmed she had been there until 2 A.M.

"I made a couple calls," I said. "Procedure."

"I'm glad you're so thorough." She sounded like she meant it. "What about Carlyle?"

I sighed. It had been a long day, followed by rounds of whining from both Dad and Chela when I told them I would have to miss dinner because of an appointment.

"Still working on it. I racked up a lot of mileage trying to find Carlyle and his friends, but they're all missing. I saw one pissed-off wife and two pissed-off girlfriends. One of the guys—Brandon—made an appearance at home Tuesday night to get some clothes. His wife says he stank of whiskey and pot." Brandon's wife hadn't looked as willing to lie as Alma, and she was clearly distraught about his behavior. She said her husband had been at home Sunday night, with her sister there to vouch for the story. Like Alma, she had conceded that her husband sometimes "took off" when T.D. and his friends were involved. But despite the friends' suspicious behavior, neither of the other women had been interviewed by the police.

"They're holed up somewhere together," Melanie said. "I knew it. It's been that way since college. Their whole Heat brotherhood is just an excuse to disappear when they feel like it. If T.D. was here, he'd kick all their asses—leaving all this stress on me . . ." She was already backing away from the notion that Carlyle might have killed T.D. She didn't want to believe it.

Soon, I might have to tell her what Jeanine had said. But not yet. I wanted her sharp and focused for our meeting at Senator Hankins's house.

We took Melanie's car. Her front seat was immaculate, brown leather seats shining, but the backseat looked like a mobile file cabinet, stacked with boxes and papers. We would have to work to make room for her niece and nephew.

T.D.'s mother hadn't been exaggerating when she told me how close the Jackson and Hankins families were; they lived in the same neighborhood, within only blocks. Almost walking distance. Once upon a time, that had been cozy—now I was sure both families wished they were a continent apart, except for the grandchildren who kept them tethered.

I looked at my watch. It was still a quarter to seven. "We're early."

Melanie smiled grimly. "We'll have more time this way."

The Hankins house was roughly the same size as the Jackson house—about six thousand square feet, I guessed—but it was colonial-style instead of Tudor, with whitewashed wooden columns, a wide porch, and a quaint porch swing that evoked memories of *Gone With the Wind*. A child's Huffy racing bike lay on its side on the porch, beside a large plastic box brimming with sports equipment. It was easy to see where the children spent most of their time.

As we climbed the porch, Melanie followed my eyes. "The kids have been living here since Chantelle died. Uncle Em and Aunt Evie have to fight for every minute with them. It's about to get ugly now—in his will, T.D. said he wanted them with me." Her voice was low.

"What will you do?"

Melanie shook her head. "I don't know. Whatever's best. We have a funeral first." She rang the doorbell, and three sober tones chimed through the house.

There was a patter of footsteps, and the door was flung open.

Maya Jackson was much taller than she'd looked in her photo in T.D. Jackson's den, the top of her head reaching Melanie's shoulder. She had an oval face, and long, relaxed hair parted into ponytails. The sturdy thirteen-year-old grinned. The grin surprised me.

"Auntie Mel!" she cried, and flung her arms around Melanie.

Aunt and niece shared a long, swaying embrace in the doorway, while Mel smoothed Maya's hair back with her fingers, kissing her forehead; I could see a mother lurking within Melanie. I felt like an intruder standing so close to them, so I hung back toward the swing. They stayed in the doorway a long time, as if Maya was reluctant to bring Melanie inside. The thought of the family pressures on that kid were too sad to dwell on.

Finally, Maya Jackson looked my way. Her eyes were clear and aware, not nearly as trodden as I had expected from a child whose father had just died.

"Where's Simon?" Maya said, her knowing eyes fixed on me. Her intuition was eerie.

"Simon will be back tomorrow," Melanie said. "This is a friend of mine—Tennyson."

Maya didn't greet me. "There's a poet named Tennyson," she said, and took Melanie's hand to pull her inside. Those private-school dollars weren't being wasted.

"She's named after a poet, too," Melanie told me. "Maya Angelou."

The Hankins house was so cluttered that it seemed smaller than it was, teeming with unique furniture and artifacts, many of them African and Caribbean. Incense had been burning recently. Wooden floors complemented wooden chairs and wooden figurines and masks throughout the house.

The family was well traveled. Above the table in the foyer, I saw a photo of Donald Hankins posing with Nelson Mandela. April would be envious; her biggest dream in South Africa was to have her chance to meet Mandela. One call from Hankins might get it done, but I wasn't there to curry favors.

A slightly plump woman in a plain red dress came hurrying down the stairs. I recognized her from her stoic gaze during the Jackson trial: Chantelle's mother. Mother and daughter shared the distinctively shaped face that Chantelle had bestowed on Maya.

"Is it seven already?" Loretta Hankins said.

"Sorry, Retta," Melanie said. "We're early."

Retta smiled widely, trying too hard, both hands waving dismissively. "It's not a problem, darling. Junior's just not quite ready, but I'll give him a nudge." She reached toward Melanie for a mechanical hug. I guessed that Retta Hankins knew full well what T.D.'s will said about custody of the children, and she was going out of her way to keep Melanie placated. That was probably the only reason I'd been invited.

Retta's smile faltered as she turned to me, but she glued it back on. She patted Maya's shoulder. "Go on up and check on Junior, baby. He's looking for his shoes."

Maya cast a last glance at me before she left. Her eyes seemed to say *I know why you're here, and nobody wants to talk about it in front of me, but don't think I'm stupid.* Like Chela, Maya was one of those kids who had wisdom beyond her years. Life had beaten it into her. As she walked away, I heard her gum pop.

"That Mel?" a man's voice boomed. I saw movement out of the corner of my eye.

Donald Hankins was peeking from around the corner beyond an upright piano, wearing a white chef's apron over his dress shirt and slacks. He'd raised a plastic spatula as if it was a bludgeon, but his grin was luminous, so natural I thought I'd earned it. I suddenly smelled gently frying food. Spicy fish. Corn bread. His house smelled like a church basement.

In a glance, I understood why Donald Hankins thought he had a shot at the governor's office. His hair was closely shaved, his mustache full but meticulously clipped. He had the same bottled charisma T.D. had mastered, the kind I could focus like a flashlight beam, while his filled the room. He didn't make a motion that wasn't calculated for effect. He was smooth and fluid and already my best friend. He looked happier to see me than Judge Jackson ever had.

"Hey, man," he said, hand outstretched. "Don Hankins."

"Senator," I said, shaking his hand.

"Mel, Junior's a mess today," Hankins said. "He really needs you up there."

Immediately, Melanie's eyes flew toward the stairs. *Shit*, I thought. I'd hoped she would be present for part of my conversation with Hankins, but he had just sent her out of the room.

"Guess I better go see him," she said.

The worst way to be played is to *know* you're being played—and still be unable to avoid the play. After an apologetic gaze toward me, Melanie was gone. Retta Hankins had vanished, too, when I wasn't paying attention. Her duty was done.

Hankins waved with the spatula. "Come on in the kitchen with me. Let's talk."

The custom kitchen was three times the size of mine, equipped like a small restaurant. Spotless pots and pans hung in regimented rows above the marble counters. Every corner gleamed with cutlery. I could cook my ass off in that kitchen.

Hankins went to the stove, where fish was frying in a small pan. Whole fish, not fillets, heads intact. As he flipped the fish, I felt the déjà vu of standing in the kitchen with my father, except that Donald Hankins was much heartier. I wished I hadn't had to miss dinner at home.

"We're having catfish, but I'm 'fraid it's just enough for me and Retta."

"I wouldn't dream of imposing, sir."

Donald Hankins looked at me over his shoulder. He chuckled, jabbing his spatula toward me. "Now we both know that's not true, or you wouldn't be here in my home at dinnertime. I may be a politician, but I don't truck in bullshit. I hope you don't either."

"Fine by me."

"Good. Mel's horseshit aside, I know why you're here, so we'll talk like two men. Grab me a beer out of that fridge."

I opened the large refrigerator and found a row dedicated to Amstel Light. The other rows were crammed with colorfully labeled children's foods.

"You might as well have one, too," he said. "We're short on fish, but there's beer to spare."

I took him up on his offer. As I sat at the barstool counter to drink my beer, I noticed the mail. A Southern California State Alumni magazine was at the top of the pile, addressed to Hankins. The cover shot was a football receiver leaping for a photogenic catch at Spartans Stadium. I thumbed through the magazine. Hankins pretended not to notice, but I felt his body tensing from two yards away. I put his magazine down.

"I was at SoCal a couple years in the eighties," I said. "You a Spartan, too?"

He laughed. "Shoot. A hundred years ago."

I gazed at his shoulders, trying to imagine him forty years younger. Donald Hankins was big enough to have been an athlete. "Play any ball?" I said.

" 'Lil' bit," he said. "Hand me that pepper, would you?" He nodded at a spice bottle arm's reach from me on the counter. I gave him the ground red pepper, and he sprinkled it liberally before handing it back. "Right cabinet. At the top."

I was tiring of his tasks, but I put the pepper away. I recognized his ploy, and it was clever; by keeping me occupied, he could control the conversation while at the same time creating perceived rapport. I couldn't have done it better myself.

"You know what a sociopath is?" Donald Hankins said suddenly. He was concentrating on the frying pan, which sizzled so loudly that I wasn't sure I'd heard him right.

"Sir?"

"A sociopath," he repeated. "A person who looks like you or me, but who has no feelings for other people. He has no concept of right or wrong. He is . . . dead inside."

"Sounds right."

After moving the pan to another burner, Hankins took off his apron, folded it across the counter, and turned to look at me. His chest was broader than it had seemed. Even leaning casually against the kitchen counter, he was taller than I am. His eyes didn't blink. "My daughter, Chantelle—my only child on this earth—was married to a sociopath. She was *murdered* by a sociopath." As he said it, one eye fought wincing. "His name was T.D. Jackson."

"Yessir," I said. "I'm afraid that may be true."

"I'll tell you in plain English, and I've said it before: T.D. Jackson killed my daughter. So if you're standing there judging me because I haven't shed any tears over his recent departure, I just told you why. If you were in my place, you'd be dancing a damn jig."

"I don't doubt it."

Donald Hankins shared a conspiratorial grin. "And I'll tell you this, too: That beautiful little girl you met—Maya? She isn't shedding any tears either. That was her *father* . . . and yet she understands she is better off without him. A child! Now, that should really tell you something."

I took a swallow of beer. It was sharp and cold, but my mouth was sour. "Maybe she had reason to think her father killed her mother. Or, someone encouraged her to believe that."

Hankins's grin vanished. "Retta and I broke our hearts every day trying not to bad-mouth that monster in front of those kids. And Junior, well, he's a different story. He's younger, and it takes a whole lot to make a boy that age look at his father cross-eyed. I feel bad for Junior—tell you the truth, Junior is the *only* reason I feel bad. I wish he didn't have that bastard's name." For the first time, I saw bitter grief on his face. He took a long swig of beer. "Son of a bitch."

I raised my bottle in a toast. "The son of a bitch is dead now."

He clinked our bottles. "I only wish I'd seen it, and I wish he'd done it sooner."

We both drank to that, Hankins gazing beyond me at nothing. Where his mind was, I never want to know. When I lowered my bottle, half my beer was gone. I wanted to go on toasting T.D.'s death, but I had work to do.

"Did T.D. ever hurt his kids?" I said. If the death of his daughter wasn't motive enough for Hankins to have T.D. killed, perhaps concern for his grandchildren was.

"The way he talked to Maya sometimes was shameful. She told Retta he called her a 'little bitch.' " I felt my own surge of anger. No girl deserved that from her father, much less a child as young as Maya. "Reminded him of Chantelle, I guess. They fought like cats and dogs."

"What about physically?"

"Maya's denied it, but I wonder," he said. "Probably just a matter of time."

"No danger of that happening now."

He gave a dour chuckle. "Damn right there isn't."

"Senator, there's just one thing . . . If T.D. Jackson was a sociopath—and I think there's a good chance he was—why would he kill himself? You said they don't feel guilt."

Hankins laughed. "*Guilt?* You still don't get it, my man. T.D. was about to lose everything he owned in the civil trial. He knew that, and T.D. Jackson couldn't stand to lose his shit. That's why he killed Chantelle. That's why he blew his brains out. He was a greedy motherfucker." Donald Hankins was sounding less like California's future governor and more like a buddy from the corner bar around the way.

"How could he be sure he would lose the civil trial?"

"Mazzoni's office fucked up the criminal prosecution, but lightning doesn't strike twice."

I raised my bottle. "What the system can't fix . . . God can. Or someone can, anyway."

A glimmer of enlightenment across the senator's face. He had just decided not to underestimate me either. He took another swig, with a lopsided smile. "I know a couple things about you, son," he said.

I didn't answer, waiting.

"You're Preach Hardwick's boy, ain't you?" he went on. I had never heard anyone call my father Preach except his men at Hollywood division. "Keeping up the family tradition."

"What tradition is that, Senator?"

"Trying to crawl up my ass with a flashlight." He winked. "I guarantee you, there's nothing worth finding up there. The man shot himself. Melanie's blind as a bat where T.D. is concerned—I'm sure you've seen that by now. I won't judge Emory and Evangeline, because I've been where they are. Take them for all you can, I guess, but have some decency about it."

"I take it you and your wife were at home Sunday night," I said as casually as I could.

"Sometimes I don't get any sleep in Sacramento. So when I'm at home, I make it a point to be in bed by ten thirty. Retta was right beside me. She's a gracious lady, but there are limits . . . so you'll have to permit me to speak for both of us."

His grin was gone, replaced by solemn earnestness. He was definitely an actor, too, as all good politicians are. So far, everyone had a spouse or bedmate willing to vouch for them. It was hard to prove, but it was harder to disprove.

"The kids were here, too?"

Hankins chuckled. "You're reaching, son."

"Just curious, Senator."

"Of course they were here. They live here." Sharpness crept into his voice.

With a custody dispute looming, I cursed myself for bringing up T.D.'s children. It was too late to salvage casual conversation, but I backed off to give it a try.

"What position did you play?" I said. "Back at SoCal?"

Hankins's face calcified, and he suddenly looked like a man who had never cracked a smile. My hindbrain noticed that a cutlery rack and a carving knife were within his arm's reach. He reverted quickly, but for a flash his face had been frightening.

"Receiver." His voice was tight.

"Judge Jackson played, too. Were you on the same team?"

"A year or two," he said, and he calmly turned back to his frying pan. "Mr. Hardwick, food's ready. It's time for me and my wife to enjoy our meal—and a toast to the departed. If you'll excuse me." Over his shoulder, he gave me a last grin.

Melanie and the kids were ready and waiting in the foyer. Tommy Jackson was wearing a 49ers baseball cap, and he never raised his head high enough for me to see his eyes. He held Melanie's hand, his feet shuffling listlessly. Maya reminded me of Chela again, her ears fused to an iPod as if the world and its offenses did not exist.

Melanie's eyes asked me if I had gotten what I came for, and I nodded. I had something—I just wasn't sure what.

Retta Hankins tried a last, worn smile at the door. "Pleasure to meet you," she lied, her smile fading before she'd fully turned her face away. Donald Hankins never emerged from the kitchen to wish us good-bye at the door. The food smelled great, but the fumes in that house were toxic. I was glad to go back outside.

Maya helped us unload boxes from the backseat to make room for two passengers, although Melanie's trunk was stuffed with files already. For someone as work-focused as Melanie, it would be a huge adjustment if she decided to raise those two kids full-time. I had Dad to help me, and I was still struggling with one kid. Maybe even failing.

As Melanie drove, Maya's eyes watched me in the rearview mirror from the backseat, where she sat beside her brother. I wanted to ask her about her father, but Melanie tapped my knee as soon as she caught me gazing at Maya's reflection: *Forget it.*

"When's Simon coming home?" Maya said. She hadn't spoken since we left the house.

"Tomorrow," Melanie said. "Why do you keep asking about Simon?"

Maya didn't answer, her eyes still on me. That kid gave me a chill, between her fledgling psychic abilities and the utter lack of sorrow in her eyes. If she hadn't been at her grandparents' house the night T.D. died, Maya Jackson might have made it to my list of suspects. Not that a thirteen-year-old could stage a suicide. *Could she?*

Maya's gum snapped again, a defiant sound. I looked away from her untroubled eyes.

Evangeline Jackson was waiting under the bright porch light on her front stoop. Both children rushed out of the car to run to her outstretched arms. Maya's long legs pumped as she climbed the yard's incline, running hard. Tommy was sobbing when he reached their grandmother, and she hugged him, shushing him until she was crying, too. Mrs. Jackson hurried them inside, closing the door. In the car, Melanie and I sat feeling sorry for all of them.

"Well?" Melanie said. "What did you get from him?"

"Not sure yet. You never told me that Hankins and your uncle played for the Spartans together," I said. Evangeline Jackson had told me the two families were close, but no one had mentioned that the men's ties went back forty years.

Melanie shrugged. "I didn't think of it. That's when they first met, back in the sixties. Their team won a bowl game. Why?"

"Seemed like a sore subject."

"Those two aren't speaking since Chantelle died, unless they have to. I'm sure he didn't like hearing Uncle Em's name come up."

Sounded reasonable, but my instincts knew better. A man who valued complete control over his facial expressions had faltered when I brought up his glory days. Judge Jackson had changed the subject when I asked him about his football days, too. The football players I know aren't shy about reminiscing, and winning a bowl game usually means bragging rights for life.

I opened my notebook and wrote SPARTAN TEAM—1960s. JACKSON. HANKINS. I had a hundred other leads to follow up on, but I underlined it twice.

"Will I see you at the funeral Sunday?" Melanie said.

"My best chance to find the Heat, I hope," I said. "Think Carlyle will be there?"

"If not"—she stared at her lap, her profile heartbreaking—"something's wrong."

Something was already wrong. I wanted to say more, but silence seemed wiser. With her fiancé coming home the next day and a funeral on Sunday, Melanie had enough on her mind.

"Keep an eye on Maya," I said. "She's pissed off at her dad. It has to go somewhere."

Melanie nodded. "I know. We've already got them both in therapy. I wish T.D. had gotten therapy when he was a kid."

"Why?"

Melanie sighed. "Did you see how Aunt Evie just hugged the kids? I almost never saw her hug T.D. like that. She just corrected him: 'Don't do this, don't do that.' She's much better with her grandkids, but T.D. never felt like he could make her happy. Between that and Uncle Em's expectations, he always felt like a failure. Never good enough."

Hankins was right: When it came to her cousin, Melanie was blind. Sooner or later, Melanie would have to let go of her memory of T.D. as a child and accept his misdeeds as a man.

"Hankins thinks T.D. might have started hitting the kids," I said.

Melanie shook her head, irritated at the suggestion. "Never."

"But you know he called Maya names? Cursed at her?"

Reluctantly, Melanie nodded. "At the end, I finally convinced T.D. he wasn't fit to be a father by himself. He wasn't willing to give up his traveling, his bad habits. And, yes, sometimes he crossed the line. He and Maya . . ." She sighed. "Maya and Chantelle were so close—plus, Maya was old enough to read the newspapers after her mother died. She knew what her friends and their parents were saying. One day she decided the stories were true, and it was never the same with her and T.D. He asked me to move the kids in with me and Simon, and Simon had already agreed. We were going to do it after Christmas. T.D. knew that Donald and Retta were poisoning his children against him. That hurt him so much."

"Why did Hankins get custody instead of T.D.'s parents?"

"Please," Melanie said. "T.D. was under arrest, Ten. Then the trial? The custody hearing was a kangaroo court. His parents had no chance. Even with his will, I don't know what a judge will say now . . ." Her eyes shimmered with tears, but no tears fell. "I'm so tired of this. I just want this nightmare to go away."

Any assurance to Melanie that night would have been an outright lie.

SEVENTEEN

FRIDAY, OCTOBER 24

While Marcela was out with Dad at his physical therapy, and Chela was at school, I spent hours at home Friday making telephone calls and doing research as I tried to find Carlyle. Not a trace. I tried hotel operators, asking for Carlyle and his friends by name. I tried calling my old sources in hotel security offices in Los Angeles and Las Vegas, but many of the personnel I had known from my bodyguard days had moved on. Even tabloids like *TMZ* hadn't sniffed out Carlyle, whose appearance in the wake of T.D.'s death would have excited the paparazzi. Either Carlyle and his friends were trying not to be found, or I was wasting my time. Or both.

Melanie checked in on me every two hours, and she sounded more disappointed every time I gave her my report. No news. The reserve in her voice reminded me that Simon was probably back home. I hoped Simon was giving her a place to rest her head.

While I waited for returned calls, I was nagged by the memory of the way Donald Hankins's face had changed when I asked about his football years. The internet is a curious man's best friend, so I hit my computer.

As a former SoCal student, what I learned during a cursory Google surprised me: SoCal State's appearance at the Sunshine Bowl in 1967 had been a major event in college football—not only mentioned extensively on the university's website, but described on dozens of hard-core college football fan sites. The matchup between Southern California State and Florida University in Tallahassee had been dubbed *The Stomp in the Swamp* by SoCal's student newspaper. A *New York Times* sports columnist, reminiscing about the game as recently as five years before, said "that one January day embodied the spirit of the social change in the 1960s, demonstrating to a nation that segregation's stranglehold on America would not endure."

The Florida team had been all-white, a vestige of the days of segregated education in the South. SoCal State's team had featured an integrated roster—and many of the key plays had come at the hands of black players who, the *New York Times* columnist observed, "played four quarters beyond their abilities in the heart of the South, as if Dr. King's dream relied upon it."

Had Judge Jackson or Donald Hankins played on that team?

My answer came on SoCal's football website—touting "Our Glorious Heritage" in purple and white—which featured a large photograph of the game-winning reception from the 1967 Sunshine Bowl. The catch looked as graceful as any footage of T.D. Jackson, a long body leaping into the air to catch a ball that should have been out of reach. The photo showed the back of the player's jersey: Number 9. HANKINS, the name read.

I checked the caption to be sure: The player was identified as Donald Hankins, a senior.

The article didn't mention all of the players' names, but it singled out twelve: Among the standout players were Emory Jackson and Donald Hankins. I printed out the article and wrote out the other names, none of which was familiar, but I Googled them all. The team's quarterback, a white player named Frank Blythewood, had gone on to play for the Miami Dolphins for a few seasons under Bob Griese's shadow, but none of the other names had withstood history. Not for football, anyway.

Five of the names were so common that they were useless—like David Smith—so I lost their internet trail. Another name, Wallace Rubens, turned up on property records in Florida, but I had no idea if he was the same player listed from the game. But I found two players who were still local: A former SoCal offensive linesman, Dominic Micelletto, who owned a car dealership in Thousand Oaks, and a former running back, Randolph Dwyer, who was listed on an Ojai High School website as a division-winning varsity football coach. Dwyer's name was accompanied by a photo of a bespectacled black man with a shaved head and a pleasant smile. In his sixties, but he looked very fit. His bio confirmed that he had played for Southern California State, although it neglected to mention the Sunshine Bowl.

I underlined his name. Dwyer had no doubt been tight with Jackson and Hankins. From the sound of it, the black SoCal players who went to Tallahassee had a day to remember.

Except that none of them went out of their way to talk about it—or even mentioned it anywhere on the internet. Given the rancor between the Jackson and Hankins families, I could understand why they didn't want to stroll down memory lane with me, but both men were prominent, and they never mentioned the Sunshine Bowl, period.

A *Los Angeles Times* profile of Hankins the year before Chantelle's death described him as "remarkably modest" about his SoCal football years, mentioning the bowl game only in passing. Scores of newspapers, magazines and blogs credited Judge Jackson's football history for inspiring T.D.'s love of the game. But Judge Jackson had rarely offered direct quotes or reminiscences. What had Judge Jackson said to me in his study? *We thought we were doin' something.*

That went beyond modesty, I realized. It was outright evasion.

By contrast, SoCal's white quarterback had been featured on a "Where Are They Now?" segment HBO Sports had taped as recently as 1997, on the game's thirtieth anniversary. And Micelletto's car dealership ads billed him as "A Former SoCal Football Star."

Why the silence from the team's black players? Had their standout performances in the game simply been overlooked . . . or had that game been too much like a war? Growing up with Dad had taught me that veterans often don't like to talk about their battles.

Whatever it was, my gut told me that I couldn't afford to ignore it.

I wrote down <u>1967</u> and underlined it twice.

SATURDAY, OCTOBER 25

Marcela didn't come on weekends unless it was to force Dad to go to a movie, so we were on our own for two days. No buffers, and it was 8 A.M. Time to check on Dad. He had been tired after physical therapy Friday, as he often was, and gone straight to bed after dinner.

Downstairs, his bedroom door was closed. I gave it two quick taps.

"You up? How you doing?" He only grunted in response.

"I . . . got it," he said, but he sounded out of breath. He was trying to make his way from his bed to his wheelchair to his bathroom, always an awkward task for Dad, but he would only ask for my help as a last resort. I listened to him straining for a while, waiting.

There was a small crash from the room. Something had fallen. I heard Dad curse. "Ten?" he called. His voice was small and anxious.

I went in. One leg had made it to the wheelchair's footrest, but the chair had rolled clear of the bed, a wheel caught on the night table. Dad was splayed between his chair and the bed, clinging to the headboard for balance. The room smelled heavily of urine-dampened sheets, but any stains were hidden under his bedspread.

"Damn . . . chair," Dad said.

"Just hold on," I told him, hooking one arm around him. When I was a kid, Dad had weighed about 220 pounds; now, he might not be 160. His arms looked scrawny in his undershirt, and I hated to glimpse his legs, which were shriveling to nothing but knobby knees and bones. Marcela took him to physical therapy three times a week, but she had confided to me that it might be a lost cause. His leg muscles were more atrophied each day. Dad's main goal in life was to turn in his wheelchair for a walker—modest wishes by any standard—but even that might be beyond his reach.

A couple of hardcover books had fallen from Dad's night table, so I picked them up and put them back. One was his old King James Bible; the other was Nathan McCall's novel *Them*. Dad had a special relationship with Amazon, with new deliveries every other day, it seemed.

As soon as he was in his chair, Dad practically slapped my hand away.

"Okay . . . got it," he said. He hid his eyes from me, wheeling to the bathroom.

The bathroom was narrower than I liked, but it was the only full bathroom on the ground floor.

Dad closed the bathroom door behind him.

"Breakfast?" I said to the closed door.

"Pancakes," he said. "Twenty . . . minutes."

Dad had cut pork out of his diet, so he cooked turkey sausage patties while I cooked the pancake recipe Dad had passed on to me from Mom: a cup of self-rising flour, two eggs, just under half a cup of sugar, a dash of vanilla, and enough milk to give the batter the consistency of yogurt. Quick and easy, with no need for syrup. Heaven. Thanks, Mom.

While we made pancakes, I had the chance to tell Dad about my visit to Senator Hankins. I hadn't told him about the bullet hole we found at T.D.'s house—mostly because I knew he would insist I share the information with the police. Besides, since I'd found potential evidence of a murder, Dad would advise me to step away from the case and not risk getting entangled in the investigation myself, like with Serena. Dad was pragmatic enough for both of us.

Hankins was safer. Dad listened intently, chuckling when I mentioned the catfish.

"Hasn't . . . changed," Dad said, but he only waved his hand when I asked him to elaborate. Not important. He nodded when I asked if he remembered SoCal going to the Sunshine Bowl in 1967, but he offered no further observations. He didn't seem inspired by the football trail.

What trail? I had no trail. All I had was restless brain cells because I couldn't find Carlyle Simms. I hated funerals—and T.D.'s funeral the next day would be a very small family gathering, the worst kind of hypocritical intrusion for me—but I would have to go. It was bad enough to go a funeral, but I probably would meet Melanie's fiancé, as if a miserable day needed improvements for either of us. *You better show up, Carlyle, you SOB*, I thought.

Be careful what you wish for.

Chela smelled pancakes from her room, the only thing that could rouse her from bed before noon on a Saturday. It was a long-standing family tradition: Dad served a hot breakfast at 9 A.M. on the weekends, and there was no such thing as missing Dad's breakfast.

Chela came downstairs bare-legged in a Barack the Vote T-shirt, her hair mussed from sleep. She smiled for Dad and kissed his cheek, but she didn't share her smile with me.

"You must think you're real funny," Chela said to me after Dad blessed the food.

"What?"

"Why'd you tell that geek I would go to the dance with him?"

Silently, I groaned. I had hoped that Chela would succumb to peer pressure once she realized I had accepted Bernard Faison's invitation to the homecoming dance on her behalf. Instead, I had set that boy up for humiliation.

Chela turned to Dad to complain. "Captain, he not only takes my cell phone, right? But now he's, like, taking my calls and telling people I'm going to the dance with them when I am *not*. It's wrong on so many levels."

Dad looked up at me: *Is that true?*

"I'll give you the phone back—just the iPhone," I told Chela. "But don't trash that guy. He's a nice kid. It's just a dance, Chela. What's the big deal?"

Her eyes sparked at me. "Number one, people will see us together. Number two, you're trying to control my life. And number three, in case you haven't noticed, I don't even own a dress—and girls who wear those foo-foo dresses like they're little princesses looking for Prince Charming are losers. Can you even see me in one of those?"

"Yes," I said. "Actually, I can. I'll get you a dress."

"Did you not hear a word I just said? Those dresses are for losers."

Finally, Dad spoke up: "Why'd . . . he take . . . your phone?"

That brought silence from both of us. Chela looked at me with terror, dreading my answer, and I saw a merry twinkle in Dad's eye. He knew he had just given me leverage. Dad wanted her to go to the dance, too.

"Just this one dance," I said. "Sorry I screwed up, but cut the kid a break. Please?"

Chela glared.

Dad nodded toward the foyer. "Paper," he told Chela. On weekends, he lingered at the table to read his *Los Angeles Times* over two leisurely cups of coffee, a habit that had endured since I was a kid. But now, Chela was the newly designated newspaper collector. I had a younger sibling, at long last. Better late than never.

"You gonna put on some more clothes before you go out in public?" I said, as she walked away. Her T-shirt barely reached her thighs, and she looked like all legs. Chela gave me a *yeah, right* look before she vanished into the foyer and unlocked the front door. I hoped she was wearing underwear, or the neighbors would get a peep show.

As soon as Chela got up from the table, Dad reached for the remote and switched on the TV. I could time him like a stopwatch; he didn't feel at ease alone with me. Maybe he was still embarrassed I'd had to help him out of bed. Dad punished me for his moments of helplessness.

After a story about casualties in Iraq and a political update, CNN reported that T.D. Jackson's funeral would be on Sunday. Yet again, Lieutenant Nelson appeared on camera against a Los Angeles backdrop, a set in the West Coast studio.

". . . ongoing investigation, but all signs indicate suicide," Nelson said on-screen.

"It's . . . Nelson," Dad said, and turned the volume up.

I kept forgetting to mention to Dad that Lieutenant Nelson, his old protégé at Hollywood division, had questioned me after Serena's murder. Nelson had personally executed a search warrant at our very house, right before Dad moved in. Nelson also knew my past in a way I didn't want my father to, and I tried to keep them as far from each other as possible. Now we were all in the same room; that brother could make me squirm even when he wasn't really there.

"The key in a case like T.D. Jackson's," Nelson said wisely, "is not to be swayed by the glare of the public eye. Just like Elvis, Tupac, and Shareef before him, the mystique of celebrity status means there will be questions and intrigue about his death for years to come . . ."

"He knows . . . it's . . . too . . . early," Dad complained. "No . . . tox screen."

T.D. Jackson's blood toxicology report wouldn't be ready for at least a week, or more. Even a celebrity death has to deal with backlogs, and until the medical examiner finished his work, the police would have no idea what was in T.D.'s bloodstream when he died. Still, I saw pride in my father's face as he watched Nelson. I had to admit that he looked and sounded good on TV. Full of shit or not, Nelson was representing the department well.

"You should call him," I heard myself say despite myself. "Get together for lunch."

Dad gave me a full-out glare.

"I'm sure he'd love to hear from you."

But Dad shook his head. He hated visits from his cop friends, which were scarce anyway. No one had come by in a year. The fear that he was dying had scared Dad's friends away in droves—except for Dolinski, who called once in a while, and his friends from church. Dad was partially to blame. He hated to leave the house, and the only companion he needed was the TV. Dad had always considered other people a distraction from his thoughts.

"Dad, I'm not saying you should sweat him about Jackson," I said. I kept my voice low for Chela's sake, until I remembered she'd gone outside to get the paper. "I know you want to keep him clear. Just call him and get together to shoot the shit. You know, like people who knew each other fifteen years."

Dad shook his head again. "Not . . . now."

After a frustrated sigh, he found a napkin and scribbled on it with a pen: NOT WHILE YOU'RE WORKING HIS CASE. TOO RISKY. IF YOU GET SLOPPY, NELSON'S SMART ENOUGH TO MAKE TROUBLE FOR YOU. I'M LYING LOW.

Reading his note, I chuckled. He was lying low, all right—so low he had practically buried himself. I almost said it aloud.

"Where's that . . . paper?" Dad said, glancing toward the foyer.

I should have realized sooner that Chela had been outside for five minutes, or longer. The paper was usually under my car in the driveway—I swear the guy aimed for the most inconvenient spot—but it didn't take five minutes to walk a dozen paces from the door.

What now? I thought. I might have had a psychic moment. I just knew. When I got up to check on Chela, I was moving fast. In the foyer, I heard Chela laughing as she approached the door from the other side. "Oh my God, he's gonna freak—" she was saying.

Who's she talking to? I wondered, just as my door came flying open.

The sun was shining outside, but in the foyer there were only shadows. The light from the doorway was blocked.

Tiny Chela stood in front of me with a ridiculously misplaced grin. Behind her—towering over her—were three behemoths who looked twice their size in the small space of my foyer.

Carlyle Simms was standing in my house, his eyes laser-locked on mine, with death in his glare. Brandon Jakes and Lee Quarry, T.D.'s other two buddies from the Tau fund-raiser, flanked Carlyle, their meaty arms folded. They were all wearing sweatshirts and track pants. I smelled perspiration and beer in their skin. I hoped my living room wasn't about to become a war zone.

"Ten, look who it is!" Chela announced, excited. "Carlyle Simms! I recognized him from TV. How come you never told me you were friends with T.D. Jackson? He lived in your *dorm*?" Her eyes shone at me with new regard.

I heard a loud bump from the dining room; probably Dad's chair knocking against the table. Dad couldn't walk, but his hearing was fine. I didn't mistake what I saw next: Lee fished his hand toward the back of his waistband, startled by the sound.

The Heat was packing heat.

I've never had an emotional whiplash like it—eating pancakes with my family one minute, nerves frying with controlled adrenaline the next. Carlyle Simms had ambushed me right where I lived. My Glock was upstairs in my night table, a million miles away. If Carlyle Simms and his crew had anything to do with the death of T.D. Jackson, our lives were nothing to them. I went cold. For a moment, everything seemed to be happening in slow motion. *Tachypsychia*, it's called. If you've never experienced it, it's hard to explain how it feels.

My heart thumped my ribs, but I grinned as if I was as happy to see them as Chela expected me to be. I showed them my empty hands while reaching toward Carlyle for a friendly handshake. "Hey, man. What a surprise."

Carl squeezed my hand hard enough to paralyze tendons. "Heard you were looking for me," Carlyle said. "So, here I am."

Another loud bump came from the dining room.

Lee angled himself as if to walk past us, farther into the house. His hand was still hidden behind him. Dad was spooking him. Not good.

"That's my dad," I said to Lee, silently begging for calm. "He's in a wheelchair. It's cool. Hey, Dad? It's Carlyle Simms and the guys. T.D.'s friends."

I was a good enough actor to keep the murder out of my voice, but not by much.

Chela shot me a questioning gaze before sick realization flattened her face. Despite my persistent smile, she knew me well enough to recognize that she'd blown it somehow, even if she had no idea of the magnitude. Chela and I both knew she had made similar mistakes in judgment in the past—and the last one had nearly gotten me killed.

I heard Dad's chair rolling closer, then he appeared at the other end of the foyer. Dad's head was listing to the side, as if he were frailer than he was, but his eyes could match any man's vigor. Five years ago, my father's eyes would have given Carlyle reason to walk right back out the way he came in.

Carlyle grinned at my father. "Hey, Pops," he said. "We won't be long. We just came to sit and visit with our old friend a while."

Lee brushed against me as he walked past, not waiting for an invitation. The unfriendly bump would have knocked me off-balance if I hadn't relaxed and exhaled. He smirked, never realizing my center of balance was still intact. He smoothed his sweatshirt back to conceal his weapon, but I saw the gleam of nickel plating. *Fuck.* I hate it when I'm right.

I wrapped my arm around Chela's shoulder, pulling her closer. I cursed her bare legs. If anyone laid a finger on her, Carlyle was going to die. I could feel the animal in the back of my head promising that. The horrifying thing is that it didn't completely care what happened later.

"Nice place, man," Brandon said, admiring the Sidney Poitier one-sheets framed on the foyer wall. He lingered in front of *A Raisin in the Sun*. "Gotta love Sidney, right? They call me *Mister* Tibbs.'" Wrong movie, but I didn't correct him.

Carlyle stood over Dad, who sat directly in his path to the living room. "What's wrong, old-school?" Carlyle said. "You don't speak to guests?"

Dad's eyes spat fire, and I wanted to crush Carlyle's trachea. Instead, I said, "He had a stroke, and he's not having a good day. Can we go outside?"

The grin Carlyle gave me over his shoulder easily could have been Chantelle Jackson's last sight. "Naw, man, I think we better stay right here. I apologize for my bad manners. It ain't right to show up and surprise a man at his home, huh?"

"Coffee smells good," Lee said. "What you think, C?"

"I think I'd love a cup of coffee," Carlyle said.

Gently, I patted Chela's back. "Get them some coffee," I said.

She looked up at me with questions, but I gave her a nudge and was relieved when she didn't object. Chela needed a compass and a map in the kitchen, but at least she'd be out of the way. I was dismayed when Brandon ambled behind Chela, watching her. They weren't about to leave her unattended. Brandon was half-leering as he leaned across the counter to watch Chela, and I could barely keep my eyes off them. When Chela reached up to look for coffee mugs in the cabinet, her T-shirt rose high across her back thighs. My anxious fingers twitched.

"*Hey,*" Carlyle said, his face two inches from mine. He lowered his voice for my hearing, and I smelled his funky beer breath. If they were drunk at nine thirty in the morning, we were in bigger trouble than I thought. "Why you riding my ass so hard?"

"Let's take a walk," I said, one last effort to get them out of my house.

"I like it here," Carlyle said. "Since we're so tight."

"Melanie's been worried about you," I said. "I was just trying to track you down, that's all, man. There's a funeral tomorrow."

"Could be a whole lot of funerals tomorrow," Carlyle said privately, to my bad ear. But trust me, I heard every word.

Lee grabbed the handles of my father's wheelchair and pushed him toward the sofa. Dad hates being pushed without permission, but he didn't move except to slump even farther into his seat, a pained look on his face. I hoped it was just an act; otherwise, my father might be having a heart attack.

"Dad?" I said.

Dad nodded to say he was fine, but he didn't look fine. Far from it.

I couldn't tell if any of the others had weapons. Men that size don't need guns to be lethal. But even without risk of weapons, I couldn't take all three of them. There was only one good move, and it had to be perfect.

"Let's sit down," I said. I turned off the TV, which was too loud. If there was a scream or a gunshot, I wanted one of my neighbors to hear it. Mrs. Katz across the street complained about Chela's loud music on a regular basis. Maybe she could finally make herself useful.

Carlyle sat in the easy chair near the fireplace, where he could see the living room, breakfast table, and kitchen. I sat at the center of the sofa, where I could keep all three of them within my peripheral vision.

"Why'd you come to my house talking shit about T.D.?" Carlyle said.

"Man, I was just looking for you, like I said. I wasn't talking—"

Carlyle's eyes narrowed. "You calling my lady a liar?"

All three men watched me, waiting. Lee was tapping the end of my father's wooden rolling pin across the kitchen counter.

I fought to keep the anger from boiling over into crazy. Crazy wouldn't help anyone. "Look," I said, my voice a lullaby. "I meant no disrespect. I just said . . ."

" 'T.D. was high-maintenance,' " Carlyle finished. *Shit.* Had Alma given him a transcript? "That's how you're gonna trash-talk our brother the same week he died?"

"I meant no disrespect," I repeated, appalled to hear the same words from my mouth a second time. Dammit, my rational mind was shutting down, shorting out. I looked at him, and instead of a man, I was seeing a silhouette painted on a pane of glass, with vulnerable areas painted on like splotches of red paint. Most of the room was dimming, but certain things loomed brightly: the fireplace poker. A butter knife on the table. A glass figurine the size and heft of a baseball.

The air felt thick, and red, and hot.

Brandon's voice rumbled beside me. "Guess you didn't mean any disrespect when you told T.D. to go fuck himself either, huh?"

That fund-raiser was back to haunt me. When you've had your ass kicked once or twice, you learn to smell violence simmering in the air. These guys had come with a purpose; the only question left was how many of us were going to get hurt.

"Who wants cream and sugar?" Chela called cheerfully from the kitchen.

I held my breath. The façade of politeness was the only thing stopping the blood flow. By then, Chela knew it, too, and I was glad that kid was street-savvy. I couldn't stand the position I had put her in, but I needed her to use every weapon she had.

Brandon and Lee waited for Carlyle, who was chewing his lip, in deep thought.

"Lots of cream," Carlyle said. "Lots of sugar."

"I like an itty-bitty cup myself—with a little cream, sexy thing," Lee told Chela. His steady gaze studied her pale brown legs up and down.

"Really?" Chela said with a smile. "I like mine really big and really *black*."

Brandon gave a start, as if he would fall off of his stool. Then he laughed. Lee chuckled, too. But Carlyle wasn't laughing, only waiting for my reaction. If they baited me, and I attacked first, they could call whatever happened next self-defense.

I deliberately softened my face, relaxed my shoulders, and smiled. Even in their agitated state, I watched their postures become slightly less aggressive. There is a phenomenon in animal relationships that goes deeper than conscious thought: Members of a herd have a tendency to match each other's actions and moods, and humans are herd beasts.

"I didn't say anything like that to T.D.," I answered Carlyle. "And it's not what I meant. I had a television gig, that's all. Shit, I can't think of anything I'd rather do than hang with T.D. Jackson. The pussy alone would have been worth it, man."

My father flinched when I said that P-word in front of Chela, but it had the desired effect: Brandon laughed again. "Got that right, bruh."

Even Carlyle's cheeks pooched a little. Just a little. Maybe enough.

Chela brought Carlyle's coffee first, walking with a self-confident sway across the room. I braced for Carlyle to throw the hot liquid in my face. Instead, he sipped.

"Is it okay?" Chela hovered, the perfect hostess. She ventured a quick gaze at me, and I gave her a grateful smile. *Good girl.* Chela probably would have put Drano in their coffee if Lee hadn't been watching her.

Carlyle nodded, his eyes never blinking away from mine. "You believe that horseshit on TV?" he said. "T.D. Jackson's a bitch who's gonna shoot himself?"

"Shit, hell no," I said. "LAPD can go fuck themselves." Another nod from the boyz. I was making up a little ground.

Careful. Careful. Maybe everybody lives through this.

While I spoke, Chela hurried away, bringing Brandon's coffee next.

I took a chance and went on: "That's why I told Mel I'm not gonna rest until I find the asshole who did this. Just like with Afrodite. And when I do, I'll call you guys first. No cops."

Brandon grunted. He liked that idea. A lot.

But Carlyle didn't look impressed. "Big talk after the man's dead. He begged you. We were all sitting around talking about it—we've never seen T.D. beg nobody like that. And then Alma tells me you came to my house talking shit." Brandon and Lee made disapproving sounds, remembering their anger. Carlyle wasn't going to give me a way out.

"It's not like that, Carlyle," I said, trying anyway. "Who am I to talk shit about T.D. Jackson? He was a legend. I know how hard T.D. worked his whole life to make his dad proud."

"Goddamned right about that," Lee said.

"And I get why you guys are pissed off," I went on. "You and T.D. were more than friends. You were brothers, like you said. Heat."

Brandon held up two fingers. "*Two* generations. Heat looks out for Heat. Always."

The three of them stirred. I had touched a nerve; I just needed to work it in my favor. "We *will* find the motherfucker who did this," I said, trying to rally them to my side.

"You talk a whole lot of shit, Hardwick," Carlyle said. "So what you got, then? You know so much. Who did it?"

I hesitated, recognizing a trap. If I announced to T.D.'s killer—or killers—that I had found evidence, I might as well pull the trigger myself. The entire visit could have been designed to find out what I'd learned.

I'll never know what I would have said. There was no more polite conversation.

As Chela walked past Lee back toward the kitchen, he reached over and gently slapped her on the ass, grinning at her as he made his play. It was more of a tap; the kind of casual contact countless barmaids and waitresses have endured through the ages. But this was *Chela*—and for all he knew, she was my daughter. That brother must have lost his damn mind. The sound of his palm snapping against her bare flesh rattled the room like an explosion. My eyes filmed over red. There was no real way out. Not now.

I laughed, and I almost believed it myself.

"Let me help you with that," I said to Chela, stepping toward her, a smile on my face, hands open, my best *gee-I'm-such-a-harmless-beta* voice in play.

I took one step, and then I crouched and shot a heel thrust kick into Lee's knee. Muscle is one thing, tendons and ligaments are another. *Force equals mass times acceleration. Pressure equals force divided by surface area.* Dropping my 190 pounds as I slid toward him focused enough force into the ten square inches of the side of my right foot that I could have hurt someone twice his size.

He buckled, losing balance, and I went in, spun him, and yanked the gun out of his waistband as I did. My left arm snaked around his throat, left fingers worming around the muscle to clamp onto his windpipe. If he twitched, I was going to dislocate it and let him strangle on his own blood, I swear to God. Brandon was on me in an instant, but I ducked his swing and smashed the butt into his nose. It burst like a tomato, splattering blood across his face and dropping him to his knees.

I had the hammer back, the gun aimed squarely in the center of Carlyle's face. *Game, set, match.* Damn, I'm good.

Then I looked at Carlyle's face. It bore a certain grudging respect, but no fear at all. That didn't make sense, unless . . .

Oh, shit. I shifted my gaze to the gun, a J-frame .38 Smith and Wesson revolver. I've held them before. A snag-proof titanium "pocket" revolver that only weighs 10.8. Unloaded. One of the lightest self-defense weapons with any stopping power, and I could feel that it didn't weigh over eleven ounces. I glanced at the cylinder.

"No bullets, asshole," Carlyle hissed. "This *was* going to be a friendly little talk."

A bluff. The gun had been a bluff.

Brandon rolled away from me. I still had Lee in a controlled choke, but that might not be enough leverage on his buddies. Dammit, I had just raised the stakes, and revealed my capabilities. They were going to regroup, and this time, they wouldn't underestimate me.

I heard a commotion from Dad's wheelchair, and I prayed he had a plan. As fast as he could move in that thing, maybe he could make it to the door!

"My turn," Carlyle said.

I was calculating moves and odds when a man's voice roared: "*Step back! DO IT!*"

Someone must have called the police, I thought. Damn, they were fast, too.

No police. Dad sat in his wheelchair, leveling his massive .44 at Carlyle with two hands. Susie, he called his gun. I hadn't seen Susie in a long time, and it had been longer since Dad had held her. Susie was shaking so badly in his hands, I wanted to duck, too.

"Hey, hey . . ." Carlyle said, alarmed, arms raised. "Don't hurt yourself, old man."

"This one . . . ain't empty," Dad said, breathing hard.

Guns are the ultimate equalizer. Dad looked like a frail husk in that wheelchair, but the dynamic in the room had shifted. With the unsteady barrel staring them down, Carlyle, Brandon, and Lee were checkmated. I didn't ask for Dad to give me his gun for my steadier hand, and I didn't run upstairs for my Glock. Dad had it handled.

"Thirty years on the force," I said. "His hand's shaking, and he's been in a bad mood since his stroke—you do *not* want to piss him off. So here's what's gonna happen: Ya'll are about to get the fuck out of my house. But first, we're gonna finish the conversation you started."

"Fuckheads!" Chela chimed in, tugging her T-shirt down to hide her upper thighs. Her face was red with embarrassment and rage.

I had an opportunity. After all, I had been looking for Carlyle Simms for days, and here he was. But I couldn't have him arrested for murder. It was all hearsay, and I couldn't betray Jeanine. Would the police even book him, given their humiliating inability to convict T.D? No. I couldn't let him know what I knew. I was going to nail this bastard, but I had to find the right way to do it.

"Chela?" I said gently. "Go upstairs, hon. Lock yourself up somewhere safe. Have a phone ready to call the cops if anything smells wrong."

Without a glance back, Chela scampered away, still pulling her shirt down.

"I'm gonna remember this," Carlyle Simms promised me.

"You'd be a fool to forget it," I said. I gave Lee's throat a final tweak and push-kicked him sprawling onto his face. That felt good. I walked behind Dad's wheelchair; I had sense enough not to interfere with his line of fire. "Now try to remember where you've been this week."

"None of your damn business," Carlyle said.

"Talk," Dad said in his old voice, the one I remembered. His gun stayed on Carlyle.

Carlyle held up his arm to shield his face. "Watch it, old-school. Shit. All right—we were over at the Bel-Air. That's where we got a suite after T.D. won his Heisman. Memories, that's all. Check the desk. I use the name Dorsey Thomas. We needed some time."

Or they were hiding from someone, I thought. Dorsey Thomas was T.D.'s first and middle names, transposed. If any of them had killed T.D., booking their room under his name had been stupid, unless they were trying to get caught.

"You asked me who killed T.D.? I don't know yet," I said. "But you can bet your ass it's payback for Chantelle."

Carlyle blinked twice, which looked to me like Morse code for *I helped T.D. kill her. And then I killed T.D. to cover my ass.* Just maybe.

"You know a Ronald or Roland who works for Donald Hankins?" I asked them. "Big guy? Name starts with an R?"

It's not often that a black man's face goes chalky, but Carlyle's did. Lee and Brandon only shrugged, but the name meant something to Carlyle.

"Naw," Carlyle said, although he wasn't the liar T.D. Jackson had been. I didn't know whether or not he'd killed T.D, but I had something on him.

"Well, watch out for him, bruh," I told Carlyle. "I hear he makes problems go away."

Brandon levered himself up from the floor, eyes blazing and blood drooling between the fingers he held to his face. But none of the men spoke again, transfixed by the wobbly gun in Dad's hands. Lee raised a pillow from my sofa to his abdomen, his shield from an errant bullet.

My father's breathing had quickened, so I decided to relieve him. I nodded toward the door. "Go on," I told T.D.'s friends. "Get out. One at a time. Slow. And call Mel to give her some support, you selfish bastards."

I pushed Dad's wheelchair while Dad kept his gun trained on the retreating men. I noticed that the gun was shaking a lot less now that their backs were turned—Dad had been playing possum from start to finish.

Once my intruders were outside, I triple-locked the front door.

Through the peephole, I watched them climb into a black SUV. A Jeep Cherokee. Carlyle started the engine.

I grinned back at Dad. "When did you get Susie?" I asked him.

Dad flashed me a smile I hadn't seen from him in too long to remember. He still had his own teeth; they looked just like mine, a mirror. "When Chela said . . . Carlyle's name."

Damn, he was fast in that chair! Dad had made it to his room to fetch Susie as soon as they showed up at the door. "You had it the whole time? Why'd you wait so long?"

"Wanted to see . . . what you were gon' do."

I stared. Then I laughed ruefully. "And?"

"Seen worse," Dad laughed, and his laughs were even rarer. Then, Dad's smile faded as concern shadowed his face. "Didn't see . . . the other . . . gun, though."

"That's why there's two of us."

And we were both grinning again. Strange as it sounds, it felt like Dad and I had just met each other and thought maybe we wouldn't mind hanging out. I heard the roar of Carlyle's SUV outside. Through the peephole, I watched him drive away.

I secured the other doors before I went upstairs to find Chela. She was in her room, and she had finally dressed, wearing baggy black jeans to match her T-shirt. I chafed at the memory of how Lee had touched her, but Chela wouldn't let me fuss over her, brushing me away.

"Ten, what the fuck? Tell me what the hell's going on, so I won't get you killed."

So, I told her. Some of it, anyway. Enough to keep us safe in case of unexpected visitors. Then I went to my bathroom and splashed my face with cold water. My hands shook so hard I had to grip the edge of the basin, staring into the mirror at eyes filled with uneasy knowledge. That had been close. Too damned close. If I was going to walk this road, I had to be more careful in the future.

An hour after Carlyle left, I got a text message from Melanie: C CALLED. DON'T KNOW WHAT U DID, BUT THANKS. I was glad to have done something for her, and even happier that I could skip T.D. Jackson's funeral. I wanted to spend the weekend with my own family.

Breakfast hadn't gone so well, so we made different plans for lunch. For the first time since Dad had moved in with us, we all ate out.

EIGHTEEN

Monday morning, Dad surprised me. After Chela left for school, he
told me he'd asked Marcela not to come in until the afternoon. He sat
with a small black satchel in his lap that he'd always used as a briefcase,
his father's medical bag from the 1930s. Dad was shaved and dressed
in a formal light blue shirt, black sweater vest, and slacks, as if he were
ready for church.

"What's the occasion?" I said.

"You . . . working . . . today?"

I was planning to drive to Pomona to talk to Miguel Salvador,
T.D.'s brother-in-law, and then to Ojai to find Randolph Dwyer,
the high school football coach who played with Donald Hankins
and Judge Jackson in the 1960s. Both were more obscure leads, but I
had already burned too much energy on Carlyle. I had to make sure I
wasn't overlooking anything.

"Why?" I asked him.

He shrugged. "Thought I'd . . . ride, too," he said. "Fresh air."

Saturday had been a milestone for us, but I groaned inside. It was hard enough to drive to interviews between Los Angeles and Ventura Counties on a weekday, but Dad would need tending, and I wanted to be focused on T.D. Jackson. Even finding food suitable for Dad would be a hassle. No In-N-Out Burger for him. His heart couldn't handle the grease.

"Been a long time since I needed a babysitter, Dad."

"More like . . . a . . . partner," he said, eyes gleaming. "Homicide cops . . . travel in pairs."

Call me dense, but that was the first time I got it: After our encounter with Carlyle Simms, Dad wanted to help with the case. Wheelchair or not, he was feeling more alive than he had in years.

"You bringing Susie?" I said, smiling. He still had his concealed weapons permit.

He patted his satchel. "Maybe."

Outside, I helped Dad into my car's low bucket seats and folded his wheelchair into my trunk like it was an everyday thing, and Dad paid me no mind. We were finally both learning how to accept life for what it was, not what we wanted it to be.

I started the car. "Driver is deejay," I said. The rule April and I had lived by.

"Just no . . . rap."

So much for Snoop's *Doggy Style*, which had been in my CD player for a week; it never gets old, and I could hear it fine with one ear. But KJLH 102.3 worked for us, too, between Al Green, Alicia Keys, and Stevie Wonder. I wished it was a Thursday, when Stevie was in the studio for the morning show—I've met him, and he's as gracious as they come.

Driving with Dad was the best I'd felt since April had left, like taking an unexpected vacation. I wished we had thought of it sooner.

The traffic gods were merciful, so it took us less than an hour to drive the forty-five miles to Pomona, almost a straight shot on the 210, with peaceful views of the San Gabriel Mountains. Southern California's mountain ranges can't touch the lush green of the Pacific Northwest and its constant infusion of rainfall, but I saw plenty of green peeking through. Much of Pomona itself is less scenic than the drive, but there is evidence of past splendor within the crush of strip malls. We found Salvador's restaurant easily on the corner, with a giant revolving chicken on the roof to aid us. I had called Friday, and an unwitting teenager had told me that the best time to find Salvador was in the morning.

I could smell a flock of chickens roasting even from the parking lot.

"Coming in?" I asked Dad.

"What you . . . think?" He picked up his black satchel.

The handicapped ramp looked about ten years newer than the rest of the building—thank goodness for access laws—and I pushed Dad inside with ease. Los Angeles Country's health department grades its restaurants, and the letter on the door was a "B," not an "A." Personally, I never eat anywhere that isn't ranked at the top of the class. No takeout for me that day.

Miguel Salvador was tending a dozen spits of roasting chickens near the register. He was wiry and about forty, with a shaved head to hide his balding scalp. He looked tired and pissed off, but when I told him why we were there, he broke into a grin.

"Yeah, yeah," he said, shaking my hand as if I were personally responsible for T.D.'s death. He took off his gloves and walked around the counter to shake Dad's hand, too, a rare gesture. Most people treat people in wheelchairs as if they're invisible.

"This is really something, right? The guy's finally dead. Shot himself. Fucking *puta*. Sorry I'm cussing so bad, *abuelo*, forgive me, but I've prayed for this day." As proof, he pointed out a large shrine behind his counter; a collage of photos of his brother, who looked nothing like him, and a colorful glass-encased novena candle honoring San Miguel. His brother looked boyish and vigorous, and Miguel looked careworn. His brother's death was never far from Miguel Salvador's thoughts. That's the tyranny of murder; it deepens the loss.

"Come on, have a seat. I served lunch free to everyone last Monday. If I didn't need the money, I would have shut down this place all last week. I told my kids, 'From now on, we will always honor this moment in time—the day T.D. Jackson finally did the right thing.'"

I wasn't sure a family ritual celebrating a man's suicide was healthy for kids, but Salvador definitely hadn't changed since his police interview. No wonder the detectives had noted how he was grinning from ear to ear. I didn't have to ask Salvador any questions. After bringing us complimentary glasses of iced tea, he did most of the talking.

"You know the truth, *hombre*? I wish I'd had the balls. When I wrote that letter to T.D., yeah, I was stupid to mail it, but I meant every word. You beat a man to death like a dog when his hands are tied behind his back?" He paused to thrust his hands behind him and crouch, imitating his brother's death pose. "You shoot a woman in the head? Be a man, I said. Come see me and be a man. But I have a cousin doing fifteen in Chino, and it's not for me. He kept telling me, 'Don't do it, man. Don't end up like me.'

"So I lit candles, I prayed. *Dios mio*, the acquittal almost killed me. Can you *believe* that? I thought maybe, just maybe, the acquittal was a test for me. Maybe there was no way to escape my destiny. But then he shoots himself!" Miguel Salvador shook his head, tears misting his eyes. He crossed himself. "There is a God. I mean that. Christ is king."

I already knew from the murder book that Salvador claimed he'd been in San Francisco for a friend's wedding the night T.D. died, and he showed us photos from the reception in his digital camera. Everyone in the photos was grinning as if they'd already heard the news.

Miguel Salvador seemed like one happy man, but his eyes told me how much pain churned underneath. He was half out of his mind. His joy would never be as real as his brother's death, no matter how hard he tried.

Dad and I had driven an hour for an interview that lasted ten minutes.

"Some folks . . . got no . . . sense," Dad said, shaking his head once we were back in the car.

"Do we take a closer look at him?" I felt like a real cop, and Dad was my C.O. "If it wasn't him, maybe a relative? Or he hired someone?"

"What's your . . . gut?"

I glanced back at the restaurant window, where Miguel was watching us leave. He waved a white dish towel, still grinning. He'd seemed sorry to lose his chance to revel.

"Nah," I said. "Happy isn't a crime."

"Half the country . . . would be in jail," Dad said, agreeing. "Let's go . . . to Ojai."

As I jumped on the 210 to begin the drive northwest, I suddenly realized that if Dad was going to accompany me on interviews, he needed to know what I knew. Everything.

"I haven't told you some things about the case, Dad . . ." I began.

Dad chuckled. " 'Course not. You like . . . secrets."

That stung, whether or not Dad was trying. I'd been keeping secrets from him since I was thirteen, probably before then. I'd blamed Dad for our shortcomings—he was so busy, so demanding, so inflexible—but how could he get to know someone who wouldn't talk to him?

I finally told him about my visit to T.D. Jackson's house—and the bullet hole hidden in the study. I kept my eyes on the road, as nervous about checking Dad's facial expression as I had been when I was a kid.

"That wasn't . . . smart," Dad said.

"No, sir."

"There's . . . rules. Procedures. We're not through . . . with this."

Shit. I wished I had kept my mouth shut. Just because Dad had asked to spend the day with me didn't mean he had changed into someone who could let that slide.

Dad sighed. "You shoulda . . . stayed in . . . the academy."

I might have graduated from the police academy after I dropped out of college, if I ever finished anything I started. How many ways would my life have been different? I'd put off getting to know myself until I was almost forty. That was why April was in South Africa; she was eleven years younger and already knew who she was.

I wasn't a part of that future. Where she was going.

"I know," I said dully.

"But . . . that was . . . solid work."

I glanced at him, but Dad was staring straight ahead, at the windshield.

That means a lot coming from you, Dad. I almost said it. I have no idea why I couldn't.

You never know when you won't have another chance.

The drive between Pomona and Ojai is two hours, but its virtues outweigh its drawbacks. The route is dotted with quaint towns and tourist-oriented shops, and one stretch of the 101 gave us such a perfect peek at the Pacific that I nudged Dad to wake him. On two-lane Casitas Vista Road, rocky cliffs bordered one side of the road, and since there isn't much north of Ojai except the Los Padres National Forest, it felt a little like driving toward a preserve. Or driving back in time. With the landscape glistening from rainfall we'd just missed, we passed fruit groves and sprawling ranches with split-rail fences. We passed Lake Casitas, a tranquil lakefront park that seems to spread for miles. Postcard photos everywhere.

Ojai has a population of less than ten thousand, and it feels much smaller. In Frank Capra's *Lost Horizon*, Ojai stood in for Shangri La. Downtown is nestled in the bowl of the Topa Topa and Sulphur Mountain Ranges, and sunset in Ojai is a filmmaker's paradise. The setting sun turns the Topa Topa Bluff bright pink. On Signal Street, mom-and-pop shops neighbor a post office built to look like a grand white Spanish mission church, an homage to the region's past. Galleries and artists abound. Ojai has long been a favorite refuge of actors trying to escape Hollywood; or for people who want to escape, period.

Dad was sleeping again by the time I pulled into the school parking lot. I woke him without a word, and he prepared to get out of the car. This time, he left his black satchel in the trunk—no guns allowed on school property.

The high school looked large enough for a thousand students. Inside, posters celebrated the school's music program and the football team, almost with equal fervor. OJAI #1!!!!!, a hand-painted banner screamed. An eight-by-ten staff photograph of Dwyer, the same one I'd seen on the school website, hung in a display cabinet alongside football trophies heralding division championships.

The halls were nearly deserted. The one student in sight, a girl in jeans and a school sweatshirt, headed straight for us with a helpful smile.

"Are you looking for the main office?" The girl was probably Chela's age, but she looked years younger. Her dark eyes still held on to a childlike brightness. "Straight down on the right." After I thanked her, she walked away with confidence and purpose, on her way somewhere.

The female assistant principal was stout and ruddy-faced, with short-cropped hair that reminded me of Jeanine's, in a blouse that paid homage to 1960s tie-dye. I hadn't called before we arrived, but Ms. Renault was polite and efficient as she talked us through the bureaucracy of a school visit in the age of Columbine and Virginia Tech. Names, identification, signatures.

Still, she seemed to assume we knew Coach Dwyer, maybe because Dad looked like he must be an aging relative. Rather than asking us to wait thirty minutes for the next bell, she said we should go straight to the practice field, where Dwyer was teaching a P.E. class.

"I don't know where the office aide ran off to," she said, "but I can take you myself."

The school was gorgeous out back, with an arresting view of the mountains. It looked more like a retreat than a school. Not a bad place to spend the high school years. I wondered if maybe Chela needed to be raised in a place more like Ojai.

"There he is," Ms. Renault said, pointing out Randolph Dwyer in the lush field about forty yards from where we stood behind the school. Male and female students were scrimmaging in a game of flag football. Some of those girls looked husky enough to play for varsity.

Things had changed since I was in high school.

Dwyer was easy to spot, since he stood a head over everyone near him, and he was one of only three people with brown skin anywhere in sight. His stomach had a slight paunch, and he was a big man who had let his shoulders slouch over time. Dwyer blew his whistle and called out to a student. The play stopped dead, and half the students groaned before lining up for a new snap. The quarterback flung her blond ponytail in a circle while she barked out signals to her line, changing the play.

Yep, things had definitely changed.

"Might be a little tough moving the wheelchair across the grass," Ms. Renault said. The walk seemed to have winded her. "I could go grab Coach Dwyer and bring him over . . ."

"Thanks," Dad said. "We'll be fine."

After a half second's consideration, she left us alone at the edge of the field.

I knew it wouldn't be Dwyer's best time for an interview, but I didn't have a choice. If I waited until after Dwyer's classes, I wouldn't get home in time to pick up Chela after school—and I needed to, just in case our troubles with Carlyle weren't over. I had to talk to Dwyer, and the telephone wouldn't be good enough. I wanted to watch his face.

We were meeting him cold, so he wasn't expecting us.

Dad's wheelchair was hell to push on the grass, but I hunkered down. We made a trail in the slightly overgrown stalks as we walked closer to Dwyer and his students. Luckily, he saw us coming. He signaled to one of his students and walked toward us. The kids played on.

Dwyer wore a white school shirt and blue shorts that looked exactly like the ones my high school P.E. teacher had worn. He was a bit heavy but had a remarkably youthful face for his age. Reaching us, he shielded his face from the sun with a clipboard.

"Help you?" he said.

"Coach, I'm sorry to surprise you at work. I'm Tennyson Hardwick, and this is my father—retired LAPD police captain Richard Hardwick."

Dad once told me there are two kinds of people, when it comes to the word *police:* those who grin, roll up their sleeves and say "How can I help you, Officer?" and those who don't. Dwyer was one of the latter. He stood like a statue in the hazy sunlight, waiting for the rest.

"You've heard about the death of T.D. Jackson . . ." I went on.

Dwyer nodded, lowering his clipboard so I could see his face more clearly. Behind his wire-rimmed glasses, his eyes were strikingly large, with an attentive quality that reminded me of Forest Whitaker. "Yes," he said, nodding. His lips pinched out the word. "Tragedy."

Like Dad, he wasn't long-winded. He glanced back over his shoulder at the kids, and I knew we wouldn't have his attention long. Three or four boys who weren't playing lingered nearby, sniggering, trying not to look like they were eavesdropping. The name T.D. Jackson had stopped them in their tracks. From their size, they might be from Dwyer's varsity team.

I chose the straightforward approach, keeping my voice low.

"I'm trying to do a favor for a friend," I said.

"What friend?" Dwyer asked.

"I'm not at liberty to say. But I can tell you that I have nothing but the best intentions toward all the families and friends connected in this matter."

Distantly, someone was practicing a tuba. Dwyer gazed at me, chewing at the side of his cheek . . . and then nodded. "Go on."

"Unnamed sources in the police suggest suicide—but we want a few folks who knew T.D. to tell us what they think."

Dwyer nodded. He understood; even seemed to approve. "I was surprised by that."

I pulled my notebook out of my back pocket.

"I didn't know T.D. well," he said. "I was invited to a couple social gatherings—his wedding, way back . . ." His voice cracked. "I knew his parents better. Long ago."

"Are you close to the Jackson family?"

He shrugged. "I wouldn't say that. It's a long acquaintance, but not deep. I'll always care about Emory and Evangeline, so this news hurt my heart. Chantelle, too, of course. I can't imagine losing one of mine—a student, much less my own child."

As Dwyer shifted and his shirtsleeve rode higher on his arm, I saw something that made me forget my next question: He had a keloid scar almost identical to T.D. Jackson's, but it was on his upper arm. Dwyer had branded himself, too. I remembered Carlyle's words on Saturday: *Two generations. Heat looks out for Heat. Always.*

"You knew Emory Jackson from your days on the Spartans." I said it like it was common knowledge. "The Heat."

A long, slow shadow crept across Dwyer's face. Beside me, my father nudged the back of my leg, in case I'd missed it.

Dwyer crossed his arms, body language for *Back off.* "Yes," he said, his voice tight again. "Been a while since I've seen them. Ten years? Maybe longer, since T.D.'s wedding."

"That was an amazing team," I said. "I'm a Spartan, too. My dad saw you play at Spartans Stadium."

"That right?" For the first time, Dwyer gave a wistful smile as he glanced at Dad. Dwyer's arms stayed crossed, but he seemed to relax. However distant, we were family now.

"You were . . . magic," Dad said. "Whole . . . team."

"The Sunshine Bowl!" I said, patting Dwyer's shoulder. "Beautiful, man."

Dwyer's smile grew boyish, part bashfulness and part pride. "We had a hell of a year," he said. "Some of it was luck, but we had a hell of a year."

"I saw that HBO thing on Blythewood," I said. "What's up with that? He sounded like he played the game by himself. Where were the rest of ya'll?"

"Guess they can't call everybody," Dwyer said dismissively.

"Same old . . . same old," Dad said. "They used to think . . . black folks . . . couldn't . . . play." Dad spoke as if he was giving a history lesson, and I guess he was. Aside from his doctors or therapists, I hadn't heard Dad speak at such length to a stranger since his stroke. Dad was pushing himself beyond his comfort zone to do the job. "These kids today . . . don't know. I 'member . . . they'd . . . bench the black players . . . for games . . . in the South. 'Member?"

Dwyer nodded, but he didn't uncross his arms. "Everyone had to be on their best behavior in those days. Like we were all Jackie Robinson."

"Wouldn't give Jim Brown . . . the Heisman," Dad said, and slapped his arm rest for effect. "Still burns me . . . to this day." Brown had been a four-sport star in high school: Football, basketball, lacrosse, and track. I couldn't count the number of rants I'd heard about the injustice of his fifth-place ranking in the Heismans in 1956.

Dwyer nodded, his face clouding.

"Then comes the Sunshine Bowl in 1967," I said, following Dad's lead. "So Cal State's black players *carried* that game. There was Emory Jackson . . ."

"Hankins," Dad said, as if reminding me. He tried to snap his fingers. "Who . . . else?"

We both looked at Dwyer.

"Bear," Dwyer said. "Nobody would have done nothin' that day without Wallace."

"That's right! Wallace. . . ." I angled for the full name.

Dwyer hesitated, but only an instant. "Wallace Rubens. Number six. He kept Blythewood off his ass all day. Gave him that pocket." I had come across that name in the list of players for the bowl-winning team. The internet had said something about Florida.

"What happened? Why'd I never hear about him?"

His face clouded. "Injury. Never really came back from it."

There was something fluttering around the periphery there. I had the odd sense that that was the edge of a truth . . . and if I pushed any further, I was going to get a lie.

"Was Wallace in the Heat, too?" I said, indicating the H-shaped scar on his upper arm. "And Hankins?"

Self-conscious, Dwyer pulled his sleeve down. His face tensed again. He would have worn long sleeves if he had known we were coming.

"It was a social club," Dwyer said with a shrug, which I guessed meant *yes*. "A brotherhood, you might call it. Back then there never were but a few black players on any big college team, and it was tough."

Dad nodded. "You right . . . about that. Tough . . . everywhere."

"We called ourselves Heat," Dwyer said. "Heat forges iron, that kind of thing. We made each other stronger. We knew some of the people watching those games wanted us to fail because of our skin color. Not every school would play teams from a segregated division, but SoCal State did."

"Bet . . . ya'll . . . caught hell down there," my father said. "In Florida. Wasn't just . . . orange trees and . . . beaches. Huh?"

Dwyer looked at my father as if he was seeing a ghost. He stood frozen for a full two seconds before he answered. "Wasn't so bad," he said.

His first obvious lie, or a conveniently misplaced memory. The *New York Times* column had said the white Florida University fans jeered loudly, spewing racial filth from the stands. Dwyer looked back over his shoulder at his students on the field, who played with less vigor whenever his back was turned. "Julie!" Dwyer called sharply. "Do that snap again!"

When he turned back to us, he ran his hand across his close-cropped scalp. "Who did you say sent you here?"

"T.D.'s friends hired a lawyer," I said. "The lawyer is a friend of mine."

Dwyer nodded, but didn't speak. He didn't look satisfied. He glanced at his watch. Dwyer was about to say *Sorry, can't talk right now.* His desire to get clear of us was so strong that I could feel his aura pulling away. A light drizzle had begun, promising to get stronger.

"One last thing . . ." I said, and Dwyer looked at me, hopeful, his eyes weary. "Can you think of anyone who might have wanted to kill T.D. Jackson?"

Dwyer sighed, looking pained. "I can't speculate on that. Like I said, I wasn't close . . ."

"Do you know of a Roland or Ronald who might have worked for Senator Hankins? A big man with a name beginning with an R?" He looked at me blankly. I realized I'd always assumed the R name was a first name, but it might be a surname. Hearing my question aloud made me think of it: "Did Wallace Rubens ever work for Donald Hankins?"

Dwyer's eyes looked like they could sink from his face, a well of sadness. He took two steps away, walking backward. "I'm sorry if you drove a long way," he said. "I'm really not the person you want to talk to."

"Coach, I'm only—"

He cut me off. "I've lived in Ojai thirty years. I have a wife, two sons, and a quiet life. We win a few games, but I've never reached for those heights like Don and Emory. I coach high school football, that's all. I haven't kept up with my old team—just that wedding, like I said. I don't know how to help you. I wish you wouldn't come back here."

"Coach," I said gently. "What happened in 1967?"

He looked at me as if I'd just broken a promise. When he spoke again, his voice was flat and lifeless. "We won a game," he said.

Dwyer turned and left us. His eavesdropping students trotted after him, as if they were a protection detail. The kids gave us wary glances over their shoulders; they'd seen the change in Dwyer, too, and they didn't like it. Walking away, Dwyer never looked back. He blew his whistle to rally his kids, and they flocked around him, some of them sitting at his feet. Dwyer was beloved at his school.

"Good call," Dad said, as I turned his wheelchair around in the grass.

"You got him to say more than he wanted to," I said. "You opened him right up."

We were a mutual admiration society.

I wrote down the name *Wallace Rubens*, then *Heat*, and underlined the words three times. I had found gold in Ojai.

Now I just had to mine it.

NINETEEN

I PICKED UP TWO TUNA SANDWICHES with bean sprouts at a local health-food deli, and we started the drive back toward home. By the time we left downtown Ojai, it was raining hard.

As soon as I made it back to Casitas Vista Road, Dad started dozing. Half his sandwich lay uneaten in the plastic box in his lap. I'd hoped to pick his brain on the Sunshine Bowl, especially with his perspective on history, but Dad's energy faded fast because of his medications. So much for my Crockett and Tubbs fantasy.

Instead, I picked up my cell phone to track down one hunch while it was fresh.

"Burnside," the reporter's voice answered. He sounded harried. One of us had a bad cell signal, so his voice phased in and out.

"It's April's friend, Tennyson Hardwick. I won't keep you, but I have a question."

"I'm in a meeting, but you're April's friend, so I'm listening."

For the first time, I wondered exactly how deep Burnside's fondness for April was. Would he make a move now that she was available? I knew nothing about the man, but my tide of thoughts almost made me forget why I'd called. *So this is what it feels like to be jealous.* The feeling was brand-new, and I didn't like it.

"The thug you think worked for Senator Hankins . . . the big guy?" I said. "Could his name have been Rubens?"

"*Rubens.* Yeah. Walter or Wallace," Burnside said. "That's the name."

I blinked, surprised by his certainty. "You said it was Roland or Ronald."

"I was wrong," he said. "It was Rubens. I have an uncle named Rubin, and I remember it now. What do you have on him?" I heard the familiar reporter's hunger in his voice, but I had promised April the story.

"Nothing yet," I said. "They played some football together, that's all."

I mentioned football in case Burnside knew anything about the Sunshine Bowl, but he didn't take the bait. Or, maybe his generosity in the information trade only went as far as mine.

"If you find anything worth knowing, don't forget my number," Burnside said. "I'd love to know if this has any legs before Hankins announces his governor's run."

You and me both, I thought.

I clicked off the phone. With the rain, cliffs, and mountains to lull me, my mind sorted through the pieces: Wallace Rubens had been part of a Heat brotherhood that tied together Jackson, Hankins, and Dwyer. No one in the 1967 Heat liked to talk about their team, or their association. Why? According to the reporter, Rubens had been arrested twelve years before for trespassing against one of Hankins's political foes. Two years later, Rubens was possibly implicated in the brake-tampering death of another Hankins opponent.

Maybe Rubens was his old friend's hammer.

"Dad?" I modulated my voice so that I would only wake him if he was dozing lightly.

My father's eyes snapped open. He was tired, but on alert. "Hnh?" He took a bite out of his sandwich as if he hadn't been sleeping for ten minutes.

"You remember that case involving Donald Hankins? The trespassing thing?"

Dad shook his head. "Not much. I 'member . . . a car accident."

"Right. But a reporter told me the name Wallace Rubens came up in a trespassing case a couple years before that. Let's say this same Rubens tampered with brakes and got somebody killed, all in service to his old friend, Hankins. Is Hankins ambitious enough for that?"

"You . . . never know," Dad said. "Folks . . . said it. Rumors."

"How hard did the chief's office work to keep car accident quiet?"

"We got . . . a couple calls," he said. "One call's . . . enough."

"So that incident was never fully investigated."

Dad sighed. "I never thought so."

There was an elegance to the idea. It brimmed with possibilities. I was worried about sounding silly to Dad's seasoned ear, but I went on. "You know Judge Jackson from the NAACP. What does he think of Hankins?"

"Never has . . . much . . . to say. Damning . . . with faint praise."

"Jackson, a judge, might have thought Hankins was too dirty," I said. "Maybe even violent. I'm sure they talked about that car accident. Their children were married, so they were stuck in social circles. But bring up their football days, and they all shut down."

My theory didn't explain the look on Dwyer's face when Dad asked him about Florida. I didn't have everything yet. But I had enough to fire up our imaginations.

"Then . . ." Dad began. "T.D. Jackson . . . kills . . . Chantelle Hankins."

I had him. Dad's mind was gnawing it over.

"And gets acquitted. Maybe that drives Hankins to ask his old friend to fix another problem. Would Wallace Rubens kill the son of a teammate?"

"Depends on . . . the reason."

"Hankins and Rubens figured T.D.'s acquittal was a hell of a good reason. And maybe Dwyer knows, or at least suspects. That's why he clammed up so fast about the Heat."

Wallace Rubens was beginning to feel like a viable suspect. *Maybe Carlyle helped T.D. kill Chantelle, but he's in the clear for T.D.'s murder.*

That's exactly what I was thinking when the black SUV roared behind me on a road that had been deserted an instant before. I saw the SUV before I heard it. The brights were on behind me, the massive grill bearing down.

"Hold o—"

That was all I had time to say to Dad before the violent jolt and a crash from my rear bumper. The tires skated on the slick road beneath us, but my hands grasped the wheel and held fast, so my car never strayed from my lane. The ridge yawned beyond the barrier, only a lane away; close to a thirty-foot plunge.

"Shit," I said. "Who the fuck—" Was it a drunk driver?

I gunned my accelerator, but my eyes couldn't leave the twisting road. Dad grabbed his safety bar and checked his side mirror. "Carlyle," Dad said. "I see 'im."

I risked a quick glance at my rearview mirror, and Dad was right: There were two men riding high behind us in the SUV's berth, but the driver was Carlyle Simms. The passenger might be Lee or Brandon. Had they been in Ojai, or had they followed us?

"Saw him . . . in Pomona," Dad said. "Wasn't sure."

I groaned. "We have *got* to work on our communication."

As I rounded a curve at eighty and gaining speed, the Jeep Cherokee charged after us, its massive tires screaming on the damp roadway. The seclusion was suddenly anything but tranquil. There were occasional farmhouses in view from a distance, but no other cars were visible in either direction. And not a single person in sight. As the SUV rode my bumper and tried to overtake me, there was no one else to tell the tale.

Carlyle's Cherokee was twice the size of my Beemer. Another well-placed tap with his thirty-five-hundred-pound monster could send us flying. If we didn't land in the ravine on one side, we would smash against a rocky cliff on the other. I was boxed in. Between the isolation and the sudden rainfall, Carlyle had chosen his time well.

"Dad, hold on," I said. "And I mean *tight*. This asshole's trying to kill us."

"No shit," Dad said, craning to look over his shoulder.

I suddenly wished we hadn't banished Susie to the trunk.

The Jeep roared, ramming us from behind again. This time, my hands were so steady on the wheel that I barely swerved, instinctively compensating for the sudden impact. My training in Colorado was about to pay off. Thanks, Alice.

But I hated the sound of my taillights crunching and trunk crumpling. Totaled already, and I'd just had my car painted two months before. Damn, I loved that car. Maybe that shouldn't have been going through my mind right then—but let me tell you, it was.

My heart was in overdrive, but by then I was pissed.

The ravine looked like a longer drop to a rocky grave every time I glanced at it, and the barrier would only slow us down long enough to realize we were about to die. If we rolled, we were done. The convertible top would give us no more protection than an eggshell. And air bags wouldn't be much help.

"We gotta . . . shake 'im, Ten" Dad said.

"No shit, Dad."

We rounded another curve, the two vehicles' tires whining in harmony. Clear, empty roadway stretched another forty yards before the next curve ahead. Carlyle gave up trying to hit us from behind. His Cherokee let out a guttural snarl as he steered into the empty traffic lane to pull alongside me. BMW 325i's aren't slow, but neither is the Jeep Cherokee SRT-8. For a big vehicle, it was supernaturally fast.

We were in a race.

I glanced at the passenger side in time to see the Jeep take a clumsy swerve toward us as Carlyle tested himself. A practice swerve, working up his nerve. He wanted to hit me, but he didn't want to roll over in the process. I could almost hear him thinking.

"Shit, shit, shit . . ." I whispered through gritted teeth.

I couldn't look over at Carlyle. If I blinked, we might crash.

While Carlyle seemed to hesitate, slowing slightly, I pressed harder on the accelerator, hugging the rock face on my side as close as I could. Pebbles churned beneath my tires. Through my side window, blades of grass growing on the cliff were close enough to touch, just inches away. A large jutting branch squealed against my car's body on the driver's side, and I let out a frustrated yell. Anything I did to evade Carlyle might only kill us faster. On the other hand, if I could tempt him into a pursuit at velocities beyond his command . . . physics might do my job for me.

Carlyle crept neck and neck with me as if it was effortless. Out of the corner of my eye, I saw the large black blur of his Jeep inching closer to Dad's side, making another run at us. Dad saw it too: He folded himself into a defensive position, his arms cradling his head.

He's an old man, you cold-ass motherfucker, I thought, trying to bargain with Carlyle telepathically.

Some moments are life's last snapshot, and that one looked like ours.

I couldn't pull ahead. Instead, I jammed on my brakes and said a prayer.

The tires held their traction on the road. One prayer answered. I slipped back from Carlyle, but not quite fast enough. He clipped my hood, and my car shook as my entire driver's side scraped against the rocks, so hard I was sure the body would puncture and my window would break. Stones *pinged* against the windshield.

Please don't let me lose one of the tires. I clung to the steering wheel like the lifeline it was, my foot still planted on the brakes. I held it rock-steady, fighting against what felt like the full weight of Carlyle's vehicle. My teeth were gritted so hard that my molars hurt. When a few inches finally opened up between us, I jerked my steering wheel toward the Jeep to give Carlyle something to think about.

As I'd hoped, a hard *thunk* was enough to jar Carlyle's concentration. He veered back into his lane, toward the barrier. I hoped he had a nice view of the ravine. Carlyle's brakes screamed as he skidded on the road. For an instant, I was sure he was going to tumble over the ravine himself—prayed for it, really—but he regained control and aimed his nose back at me. While he recovered, he'd fallen fifteen yards behind.

We turned a corner around a curve, with another curve and an empty road waiting ahead. I calculated the distance and my speed, ready for an experiment in physics.

"Dad . . . I have to do something crazy." What I meant was, *Dad, I'm gonna get our asses killed.* No time to clarify. "Just trust me."

"Do it . . . fast."

Adrenaline turned my thoughts into a blizzard, but I gunned the accelerator. My car jolted forward like a bronco, snapping our necks back.

"Come on, come on, come on . . ." I whispered to my car.

We sped. The speedometer passed ninety-five.

I glanced in my rearview mirror. We'd pulled so far ahead that the curve in the road had taken Carlyle out of sight, but it would have been a fool's prayer to believe we had lost him. Carlyle was coming.

Now or never, I told myself.

I turned the steering wheel, hit the brakes, and wanted to close my eyes.

My brakes cried out as if they were heralding our deaths. The damp road sent my tires into a spin, but I controlled it. Just barely. This time, I couldn't shout or curse. No time. The world narrowed to my windshield: I saw us pulling clear of the rocks as we spun, but we were sliding toward the barrier and its long drop. I pumped the brakes gently and fought the instinct to oversteer; instead, I nudged my wheel. *Come on, come on, come on . . .*

My rear bumper crashed into the barrier, and the rear tires bumped off of the road. Another foot back, and we would be airborne.

Instead, we rocked to a stop. We were facing the opposite direction, just in time to see Carlyle rounding the corner straight toward us.

I hit the gas, and my back tires spat mud before they climbed back to the road. I sped straight toward Carlyle's headlights.

"You wanna play, asshole?" I said. "Let's play."

Dad folded himself up again, bracing for impact. "Shit," he said.

Carlyle Simms had probably believed since junior high school that he was the baddest motherfucker he knew, but his face through the windshield told a different story. Carlyle was slack-jawed and shocked. He hadn't expected me to come back for him.

I grinned at him and floored it.

Sometimes a moment gets hewed down to such essentials that fear and worry vanish into a whirlpool of pure intention. I wasn't feeling, only thinking: If he swerved right, I would swerve left. If he swerved left, I would swerve right. My imagination painted my pathways in bright gold.

As I roared toward Carlyle's Jeep, I felt like I was charging an elephant. In a battle between an SUV and a convertible, the odds in size are depressing.

But I had the advantage, and Carlyle knew it. His only sane option was to hit his brakes and trust me to evade him. If he didn't, the slightest mistake would flip him over, or he might flip over whether or not he made a mistake. That's the thing: SUVs flip over.

Just like all those studies have warned.

Carlyle waited until I was within fifteen yards before he braked, and by then he'd waited so long that he couldn't help trying to steer clear of me. I'd panicked him so much that he steered too hard, too fast.

A nightmare scenario unfolded in my windshield like a horror movie: Carlyle's frenzied steering had sent him out of control—his Jeep skittered, then skidded, fishtailing toward us.

Right, steer left. Left, steer right.

I was close enough to see the dealership's logo glittering from the side of Carlyle's rear flank by the time I decided to steer left, toward the drop-off. My brakes squealed from a love tap, and I felt my back tires trying to break free of my control.

The rest was what Dad would call giving it up to God. You do everything you know how to do, but eventually death catches up to you. I thought of Chela, and felt sad for her. Dad reached out instinctively, his arm planted across my chest, trying to hold me in my seat the way he had when I was a child.

The roar of Carlyle's brakes sounded like an approaching hurricane.

One . . . two . . . three . . . We were still on the road. As my life's purpose narrowed to controlling my car, images came to me in flashes, obstacles to avoid: The guardrail alarmingly close on the driver's side. A cloud of smoke from Carlyle's brakes. The underbelly of Carlyle's Jeep as he capsized on the road, spinning toward the rocks.

In my rearview mirror, I saw Carlyle's overturned Jeep spinning, but I had to look back at the road. A *crash* behind us told me how hard the impact was. The Jeep seemed to bounce, and more skidding told me that Carlyle's ride wasn't over. This time, he was headed toward the cliff.

As I tried to fight myself out of a skid, an oncoming Winnebago appeared suddenly from around the corner, in my path. The appearance of another car had always been inevitable, but that might have been the worst time, and the worst kind. I forgot Carlyle's troubles while I tried to resolve my own.

The Winnebago's driver gave it up to God, too. He braked, bringing a much-more-unwieldy vehicle to a controlled stop. She must have figured it was my job to evade her, or we were both fucked. The strategy paid off: I steered well clear of the Winnebago and stopped as close to the rocks as I could, pulled halfway out of the traffic lane.

If Dad hadn't been with me, I might have parked across the lanes to stop the traffic flow—but my first priority was to make sure that he wasn't having a heart attack. Dad was breathing in slightly hitching gasps. I don't know how long he had been breathing like that, but it was the first time I could afford to notice.

"Dad?" I said.

He waved me away. "I'm . . . all right." He breathed again, wincing.

"No chest pain?"

"No. Just . . . startled."

I wasn't sure I could believe him, but I didn't have a choice. I glanced around the bend, and I saw Carlyle's SUV rocking on the cliff behind us. The barrier had already been torn, but either Carlyle's willpower or pure fortune had kept him from plummeting down.

But gravity was doing its best.

Shit. The Jeep was going to fall. I had just started running toward the Jeep when I heard something metallic groan, and the Jeep tumbled down with a horrific bounce.

No way they'll survive that, I thought. *No way.*

Carlyle had whiplashed my emotions again: A moment before, I'd been wishing him dead; now I was praying for his survival.

The height was dizzying when I reached the edge of the cliff—I have a touch of vertigo, which kicks in at inconvenient times. I came close to swaying. I saw the Jeep right away, to my left: It had landed on a wide ledge twenty feet down rather than plummeting down another thirty.

The nose of the Jeep was upturned, facing me, one broken headlight still bright, one out. The glass in the windshield had broken out entirely. Both airbags had deployed, so I couldn't see Carlyle or his passenger behind the massive balloons.

And it was scalable. Steep at one point, but I could get down there without a rope.

Was the Jeep going to burn? The hood was steaming, but I didn't smell gasoline, and I didn't see smoke. Carlyle was luckier than he deserved.

I turned and ran back toward the parked Winnebago, waving my arms. The driver had climbed out, a portly woman wearing a fishing cap in hunter's camo.

"Oh, my goodness!" she said. "I just saw them go over—"

"Do you have flares?" I said.

"Of course I do." She sounded almost offended by the question.

"Put them out—we need to make sure nobody else goes over," I said, then I pointed out my Beemer, which was unrecognizable from twenty yards. "Make sure nobody hits that car. My dad's in there. He can't walk."

"Oh, my goodness!" she said again, in shock. Her cheeks flushed bright red.

I turned to run back toward Carlyle's Jeep.

"Could he still be alive?" the woman called after me.

"Flares!" I said. I wanted her to keep her mind on my car and my father.

I half slid, half climbed down a few choice rocks to make it to the ledge that had prevented Carlyle Simms from exploding at the bottom of the ravine. Now that I was closer to the car, I thought I might smell smoke. I should have brought the fire extinguisher out of my trunk, I realized. *Except that Carlyle smashed your trunk into an accordion, so I guess that's on him.*

The Jeep had reached a secure berth, I realized, its rear nestled firmly between boulders that weren't going anywhere. It didn't look like I was in danger of tumbling down with him.

I reached the driver's side first, and my illusions were lost.

Carlyle's empty eyes stared from a bloody mess of crushed flesh and bone. His head lolled at an angle damned near perpendicular to his spine. The driver's-side front window was spiderwebbed, cratered, and splattered red. Someone hadn't been wearing his seatbelt. So much for his interview.

I heard a groan. Another glance at Carlyle's face reminded me that the groan wasn't from him. I squeezed between the hood of the car and the rocks to make it to the passenger side.

Lee Quarry was groggy but alive. Not surprisingly, his seat belt was buckled. His face didn't have a scratch, but when he saw mine, his eyes went wide. I tried to forget how he had put his hands on

Chela, but suddenly I was pissed about my car again. And my father's breathing.

Lee's head was already lolling, but his eyes widened with panic as they focused on me.

"Naw, man, wait—" He tried to wriggle away, but he was trapped behind his airbag and too disoriented to free himself from his seat belt.

"Let me see your hands," I said.

"Shit, man—my arm's broken!"

"Carlyle's neck is broken. Something really bad could happen to you before the ambulance gets here. Why'd you try to kill me?"

Lee raised his arms over the airbag, within my sight. His left arm was misshapen, dangling lower, but he kept it raised with gritted teeth. They weren't called Heat for nothing.

"Man, that was Carlyle," he said, fighting a sob. "Is his neck really broke?"

"Let's just say you'll save a stamp this Christmas," I told him. "Answer my question."

Lee fought to compose himself, blinking several times as he stared into my eyes. He knew his life was in my hands; if he'd been in my place, he would have killed me already.

"OK, man, look . . ." Lee said. "Carlyle said he was gonna follow you, that's all. I never thought that crazy motherfucker would try to crash into you. Shit—he almost got me killed!"

Funny how the survivor is always the innocent one.

"Why's Carlyle following me?" I said.

"He said you were trying to trash T.D.," he said. "Trying to get all that shit with Chantelle stirred up again."

"Did Carlyle help T.D. kill Chantelle?"

A light flared way back in Lee's eyes. "Man, I don't know," Lee said. "I wasn't there."

"But you know they did it. As close as you guys were? You're full of shit. Even if they didn't say a word, you knew as soon as you saw them. You could see it."

Lee stayed firm, his features hardening. "Like I said, I do not know. I was not there. Can you let me out of this damn car before we blow up?"

"Did Carlyle kill T.D.?"

"Fuck you, man. Carlyle loved T.D."

"Then who killed him?"

"Shit, if I knew that, he'd be on the news. Let me the fuck out of here, man."

"What do you know about Wallace Rubens?"

"Who?"

No light in Lee's eyes that time; the name didn't mean anything to him. But Wallace Rubens had meant something to Carlyle—his face had told me that when he came to my house.

Dammit. Carlyle might have been my best chance to find out who killed T.D., and the son of a bitch had just made me kill him. That might not be exactly what happened, but that was the way it felt. The smell of Carlyle's blood made me feel sick to my stomach.

I opened Lee's door and helped him out of the Jeep.

Above us, the police were waiting.

I was relieved when Melanie picked up her phone. "You got something?" she said, anxious. Melanie sounded desperate for me to finish it, somehow. Make the pain stop.

The rain was back to a drizzle. A trickle of traffic passed as a Ventura County sheriff's deputy officiated from the center lane. By then, the Winnebago was long gone. I watched as my father's gurney was lifted into the back of the Lifeline ambulance that was parked as close to the shoulder as it could get. Dad lay staring straight up at the sky, full of resignation. He looked smaller than he had seemed in my car. We hadn't expected to have to talk to doctors today.

"Bad news," I told Melanie. "I'd tell you in person, but I don't want you to hear it on TV."

Melanie's line filled with silent dread. Her silence was a torrent of questions.

I told her Carlyle was dead, and how he'd attacked me and my father on the road.

"No!" she said. "Ten, no." A plea to confess I was only joking.

"It doesn't mean he killed your cousin, but it sure doesn't look good," I said. "We knew this might be coming, Mel."

The wheels to my father's gurney rattled across the ambulance floor. The white-shirted attendant waved at me to climb in behind him. The only thing worse than taking Dad to a doctor was riding with him in an ambulance. I climbed in, swinging myself inside with the handrail with one hand, on my phone with the other. I knew the drill by then.

Chest pains don't mean it's a heart attack, I wanted to say as I stared down at Dad's face, chiseled tight as he tried not to sink into fear. If I fussed over Dad, it only scared him. I thought it might be better for Dad if I stayed on the phone. Casual. Just a routine trip to the hospital.

"Maybe you should call his girlfriend," I told Melanie. I remembered how protective Alma had been of her home; the honor-roll bumper sticker on her car. "In case Lee doesn't."

"Oh, God," she said, her realization deepening. "Alma and the boys! And these kids. He's Uncle Carlyle to them. They just saw him at their father's funeral yesterday."

"We'll talk more about this soon. I'm on my way to the hospital."

"I'm sorry—are you all right?" Melanie sounded deeply concerned. "Your dad?"

"We're lucky to be alive, so we're fine. I'll call you later. I'm really sorry, Mel."

"God, I'm sorry, too," she said, soothing me. Somehow, Melanie and I couldn't keep from crashing into each other. It was starting to bruise.

In the Ojai Valley Community Hospital emergency room, the doctor sounded certain that the chest pains were only Dad's recurring angina, not a heart attack. Sure enough, after my father got a dose of nitro, the pain went away. Still, it reminded me too much of waking in the middle of an old, ugly dream.

Marcela arrived with Chela by five o'clock. Marcela conferred by phone with my cousin Reggie and agreed that Dad should stay overnight for observation. It pays to have medical experts close to the family.

Since Dad wanted to go home, he wasn't speaking to us before long. In some ways, the episode on the road with Carlyle Simms was buried by its aftermath at the hospital. Marcela sat beside Dad's bed, holding his hand openly, maybe for the first time, but he was so angry that he barely looked at her. Dad's face was drawn and weary. He hated hospitals. To me, he looked like a scared old man again. Even Marcela's chiding and Chela's cooing couldn't loosen up Dad's face.

For once, the television was turned off. The news isn't as entertaining when the top story is about you. For dinner, Chela, Marcela, and I ate burgers from the cafeteria—hospital cafeterias generally have fast food to give patients and staff alike comfort from stress. We stayed in Dad's room until nine, when he head nurse insisted that regulations required us to leave.

"I'll be back in the morning, Dad," I told him, standing over his bed.

"Foolishness," Dad said, just to make sure his point had been made. He wanted to sleep in his own bed. He didn't want to be alone. The way Dad refused to look me in the eye cut more than it usually did, but I understood. My ear buzzed, at the same instant I remembered the sight of the ravine spinning past my windshield.

"I'm sorry about all of this. Truly. I love you, man." As if I said it every day.

Dad looked straight past me, so I gave up and headed for his door. Finally, Dad called after me. "LAPD will . . . call. Nelson. Be . . . careful."

Dad's way of saying *I love you, too.*

And he had a point. In Ventura County, I was only a witness in a traffic fatality. There was no point in pressing attempted murder charges against a dead man, so I let it go as road rage. But to Lieutenant Rodrick Nelson, I was suddenly a fly in his ointment. A loose end in the T.D. Jackson case. Nelson knew my number; I was surprised he hadn't called me already.

As I was walking out of the door, I got a text message. CAN YOU COME BY UNCLE EM'S TONITE? NO MATTER HOW LATE? Melanie. Shit. It was late, and I was miles beyond tired.

"We better watch out," Marcela muttered suddenly. "Reporters ahead."

She was right; a gaggle of paparazzi with huge cameras were making their way down the hospital's hall, trying to catch a glimpse of the people who had walked away from the accident that killed Carlyle Simms. Lee was in a nearby room, too, so the entire cast was in place.

"Leeches," Chela said, as if she'd been a starlet all her life.

"This way," I said, and we ducked into an elevator.

A long way around took us to the parking lot. I searched for my car under the lights, until I realized it was on its way to the scrapyard, except for a few things I'd saved from the trunk. My car was gone. I'd driven that car for fifteen years, and she'd always made me happy. If I hadn't already been numb, I would have felt grief. Compared to the memory of my lost car, Marcela's Rabbit looked puny and sad.

"Hey, Ten."

The voice behind me was friendly, but I didn't have any friends nearby. Besides, I knew that voice well; I had just heard him on CNN that weekend.

"It's late, Lieutenant Nelson," I said. "I thought supervisors don't get paid OT."

Lieutenant Rodrick Nelson hadn't come straight from his office, because he was wearing only a black pullover and khakis, not his usual Brooks Brothers routine. Still, with his badge and gun in plain view, Nelson stank so badly of *cop* that Chela practically dived into Marcela's car. Marcela climbed into her driver's seat, wary, too. But she didn't start the engine.

"Maybe you can answer a question for me," Nelson said, standing about an inch beyond acceptable personal space. He had two inches of height on me. "Why does your name keep coming up in my cases?"

"What cases, Lieutenant?"

"Afrodite. And T.D. Jackson."

"His suicide?"

"Don't be too smart, Hardwick." It seemed to hurt his mouth to use my father's name in reference to me. He leaned close enough for me to smell his dinner. Men only stand that close to each other when they're ready to fight, and you can't win a fight with a cop: They have too many beefy, armed brothers and sisters and cousins in blue, all waiting to pile on.

"If you think I'm gonna believe that you and your dead homeboy just happened to be hanging out in Ojai today, you've confused me for someone with his head up his ass," Nelson said. "Lee's a shitty liar. What were you and Carlyle doing up here?"

"Just taking a drive with my father, Lieutenant."

He smiled at me, almost a leer. "If there's a word that describes Richard Allen Hardwick, it's *forthright*. I watched him shoot his career in the balls every other week because he never mastered the art of bullshit. So I'll go see what Preach has to say about your drive."

So far, Dad had been spared a police interview because of his health, and I'd hoped to convince him to corroborate my version of the crash. Lee and I had come up with a simple story of bad tempers, with Carlyle at fault. Would Dad lie to his own protégé's face? I wished I could explain to Lieutenant Nelson that his old mentor had just suffered a hell of a day and didn't need the aggravation of an interrogation, but that would only prod him on. Nelson's tenacity was what Dad had loved most about him.

"So now you want your visit?" I said with an acid smile. "Took you a minute, considering how much you owe him. But better late than never, I guess."

Nelson's face told me I'd drawn blood. I'd been waiting a long time to tell Rodrick Nelson what I thought of his cowardice; he hadn't visited my father once. Nelson and I barely knew each other, but we knew where to land the punches. Dad was our best weapon.

"How were you involved with T.D. Jackson, Ten?" Nelson said, his voice softening as if to say *Tell me now so I can help you out of this.* Nelson tried to be both good cop and bad cop. It wasn't a good fit for him.

If I'd really fucked up, Nelson had some kind of evidence to arrest me for something bogus. If not, I wasn't going to stick around. I climbed into Marcela's car, closed my door, and rolled my window down. I nodded to Marcela, and she started the engine.

"Let him get some sleep, Nelson. They call it a hospital for a reason."

Nelson is one of the biggest assholes I've ever known, but he somehow gives the impression that if you dig deep enough through the granite, you'll strike a vein of warm flesh. He knew better than to bother Dad that night. But it would depend on how important he thought it was.

When Nelson leaned close to the window, I heard Chela shrink back into her seat. *Cool it, girl*, I thought. *To him, you look like Marcela's daughter.* I'd been avoiding official scrutiny on the matter of Chela for more than a year, and Nelson would be scrutiny of the worst kind.

But Nelson barely glanced at Chela or Marcela. They were invisible. He had eyes only for me, his hand clamped to my door. "You better come see me at 10 A.M. sharp, smart-ass, or I'm slapping you with obstruction. For every ten minutes you're late, I'll find something else to charge you with. I can get very fucking creative."

Marcela looked taken aback. She sat frozen, as if he was addressing her. Nelson wanted to humiliate me in front of my family. My philosophy is that you can't humiliate a man without his permission. But I kept my thoughts to myself.

"And you'll back off Dad tonight?" I said.

"I didn't say that. This wasn't a negotiation."

I would have said *Fuck you* before *Yessir*, so I opted for silence. *Shit.* My life was messy enough without cops. Nelson was as a better interrogator than I was an actor, and his instincts were usually sharp, just as Dad had always said. I didn't fool Nelson, somehow. Besides, depending on what Dad told him, I might be charged with obstruction no matter what. I didn't think Dad would sell me out, but he was tired. And he was Dad. He might make a mistake.

I definitely had.

Marcela backed out of the parking space, careful to avoid Nelson, who stood there like an oak watching me, trying to figure it out. I wondered how long it would take.

There was stone silence in the car as we pulled out of the hospital driveway. Marcela kept checking her rearview mirror, as if she expected police lights to flash behind us. I held my breath every time her eyes left the dark, curvy road.

"Slow down," I said more than once. I almost asked her to let me drive.

We didn't talk about Dad and his angina. We were telling ourselves we were sure he would be fine by morning. We never discussed getting a hotel room in Ojai overnight. Dad would be fine. We worked it out in our own heads as we left him behind.

I couldn't wait to get to bed, but I dreaded the morning. The last time I'd met with Lieutenant Nelson, I'd been handcuffed in an interrogation room. A cold one. I'd been lucky to walk back outside again.

"Ten?" Chela said quietly after we were on the road. "Is that cop gonna arrest you?"

Telepathy. An optimistic lie came to the surface first, but then I remembered that I was trying to tell the truth whenever I could. It's a harder habit.

"He'd like to," I said.

"That's nonsense," Marcela said. "That man came to your *house*. Tried to kill you today!" I wondered how much Dad had told Marcela after Carlyle's visit Saturday. The circle of people who were privy to my business was getting larger and larger.

"There's a little more to it than that, Marcela," I said.

"Ten's on a big case," Chela explained with pride. "But you can't talk about it."

"T.D. Jackson?" Marcela's voice was needlessly hushed.

I only nodded and looked at my watch, too tired for conversation. I was sick of T.D. Jackson's name. It was after nine, and we still had a long drive. It would be late when we got home, but my second car was waiting. I had to make another trip. Alone.

Lieutenant Nelson wanted to see me in the morning, so I had no choice.

I had to see Judge Jackson that night.

TWENTY

IT WAS MIDNIGHT. I hadn't slept well in days, so I might as well have sleepwalked my way to Judge Jackson's door. Even with my feet on the concrete porch, I could feel the earth moving beneath me. Images of the road in Ojai strobed across my mind.

I would be all right in the morning, but I was still rattled that night.

Melanie answered the door, and the ray of concern across her face soothed my nerves. She grabbed my arm, cupping it at the elbow, and electricity jittered through me. "Ten, I'm so glad you're all right," she said. "And your dad?"

"He's fine." Short and sweet. I rarely talk about my personal life on a job, if I can help it.

"Thank God. I'm too stunned to think right now. It's like we stepped into Hell."

I was about to offer her a merciful shoulder to lean on when I noticed a white man standing just inside the foyer, waiting with his hands thrust into his pockets. He was taller than he'd looked in his photo. Simon. He looked tired and hollow-eyed. I was so off my game that I drew away from Melanie a little too hastily when I saw him. Simon was too polite to be obvious, but he must have seen something in my face. Either Melanie hadn't noticed my gaffe, or she was too upset to care. They both looked miserable, but I hoped it would pass.

Melanie closed the door behind me, explaining that we had to keep our voices down because the children were sleeping upstairs. "We haven't told them yet," she said. "I don't know how I can. He was Uncle C."

"It's all right," Simon said, enfolding her in his arms. "An hour at a time. Let's get you home." Simon had a take-charge demeanor without sounding bossy. Melanie forgot to introduce us, so Simon held out his hand to me. "Simon Gadbury. I'm Melanie's fiancé."

And don't forget it, he managed to say with his eyes, without losing his polite smile.

I envied him, but I liked him. He seemed to want to take care of her.

"Melanie felt she had to wait for you," he said, almost accusing.

"I want my briefing first," Melanie told me, ignoring Simon's chide. "Then I'll take you upstairs so you can talk to Uncle Em."

Great. Now I had to go through it twice.

"Upstairs?"

"His room," Melanie said. "He's had the flu. I'm sure it's stress. Sunday was . . ." She didn't finish, avoiding her memories of the horrors T.D.'s funeral had held. "It takes a toll."

"I hate to disturb Mrs. Jackson this late, Mel," I said. "Can't he come down?"

"Her room's clear across the house," Melanie said. "She's been in bed since nine thirty."

If separate bedrooms were Melanie's family tradition, Simon was in trouble. Maybe it was the secret to a long, happy union, but I didn't think so. I wondered how long the Jacksons had been sleeping apart, and why.

"Tell me what happened," Melanie said. "The news said it was road rage. . . . ?"

We sat on the kitchen barstools while I described my encounters with Carlyle Simms, beginning at my house on Saturday and ending on the 150. Stripped of needless details, it took only five minutes, but it felt more like years.

Melanie nodded with whispers of "okay, okay" every once in a while, but was mostly silent. She winced when I described how the Cherokee had flipped over the barrier, her eyes rapt with the horrific vision. By the time I finished, her face seemed to have aged. It suddenly occurred to me that Melanie probably had a fling with Carlyle once, or maybe more than a fling. I saw something dimming in her face.

"Mel, that's enough," Simon said, cutting me off when I got to the airbag. He looked at me, hoping for an ally. "She never sleeps. Soon she'll be sick like her uncle. What she needs most right now is a bed."

Melanie looked irritated, but she stood. "All right, we'll go. I'll just take him upstairs." Her voice was hoarse.

I followed Melanie's ghostly walk across the house to the staircase, careful not to make a sound. Neither of us spoke on the stairs. Melanie pointed out two rooms closest to the landing, both with closed doors, and raised her finger to her mouth: *shhhh*. Colorful crafts taped to the doors told me that the children slept there; one of three houses they had called home. Children that wounded would have a hard time, and mothering them wouldn't be easy. Melanie's life would be as chaotic as mine, I realized. Maybe more.

Upstairs, the Jacksons preened a bit more—this wing had marble tile and an impressive four-foot replica of Rodin's *Thinker* beneath recessed lighting at the end of the hall. The nude sculpture sat in perpetual thought, elbow resting between his chin and his knee. Melanie led me toward the statue.

A bedroom door beside it was cracked open, and I heard the very faint sound of television news. Judge Jackson's room. With a wing separating us from the other rooms, Melanie felt free to pick up my hand and hold it between her palms. Her skin seemed fevered, or maybe it only felt that way to me.

"I'm glad you weren't hurt," she said. Her voice was so soft that I had to aim my good ear. "That's the only good news."

"I really wanted to find him alive, Mel. I swear."

She nodded. "Thank you. That helps."

I knew the judge was waiting, but Melanie held on. I wanted to tell her that Simon seemed like a nice guy, but it didn't feel like the right thing to say while she was holding my hand.

"I heard from your agent," she said. "I'll call you about your lawsuit."

Lynda Jewell and FilmQuest Studios resided on a faraway planet that night. "Don't worry about that. You're busy with life right now."

"No, I want to, Ten," she said. "Working helps. So I'll be in touch. I still owe you."

Sometimes two people meet in the wrong place, at the wrong time. It happened with me and Serena, and with me and Alice long before. I was beginning to realize it might have happened with me and April. It's a feeling you notice, an instinctive yearning for something that seems close enough to touch, but is still out of reach. It's best not to take it too seriously, even if the feeling is as real as your own skin. If it can't work, it won't.

I gently slipped my hand away. "Simon seems like a really decent guy." It blurted out by itself. I don't like to sleep with married women;

I've *slept with* too many. And I didn't like the memory of how easily Melanie made me throw away better judgment.

"He's more than decent," Melanie said. She smiled, reflecting on the man downstairs. "He's a natural with the kids. And he's crazy about me."

"Of course he is."

She mustered a full smile, a treat of white teeth. I hadn't known Melanie long, but I was glad we were friends again. By then, Simon had come up to find her. Simon's no fool. He stuck his head around the corner from the hall near the stairs, waving to be sure we saw him. My last gaze with Melanie was cut short. I was glad he hadn't seen her holding my hand.

Melanie finally knocked lightly on the door. "Uncle Em?"

"Send him in," the judge called.

Judge Jackson was sitting at the edge of his bed in faded slippers and crimson satin pajamas suitable for company. The furniture was Louis XIV, masculine and mannered. His walls were covered in framed prints and oil paintings, many of museum quality. One was a dark, richly hued painting of two spotted dogs staring each other down beside the carcass of a dead hare; the image brought T.D. and Carlyle to mind. GUSTAVE CORBET, a placard beneath the painting read, with a notation that the original was on display at New York's Metropolitan Museum of Art. Detailed. Judge Jackson was a true art lover.

And a book lover. There were more bookshelves in his bedroom than in his office. No legal books: only encyclopedias, classics, and history volumes. In a glance, I noticed books by Colin Powell, Thurgood Marshall, and Cornel West. From what I'd seen at T.D.'s house, Judge Jackson hadn't passed on his love of art and reading—unless I counted the magazines in T.D.'s sex drawer. Father and son had been very different.

Judge Jackson had kept a separate bedroom for years; that was obvious. There was no trace of his wife, or any family. I couldn't even spot any photos of T.D. This bedroom belonged to Judge Jackson alone.

His eyes were bloodshot. He looked like a man who was up later than he wanted to be; I'm sure I looked the same way. "I'm sorry," I said. "The message said no matter how late."

He nodded. "Can't be helped. Don't come too close—damn flu." He coughed into a woven handkerchief and slipped it into his robe's pocket. "Close my door, please."

On his television set, eight miniature screens from news channels played at once. Most of the channels were flashing pictures of T.D. Jackson, Carlyle Simms, and the accident scene outside of Ojai. A glimpse of the ravine made my stomach curdle. I stood with my back to the television screen.

"Drink?" Judge Jackson asked. He pointed out the minibar beside his fireplace.

"Better not." A drink would knock me unconscious.

His sigh sounded like it hurt him to breathe. "It was rough out there, looks like."

"Yessir. Pretty rough."

"Mel says Captain Hardwick was with you."

"Our first real drive together since his stroke." I don't know why I told him that; maybe because he knew Dad. "But he's all right."

"Thank the Lord Jesus. That would have been too heavy on my conscience."

His conscience would be heavy anyway. Judge Jackson looked like a man who was up later than he wanted to be, and I'm sure I looked the same way. I took a seat in the armoire across from where he sat at the edge of his bed, his feet side by side on his rug, tense but prepared.

"Where did they meet?" I asked him.

"Pop Warner ball. Best friends from a long time back." His voice fractured, and he sighed that terrible sigh again. His lungs mewled. "Their friends dictate all. Remember that, if you have children. Carlyle had a quality—I see it on the bench every day—where he didn't understand the need to play fair. To do *right*." He sounded so offended, I imagined he might also be talking about Hankins, an old friend who had surely disappointed him.

Judge Jackson went on: "It is dangerous to forget how important it is in life to be fair. It sounds like such a simple thing, but without the appearance, if not the presence of fair play, society crumbles. Yes, I came to view Carlyle as family over time, but I used to tell T.D. to remember Carlyle was part wolf. It was the way he was raised—an abusive mother, that sort of thing. I just never thought . . ." He stopped, coughing. He sipped from a mug he held in his lap.

An abusive mother. That would have explained Carlyle's rage toward women. T.D. had been pissed at Chantelle when she deserted him for another man, but he'd saved his greater rage for her lover. T.D. had made Chantelle watch while he beat Arturo to death, then Carlyle had shot her in the head while she screamed. Teamwork.

"I can come back in the morning, sir."

He shook his head, firm. "No. I want to go to bed knowing. Tell me."

I wasn't sure what I planned to tell him. I remembered Mrs. Jackson asking me in the garden not to tell her husband anything he didn't need to know. But there was no such thing. Judge Jackson was paying me to tell him what no one else could.

"Sir, I think Carlyle and T.D. were responsible for Chantelle's death. Together. I spoke to a witness who heard Carlyle confess his involvement—"

"Then it was *he*," Judge Jackson said, his face clouding. "Carlyle killed her, not T.D.!" He came to his feet, almost forgetting not to raise his voice. He picked up a remote and switched on soft music to mask our voices. Miles Davis's *Kind of Blue* played, sultry and lovely, a staple in any jazz aficionado's collection. I hoped Judge Jackson wouldn't deplore the sound of Miles after our meeting that night. I hoped Miles wouldn't always remind him.

"I have to agree with T.D.'s criminal defense on this," I said. "The job was too big for one man. They had to restrain two adults, and Salvador was a former probation officer, so he might not have gone down easy. I don't know who goaded who, or who wanted it more, but T.D. and Carlyle did it together. T.D.'s blood was found at the murder scene. The defense poked holes in the blood evidence, but we both know it bolsters my theory. If you press T.D.'s friend Lee, you might get something. I bet Alma suspects, too. Now that T.D. and Carlyle are both dead, they might be more willing to tell the truth."

Judge Jackson closed his eyes. I doubted that I'd said anything his Evil Voice hadn't told him all along. He had known what he might learn from the time he hired me.

Melanie hadn't asked me if I thought Carlyle killed T.D., I realized. That was odd, given how much we had focused on him before the funeral. Maybe she was planning to hear the story from her uncle—or maybe she didn't want to hear it at all.

I paused a moment and went on: "Murder forms a lifetime bond, Judge Jackson."

The judge's eyes flew open, as if I were a prophet. "What do you mean?"

"There's no statute of limitations. It can come back to haunt you at any time. Let's assume neither of them had ever killed anyone before. T.D. had a stressful trial, and it was about to start all over again. It might have brought them closer together, or it might have driven them apart. Maybe one of them had more remorse. Maybe T.D. wanted to confess."

I didn't believe that for a minute. More likely, T.D. hadn't wanted to take the fall by himself—but it was a prettier picture to paint for his father. Whatever the reason, whatever had happened and whatever was *going* to happen, it was easy to imagine Carlyle and T.D. with plenty to argue about.

Judge Jackson nodded, mulling the scenario over. His son had fallen, but he had died seeking redemption. The judge's loose cheeks trembled with the thought of T.D.'s courage.

"We told you there's a bullet hole in the wall in the room where T.D. died. Maybe Carlyle came inside that night. They went to his study—T.D. sitting at his desk, and Carlyle in the easy chair. Carlyle got to T.D.'s gun. He kept one in his desk. They struggled. A bullet went wild. The next one didn't. Carlyle's secret is safe." The longer I thought about it, the better it sounded. Maybe Randolph Dwyer hadn't led me anywhere except back to Carlyle.

"Then you came along," Judge Jackson said. He was following the scenario just fine. "He heard you were asking questions . . ."

"I spooked him. He panicked. I'm not a cop, so he came straight at me."

Judge Jackson stared toward the fireplace's gray ashes. The room was slightly chilly, but he hadn't started a fire. I saw artificial logs neatly stacked in the bin, so I squatted beside the fireplace door and chose a meaty one to burn. The whole house was too cold.

At least I could grant one of his wife's requests, I thought. I could give him a way out.

"You could get all the way down to the sticky bottom of it, Judge Jackson. Maybe you could learn all the ugly details," I said, easing him down as gently as I could. I laid the last words down like a baby at his feet: "Or, you could leave it alone. They're all gone."

"So what's the point?" he agreed, nearly whispering. "There's no point."

The log was smoking, and a bed of sparks billowed into flame. I love to watch fires born. I hoped we were both through the worst of the night.

"There's one other possibility," I said. "It's remote. And it doesn't change my belief about what happened to Chantelle. But it may mean something else happened to T.D."

"Maybe Carlyle didn't kill him?"

"It's possible. Maybe today only had to do with Chantelle, and he was afraid I knew."

Judge Jackson nodded. "We'd all rather think it wasn't Carlyle. That cuts from a different direction. I'd never have believed it could feel worse . . . but there's a line from Shakespeare, in *Titus Andronicus*, when Aaron the Moor boasts of his evil deeds: 'Oft I have digg'd up dead men from their graves, / And set them upright at their dear friends' doors, / Even when their sorrows were almost forgot . . .' "

His voice trailed off, and he drained his mug. With everything else failing him, he was trying to find solace in his mind.

"Judge Jackson, what do you know about Wallace Rubens? Isn't he down in Florida now?"

His lips fell apart. He stared at me without blinking so long, I wondered if he was having what is euphemistically referred to as "a senior moment." "What about Rubens?" he said finally.

"He's your old teammate. Heat." Judge Jackson nodded vaguely, but offered nothing. His silence was stark and impenetrable, so I went on. "He may have done some work for Donald Hankins. Intimidation. Maybe more. You probably heard rumors."

"Where is this going?" he said.

"If that's true . . . it's not impossible to believe Rubens might have done another favor for Hankins."

The judge broke eye contact. *That hit home.*

"They had a lot of history," I continued. "What was their relationship like back in 1967?"

Judge Jackson sat up so abruptly that his mug fell and cracked on the Moroccan rug. Judge Jackson's fingers trembled while I helped him pick up the larger pieces. Several others were too small to collect; he would have to walk carefully until it was cleaned up.

Judge Jackson had barely flinched when I told him I thought his son was a murderer—but when I asked him about the Sunshine Bowl, I'd shaken him up. The name Wallace Rubens carried weight and power; everyone I met who'd known him was afraid to talk about him.

"It was long ago," he said curtly. "Another time."

"I've noticed that no one likes to talk about that time—especially the Sunshine Bowl. I was in Ojai to see Randolph Dwyer today, but he's not the type to live in the past either."

Judge Jackson's gaze looked eager to ask me what I'd discussed with Randolph Dwyer. Instead, he propped himself up on one knee and groaned to stand. He threw the pieces of the broken mug he held in his trash. He paused as if he was tired, then he wiped away shards of glass from his palms.

Judge Jackson sat at a small desk and pulled open a drawer. Inside, he found two thick manila envelopes. Heavy. He tossed them to the floor, atop the slivers from the broken mug.

"I promised fifty thousand for a name and a lead. You've given me more than I asked for, but I'm afraid I can only pay what we agreed. The balance is all there."

The scent of money made it easier not to care about the rest of the story. If the secret was as old as the 1960s, they had kept quiet a long time. I hadn't even been born. It was none of my business.

"If it was Rubens," I said anyway, "he might pose a public hazard. It may not be his first time. So there's a good chance it won't be his last."

Judge Jackson nodded. "Thank you again. I couldn't be happier with your service, Mr. Hardwick. Please forward the repair bill for your car."

Unfortunately, there are some things money can't fix. I lingered just inside the judge's bedroom door, my voice more hushed because I was closer to the hall and the sleeping children.

"This has nothing to do with you, but I'm telling you for the sake of candor. Carlyle's stunt today brought me under Lieutenant Rodrick Nelson's nose. He wants to talk to me tomorrow, so I'll be inside RHD. He has no grounds for anything against me—that I know of." It was an all-important clarification. If the judge was planning any unhappy surprises for Rubens in retaliation, he'd be smarter to think twice.

Judge Jackson only blinked. "I would hope that's a problem Captain Hardwick could help you solve." Meaning: *Don't even THINK about mentioning me.*

"Of course," I said, wondering what Dad had told Nelson at the hospital. The thought of Nelson perched over my father's bed like a vulture infuriated me.

Judge Jackson closed his desk drawer. "You were hired with certain preconditions."

"I remember."

"I'm sure you know how to conduct yourself."

"Yessir, I do."

But he was no longer listening, his glassy eyes vacant.

Judge Emory Jackson had already forgotten my name.

TWENTY-ONE

TUESDAY, OCTOBER 28

I felt eyes following me as a wide-hipped female detective nearly as tall as me led me through division headquarters to Lieutenant Nelson's office. It reminded me of that last day on the set of *Homeland*, except that these stares were from people wearing guns with bullets, not blanks.

It's not a good way to start the day.

I almost nodded when I saw Hal Dolinski at an espresso machine, staring at me alongside a black woman I didn't know. Dolinski looked like he'd gained ten pounds since my last run-in with RHD. He'd worked with my father, and he'd helped me with inside information after I got snagged in Serena's murder, but Dolinksi's face showed nothing but blank curiosity. He was keeping far away from this one. Casually, he refilled his coffee mug before I was even out of sight.

I bet Dolinski's the one who copied that murder book. The nagging thought came back.

Nelson's office was larger than I expected, with a halfway-decent view of the business end of the city of Los Angeles, away from the tourist spots. His office was empty, so I made a quick assessment: It had a lived-in quality my father had never cared about: certificates, plaques and photos. I saw a photo of Nelson with an attractive woman who looked Japanese, alongside two girls and a boy so beautiful that they could have launched a modeling agency. During an argument years before, my father had told me I didn't have an ounce of what Lieutenant Nelson had. The photo of Nelson's family reminded me of how true that was.

Nelson arrived within thirty seconds of me, closing his door behind us.

"Are you a problem for me?" Nelson asked, taking off a jacket he was careful not to wrinkle as he hung it on the coatrack behind his door. His badge gleamed silver from his belt.

"I'm sure as hell not trying to be."

"What happened in Ojai, Tennyson?" So far, he sounded civil.

"A drunk asshole nearly ran me off the road." Carlyle's blood toxicology might not show drugs or alcohol in his blood, but I figured the odds were good.

"A drunk asshole who just happened to be T.D. Jackson's best friend. The week after T.D.'s death."

"A suicide, from what I hear."

Nelson walked close enough to loom over me in my chair. His eyes wrestled with his impulses to do me bodily harm. "Are you fucking with my case?"

"What case, Lieutenant?" I said. "You said it's open-and-shut. Didn't I see you on TV?"

I'd lectured myself for twenty minutes on what to say and what not to say, but something about Nelson always made me ad-lib. Nelson's lips pursed. He studied my eyes long enough to figure out that I knew something.

When Nelson sighed down on me, I smelled coffee on his breath. The uninitiated might think the brother would be grateful I'd helped him solve Serena's murder, but that's not how it works at LAPD. With territorial bickering between squads, divisions, and agencies, cops have zero tolerance for outsiders. Besides the threat of making real cops look bad, a do-gooding citizen or private dick can blow a case and get real cops killed.

Except that we both knew Nelson was already blowing the case fine without me.

"I need to pick up my father, who's in the hospital up in Ojai. You might have heard."

"I did hear. He's there because his dumb-ass wannabe son put him there." The anger in his voice was genuine; he felt protective of my father. Nelson's punches landed, too.

"Well, Dad's a forthright guy, so I guess he told you everything you need to know."

Touché, asshole. Dad and I hadn't been able to talk long before I left to meet Nelson—and the telephone was always frustrating for both of us—but Dad confirmed that he hadn't said anything to link me to Carlyle. *Stick to your story,* he said.

Dad had lied to his own man. With Nelson's instincts, he probably knew it. Had to hurt.

Nelson summoned his patience, and his chest deflated, concealing his anger. Good-cop mode. "Tell me what you had on Carlyle, Ten. Did he go after you? Why?"

I shrugged. "Maybe I forgot to signal before I changed lanes."

"Did he kill Jackson?" Nelson's voice was low, a hush.

"You and your forensics experts searched the room. I'm sure you would have found evidence if someone was with T.D. when he died."

In a flash, Nelson put his finger in my face, almost touching my nose. I hate that, but I didn't dare push him away. Nelson wanted to provoke me as much as Carlyle had. If I made a mistake with Nelson, my father would die long before I stopped showering with tattooed felons.

Nelson might have been reading my mind. "If I find out you've breached my investigation, your pretty face is gonna be popular at Lancaster. You can take up your old trade—dick for cigarettes. Blow jobs for Baby Ruth bars. Just don't expect those guys to pay for your services."

Pure provocation: He knew I'd never resorted to that. Women only. I moved my head to the side, but his finger came in close again. That time, my hand twitched as I almost batted at it. "Man, that's not cool," I said.

The finger didn't move. "What did you get on Carlyle?"

"Tread marks," I said. "Stop wasting my time."

Nelson jabbed his finger toward my eye, and that time I grabbed his finger and crushed down. "Keep it out of my face," I said quietly, and then released it.

"*What's* this, you stupid shit?" Nelson said. His free hand flew toward the butt of his gun. Cops don't like to be touched. To put it mildly.

Hand still poised over his gun, Nelson stepped back and cocked his head, staring down at me with a startled gleam in his eye, wondering if he would have to shoot me. When my expression didn't change, he made an odd hissing sound.

"You just made my week," he said.

"Nelson . . ." I couldn't make myself apologize, but I knew I had to say something. "You think I'm a lowlife piece of shit. Preach deserved better. Fine. But I'm not your problem."

"You've got five seconds to tell me who is."

"I heard a rumor he might have helped T.D. that night in the garage."

"A rumor from who?"

"Just a rumor," I said. Our eyes locked, and then disengaged.

"And your interest in this is exactly what?"

"I'm working on a script," I said. "Just research."

"Research." We both knew I was lying, but he wanted to know where I was going. We were behind a closed door, and without a witness, we could still pretend I hadn't touched him.

"Since I know you searched the room where T.D. died *thoroughly* . . ." I said again, speaking slowly, "Behind the certificates . . . under the chairs. Everything. And you probably already talked to the USC kid across the street who heard *two* gunshots that night . . ." Nelson's eyebrows jumped. ". . . there's nothing else you need from me."

I didn't mention the bullet hole specifically. I still might need plausible deniability. But Nelson understood. He planted his hands on his hips, away from his gun. I felt every muscle relax; only then did I realize I'd been sitting like a stone.

"Did you contaminate my scene?" Nelson said.

"If I had, you'd never get a conviction, would you?"

"Carlyle Simms is dead."

"Road rage is a terrible thing."

Nelson's eyes were pure loathing, but not all of it was aimed at me. He hated knowing I'd found something he'd missed.

"Get out of my office," he said. "And stay away from my case."

I stood up and kept a healthy distance from him, hands in plain sight. As I backed toward Nelson's door, I felt like I was inching out of a cage. "Thanks, Nelson."

"Fuck you," he said. "This one's for Preach. You've put him through enough shit."

From the way his voice wavered when he used Dad's nickname, I guessed that Lieutenant Nelson hadn't liked what he'd seen at the hospital. *Welcome to the club*, I thought.

But I let Nelson have the last word. Hell, I agreed with him.

I practically held my breath until I was back on the sidewalk outside.

My meeting with Nelson killed the last of my curiosity, so I was glad to leave the T.D. Jackson case behind me. T.D.'s life was so noisy that it had overpowered mine, even in death.

I called Marcela and told her I would pick Dad up from the hospital in Ojai alone. She bristled when I insisted, but I wanted to have time with him. The way things looked between Dad and Marcela, I wasn't going to have him to myself very often.

Call me selfish, but this drive was ours. The last one had been interrupted.

Dad's doctor had already signed off on him, so Dad was dressed and waiting in the lobby. I got him away from that building as quickly as we could. With no maniac trying to crash into us, Casitas Vista Road was as lovely a drive as it could have been the day before. We both noticed the broken barrier where Carlyle had died, with skid marks left to mark the spot.

"I'm sorry you had to lie to Nelson," I said.

"I told him . . . I was asleep. He didn't . . . believe me. Of course."

I told Dad about my interview with Nelson, and about my conversation with Judge Jackson the night before. He was especially intrigued by Jackson's reaction to Wallace Rubens. We had been onto something, then our case had literally driven off of the road.

Dad hadn't said much else, but I hoped his anger had melted. He seemed to be in a good mood, enjoying the sunlight and the view. Any day he left a hospital was a day to celebrate.

My mood was improving, too, maybe because of the cash in the trunk of my car.

"You take . . . the money?" Dad said.

"Of course," I said, smiling. "You'll get your cut, partner."

Dad shook his head, lips pursed. "I don't want . . . that money." His eyes were resolute. The judgment in his tone hit a nerve.

"So I shouldn't have taken his money for doing what he paid me to do?"

"What was . . . the point . . . of the job?"

"He wanted a theory, a name. I gave him that."

"A . . . fantasy. A story."

"The man's dead, Dad. We both saw him drive himself off a cliff. End of the line. And these old-school Heat players are wrapped up tight, so all we get is a story. A theory. What did you expect to find?"

"Couldn't say," Dad said. "But . . . I was looking for the truth."

Vintage Dad—the self-righteous voice of my childhood always demanding the unreasonable. First he'd warned me to stay away from Nelson's case, and now he was trying to push me back in. Did he expect me to track down the widow in Toronto who thought Wallace

Rubens killed her husband? Fly to Florida to interview Rubens my-self? That was LAPD's job.

"Hey, let your boy solve it," I said. "I pointed him in the right di-rection."

"Don't play . . . games . . . with Nelson."

"He's the one playing games, Dad. If he can't stand up to pres-sure from the chief to let Jackson's murder slide, that's his problem. I'm done with it."

Dad looked back at his alluring window view. "Hankins . . . always wins."

"True. He'll be Governor Hankins before long."

Dad exhaled with a disgusted snort, his face sour. "I thought . . . I lied for a reason, Ten."

"I'm grateful, Dad, but I didn't ask you to lie. And I had nothing to do with letting Don Hankins skate past his brake-tampering prob-lem, so it's not up to me to wrap it up."

My own words surprised me. Maybe I suspected that Dad had a role in the Hankins incident in '99, even if it was just squashing spec-ulation. Nelson and I both had believed Dad was uncompromising, and now we both knew better. If I spent my life trying to mend every-one's tragedies, present *and* past, I would never have peace.

"You're right, Ten," Dad said. "I made . . . a mistake. Mis-takes . . . come back."

"This I know, sir."

The car was silent for a long time, but we didn't turn on the ra-dio to compete with the landscape. It was a clear day, and the sun was high in the noontime sky. Without T.D. Jackson to bind us, Dad and I might not talk much for a while. But now we both knew we could.

Every time T.D. Jackson's name came into my mind, I forced my-self to stare at the mountains—and his memory was gone. The same trick worked when my thoughts tried to detour to Lieutenant Nelson or Melanie. Even April. I was free! The feeling hit me all at once, and my spirits flew, making me grin as I raced toward home. My life was mine again, Dad had survived his latest brush with a hospital, and I had a mountain of cash. The week had started as a catastrophe, but it was taking a radical turn.

"... money on your taxes," Dad said, but my ear missed the first part.

For once, I didn't mind.

I surprised Chela at the curb after school, and we ended up at the Beverly Center Mall in Beverly Hills. I didn't know anything about shopping for high school formalwear, but the familiar couture shops on Rodeo Drive would have been overkill for a high school dance, no matter how much money I'd been handed by the judge. I spoiled that girl, but I had limits.

"Screw shopping for a dress, Ten," Chela said as we walked toward Bloomingdale's. The mall is funky, overlooking Hollywood. "Let's go buy a *car*."

"Tomorrow. The dance is in three days, so that's the priority. It's not just a dress—it's a whole package. Shoes, hair, accessories. It's a production." I had escorted women to more awards shows than I could count, and I knew the drill.

"You have no idea how incredibly gay you sound."

"Whatever it takes," I said, laughing. "We're gonna do this right."

I loved my new life. Chela and I were hanging out at the mall, mingling with carefree shoppers. My phone was off. *Freedom.* That was my mantra that day.

We made it inside. One threshold crossed. My eyes cross in department stores, like most men, but this was for Chela. In the formal-wear section, the collection of taffeta, chiffon, lace, and beads stopped Chela in her tracks as soon as it came into sight. The dresses radiated queenliness.

"Oh, *hell* no," Chela said.

"Just find something that works for you, Chela."

"I'll try on one dress, and we're gone."

"At least five, or don't bother. For something like this, girls try on twenty dresses sometimes, Chela."

"Yes—very shallow, lame girls. Chela does not wear dresses like these. Not in a million years."

When the store employee dashed over to see if she could help us, I waved her back. Extra pressure wouldn't help. Chela would only find something she liked on her own.

"I'll get you started with one," I said. "You pick the other four."

"I'm not going to that dance anyway."

I ignored her. She knew she was going, so that argument was stale. Instead, I headed to the racks and looked through the dresses. There were several short dresses I thought might work, but I deliber-ately chose a long chiffon gown in pastel rainbow hues, knowing she wouldn't like it. Even if I only girded her tastes in opposition to mine, at least she would be thinking about it.

"So I guess I'll have sex with him," Chela said casually. "That's what people do after these dances, right? They get all dressed up, then they get a motel room?"

"I'd be surprised if he has any plans like that."

"Who said anything about *his* plans?"

Chela was trying her best to get under my skin, but I didn't let it work. Instead, I handed her the rainbow gown. Her eyes flashed.

"You're kidding, right?" she said. "You better be kidding."

When I didn't answer, she plowed into the racks herself. Hangers squealed as she raced through the dresses. One black dress fell to the floor, but I picked it up and hung it up again.

"You said you don't know him that well," I said. "Isn't it a little early for sex?"

"I've known him since the beginning of the year. He's in my trig class, too."

I realized Chela might be serious: She'd agreed to go to the homecoming dance with Bernard, and now she was trying to figure out what else the ritual entailed. Out of faith, Chela had fashioned a new life and new rules, but she still felt lost. I kept forgetting that.

Suddenly, I saw the dress: It was a minidress, not floor-length, such a pale powder color that it was almost white. An elegant bubble dress that hung from the neck. It wouldn't fit her too snugly, so she wouldn't feel too exposed even as she would look stunning. The dress had three rows of large mock crystals at the neckline—striking but not too girly.

Chela followed my eyes. "Forget it," she said. "Cute, but it's white. Not Chela's color."

"Off-white." I held it up to her neck, and the dress leaped out against her brown skin. One of the crystals sparkled dully against her chin. Beautiful. "At least put it on the list."

She shook her head, so I backed off and hung it in plain sight. Once she'd tried on a few others, she might come back to it.

"He eats lunch with me sometimes," Chela went on. "He makes me laugh my ass off."

As I thought, she liked Bernard more than she'd let on. "So . . . you think you should have sex with him because he's funny?"

"Well, what do people wait for? He's hot and funny, we're all dressed up—why not?"

"Does he have a job?"

Chela shot me a look. "At a movie theater, like minimum wage. But he's *sixteen*. We're going to a dance, Ten—we're not getting married."

I shrugged. "When I was in high school, Dad found a box of condoms in my backpack. He told me, 'When you're ready to take care of a baby, you're ready to have sex.' "

"He told *me* to wait until I'm married."

"He didn't bother with that for me. But sure, you can try it."

"Yeah, right—as in *never*," Chela said.

"Listen, I just think you should wait for the right guy, the right time. Bernard sounds cool, he asked you to a dance, but he's not even your boyfriend."

"Well, he is now. That's what everyone's saying, thanks to you."

"Chela, I'm talking about a relationship. *Love*, right? You love him, he loves you."

"What if you just want to get laid?" Her voice was loud enough that a bookish-looking woman in the neighboring section glanced over.

I tried not to let her throw me. "So what? You still need to both be set up—you've got an education, you've got a job. Maybe then you'll be ready."

"Like I said before . . . that sounds like never. I'm going to the dressing room."

Chela had five dresses across her arm. In a glance, none of them appealed to me, but it was a start. As Chela went to the dressing rooms by herself, I wished April were home, and that Chela had gotten along with her better. April's absence felt sharp, suddenly.

"Are you gonna come out and let me see how they look?" I called after her.

"No way!"

But within five minutes, Chela shuffled back in a floral print dress so long on her that it dragged on the floor. She gazed at herself in the boutique's array of three full-length mirrors. From the colors to the pattern, the dress was hideous.

"You like that?" I said.

"No. They all suck, Ten. I told you."

"Let me see another one. That green one . . . ? "

Chela didn't move, preoccupied with staring at her shoulders from different angles. She seemed to like the spaghetti straps. Even in a terrible dress, she saw herself with fresh eyes.

"Now it's my turn to get into *your* business," Chela said to her reflection. At first, I wasn't sure she was talking to me. "I hope you won't let that cop scare you off, Ten."

Freedom. My mantra came to a halt in my head.

"Who?" I said. "Nobody's scaring me off."

She gazed at me skeptically in the mirror, addressing my reflection. "So who killed T.D. Jackson? I thought maybe that cop scared you off the case."

"Carlyle Simms probably did it, but I'm not a psychic, Chela. I had a job, I did it, I got paid. Nobody's scaring me off." I had to repeat myself. Her idea that Nelson scared me was ridiculous, almost laughable. I had to make sure she got her facts straight.

Chela turned to look me in the eye. Then she gathered the folds of her dress so she wouldn't trip on her walk back to the dressing room. "Maybe," she said. "Carlyle was an asshole, for sure. But it didn't seem like he'd killed T.D. to me."

Me either. That was the thing.

The other thing was, I had let Nelson scare me off. *Shit.* So much for my freedom.

While Chela was in the dressing room, I turned on my phone and tried April's number before it got too late in South Africa. I hadn't realized I was going to call her until I was dialing the number I'd stored on my phone. There was no answer in her room, so I left a message asking her to call me. I told her it had to do with my case. Maybe it did have to do with the case, or maybe I just wanted to talk to her. I didn't care. I wondered where she was so late.

When Chela emerged from the dressing room again, she was back in her drab school clothes. Empty-handed. "I told you I would only try on one," she said.

"You're getting a dress for this dance, Chela."

"Fine." She whipped a dress off of the rack—the same powder dress I'd pointed out to her, the one I'd thought would make her look beautiful. "This one."

"Great. Try it on." If it didn't fit later, that was an excuse to avoid the dance.

She held up the dress, studying it. "It'll fit," she said. "Chela would never wear a dress like this . . . but Lauren might, I guess."

"Who's Lauren?"

Chela gazed at me with wide-open eyes, expecting me to understand something important. Her bottom lip trembled, but she didn't answer.

"Is . . . Lauren your real name?" I asked so quietly that only the two of us heard.

Chela smiled ruefully and nodded. "Lauren Estelle McLawhorn. Try not to vomit."

She was a runaway. Chela was her street name. She might not have told anyone her real name since she left her dead grandmother's house and arrived in California as a pedophile's passenger, or she would have been found by now. She had just told me something she had never expected to reveal. She had buried both Lauren and her grandmother back in Minnesota.

"Lauren's a great name," I said. "She'll look great in that dress."

Chela lowered her eyes and pulled out the dress's tag. "It's almost four hundred dollars. Is that a problem?"

"Not if Bloomingdale's still takes cash."

Chela grinned up at me. "Then Lauren needs shoes, too."

TWENTY-TWO

DIRECTORY ASSISTANCE IN TORONTO was no help finding Laura Ebersole—her number was unlisted—but Craigslist came through. Google picked up a two-month-old ad posted by a Laura Ebersole in Toronto with a vintage Moog Liberation keyboard for sale. The ad didn't provide a telephone number, but it listed a Gmail address.

I sent a short note, first apologizing in case my note reached the wrong person: *You don't know me, but I recently spoke to a reporter who was investigating your husband's death. My father is a retired LAPD police captain, and we are conducting an informal investigation. We are especially interested in this case because of Donald Hankins's bid for the governor's office.*

Never write anything in an email you want kept a secret. With the magic of forwarding and websites, an email sent anywhere can end up everywhere. But I was willing to take the chance. In a way, sending that email was a declaration.

I sent the email at seven, hoping I might hear back in a couple of hours, or by morning.

Within fifteen minutes, my cell phone rang from a caller in the 416 area code. Toronto. I had just started washing dishes.

"Is there news?" a woman's voice said. That was her only greeting when I answered.

"Laura Ebersole?"

"Yes," she said impatiently. "Is there news?"

The urgency in her voice made me feel guilty for raising her hopes. She sounded as if he'd been waiting for her phone to ring for nearly a decade. My email might have given her the impression that a team of investigators was hot on solving her husband's case.

"No, there's no news," I said, and her sigh was more angry than disappointed. "Sorry. But like I said, we're asking some questions. Can you hold on? I'll put you on speaker. I want my father in on this call."

I muted my phone while I told Dad who I was talking to. Dad looked surprised, but he flicked off *Judge Joe Brown*. Dad wanted to hear this.

"You're the police?" her voice crackled over my speaker.

"Retired," my dad said.

"What?" She hadn't understood him.

I held the phone closer, and Dad leaned toward the speaker. "*Retired*," he said. "But I remember . . . this case. Hollywood Hills."

"Yes!" Laura exclaimed. "I can't believe this. For six months after my husband died, LAPD treats me like I'm a fanatic, some crazy person, and now a retired captain calls and says, 'Oh yeah, I knew all about it.' What is this?" She sounded angrier now.

"You're right," Dad said. "You were . . . dismissed."

"And I know why," she said. "No one wanted to touch the Golden Goose."

A shimmer of grief in my father's eyes told me she might be more right than she knew.

"Mrs. Ebersole . . ." I said. "I wish I could change what happened to your husband, and to you, but I can't. All we can do now is try to find any pieces that haven't been lost. You're mad because no one wanted to listen? Well, we want to listen. But we'll need you to talk to us."

"Why now? Ten goddamn years later?"

I considered mentioning the T.D. Jackson angle and decided against it. It confused the issue. "Because if Donald Hankins had anything to do with Chad's death," I said, using her dead husband's name, "we don't want him elected governor of this state. That would be an outrage to his memory."

She didn't say anything for so long that I thought I'd dropped the call.

Then I heard her sob. I'd broken through. After that, it wasn't a question of getting her to talk—it was how to get her to stop.

I wish I had called her as soon as I heard her name.

"My husband wasn't a perfect man. I've never tried to hide that. He had some attitudes I abhorred, and there were times they came between us. I know he said and did things did he shouldn't have done. He got into a fight at a Lakers game once when he was in law school, and yes, he did call the guy who knocked out his back tooth the N-word. Did that word come out of his mouth when he went to see Donald Hankins? You know what—it's possible. But last I checked, calling somebody names wasn't grounds for death."

I glanced at Dad, and he shrugged. Neither of us had ever heard any assertions of Chad Ebersole making racial epithets against Hankins. Burnside might have known and forgotten, or maybe he hadn't thought it was important. While I assured Laura that there was no death penalty for calling someone "the N-word," I was glad that the telephone masked our ethnicity. If she was afraid of offending us, she might not be as candid.

"Too many people take political correctness to absurdity," I said.

"Tell me something I don't know. It's not a gun. It's not a knife. It's a *word*, for God's sake. If someone calls me a bitch, am I supposed to report a hate crime? Call out the National Guard? Anyway, can I see Chad mouthing off at Hankins, calling him a 'pushy nigger'? Maybe it happened like that. But that had nothing to do with the zoning. We'd invested in that property for five years. Hankins was trying to push us out so he could install his own people and develop the land. That's a matter of public record. The CEO was Hankins's *friend*."

She paused, waiting for us to share her indignation. On her cue, Dad grunted with disgust and I told her the deal stank. Unfortunately, there are scores of political deals like it. They don't usually end up getting people killed.

"Who told you about that alleged exchange between Hankins and your husband?" I said.

"That guy," she said. "The one who called the house. The venom! Chad let me listen to their whole conversation, and I took notes. A black guy, I think."

"But not Hankins?"

"No. The voice was . . . coarser. Less cultivated."

"Was there . . . a regional accent?"

"Yes. Southern, I think."

Imagine that. "What did he say?"

"He kept saying, 'You should be mindful who you call a nigger. Some pushy niggers can push back.' "

Maybe it was only in the spirit of recitation, but Laura was much more comfortable repeating the word "nigger" than most whites I knew. Most people spoke low or turned the word over in their mouths like raw food—not that it came up often. The sound of it grated on my good ear.

"And then I'll never forget this: This man says, 'You need to get right. Maybe you should reduce your work load a little. I think you might know a project it'd be better to let slide.' "

"I bet. And did Chad back down?"

"He hired a bodyguard." She made a disgusted sound. "Man was huge, but useless."

"Useless?"

"I know there was a confrontation at the construction site. Chad wouldn't talk about it, except to mutter something about a 'fucking black rhino' of a man. But I know that the bodyguard and a beefy construction worker were both beaten pretty badly. I think it was the man who talked on the phone. Chad was angry, and frightened, but he still wouldn't back down."

"And he had an accident."

"Two weeks almost to the day after that phone call. Maybe five days after the fight. Chad was dead. I kept trying to tell the police, and they treated me like I was a spokesman for the Ku Klux Klan. Some kind of skinhead kook.

"I brought in my own expert to examine those brakes. And guess what: The next time we come to the lot, the car's been scrapped. Right out of the evidence lot."

Dad nodded sadly. He remembered that, apparently.

"Why did you leave California?"

She paused. "Police harassment," she said finally.

"What . . . kind?" Dad said, sitting straight up in his wheel-chair.

"I just kept noticing there was a cop car in my rear-view mirror everywhere I went. Or parked down the street. Dumb me, I thought it was extra protection—until I got pulled over on a DUI practically in my own driveway. I was just going down the street to the grocery store . . ."

"Had you been drinking?"

"Yes," she said. "I had a problem back then, and my goddamned husband had just been murdered. So go figure, I had a few drinks. I'd had a DUI in college, too, back in Michigan, and all of a sudden I was Public Enemy Number One. One of the cops took me aside—not a patrol cop, but someone in a shirt and tie—and he told me that if I didn't stop making unfounded accusations about Hankins killing Chad, I was going to jail. I almost fainted. *I* would go to jail!"

Her description of the detective was useless: white guy, dark-haired, long face. Dad only shook his head. It could have been anyone. Laura had been drinking, after all.

"Can you excuse me a second?" Laura said, suddenly overwhelmed by shame and memories. In her absence, Dad sighed and rubbed his temple with his index finger.

I muted my phone. "Sound plausible?"

He nodded. "Sure. Just don't know . . . who."

"LAPD ran her out of town," I said. "Not Rubens. Shit."

The black man with the heavy, Southern voice. A brawl that broke a construction worker and a professional bodyguard. Someone who danced to Hankins's tune and might have fixed a man's brakes.

"Hello?" Laura was back. She called out twice more.

I had spoken half a sentence before Dad gestured to remind me that I still had the "mute" button on. "I'm here," I said.

"So after the DUI incident, I had a dream. Chad came to visit me. I'd never believed in that garbage, but I swear it was him. Six months, and it was my first dream about him since he died. He reminded me what a great time we'd had in Toronto, and how we'd always talked about moving there. I said I couldn't move now . . . and he looked me straight in the eye and said, 'Yes you can, Laura. You just pack and go.' He gave me *permission*. He set me free."

Now I had a glimpse of how Laura Ebersole had coped with the loss of her husband and the pressure from LAPD. Whether it was her husband's ghost or her own unconscious mind, she realized she didn't want to spend her life, or go to jail, trying to avenge him.

But Chad's ghost couldn't help me.

"Listen," I said, trying to move her back to the realm of the living, "the reporter told me your husband had a personal encounter with someone who threatened him. Is that true?"

She sniffed and blew her nose. "That's the other thing! This was before that phone call. Chad said a black man was waiting beside his car after work, right in the parking lot. He told him to back off the zoning issue."

"What did he look like?" For the first time, I readied a pen to take notes.

"He was very big, Chad said. Like a construction worker, he said. Or an athlete. A black male. Maybe six-three or six-four."

"How old was he?"

"Chad mentioned he was in his fifties, maybe. From a distance, he barely noticed the guy—he said he didn't look like the type to be a problem. Well dressed. Middle-aged. But as soon as Chad got close, he said there was a look in his eyes . . ."

I almost sighed in frustration. The description of his age and size were promising, but I wasn't going to fly to Florida looking for Rubens because of a widow's recollection of an alleged "look" in a man's eyes.

"Forget his eyes," I said. "What did he say?"

Dad motioned—*Slow down. Be gentle.*

"He said, 'A man only needs enough about six feet of land. Anything more than that is just greed. Back off. It's not worth it.' And Chad said, 'Are you threatening me?' And he said, 'I'm just making conversation. Back off.' " She had memorized it. The transcript might be playing in her head every night. "As you can imagine, Chad got pissed. Maybe the smart thing would have been to go the police right away, but instead he drove over to Hankins's office the next day and showed him he wouldn't be pushed around."

"You pushy nigger," I repeated, just to be sure.

"If that's what he said."

"And then the phone call came?"

"The same night," she said. "Not from Hankins. The other one."

I wanted to groan. She had no idea who the man was who had confronted her husband in the parking lot, or had called on the phone. But I did.

Dad had found his writing pad, too. He scribbled and held it up for me: *DISTINGUISHING MARKS?*

"Can you tell me anything else about the way this man looked?" I asked Laura. "Did your husband mention any distinguishing marks?"

"Just that big scar," she said.

"A scar?"

"Yeah, a big one on his chest. His shirt got torn in the fight. It was like from heart surgery? A pair of lines."

"Intersecting?"

"Parallel."

My heart jumped. "Could it have been an H?"

Dad nodded, smiling. He was thinking the same thing.

"Chad said it was a scar, but I guess so. High on his chest."

I told Dad what I wanted to do as soon as I got off of the phone with Laura Ebersole, and he agreed to help me work it out. But first, more research.

I missed April's quick mind to trade ideas with, but it was the middle of the night in South Africa, and she'd never returned my earlier call. For both reasons, I wasn't going to call her back. Maybe she had decided she was tired of talking to me, or maybe she had never gotten back to her room to receive the message. I wasn't sure which scenario bothered me more.

I would have to get used to doing things on my own again.

I brought a cup of green tea into my screening room and sat at my computer. Since there was a giant movie screen behind me, I put on *Shaft* to play in the background. Dad had taken me to see *Shaft* at an art theater when I was fifteen, and it blew my mind. The theme song alone powered me through my fatigue. Hell, just like five million other black men, I thought Isaac was singing about me.

I paid for access to two membership sites to expand my research capabilities: The *Los Angeles Times* archives and Factiva. I bought a two-hundred-article Annual Pass to the *Times*, figuring I would use it again, and Factiva is a business news site run by Dow Jones, with access to business journals and wire services. Knowledge is power.

My investment wasn't wasted. After an hour at my desk, a story emerged:

For starters, Laura Ebersole hadn't told me everything she should have about her husband. His name had come up in a civil trial when a business partner was sued for breach of contract after a real estate deal gone awry in the Valley. A defendant was quoted calling Ebersole "nothing but a bully," accusing him of intimidation tactics. Change the name, and the article could have been about Donald Hankins.

Ebersole and Hankins both liked to play rough.

LAPD might have done more than threaten Laura Ebersole with a long DUI sentence—they might have had other dirt on Chad, too. If she'd kept making accusations about Hankins, evidence of her husband's past wrongdoing might have begun to surface in the news, too. After his death, the only thing Chad Ebersole had left to lose was his name. She'd given up.

Predictably, there had been a loud collision from the moment Hankins and his former business partner made a play for the property adjoining Ebersole's in Hollywood—a half a block's worth of land where Hankins's crony wanted to build a boutique hotel, changing the zoning from residential to commercial. The change would have had a wide impact, effectively killing Ebersole's plans to refurbish the apartment building he owned on the corner.

There had been a shouting match on the street between Ebersole and one of the lawyers for the company with Hankins's backing, Page/Tiger Properties. According to a short article in the *Los Angeles Times* on May 12, 1999, a Hankins staff member promised to seek charges against Ebersole after he "stormed" into the councilman's office to berate him with the "N-word." No charges had been filed, but Ebersole had made the news, at least for a day. Two weeks later, Ebersole's death had been reported on the California page: MAN DIES IN HOLLYWOOD HILLS CRASH. The story had been short, with much discussion of the night's rainfall and none at all about the possibility that Ebersole's death wasn't accidental.

Chief Randall had promised to sweep race out of LAPD politics, but it was obvious that some promises can't be kept overnight. If Ebersole's widow hounded them for six months—and even had a reporter from the *Times* calling on her behalf—someone should have looked into her story, especially after the incident at Hankins's office. Instead, under pressure from the chief, LAPD had ignored her claim with all its might. Lieutenant Nelson probably wasn't throwing T.D. Jackson's case intentionally, but he was feeling heat from Chief Randall, too. Why?

Chief Randall and Donald Hankins were friends, Dad had said.

And Hankins's role in pushing for LAPD funding in Sacramento couldn't be overestimated—he had been voted the most pro-police member of the legislature, and he had rallied his supporters behind the proposition that funneled millions to LAPD. Suddenly, LAPD's hiring freeze was over—and Chief Randall could hire an army.

So what if Chad Ebersole had help driving off a road?

So what if someone might have shot T.D. Jackson?

To Chief Lester Randall and Senator Donald Hankins, it worked out in the end. It was all for the public good. I could see how it might have happened.

Next, I moved on to Wallace Rubens.

Rather than a thug or a hit man, Rubens sounded more respectable than either Ebersole or Hankins. I would never have guessed an arrest for trespassing without the report from April's friend Casey Burnside.

He'd been mentioned in the *North Florida Business Journal* in 2002, in an article entitled "10 People Behind the Scenes." The photo was the most striking part: Wallace Rubens was a hulk of a man, broad in the face, shoulders, and chest. His grin was hearty and full-faced. He had been in his late fifties when the photo was taken, but his hair was mostly black. Still, his face was more deeply lined and looked older than either Jackson's or Hankins's. Since Rubens was dressed in a crisp Italian suit and stylish tie, there was no sign of the mark on his chest.

Still, I realized right away what Chad had meant when he told his wife about his eyes. Even when Wallace Rubens was grinning, his eyes seemed far from the surface. Sunken.

The rest of the piece was a mini biography. Rubens was the only one of the ten people profiled who didn't list a college or university; in most cases, the others profiled had attended two or three institutions, listing both graduate and undergraduate degrees. This listed SoCal University very briefly, with a mention of "played football." Not exactly Glory Days.

Name: Wallace Rubens. *Hometown:* Mercy, Florida. *Bread and Butter:* Restaurants, real estate, auto repair.

Auto repair: I'd bet he knew his way around a set of brakes.

Last Book Read: Dreams from My Father, by Barack Obama. *Hobbies:* Fishing, blues music. *Affiliations:* Mercy Rotary Club; First Baptist Church of Mercy.

If all else failed, I knew where to find him on Sunday mornings. Maybe.

But I couldn't wait until Sunday.

All I dug up on Wallace Rubens was a few property listings throughout Florida and Georgia, and the *Journal's* fluff piece, but I'd made up my mind as soon as Laura Ebersole hung up her phone. I did my best to get a good price on a flight to Florida, but it's hard to avoid getting gouged when you book so late. I bought myself a first-class ticket, round-trip. I got the ticket for under two thousand dollars and considered myself lucky.

I just had to be back in time for Chela's dance Saturday night; I had to be there to see her go in her dress. If Wallace Rubens was out of town, I'd find out what I could and come back another time.

But I had to try to see him in person. I had to know.

April called me just after midnight, while I was packing the leather duffel bag I use for weekend trips. In Johannesburg, it was seven in the morning. I pictured April arriving in her hotel room, hair tousled, after a night with someone else.

"I never notice my light flashing," she said. "Is it too late to call?"

Never, I thought. "Let me call you back," I said. "It'll be on my dime."

She didn't argue. When I called April back, I told her about Carlyle Simms. And my suspicions of Donald Hankins. I had no client to protect, so I told her everything.

"Oh, Ten!" she said. She sounded breathless, as if she were gazing at a natural disaster unfolding before her eyes. "That's big."

"Yeah."

"No, I mean *really* big. As in the story of a lifetime. Two lifetimes." She laughed, giddy. The delight in April's voice helped me imagine her smile, dimples and teeth. I smiled, too.

"I'd love to give you that story as a present," I said. "I'll do my best."

"Oooooooohhh . . . Why am I way over here?"

The question hung on the line. If April didn't know, then I didn't have the answer. Quickly, she went on. "Ten, please be careful. I'm serious. Rubens could be a stone hit man. We don't know what else he's done. He could be waiting for you."

As certain as I felt that Wallace Rubens was worth talking to, I knew there were still holes in my theory tying him to T.D.'s death. It was hard to buy Rubens as a standard hit man, no matter what Laura Ebersole said, or how his eyes looked.

"Why would a well-to-do businessman do violence for a politician and risk going to prison?" I asked April. "Maybe it could happen once—the Ebersole thing might have just escalated out of control—but multiple times? That piece doesn't sit right."

"True. And I've got one for you . . ." April said. "If Hankins is planning to run for governor, he'll need to get his campaign going. Why would someone who knows he's under extra scrutiny order a hit at a time like this?"

"He loved his daughter. He was spurred by a miscarriage of justice."

"Ten, come on—he's still a politician. Think about it."

I knew she was right. As a suspect, Rubens flew against logic on two counts. And Donald Hankins couldn't have risen to his current station without rapier instincts as a politician.

But his *daughter?* That threw all logic out the window.

"I'm really proud of you," April said. "Even though I'm petrified something will happen to you in Florida, I'm proud of the way you put this together, Ten."

"Thanks, babe."

We slid into a long silence before either of us realized it was coming.

"I'm flying into Tallahassee," I said, trying to jump-start the conversation again. "I guess I could swing by and say hello to your parents."

April's silence told me that my humor had been lost on her.

"Joking," I said.

"Oh."

"Don't worry, I won't embarrass you by bothering your parents." It flew out before I could think or pull it back. The way she'd said *oh* smarted. She hadn't tried to mask her relief.

"What?" I hoped I could pretend I hadn't said it, and she could pretend she hadn't heard. I heard a tendril of anger in her voice. "Embarrass me how? You think I'm holding that over you?" She didn't have to say what *that* was.

"April—please stop." My voice was as gentle as rainfall because I didn't want to argue.

"Stop what?"

Stop lying to yourself.

"I'm not the person you wanted me to be," I told her. "Admit that to yourself. I fell short. I disappointed you. Don't act like you have no idea what went wrong. Most people don't mind their friends dropping in on their parents."

"Ten, I'm very private . . ."

"You mean you hide things. There are some friends you tell them about; some you don't. Does your father still think you're a virgin?"

"No," she said quickly. "I just don't flaunt it in his face."

A daddy's girl. But I'd known that already. "Well, I wasn't planning to show up and announce that we used to fuck."

"Thank you for sounding so vulgar. If this is going to turn into drama, I can't handle it right now, Ten. I'm on my way to school, and I'm packing. I got assigned a family to stay with, finally. Out in Soweto."

"Will you have email?" I followed her lead. Neither of us wanted to fight.

"Yes, at school. But probably not at the house."

I wanted to ask about her access to a telephone next, but it would have sounded exactly the way I meant it. Either she would keep calling me, or she wouldn't; it was up to April now. And no matter what, the April I knew couldn't keep away from a good story.

"Don't worry," April said quickly. "I'll definitely call you to check on what happens in Florida. Just email me if you need any contacts from me."

"What do you know about Mercy?"

"I've driven past, but I don't think I've ever been there. It's one of those small towns west of Tallahassee, like Midway and Quincy. The sticks. There were lots of tobacco growers out that way. Cotton. Citrus. To you, it'll look a swamp with houses."

"So . . . no Starbucks?"

"I bet you've got family in towns just like Mercy, city boy."

She was right. My mother's family had come to California from Georgia; my father's family from Chicago, but the previous generation had come from North Carolina, where they had lived since slavery. I don't remember my grandparents, who were all dead either before I was born or when I was young. I didn't know my extended family well, mostly because of distance.

Suddenly, I realized that April and I had avoided the fight we'd almost had. I also realized that this was our longest conversation since she left.

"You haven't told me what it's like," I said. "Are you changing the world?"

She laughed. "A little at a time, maybe. Mostly I'm just trying not get lost. Teaching is *hard*. But I have the most incredible students— you wouldn't believe their stories, what their families have to sacrifice. It's so different than back at home. These kids talk about going to school like it really means something. They expect school to take them somewhere."

"American kids are hungry, too," I said.

"It seems different. I feel so appreciated."

"Of course. They're happy that a rich American woman would take such an interest."

"You know I'm not rich."

"Please. Wasn't that one of the first things you learned?"

"True, I'm blessed," she said, and sighed. "Blessed and confused. I miss you."

Missing me was harder than she thought it would be. That would have been my moment to strike, if I'd been stalking April like I stalked Melanie. But I didn't want April to come back to me when she was confused. One of us might end up angry, and I was trying to keep anger far out of the whole thing.

"I miss you, too," I said. "But I can't think of what to do about that right now. Can you?"

"No," she said, resigned. She paused. "Good luck in Florida. You deserve this one."

"So do you."

Our civility and warmth at the end didn't help. After I hung up, I felt every one of the ten thousand miles between us.

TWENTY-THREE

THURSDAY, OCTOBER 30

The first flight I could get was Thursday, and I lost the day in the air.

Even leaving on a 7 A.M. flight, which meant I missed wishing Chela good-bye before she got up for school, I didn't land in Tallahassee until after five. My second plane, from Atlanta to Tallahassee, was a little twenty-passenger jet parked out on the tarmac by its lonesome. We had to walk out. It was colder outside than I expected. Forty degrees, maybe cooler.

I wished I had brought a heavier jacket. Tallahassee isn't Miami Beach.

Tallahassee's tiny airport felt as if it was out in the wilderness, with a simple wooded road toward town. I was overjoyed when the first Applebee's came into sight. April was right about me: I'm a city boy. I grew up in L.A., and I've traveled the world, so L.A. is small enough for me.

There was no satellite radio in the rental, so I had to listen to the local fare. The sharp, noticeable accents from radio station callers reminded me that I was in the South. Deep South. I bypassed the country stations and rested on soul. To me, Aretha blended best with the thin-trunked pines and ancient oak trees draped in moss. *What the fuck am I doing here?* I thought, and Aretha's earthy clarion call reminded me that Melanie's family was in misery. While Aretha sang about a bridge over troubled water, I hoped that bridge was me.

This is where it all began, I thought as I drove down that narrow road.

In a blink, I was in a fair-sized city. At rush hour. I found myself snarled in traffic on Capital Circle Drive in Tallahassee, which is northern Florida's version of downtown Manhattan. It wasn't L.A.'s 405 by a long shot, but Tallahassee's traffic was no easier to navigate. The town was a mixture of brick façades, old colonial architecture, and strip malls, assembled around the soaring twenty-two-story state capitol building. Sitting in a lane that wasn't moving, I passed the time by entering an address in my navigator: 14620 FILLMORE STREET.

The result surprised me: I was within ten minutes of where April's parents lived.

Mercy was in another direction, headed out of town, but a detour wouldn't take long.

I'm not sure why I'd looked up the address for William R. Forrest. Or why I wanted to stop by the house on Fillmore Street before I went searching for Mercy. But the sun would be setting soon, and suddenly I wanted to see where April had come from. Maybe I thought the sight of her house would teach me something. If I was going to fix whatever was wrong with me and April, if it *could* be fixed, I needed all the evidence as I could gather.

The neighborhood was quiet, only blocks from the bustle of Florida A&M University's campus, where her father was the dean of the criminal justice department. As the sky's angry orange daylight faded, and the shadows from the pine trees stretched long, I found myself idling across the street from a one-story redbrick ranch house shaped like an L, on a street of well-kept homes.

The house had a covered porch draped in kudzu and a circular driveway, where a purple minivan was parked in front of the white-washed door. The minivan had a Barack Obama campaign sticker and a green FAMU Rattlers vanity license plate: PROF229. The yard was on a slight incline, big and lush, carpeted with pine needles. Light shone through the closed blinds in the living-room window.

I remembered April telling me that since she and her brothers had all moved out, her parents thought their old house was too big for them. Every year, April and her brothers spent four weeks at their parents' house—two in summer, and two at Christmas. It looked like a pleasant place to spend time.

I was about to drive off when the front door opened, and a silver-haired woman with a short 'fro and a white track suit came bounding outside with a large box in both hands. Her car's remote control dangled from her hand. I saw her van's lights flash as the doors unlocked.

April's mother. She raised her knee, trying to balance the box as she opened the van's passenger-side door. April said her mother was a one-woman machine, between her volunteer work at her church and her job as a social worker. April had mentioned more than once that she was afraid her mother was wearing herself down. As April's mother leaned over, the box nearly slipped from her hands. It looked heavy.

Shit. My hand was on my door handle when she got the box safely inside the van and slammed the door. Before she climbed into the passenger side of her van, I got a very good look at Gloria Forrest. Her face was fuller than April's, but so similar that it was eerie. She was April's future, and the future looked bright. April's mother was beautiful.

I tapped my horn and waved as I drove past, and she waved back with a ready smile I already recognized. She didn't know me, and it didn't matter. She was that kind of woman; the kind who would greet a stranger with a motherly smile at the end of a busy day.

As I drove away from April's street, I hoped I would see her again.

I started out for Mercy as the sky was getting dark.

With the lights of Tallahassee fading behind me, isolation set in right away. Traffic was still clogging the lanes as commuters drove home to the nearby towns, but Mercy was twenty miles northwest of Tallahassee, so traffic thinned as I got farther out. Soon, there was nothing in sight but trees on either side of Highway 10. *The Sticks*, just like April had said. I stared through my windshield at the large white moon radiating above the woods from a clear sky. The starlight's patterns hypnotized me. In L.A., it's easy to forget what a clear sky looks like.

In my rearview mirror, I noticed a pair of bright headlights approaching me fast. A huge pickup, probably a Chevy. The truck came so close that its lights filled my rearview mirror. My ear roared. It was as if Carlyle had come back from the dead.

The truck swerved to pass me in a streak of gleaming silver. The cab was crammed with boys who looked like they were in college. Someone let down a window in back. For the first time, I noticed a large Confederate flag pasted to the bed's door. A flashing red light in the back of my mind went on high alert. Genetic memory, perhaps.

Welcome to the South, I reminded myself, ready to hit the brakes.

A lanky white boy leaned over to yell at me from his window. I couldn't hear him, but I saw his lips move: *"Obamaaaaa!"* he called, and grinned, pumping his fist.

Someone stuck out a bright orange foam finger boasting #1 from Florida University, inviting me to honk and join their celebration. I didn't know if they had just come from a game or a political rally, but they were college kids having fun, driving too fast. Life, lived as an extreme sport. I honked twice, and three of them raised their arms while they cheered.

My foot relaxed. *Did you think they were on their way to a Klan rally?* I laughed out loud and called Dad to tell him the story.

"Whoa—I can't believe you still have cell reception," Chela said when she answered.

"Yeah, me neither. How's Dad?"

"He's good. Don't worry about us. Marcela's driving us crazy. She's lucky she's so cool, or she'd get on my nerves."

"I heard that!" Marcela called from a distance, and Chela laughed. Chela would never admit it, but she was giddy about Saturday's dance. *No matter what, you have to be home by Saturday night,* I reminded myself. I couldn't leave Saturday night to Marcela.

But without Marcela, I couldn't have left Dad and Chela alone. Marcela had agreed to keep an eye on Chela while I was gone, but Marcela wasn't spending the night. There was nothing I could do if Chela snuck out of the house while I was gone. Or ditched school all day. Marcela was Dad's nurse—but she was turning into a member of the family. I wished Chela had warmed up to April as easily as she had with Marcela.

But April had been different.

"Okay, well don't stay up too late. TV off by midnight," I said.

"Believe that if you want to."

"Can you put Dad on?"

"He's taking a nap."

I was disappointed. I wanted to tell him the story about the pickup truck. I wished he had been able to make the trip with me. I had left my new partner at home.

I tried to dial Len next—I hadn't talked to him in days—but my cell phone beeped. SIGNAL LOST, my phone read, at the same time my navigator's British accent informed me that I had arrived at my destination. I took the exit toward Mercy.

Mercy's exit led to a darker two-lane road, and open fields instead of trees. For what seemed like a long stretch, I didn't see any lights— no businesses, no homes. Nothing. If not for my navigator, I would have been sure I was on the wrong road.

But lights appeared like an apparition when I turned right at the dead end, where reflective letters on a green sign pointed toward Mercy. Suddenly, I saw neon signs for hotels standing higher than the treetops on tall poles meant to draw travelers from the highway. They were chains—I won't name them, but one had kept the light on—and both were charging more than a hundred dollars a night.

Might as well stay in town, I figured. The chains were clean and familiar. Nothing fancy, but no cockroaches either. Inside, the hotel was so new that it smelled like paint, and there was a dish of fresh fruit at the front desk. I was feeling lucky until the front desk clerk told me that my room would cost two hundred dollars a night.

"Everybody fills up at homecoming. Big game Saturday," said the man behind the counter, who looked Indian or Pakistani. He wore tortoiseshell glasses and a beige mock safari coat, the chain's desk uniform. "Florida University."

I felt jacked, but my stomach was growling. I gave him cash to book a room, registering under the name John Gage, the paramedic from that show *Emergency!* I watched when I was a kid. Just a precaution. "Is your restaurant open?" I said.

"No restaurant, sorry. The Domino's over in Quincy delivers."

Shit. I didn't want to spread a bad mood around, so I kept my voice pleasant. "What about in Mercy? Any restaurants?"

The clerk took a long time to answer, absorbed with typing my registration information. "The new Hardee's, maybe." He sounded distracted.

"I'm looking for some *real* food, man."

"The good food's in Tallahassee," he said. "Boston Market. Cracker Barrel. Denny's. You should have brought dinner with you." He said it as if that was common knowledge.

"Nowhere in town for a hot meal?" My tone slipped two notches, to irritation.

The clerk raised his finger, an afterthought. "Unless you like barbecue." I was afraid I'd heard wrong; the word *barbecue* made my mouth water. "There's a place in town, Pig'n-a-Poke. Off of McCormack Way. Only sign on the block with neon."

"Is it good?"

He shrugged. "Never eaten there."

If the place looked clean, I would try the beef ribs. Or chicken. Or both. But first, work.

My cell phone was still gasping for service and the hotel didn't have Ethernet in the rooms, so I hit one of the two computers in the hotel's bathroom-sized OFFICE SUITE. I'd done a property records search on Rubens, and I scanned the addresses, computing my distance on MapQuest. Man was livin' large. Most of his property was in Tallahassee, so I might be able to check those out at the end of the day. I noticed that one of his apartment buildings was in Quincy, about six miles away. Maybe I'd start there in the morning, after I sniffed around Mercy. With so little time, I had to hope it would be easiest to find him close to home.

My plane had arrived too late for me to make it to the Florida University Library archives in Tallahassee, which had been closing up at the same time I was landing, but a librarian I reached by phone had given me a temporary password and user ID. I would have access to the university's archives online for twenty-four hours. A trial membership, since I wasn't a student.

The online archives, which included access to old student newspapers, went only as far back as 1983. I surfed the site, but I didn't find much I hadn't already seen on my previous searches. The most interesting discovery, under the Bobcats Athletics section, was a photograph from the Sunshine Bowl published by the *Tallahassee Democrat* in 1967. The photo looked dramatic in black-and-white, like a still from a classic sports film:

The white SoCal quarterback is nearly falling backward, the football launching from his fingertips while a swarm of determined Florida players in dark jerseys leap at him from every direction. Right behind the quarterback, a Florida player is broadsided in midleap by a hulk of a man in a SoCal helmet, whose face is knit with thunderous will, teeth gritted.

The SoCal offensive tackle was Wallace Rubens. His face was distorted except for his nose, but his nose was enough. The photo was striking because all of the players charging the SoCal quarterback were white—and the most prominent players beating back their charge were black. I wondered how that photo had gone over in Tallahassee the morning after the game.

Florida University had thirty thousand students the year after that game, in 1968, so it had always been big. And powerful. Between current students and alumni, FU had a large influence over Tallahassee and the outlying areas.

Information on the Sunshine Bowl was otherwise scant. Universities celebrate their victories, not their losses. A link in the chat section took me to a college sports blog, where an unnamed blogger had written about the 1967 Sunshine Bowl. The anonymous entry was a

year old, but it was my first glimpse into the game from the eyes of an
FU student.

"FU tries to pretend it never happened, but I was there," he wrote.
"Hell, I was a part of it. I was as mad as everyone else, and it swept the
whole stadium that day. Don't forget about Vietnam, folks. We'd lost
Calhoun after he graduated, and nobody had recovered from that yet.
(Rocket Forever!) There was a Cinderella story, rebuilding the football
program after a hero falls. We'd gone in with so many expectations, and
nobody thought a damn about Southern Cal back then. (LOL!) I'm not
making excuses, I'm just saying we have to take it all into account. It's
easy to judge something when you weren't there.

"But let me call it like it was, since everybody else here is too chicken:
When we saw that SoCal offense, a kind of a shock went through the
stands. Remember? There'd been sit-ins and all these demonstrations in
Tallahassee, our parents saying we were about to lose everything, and
now here was this team with so many black players—four in the offense! One of them built like a truck! Holy shi**! (Show of hands: Who
had ever seen anyone like Rubins?)

"And they could play too! Run fast! Catch! Maybe we wouldn't
have noticed so much if they'd been more spread out, but they're all on
offense, like we're being attacked on our home soil. There was this chant
inside the stadium that echoed from the rooftop. Go home, Nig***!
Every play, same chant. If one of them got shaken up (and let's face it,
it was open season on those guys and the referees went blind), everybody cheered. Go home, Nig***! I was there, and a lot of you were too.
Class of '67? Class of '66? All those alums? Nobody wants to say, like it
never happened. Ain't it funny how life turns around and stares at you
in the face?

"Not exactly a proud moment. But a GREAT game! Even though
it hurt like hell to get our butts kicked, I kept looking for Rubins' name
to come up in the draft. Never did. Didn't he get hurt at that game? It

*might have killed his career. And one of them was T.D. Jackson's dad,
so THAT goes without saying—like father, like son. (What a waste of
protoplasm T.D. Jackson turned out to be, but that's another subject). I
always wondered what happened to those players. I wonder what it felt
like to be one of those black guys standing on that field with so much ha-
tred raining down."*

It felt like it was time to kill you, I thought. My teeth had clenched.
Humiliating you publicly would have been a poor second best.

When I checked my watch, it was almost nine.

I hoped the barbecue place was open late.

Mercy was almost invisible at night.

There were long stretches without streetlamps, and only occasional homes with lights burning, most of them set way back on farms.
Mercy was definitely rural. My headlights reflected against highway
signs announcing a maze of obscure roads; not that I could have seen
the roads well in the dark. Mercy's roads were noticeably bumpy, not
well paved, and my headlights warned me that they were bordered by
deep gulleys. I wouldn't be making any U-turns if I could help it. I
was glad I had my navigator.

A single stoplight shone red ahead: downtown Mercy. The businesses lining the street were dark and shuttered; most of them identified with hand-painted signs: ANTIQUES. FURNITURE. HUMAN HAIR/
WIGS!!! A plantation-style colonial building in the middle of the block
on McCormack Way was probably the town hall. There was a bronze
statue of a horse-mounted soldier in the courtyard, probably a Civil
War hero, but it was too dark to see an inscription. Mercy didn't have
much, but it was a proud of what it had.

At the gas station on the corner, Handi Mart, shopping carts and the two dozen cars parked outside told me that a lot of locals bought their groceries at the convenience store. I could only imagine what they were paying. The Handi Mart was the only place in sight that was still bustling. That, and Hardee's—the Southern version of Carl's Jr.

I turned the corner at the light and crossed the railroad tracks, following my navigator. Just that fast, downtown Mercy was gone. Darkness. More than a half mile down, as the clerk had told me, the barbecue restaurant was the only light at the end of the street. The sign blazed red in the dark, lighting the crush of cars parked beneath it: PIG'N-A-POKE.

The sign was about the size of a car tire, a bright red ring circling a cartoonish, grinning pink pig with a chef's hat and a spatula. I wondered what kind of ghoulish, self-loathing cannibal pigs they grew around there. The logo made me think of Senator Donald Hankins: I'll swear it until the day I die.

The parking lot was packed. As I bumped into the gravel lot, which bordered an overgrown field, my headlights caught a house across the street so dilapidated that I was surprised it was still standing. Its wooden walls and porch were warped and sagging. The paint was so old that it looked unpainted, and there were cracks between the planks so large that I could see them even at night. In front of the house, near the road, five older men warmed their hands around a fire in a barrel. Sparks twirled up into the night, lighting their laughing faces.

I had found the 'hood.

Nothing on the outside of Pig'n-a-Poke made me want to go inside. The long, large building was virtually windowless. A light-colored German shepherd pawing the door at the top of the concrete-block steps seemed certain he'd be invited in before long. I hated to guess what Pig'n-a-Poke's L.A. County health code grade would be. I could see why the hotel clerk had never made it there.

I carefully nudged past the big gray shepherd to go in without him. He gave me sad eyes.

Inside, the scent of spicy, slow-roasting ribs blew across my face like a spring breeze, and B.B. King was singing "Let the Good Times Roll" on a jukebox, working sweet Lucille like a back-door lover. I'd come to the right place.

But it's hard not to stand out when you don't belong. I had two days' worth of razor stubble to try to make my features less noticeable—it's a face women notice, and that isn't always an advantage—but even in a denim jacket and jeans, I stood out like the neon sign outside.

Every sister in the room seemed to notice me walk in, so their men noticed, too. The room's hum of conversation dipped down. I sat at my first chance, at a table slightly hidden by the jukebox. The waitress might never find me, but at least I wouldn't draw stares. After the room noticed that I'd sat quietly—and *alone*, girlfriends acknowledged with sly grins—the conversation went back up a decibel.

The front room was boisterous, at least forty people under red-tinged lights, like a nightclub. Most of the patrons were dressed for work, whether it was loosened ties or muddied overalls. I saw women's pressed heads of jet-black hair and exposed cleavage. Most of them had too much eye makeup, the amateur's mistake, but their faces were prettied up. The women's clothes shared a fashion code: tight. Nobody came to Pig'n-a-Poke to be on their best behavior.

I grabbed the plastic-encased menu from my table, wiping off barbecue sauce. I was glad there were towelettes at every table.

The décor inside was Southern sports bar, with sawdust on the floor. A buck's head was mounted above the bar, and the walls were plastered with football banners from FU, Florida State, and Florida A&M. Above the entrance, I saw a framed chalk drawing of a huge tobacco barn.

A man in a beige-and-brown uniform who looked like the sheriff walked in soon after me, and the dog trotted in on the sheriff's heels, tongue lolling in triumph. The dog headed for a back room, as if he knew his way around.

The sheriff scanned the room, and the only thing out of place was me.

The sheriff was the only white man in sight. He was about my age, his graying hair cut low beneath a brown cowboy hat. His tin star was so big that it looked like a movie prop. He had a friendly face, but his eyes were like blowtorches. He looked alert and fit enough for me to wonder what he was doing in Mercy instead of a bigger police department. Hometown boy done good, I thought. The back of his neck was leathery and brown from the sun.

He was never out of my sight, and I was never out of his. After he floated around backslapping, ordering a beer from the bar counter, he drifted back toward me with his bottle of Miller Lite. On sight, I'm bothered by a cop in a cowboy hat. Maybe it's the Native American in me; Cherokee on my father's side, Seminole on my mother's. I don't like armed cowboys. Especially when they're drinking beer.

The sheriff stood above my table. "What brings you here?" he said.

His accent was thick; "brings" came out "brangs." Nothing confrontational in his voice, but he was making more than small talk. He might already have decided he didn't like me, the way I didn't like his hat. If so, my visit to Mercy was off to a shitty start. The deputy's name-tag said SHERIFF J. KELLY.

"Here for the game, Sheriff." I had a different cover in mind for Rubens, but I hoped I could brush the sheriff off faster as a football fan. I was wrong.

"If you're for Texas, keep it to yourself." Sheriff Kelly didn't sound like he was joking.

"No problem. I'm a Bobcat."

"What year?"

"Never graduated," I said, trying to minimize my lies. "Dumbest mistake of my life. I try not to miss homecoming. I met my wife in school." The truth, whether ugly or beautiful, is a living thing. A fine lie, on the other hand, is a mosaic of selective, plausible details.

"So where's your wife now?" The question surprised me. The sheriff was digging deeper in my business than casual necessity would demand. Maybe I'd tacked on one detail too many.

"Not a football fan," I said. "Left her home."

"Where's home?" He sounded less and less like he was making conversation. I needed a spritz of Cop-B-Gone. For some reason, badges always sniff me out.

My home address was on my driver's license, so I decided to tell the truth in case he manufactured a reason to pull me over on my way back to the hotel. "Los Angeles."

"When the cat's away . . ." He knocked on my tabletop, as if for luck. "Try the babyback special. You be good, now."

He was only missing the word *boy* at the end, but I tried to be more amused than pissed off. *OK, I get it. This is how it works in Mercy.* I was glad I didn't live there.

"Know where I could find Wallace Rubens?" I said to the sheriff casually as he turned to leave. If Rubens had trouble with the law, the sheriff was a good place to start.

The sheriff faced me squarely again. "What for?"

"My dad told me how he played back in '67. Thought I'd like to meet him."

For half a second, the sheriff studied my eyes like he was seeing me for the first time. "If you're in Mercy long enough, you'll meet Bear sooner or later," he said, motioning to the waitress waiting behind him. "Janiece—bring this man some ribs."

The fair-skinned waitress was just shy of plump, with a healthy bust, overly greasy curls and a face that needed a smile. Her frown diminished her face, which was slightly acne-scarred. Janiece barely met my eyes, shy in my presence. I guessed that she was nearly thirty—old enough to look silly in her low-cut uniform dress: parading pink pigs wielding spatulas.

"What's he having?" Janiece asked the sheriff, as if I wasn't there.

"Babyback special," he said.

I'm not in the habit of letting other men order my food for me. It's especially irritating from a cop with a cowboy hat and an accent straight out of *Deliverance*.

"I don't like pork," I said. "I'll have beef ribs and chicken."

Sheriff Kelly winked at me, not smiling. "Suit yourself. Enjoy your stay."

I hoped he'd scratched whatever was itching. I slipped on the phony wedding band in my pocket. Then I pulled out the newspaper I'd been reading on the plane and propped it open in my hands. Every once in a while, a woman buzzed close to my table, pretending she wasn't trying to be noticed, and I pretended I didn't. Some of those women were tasty, but I wasn't hunting, so I never met their eyes. My ring sat on my finger, in plain sight.

Pig'n-a-Poke was a good-mood kind of place, filled with smiles. I watched as an overweight man wearing a dark blue jumpsuit from Minit Auto Repair was led by the hand toward the jukebox by one of the finest women in the room. The woman seemed out of his league—about twenty-two, in cherry-colored stilettos, with sturdy calves and a face I might have found in any agent's waiting room. Although the man pulled her close to sway to B.B.'s music, the way they avoided each other's eyes made me wonder if they had ever met before that night. For thirty seconds, I couldn't figure out the energy.

Then it hit me: The woman was a prostitute, and the mechanic was a potential john. Another scan of the room, and I spotted two other working girls. But the sheriff, who had taken his place at a card game on the far side of the restaurant, didn't glance in their direction. I chuckled, shaking my head. *Way to police the room, Gomer,* I thought.

Then I got it: Pig and a Poke. Part restaurant, part cathouse? That was nervy. Was the sheriff dumb as a bag of rocks, or was he bent? I guessed the latter.

I heard competing music from another open doorway off to the side, beyond the bar counter. Live blues, from the sound of it, but not professional; a jam session. Since my food hadn't arrived yet, I left my jacket on my chair and walked past the cluster of patrons at the bar to the doorway of the adjoining room, which was crammed with listeners in front of a stage. I couldn't see the musicians because everyone was standing.

The drummer's beats were loud and sloppy, and I wasn't impressed by the sour guitar. Still, I was impressed to hear live blues in a town the size of Mercy. I wished my ears were working better. Between the jukebox, the band, and the noise from the crowd, I heard mostly murmurs and babbles.

My waitress, Janiece, surprised me from my left side. She was holding a platter of chicken, ribs, and corn bread that looked big enough to feed a village and smelled like paradise. She leaned close to my ear.

"Bearzintherejamminrightnow," she said. She was a mumbler.

"Sorry, darlin'—what's that?" I said, leaning down with my good ear.

She only pursed her lips and shook her head, as if she was irritated. I followed her back to my table, where she set my plate of food down without a word. She wasn't from the school of *Can-I-get-you-*

anything-else and *Have-a-nice-day*. She was gone before I could order a drink.

But the food made me forgot the bad service. The sauce was sassy and rich, the beef so tender that the bones offered only token resistance. I decided I would eat there for lunch the next day if I could, and pick up a bottle or two of sauce to take home to Dad and Chela.

As I sat at Pig'n-a-Poke eating my first good barbecue dinner in a long time, I had no idea how close it was to my last.

TWENTY-FOUR

Daylight only confirmed how tiny Mercy was. The road between my hotel and downtown Mercy was surrounded by fields, some ripe with fluffy white cotton plants I'd never seen up close. The few homes I saw had cows, goats, horses, and chickens penned in their yards. The dirt beneath everything was dark orange clay, like the jack-o'-lanterns on every porch.

Downtown was larger than I'd thought, with stop signs to supplement the streetlight at McCormack Way. Driving away from the railroad tracks, turning left instead of right at the Handi Mart, I saw a row of more upscale business: an attorney, an accountant, and a large feed and tack. Several large colonial-style houses had been refurbished into businesses, which gave downtown a homey quality. There were a few blocks of grand older homes with verandas and tire swings; some brick, but mostly wood-frame.

On the other side of town, the area around Pig'n-a-Poke was clearly poorer, with smaller homes, mounted junk cars, and patchier lawns. The clapboard houses were built so close together that they looked stacked. I imagined it must have been especially lonely to have so little in a town that didn't offer much to look at. Only First Baptist Church of Mercy shone like a pearl.

I saw three boys running barefoot near a junk pile, and it reminded me of Soweto. South Africa had its work cut out for it, but there was work to do at home, too. I wondered what difference a teacher like April would make in a town like Mercy.

So much for Plan A: I wasn't going to see Rubens taking his morning constitutional.

I programmed my navigator and headed toward the apartment building he owned in the nearby town of Quincy. The building manager could narrow down my search.

Instead of taking the 10, my navigator concocted a maze of smaller roads to steer me toward Quincy, most of them more gravel than asphalt. The road turned muddy, and I noticed water gleaming through the tall stalks of crabgrass on both sides of my car. Grass grew defiantly in the center of the roadway, *thwapping* my undercarriage. A white-tailed deer bobbed up its head as I approached, and went back to grazing when I drove past.

April was right. I was in a swamp.

I'd also just driven into the charcoal drawing I'd seen at the Pig'n-a-Poke: Ahead, an old tobacco barn loomed beside the road, casting a shadow across the lanes. The drawing hadn't captured the sheer height of this barn, which was more a large ornament than a real barn. It was so old that a quarter of its planks were missing. I saw another barn in the distance, closer to the woodland, and it looked timeworn, too.

Tobacco money makes me queasy; it's one of the reasons I've never smoked. Turns out I'm not too fond of old tobacco land either. Even the pine trees looked stripped, as if they were recovering from a storm. No crops grew nearby, and the area looked desolate and empty. I saw a raccoon's upturned carcass by the side of the road, feet frozen high in rigor mortis. Not far beyond, a wooden cross lashed with string marked an accident victim's unlucky spot.

This is no place to die. I'm no psychic, but I'm almost sure that was my exact thought.

I noted the road from the sign: A-66. I decided I would take another route back.

Quincy was a welcome relief from the wilderness. It was much bigger than Mercy, with a Wal-Mart and CVS to herald civilization. Pat Thomas Parkway was lined with neon-lighted chains.

The address led me to an attractive apartment compound called Quincy Gardens. There were twelve cottage-style units, more attractive than any apartments I'd seen in Mercy. The cottages were shaded by old oak trees that made them look rustic. There were bright pink bougainvillea bushes growing in splendor between the cottages. It looked like a good investment.

A black man in his midtwenties was just leaving the office as I walked in. I thought he was a tenant, dressed in a long Jacksonville Jaguars sweatshirt, but he wore a ring of keys around his neck. "Shit, you scared me," he said, leaping backward. His brow creased with irritation. His country accent was thick, too.

"Who'd you think I was?"

He didn't answer, giving me a wary stare. I can't prove it, but I got the feeling that he worked for a boss with a temper. He wore round-frame glasses, his hair in short twists. "No vacancies until January. Waitin' list's pretty long," he said.

"I'm here to lease, not rent," I said. "My mother lives out this way, and I've got a Popeye's franchise back home in Philly. Who would I talk to about the adjoining parcel?" There was plenty of land on both sides of the apartments; I figured Rubens owned an adjoining tract, too.

"Wish it was me," the man said, and waved me into his small, tidy office. On the wall, I saw plaques from the Quincy City Council and Better Business Bureau. He had a nameplate reading JAMAL JONES II.

"It's zoned mixed-use, so you could do a Popeye's, no problem. You'd do big business. But the man you want to talk to is Wallace Rubens." He went to his desk to grab a Post-it. "Just give me a name and number, or an email address, and he'll hit you back."

The young man was efficient and well-informed. By the modest size of the apartment complex, I guessed that Jamal Jones II didn't spend his whole day at Quincy Gardens. He might manage Rubens's Tallahassee properties, too, or some of them. I gave him my email address, explaining that my cell phone didn't get reception in the area.

"How's the market?" I said, angling for small talk.

I hit a vein. The kid was a salesman. "Better'n you'd think. Quincy's almost a bedroom community of Tallahassee now, and town infrastructure can't keep up with the growth. Bring in a restaurant, and you'll print paper. If I was you, I'd do Applebee's, a sit-down kind of family place. The town's got fast food—just not enough *food*."

"So your boss is doing all right here."

"My boss is doing more than all right. My boss is the wealthiest black man in three counties," Jamal said, fierce loyalty blazing in his eyes. "He opened this little place because his daughter wanted to live in Quincy, so she asked him to build something nice. But do not judge Wallace Rubens by Quincy Gardens."

"Looks good to me. Is he from around here?"

"Reared in his grandmother's shack over in Mercy."

A daughter and grandmother. Rubens might own a house and other property under relatives' names, I realized. Maybe I could find his home address with some research. I didn't want it to come to that, but it would be good to know where Wallace Rubens lived.

"I respect a man with a sense of community," I said.

"Mister, Wallace Rubens helped pay for my MBA," Jamal said.

"Me and another honor student from Stephens County High. Everybody else is out for themselves, but Wallace Rubens remembers where he came from." He wanted to go on, but he stopped himself. His lips twitched, reeling a story back in.

I wanted to ask about the Sunshine Bowl, but instinct told me not to. *Take it slow.* "Now I'm *really* eager to talk to the man," I said. "But I'm only in town today."

I wanted Jamal to volunteer Rubens's telephone number, but it had to be his idea. If Wallace Rubens got a whiff that someone suspicious was asking for his number, I would never find him. Jamal seemed like a legit businessman—and I hoped he was—but if he worked for Rubens both underground *and* above ground, he was too smart for me to risk stupid mistakes.

Jamal shrugged. "It's his fishing day, so his cell phone's off. Don't know if he'll check in today or not. I just saw Mr. Rubens last night, too. He plays guitar at the barbecue place over in Mercy. Blues Jam Wednesday."

Shit. Rubens had been on the stage only twenty yards from me!

"Pig'n-a-Poke?" I said. "You're kidding. I just ate there last night."

The man smiled. "Then you just had the best ribs in the Panhandle. And you truly can appreciate the meaning of the saying, 'They can't kick you off your own stage.'"

"He owns Pig'n-a-Poke, too?" I wondered why the sheriff hadn't mentioned that when I asked about Rubens at the restaurant. Which of us had he been running interference for? I longed to ask Jamal about the working girls I thought I'd seen at the barbecue place, but I didn't.

"Yeah, yeah. A chain. One in Mercy, one in Midway. He's religious about fishing every other Friday, but Wallace Rubens is a *businessman.*"

"I hope I get the chance to do some business with him." I threw in a frustrated sigh.

Jamal checked his watch, and I checked mine. It was eleven. "Hey, it's a long shot," he said, "but swing by the Mercy Pig'n-a-Poke in about an hour. If he's done fishin' and it's time to eat, that's where Mr. Rubens is fixin' to be."

Instead of taking the back roads, I hopped on the interstate back to Mercy. That route took ten minutes longer than the shortcut, but I'd seen swamp enough for a lifetime.

While I drove along the well-paved, tree-lined highway, I admitted to myself that the emerging portrait of Wallace Rubens didn't look much like a killer. He was tight with the local police, and his businesses seemed respected even if they weren't completely above-board.

Why would Rubens risk flying all the way to L.A. to commit acts of violence? The Wallace Rubens I thought might have killed T.D. Jackson didn't fit the Wallace Rubens who lived in Mercy. They were like two different people—or a personality split straight down the middle. I had no case. *What the fuck am I doing here?*

I thought about driving straight past Mercy's exit to go to the airport. I was so eager to be back at home that my leg bounced anxiously beneath the steering wheel.

MERCY—NEXT EXIT, a highway signed warned. Like I said, I'm no psychic, but I could feel myself resisting the whole idea. But my intuition was in hyperdrive, and intuition was all I had to go on:

If I wanted to know what had happened to T.D. Jackson, I had to see Wallace Rubens.

Go in and find him. If you don't get a vibe from him, drive straight to the airport.

But seeing Wallace Rubens would be a dangerous thing to do. I *knew* it, somehow.

I signaled and took the Mercy exit.

Pig'n-a-Poke was waiting.

The barbecue joint looked worse in daylight than it had in the dark. Outside, the walls looked like flimsy corrugated tin, caked with red clay dust. Without the aid of the darkened neon sign above, the building looked more like an abandoned warehouse.

At noon, the parking lot was nearly empty. My car was the sixth one in.

The same gray-colored German shepherd trotted past me to come outside when I opened the door. He appeared so fast, I gave a start. It was a big dog. But he only sniffed the legs of my jeans and moved on.

The sawdust had been swept up, but there was no crowd to appreciate the effort. The jukebox was silent, and I didn't smell food cooking. If not for three men at the back table, I wouldn't have thought the place was open.

Three black men sat at a corner table, arguing with such passion that they might have been talking about religion *and* politics. The men were thick-bodied, in their twenties and thirties. The larger one was in a blue jumpsuit, and I realized he was the mechanic from Minit Auto Repair who'd danced in front of the jukebox. None of them glanced toward me when I walked in. All of them had drinks, but no one was eating.

The waitress, Janiece, came to greet me from the bar, practically meeting me at the door. She was the only part of Pig'n-a-Poke that looked better in daylight, even in her silly dress. She smiled and gave her hair a sassy shake. She didn't seem shy anymore.

"I was hopin' you'd be back," she said.

She might have been flirting. Nobody had told her how to adjust her posture from a slouch to a rolling strut, so the effect fell flat; but her smile was nice. I can almost always find features to appreciate on a woman's face.

"This is funny . . ." I said. "Jamal Jones just told me I need to see Wallace Rubens."

She nodded. "They were both here last night." That smile wasn't bad at all.

"So I'm the last to hear." I gave her a grin, and I saw lightning flutter behind her eyes. "Just want to talk about some land. You expect him for lunch?"

"If he's not still fishin'," she said.

The men at the table grew louder. An unusually short man stood up, waving his arms to make his point. He was barely five feet tall, but built like a fireplug. His husky voice dominated their angry volleys. I was glad they weren't pissed at me.

"Damn, they take those ball games *way too serious*," Janiece said, raising her voice so the men would hear. She beckoned me. "Come on back where it's quiet. Bear'll be 'round."

Janiece led me past the bar to the now-empty room where the jam session had been held. There were two small tables near the front, both set for customers. The stage was more professional than I'd thought, raised a foot from the ground, polished wood. Center stage, between two microphones, a gorgeous royal purple Fender stood on a guitar stand.

Rubens's guitar, I guessed. Apparently, he didn't expect anyone to walk away with it.

"On Fridays, hard lemonade's fifty cents," Janiece said. "Might as well have one, 'cuz it's the first thing he's gonna axe when he meets you: 'How'd you like the lemonade?' Mr. Rubens don't trust nobody who won't take a drink. Plus, it's his grandmama's recipe."

It was as if she'd taken a personality pill overnight. Worked fine for me, as long as it got me closer to Rubens. "Then gimme a lemonade and a beef brisket sandwich."

"Lemonade'll be right up," she said. "But we gonna need a minute for that brisket."

The performance room's walls were wood-paneled. An upright piano that looked like an antique stood against the wall beside the stage.

Janiece was back with my drink within thirty seconds. Her service had improved, too. In the next room, I heard the men at the table bellowing at each other.

I touched the piano's middle C note. The piano sounded bright, perfectly tuned. Music might build rapport with Rubens. Could be an option.

"Go on and play if you want," Janiece said. "Folks do it all the time. Just don't spill none of that lemonade on the keys." She spoke over her shoulder, on her way out.

I puckered when I tasted Grandma Rubens's hard lemonade. Too much sour, not enough sweet. But I drained my glass in case Rubens showed up and asked me how I'd liked it. I would only order one. Alcohol slows reflexes.

While I waited for my food, I strolled the large room. I noticed a framed *Jet* magazine on the wall near the piano, the middle pages spread open. The article was dated January, 1967.

Jet had written a feature about the Sunshine Bowl in 1967! The pages were slightly yellowed, but the magazine had been in the frame for years. There was a close-up of Wallace Rubens, his face enlarged from the *Tallahassee Democrat* photo I'd found on the university's website. The caption read: "(UNOFFICIAL) MOST VALUABLE PLAYER: WALLACE RUBENS." The determination on Rubens's face was mesmerizing.

The article read: "In a shameful display of desperation, Florida University fans screamed racial epithets at the Spartans, whose win was led by the Negro players on the team's offensive line, particularly Wallace Rubens (Mercy, FL). While the Negro players' concentration and discipline ruled the day, a tragic turn befell Wallace Rubens when he was seriously injured in a car accident after the game. At press time, Rubens's grandmother says it is possible that he will never be able to play football again."

My mouth felt dry, suddenly. I tried my glass, but even the ice tasted sour. *They should pay us a dollar to drink it.*

"Now, *that* was a day . . ." a voice rumbled behind me.

Wallace Rubens had come in while my back was turned.

He was only six yards behind me, so close and wide that I had to turn around to take him in. He might be in his sixties, but I imagined what it had felt like to face him across the line of scrimmage. He was still impressively big and broad, built like that black guy from *The Green Mile.* Six-foot-six, easy, but he had put on a lot of fat since his college days. It didn't sag; more like marbling, but enough marble for a good-sized fireplace.

Instinct roared that I should take a step away from his reach, but I held my ground, cursing myself for my carelessness. I would only get one mistake on this trip to Mercy, and I might have just made it.

"Was that a life-defining moment?" I said. At least Rubens had brought up the Sunshine Bowl first. I'd landed my fish already. "I'm John Gage."

Wallace's face widened by inches. " 'A life-defining moment?' "

he said, exaggerating my Yankee accent so that it sounded British. "Where you from, *John Gage*?"

"From Philly," I said, sticking to the story I'd told Jamal Jones.

"North Philly? West Philly?" His tone was friendly, but his questions were rapid-fire, on the heels of my every word.

I felt mild panic, but kept my face clear. I'd been to Philly plenty, but I wished I had chosen New York instead. When I was an escort, I spent half my time in New York.

"Mt. Airy, actually," I said, choosing an area where a high school friend lived. "We moved from Brooklyn Heights last year."

"Where you get your hair cut in Philly?"

"My wife cuts my hair."

He eyed me with a glimmer that looked almost like a smile.

"So, John Gage . . ." he said. "What do you consider a life-defining moment?"

I shrugged. "Maybe your last football game. A lot of work. A lot of dreams."

Slowly, he nodded. He pursed his lips, looking thoughtful. When he sighed, I smelled beer and cigarettes. His breathing sounded heavy for a man at rest. Sweat beaded on his skin in the folds of his neck. His earlobes were creased vertically. Man had sampled entirely too much of his own cuisine. Rubens drew his words out like dripping molasses.

"If that's your definition, the Sunshine Bowl was that."

My mind raced, but I remembered my father's advice: *Take it slow.* Rubens took my empty glass and set it on a coaster on top of the piano. "My niece says you play."

I hadn't realized that the waitress was his niece. I was glad I'd been polite to her. "I dabble some. Wouldn't call it playing."

Rubens jumped up on the stage. He had to weigh three hundred pounds, maybe sixty above fighting weight, but he carried his mass like a round black grasshopper. He picked up his guitar and draped the strap over his shoulder. He knelt to plug his guitar to the amp.

My stomach suddenly felt queasy. "I gotta warn you, I don't play blues . . ."

"What *can* you play?" he said, not looking up at me as he wired up.

"Three chords. C, F, and G. That's what I learned in seventh grade."

Wallace Rubens gave me a scolding look, lips curling in a smile. "Three chords is all you need to play blues, John Gage. Go sit down."

I didn't like the way he kept saying my name, almost mocking it. Could he know I was lying? *One call from Hankins . . .*

"All right, I'll give it a try," I said, and pulled out a wooden piano bench that whined across the hardwood floor. "But don't say I didn't warn you."

The speaker beside the stage squealed to life as Rubens tested a bluesy riff. His guitar was out of tune, but only slightly. He plucked a string, tuning. "Play the C chord. Like this . . . *bah-bah-bah, bah-bah-bah*, in six-eight time. I'll nod to count off. One, two . . ."

After fumbling to remember the C chord, I tried to match Rubens's tempo. Just when I was ready to give up, my fingers synchronized with his nodding head. I was playing it!

Rubens answered with a blazing riff up and down his guitar.

By some miracle, we sounded good.

"Okay, go to F," he said. Rubens called out three notes in the F chord, and my fingers muddled their way into the pattern. When I finally got back on the tempo, Rubens followed with another soulful solo.

"Now the G chord," Rubens said. "That's G, B, and D."

I could almost see the music staffs on my seventh-grade chalk-board again. This time, I made the key change without losing tempo. Rubens let out a hoot and followed me in G. We sounded so good that I wished someone had been there to witness it.

"*Half of life's fakin' it . . .*" Rubens sang in a baritone into the live microphone. "*The rest's just the luck of the draw . . .*"

The song made my fingers feel fevered. I was playing! Rubens had just met me, and he'd already taken me to school.

"Go back to C," Rubens said, and repeated the lyrics. I followed him in the next chord change without having to be told. "*Lord, I know Bear ain't been perfect . . . but help pull these thorns out my paw . . .*"

We ended with a flourish, almost in unison, and we couldn't help smiling. But Rubens's smile was gone so fast, it might have been my imagination.

"What you wanna ask me, son?" Rubens said, sliding his fingers up and down his strings. A series of ugly chords. "You wanna ask me about that game?"

My gut told me to back off, that I might have come on too strong. "Actually, Jamal Jones said I should talk to you about real estate in Quincy."

His guitar went silent as Rubens gazed at me. "Naw, I don't mean that. I'm talkin' 'bout how you had your nose pressed to that maga-zine story about a football game in 1967. That same story hung on my grandmother's wall until the day she died. So . . . what you wanna ask?" Emotion crept into his voice. Not anger, I didn't think—more like sadness.

"I guess I just wondered . . . where that disappointment goes."

"*Go?* It don't *go* nowhere," Rubens said.

"How do you get past it?"

"You don't," he said. "You change."

"The story said you got hurt . . ."

Rubens walked closer to me. He sat at the edge of the stage, cradling the neck of his guitar. "Car crash. My leg got broke in four places. To this day, when it gets cold, I limp."

"Sorry to hear it, man."

He only shrugged, buffing his guitar with his shirtsleeve.

"So . . . was it really an accident?" I said.

Rubens stopped buffing. "What do you mean?"

"I was just wondering how bad the town took it—losing the game like that," I said. My heart was pounding so hard that I felt dizzy. "You sure nobody rigged it? The accident?"

I winced when I heard myself say the word *rigged*, but Rubens's face didn't change. He seemed to consider it, then he shrugged his hulking shoulders. "They weren't sad about it—but nobody rigged it.

"How did—"

"The accident was triple-B. Too much Beer. Too much Balls. Not enough Brains." Wallace Rubens grunted, rocking himself to his feet. "Let's do another duet. I'll teach you three more chords." He said something else, but I missed it. At the time, I blamed my ear.

I wasn't in the mood to play, suddenly. "I don't think . . ."

Rubens caught my gaze, dead serious. "Never waste a chance to make music, son."

I didn't have the will to argue. While I sat waiting for his cue with my fingers on the keys, I noticed a plastic-covered menu standing in front of me in the sheet-music rack. Numbers caught my eyes, so blurry that I had to lean over to see them clearly.

PIG'N-A-POKE: OPEN WEEKDAYS 3 P.M. TILL 3 A.M.

I'd lost track of time, but it couldn't be later than twelve thirty. No wonder the restaurant had been so empty! Pig-n-a-Poke wasn't a lunch place. It was closed. In retrospect, it was obvious.

I suddenly realized how dizzy I was. I swayed in my seat; my toes tightened in my shoes as I pressed my soles against the floor. I felt like I was on the deck of a rocking ship.

Adrenaline drenched my pores even as I felt the weight of my muscles trying to drag me to the floor. *Shit, shit, SHIT.* I was in trouble. My heart's frantic racing only made my dizziness worse. My heart knew something was wrong.

Judging from the fast-acting effects, they'd slipped me Rohypnol or GHB, which were choice date-rape drugs: loss of judgment, motor skills and consciousness. Amnesia. From my dizziness, I'd ingested a lot. Too much. Mixed with alcohol, I would be lucky if I could stand. I thought about grabbing the nearest microphone to bash across Rubens's head, but I didn't trust my coordination. I would have to bullshit my way out of the room.

"Tell you what, man . . ." I called out to Rubens, trying to keep the slur out of my voice. I finally understood my father's daily battle. "First I'm gonna go find the bathroom."

"Other side of the bar, to the left." His voice sounded like someone gargling at the bottom of a well.

While the room swayed, I brought myself to my feet, holding the piano to keep my balance. I was breathing harder. I suddenly felt violently sick to my stomach, on the verge of vomiting. I clenched my neck muscles tight.

I felt myself take a step while Rubens played a series of chords. The loud strumming rattled inside my head. I bumped against the piano bench, which forced me to lean against the wall. I straightened as quickly as I could, hoping Rubens hadn't seen. His music went on. Either he didn't know the drug had kicked in yet, or he didn't think I could get away.

"*Half of life's fakin' it . . .*" his voice warbled. "*The rest's just the luck of the draw . . .*"

The air felt too thick to pull into my lungs, so I forgot about breathing and focused on moving one foot in front of the other. I hated to leave the wall; there was nothing but open air between where I stood and the doorway, merely a football field away.

A woman's blurry form appeared in the doorway. "You want another lemonade, baby?" Janiece called to me. She sounded as sweet as peach pie.

"Lord, I know Bear ain't lived perfect . . . But take this big ol' thorn out his paw . . ."

The room spun, and suddenly I could only see a sheet of white. The world pulled away from me, a speeding train. I stared up at the ceiling. Two fans spun above me.

The floor thundered as Wallace Rubens walked toward me from the stage. My mushy head felt like I was drifting, a child's balloon floating up against the ceiling, watching someone else's luck turn for the worse.

I couldn't see Rubens's face, but his legs were tree trunks above me.

I rolled away from him, but not far. My body cramped, and vomit spilled from my mouth. I could taste everything that had been wrong with that hard lemonade, and tried to tense my stomach, heave out more of the poison. My lungs were frozen.

"We got you, son," Wallace Rubens said quietly. With a sigh, he slapped on a green fishing cap. When he walked away, the floor thundered again. "We got you."

My memory has holes in it. The next thing I remember is the sound of angry shouts.

The three men who'd been sitting at the table in the restaurant stood over me, although none of them was looking down my way. In my imagination I broke their legs and tore out their throats, but my body wouldn't move. I vomited until my insides were on fire.

"... because *HE CAN'T THROW DEEP!*" one of the men

said, screaming. "Tell me the last goddamn time he threw a long ball! When has he done *shit* outside the pocket?"

His friends shouted him down in a chorus. I tried to kick out, but my legs lay like lead.

As the room dimmed, I saw a woman's bare calves. I could smell the lotion on her legs. She knelt beside me, and a fingertip tapped my nose. *Get help,* I whispered. Or thought.

"Sorry, baby," Janiece said.

She nudged me to my stomach with her foot, and I flopped down like a fish. Then she grabbed my hand and snaked it around my side until it rested at the small of my back. Next, my other hand. I tried to move before I heard the handcuffs, but she held on. She snapped the cuffs on like a pro. "Wish I coulda got you that brisket," Janiece said. "You woulda liked it."

I wanted to run, but I was sinking out of myself. I didn't think about Dad or Chela. Or April. The fight to stay awake was all there was.

SEE? my Evil Voice screamed in the dark. *EVERYBODY DIES—*

Just like in death, I forgot my own name.

TWENTY-FIVE

I WAS DROWNING.

I gasped, my eyes flying open as water clogged my nostrils. I spat and choked, shaking my head. I was drenched, but my face was swimming in sweetly scented air. It was dark in places, too bright in others. *Night?* Blinking at a light, I realized I'd been hearing a babble of voices, on and off, for what seemed like years. But the voices were gone.

I couldn't place the pieces that came into sight from the beam of a bright fluorescent lantern on the ground: Planks of wood. A large yellow bucket. Fast-food wrappers scattered on a leaf-covered floor. Was I indoors? Outdoors? I felt an immense space, but I couldn't get my bearings. The ground felt like it was veering from side to side.

I was sitting on a wooden stool, leaning back against a wall, my wrists tied low behind me, fastened to something intractable. My shoulders burned from being slumped in an unnatural position while bound, but the confusion felt far worse. Air was hard to come by, so I was breathing in gasps. I struggled to make out where I was—to distinguish my own limbs from the surrounding environment—blinking quickly to see in the odd bluish light. I smelled cigarette smoke, spicy and exotic.

Willpower focused my eyes, and the nearly dark room filled with colors.

A hazy, hulking figure stood over me. Wallace Rubens still wore the same overalls. His boots were caked with mud. A cigarette dangled from his fingertips. He tapped the cigarette until the glowing ash fell to the floor.

"You've been 'sleep seven hours," he said. Even his speaking voice was a singsong. "Janiece *may* have put too much pack in your punch. My bad. Hope that dose wasn't too much of a shock. One thing you'll find: I'm not one for unnecessary discomfort."

Southern hospitality.

I saw the large yellow bucket he held and realized he'd thrown water on me to wake me up. My face, T-shirt, and jeans were drenched. My stomach tried to vomit, but nothing came. I only spat as I looked around, frantic to know where I was. I was inside a wooden structure with missing planks. Rafters soared above, with vines dangling that looked like hanging moss. The scent was strong and familiar. *A tobacco barn!* I might remember the name of the road where I'd seen a decrepit barn, if I could get my brain to work . . .

I knew Rubens was a killer before he told me. His cool voice said it all.

"We coulda just held your head down in this bucket till you drowned anytime," he said with no particular interest. "That's what my godson wanted to do. Now he's had to go home for dinner, and I said we'd finish when he gets back. Demond and the rest, we all want it done and over with. But before you go, I thought we might have a little talk."

I grunted, yanking my wrists. I tried to slip my wrists through the cuffs, but they were so tight I could barely twist them against my skin. Janiece had locked me up well.

When Rubens stepped closer, I tried a swiping kick from the ground, but my sense of distance was shit. My feet missed his ankles, and the room tilted. I nearly toppled from my stool. *Shit.* The room was spinning. I couldn't trust my senses at all.

"Effects'll wear off gradually," Rubens said, taking a careful step out of range. "If you have time. If I were you, I'd try to use my brains instead. You might think up some questions . . . like, 'Why am I still breathing?' "

"Barely breathing." I exaggerated my next gasps so I would sound even weaker than I felt.

"Don't waste your fine theatrics on me, son," Rubens said. "In the spirit of honesty, I have to tell you . . . in a little while, I'm gonna bring over my shotgun and put you back to sleep. And we're gonna bury you right outside, 'bout fifty yards from here." He spoke quietly, as if reciting mundane chores. "We've got your rental car, and it's on its way God-knows-where. You're just gonna be one o' them unfortunate folks who disappears. I'm old enough to remember when that used to happen from time to time 'round this way." Rubens knelt closer, looking for my eyes. "All that . . . and you still ain't a little bit curious?"

In the odd light, Rubens looked to me like he had no eyes, only flesh above his nose. A hallucination, maybe. Reflex made me recoil. Rubens knew my future—and there was no danger I would reveal his past. If I wasn't wearing a gag, it was because there was no reasonable expectation that a casual passerby would hear me scream. He was in no hurry. Rubens had no fear of interruption. This was very, very bad, but whatever marginal odds I had diminished to zero if he killed me.

Keep him talking. Buy some time. You'll think of something . . .

"Damn right I'm curious," I said, my voice hoarse. "Tell me, then. Why am I still breathing?"

"Because I can't waste a life," he said. "Got to do what needs to be done, but I recognize the gravity." He sounded like a sociopath in a twelve-step program.

"What are you talking about?" I said. "Let me go."

"Can it, son," Rubens said. "Any more of that talk, and I'll go fetch my shotgun. I was hopin' to find out what I need to know first, so the waste ain't so bad."

Please let him be bluffing. There was no way I could tell him I thought he'd killed T.D. Jackson, not even to warn him about possible retaliation from Judge Jackson. It wouldn't help me, and it might put Judge Jackson, or Melanie, in danger. I had to stall, but my brain was mush.

"Your sheriff's fine with murder, too?" I said. "I saw he's down with the hookers in your restaurant. I just wanted to get laid! What do you want from me, man?"

Rubens shook his head. "I'm disappointed in you, son. *That's* what you're gonna say at this moment? Some bullshit 'bout my little angels? I got no hookers, man. I got dancers, and I got models, and everybody comes from fifty miles around to taste Grandmama's barbecue sauce. But what two adults negotiate behind closed doors is none o' my business. We both know that's not what brings you to town."

If Rubens knew who I was and who I'd been working for, he had to suspect why I was in Mercy. *If I'm close on T.D. Jackson, then he probably knows I heard about Ebersole, and the car accident . . .*

"You startin' to get a bigger picture?" Rubens said, as if I'd spoken aloud. "If you thought I was a dumb ol' hick out in the woods, you judged me wrong, Tennyson Hardwick. I always do my research. Just go on 'head and tell me whatever you've told Judge Jackson."

My true name from his lips sounded like a signed death certificate. My brain was barren of answers. All I knew was that I couldn't sell out Melanie's family. And I had to find a way out of my mess for Dad's sake. For Chela's. I vowed I would survive the night somehow.

"I don't know a Judge Jackson," I said, so overwrought and sincere that for a moment I believed my own lie. I tested my chains again. "This is crazy, man. Think about what you're doing! The sheriff's all right with kidnapping, too?"

After a hard sigh, Rubens suddenly walked over to his shotgun. He wasn't in a hurry, but his stride was full of purpose. He looked like he'd lost his patience.

Shit shit shit shit SHIT.

"What do you need a shotgun for?" I said. "I heard you were some kind of a wrecking machine, Rubens. Look at me, all doped up. Set me free, and let's work this out man-to-man." I had no illusion that I could take Rubens in my condition, but any chance is better than none.

Rubens didn't have his finger on the trigger when he turned around, and the shotgun was pointing toward the floor. He sat in a white folding chair a few feet from me, and propped his shotgun across his lap, caressing it like his guitar.

"You're sniffin' the wrong bush, Hardwick," Rubens said quietly. "That sheriff, Jim Kelly, is an open-minded li'l' SOB—more interested in order than law, I'll put it—but I imagine he don't look kindly on kidnapping. That said, we go back a long way, him and me. He might look the other way if he caught wind of what's gonna happen tonight . . . under the circumstances."

Under the circumstances? What would make the sheriff look the other way about my kidnapping and possible murder? My eyes searched the room, newly motivated, and I saw a pile of trash and wreckage crowding the middle of the barn. Maybe something in there would be useful to someone *without* his hands cuffed behind his back, who *wasn't* under immediate threat of a shotgun-wielding mastodon.

The gray German shepherd I'd seen at the restaurant appeared from behind the trash pile and settled at Rubens's feet. I wasn't happy to see the dog. He looked as if he wondered what flavor I was. "So where's the sheriff—" I began.

The shotgun snapped up with two barrels. "My friend said you were smart," Rubens said. His voice wavered slightly, like a man on the verge of pulling a trigger. "If you can't think of nothin' smart to ask me, I'm gonna shoot you now and tell him it was all a misunderstanding. Your choice, son."

My heartbeat galloped. I couldn't think, so I blurted the first question I thought would keep him talking: "What happened at that game in 1967?"

Rubens smiled, lowering his shotgun. He stroked the stock tenderly. He had killed more than once. Maybe more than twice. His eyes were shining; I think Rubens had always planned to kill me, but that was the first moment when he felt any peace about it.

"Man's life is a heavy burden, Hardwick, and you're about to lay yours down. We think we have some control over how many days we get. Think we can we can by on brains and luck. Nah. But you deserve the truth, so I'll give you that gift," Rubens said, crossing his legs. "I haven't told once in forty years. Not even my grandmama, and she asked me about 1967 the very day she died . . . I couldn't say it then, but I'll say it now . . ."

I could barely concentrate on his voice, inhaling as slow and deep as I could, exhaling like a silent teakettle, using oxygen to counter the effects of the drug.

As long as he kept talking, I kept breathing.

TWENTY-SIX

"I USED TO HELP PICK TOBACCO out in these fields when I was eight, nine years old," Rubens said. "Stood right here in this barn when they strung the leaves up in those rafters. Nobody in my family could *spell* college, until me. First one in my family. Football scholarship. My body could always do easy what other boys found hard. I couldn't afford a plane ticket, so I went out to California by bus. Might as well've been the other end of the earth.

"In 1967, I was a junior at SoCal. I was on the football team, where I met the finest men I've ever known: Don Hankins, Emory Jackson, and Randolph Dwyer. After the first week of practice, you couldn't pry us apart with a knife. Blood couldn'ta made us any closer.

"In those days especially, it was a culture shock, tryin' not to fall flat on our faces. So me and Don, Emory, and Randolph formed a brotherhood. We were all ballplayers and all Taus, so we made a little group inside we called the Heat. Pushed each other through practice, helped each other with schoolwork—you name it, we did it. I wouldn't have passed freshman English if not for Don Hankins, and that's a fact. When I showed up on that campus, I'm 'shamed to say

I could barely read. Don helped me pass English, and I gave him a hole to run through, if I had to dislocate my shoulder to do it. A team within the team. That was the Heat."

Rubens paused for the first time, unhooking his overalls. He pulled down the straps and began unbuttoning his shirt. Rubens was nearly lost in the fluorescent light, but with his shirt open, I saw the dark "H" on his chest, the size of a silver dollar. "We got brands, all of us. We chose where we wanted to wear the mark. I wanted mine right near my heart. They were the first family I ever had besides my grandmama. Every week, I went to Hell and back for my boys."

I found the cuffs' keyhole. To the touch, it seemed round, like regulation cuffs, but I'd bet that they weren't. If I had a paper clip, I might have a chance to pick them. If my fingers weren't numb. If my hands weren't behind my back.

Rubens went on: "Life was good, and the day we found out we were gonna play the Sunshine Bowl might still be the happiest day of I've ever had. We were heavy underdogs, but we had a point to make. Especially me—I was coming back home. When I left for college, there were still white-only signs on these water fountains. White and colored sections at the movie theaters. So to come back and play against the *Bobcats*? Negroes couldn't sit in FU's classrooms, but here we had a crack at 'em on a football field. Shit, a country boy like me had never even dreamed so big.

"It wasn't just the players who went to the Sunshine Bowl—some of the students had money, especially the Taus, and they made the trip to see the game. We had a sister sorority, and one of those ladies was like a little sister to us. We called her Bird, 'cuz her bones were like a sparrow's. Texas gal, from Waxahachie, sweet as you'd ever meet. We were all in love with Bird, but since we couldn't let a girl come between the Heat, nobody could touch her. Still, everyone knew it was me she loved. We were both country folk, spoke the same language more so than Em or Don. They'd been too sheltered. And Randy, well, he was too much a choirboy.

"But it was all innocent. I never broke the pact. We traveled in a pack, the five of us, doin' kid stuff. The drive-in. Student union. Shit, you *know* I'd follow that girl anywhere if I'm sittin' at the library on a Friday night. So it was no different when we got to Tallahassee for the game. We got in a day early, so I took 'em 'round Mercy a li'l' bit. My grandmama never forgot the day I showed up with all my friends from school on her doorstep. See, her grandmama had been born a slave . . . so Southern California University was a long way from where my family started. I don't think I ever saw her happier again, with a whole house of college kids to feed.

"But me and the guys, we knew we had a game, so we were on our best behavior. We got to the boardinghouse when we told the coach we'd be there. Lights out. Me and my brothers prayed on it, asking for strength on the field, and we went to bed."

He paused to sigh, and I was afraid his story was over. But it wasn't.

"The game got ugly, name-calling and such. Don, Emory, and Randolph were surprised. Well, being from Mercy, I knew that crowd would get riled. But Em, Don, and Randy seemed real hurt by it. People say I'm the hothead, but nothing like the way Don got pissed off during that game. Boy was made out of mad. I swear, that boy played miles better'n we'd seen him in practice, or any other game. We were all talkin' shit to the Florida players on the field—and they weren't used to Negroes who weren't 'fraid to talk back. Mind you, I knew some o' them boys. Two or three of those players were from Stephens County High, which wasn't integrated back then. Couple o' them Mercy boys pointed right at me, and said, 'You better shut your friends up 'fore they get hurt.'

"There's no feeling to describe seeing the scoreboard when the clock runs out. There we were, twenty years old, never been nowhere or done nothin', and we'd just beat the Florida University Bobcats *on their home field.* You'd have to be in the same place and time to know what that felt like. With the race thing on top of it, we all thought we were Malcolm X and Dr. King rolled up in one. We were changing the world. At long last, our day had come."

A loud rumbling sound came from outside, and a truck's brakes moaned to a stop. Headlights bled through the cracks in the planks.

I heard voices. Three or four other people had just shown up.

The dog leaped up and ran for the open barn door, tail wagging. The dog barked.

Propping himself up with his rifle as if it were a cane, Rubens stood up. He pulled his fishing cap out of his front pocket and put it on. Rubens had told he was going to kill me when his family got back from dinner. I suspected he was a man of his word.

"That's the story?" I said. "What else happened?"

Rubens held up his index finger, walking toward the door. "Hold your horses."

Outside, I heard men's voices, speaking low. Two men, maybe a woman, too. I tried to hear what they were saying, but the dog was barking.

With Rubens's back turned, I twisted my right wrist around and around, kinking the chain. If I could take all the slack out, I would have the best leverage to see if one of the links was weak. When it wouldn't twist any farther, I clinched my gut as hard as I could, exhaled slowly, and channeled every ounce of strength into my forearms and wrists, ignoring the sting as the cuffs bit into my skin. My arms felt as if I would wrench them out of my shoulder sockets.

Rubens didn't turn around. I pulled again. Just one weak link. A bad weld. A bubble in the metal. Any structural compromise for appearance above security. Anything.

"*Shit, shit, shit . . . come on, come on . . .*" I whispered, resting a moment, then twisting harder. Simultaneously, I scanned the floor for something useful; there wasn't anything within my legs' reach except pinecones, dead leaves, and scrawny twigs.

Rubens met the others in the open barn doorway. The damn dog buried his words with his yapping. Janiece appeared with a brown bag I guessed was filled with food. She was still wearing her pink piggy dress and apron from work.

". . . some bullshit, Bear," I heard one of the men say. "It's like, eight o'clock, man . . ."

"Just go on, take a few minutes and get started out back. Four, five feet. Use the jack."

I was relieved Rubens was bargaining for more time with me, until I realized he was telling them to kill time by digging my grave. Every silver lining has a cloud.

I saw Janiece peek at me from around the corner, her arms folded. She was too far to see her eyes, but she looked quickly away. I heard her ask Rubens what he wanted to drink.

"Gimme a Coke," Rubens said. "Go put my dinner by my chair."

Shit. I stopped struggling to free myself when Janiece came toward me with his soda and bag of food. Could I turn the interruption into a blessing in disguise?

"Don't get close!" Rubens called after her, and she stopped short, just when I was plotting how to capture her with my legs and bargain for my freedom. *Damn.* Rubens and the other men argued, walking out of sight. I heard the bed of a pickup truck fall open.

"Sorry," Janiece said softly.

"*Sorry?*" I whispered. "Girl, *they're gonna kill me.*" Her pity was my last hope, so I gave her an actor's tears. I spoke in a hush, my lower lip trembling. "There's gotta be something you can say. Please. I've got a kid—Chela. She was headed for trouble, but everything's working out for her. Don't let this happen. Her future's finally looking bright. Janiece, I'm begging. *Please.*"

For an instant her face froze, as if a thought was trying to surface. Then she shook her head. "When will ya'll learn not to fuck with Bear?" she said, as if it were a question she pondered each night. "You seem nice, not to mention *fine*, so yes, I'm sorry. But don't act like I made this bed for you." She stuck out her lip and turned to walk away.

So much for pity.

"Sister, *please*," I hissed. "I haven't done a single thing to this man . . ." My voice would have broken almost anyone's heart.

"Liar," Janiece said, walking off.

I yanked my wrist with frustration, biting my lip. It took all of my willpower not to yell out what I thought of her—but she might come in handy later, so I held it in. If there was a weak link in Bear's crew, Janiece was it. It was hard to watch her walk back into the night.

Outside, a chain clanked. Rubens reappeared with his shotgun resting across his shoulder. As he got closer, I smelled his perspiration from an exertion. Digging?

Rubens sat in the chair, ignoring his food. He sighed and lit a hand-rolled cigarette. He stared at me with one eyebrow raised while he put his shotgun between his knees, his hand inching toward the stock.

"What did you say to Judge Jackson?" His voice was gentle, a father confessor.

This time, a lie would only get me shot sooner. I was certain of that.

"I told him what T.D.'s mother begged me to tell him—I said he might never know what happened, and he should let his son rest in peace."

Rubens' soft, sad look said he believed me. I might have finally said the right thing. Still, he didn't take his hand off of his shotgun.

"What happened after you beat Florida?" I said. "Did you really have an accident, or was some redneck from town looking for payback?"

Rubens smiled sadly. "Don was right about you, son. You were headed straight for it."

Straight for WHAT? I felt a terrible certainty that Rubens wasn't planning to kill me merely because he'd killed T.D., or I because I might be able to implicate his buddy Hankins in an old car accident. Hankins and Rubens thought I'd stumbled on to a secret from 1967.

"Whatever it is you think I know—I don't," I said. "I just wanted to ask you some questions. I only came to Mercy because of lucky guesses, Rubens."

"All things considered, I'm not sure I'd call 'em lucky," Rubens said. But his hand fell away from the rifle, and he leaned over with a grunt to pick up his food. He pulled out a thick barbecue sandwich and bit down. Brisket. My stomach rolled.

"We were pretty much mobbed after the game, but Coach got us on the buses and sent us to the rooms," Bear went on. "If we'd stayed in our room like we were supposed to, none of the rest would've happened. Turned out, there were kids waiting outside, hoping we'd come out. Sitting there in their cars with the lights off. But we didn't know.

"Me, Emory, Don, and Randy piled into my grandmama's big ol' beat-up Dodge Dart, and we headed for Bird's aunt's house, where Bird was waiting. We'd all made a plan to go to Quincy, where we hoped we could sneak into a bar. Then we jumped on I-10 and headed west. You've seen the road—it looks much the same now. Just weren't as many cars then.

"We'd been driving fifteen minutes before we realized anyone was following. Not just one car, it turned out—two. Nine boys in all. Only one of 'em was from FU, and none of 'em were players. They were pissed off and drunk, and they wanted a little overtime, an extra down or two, you feelin' me? Near the town Midway, one of the cars drives alongside us and honks. I'd told my friends not to say anything—*Let me do the talking*, I said—but Don Hankins shouts something out of the window, playing the dozens like he would back home, and those boys took great offense to the idea of Don Hankins ass-fucking their mamas. Maybe it would have all gone to hell no matter what, but that was certainly no help."

Outside, faintly, I heard machinery chug-chug-chugging. Digging.

Think think think think think.

I unwound the cuff chain, and then wound it up the other way. Inhaled silently, tensed my body without moving my face, and *twisted.*

Rubens went on with his story. He seemed lost in his past. "Two cars against one, it didn't take 'em long to run us off the road. I was driving, and I did my best, but my grandmama's old car could barely make fifty. Next thing, we were in the woods. I grabbed a tire iron and Don had his switchblade—he always wanted to be a thug like his uncle in Chicago, I reckon—and we thought we'd show those rednecks who they were messing with. We were young and dumb and full of cum, man.

"Next thing we know, there's a shot fired. One of 'em had a gun. Shotgun, like this. Once they had the gun on us and we gave up fighting, they went after Bird. She was a fine-featured li'l' thing, turned lots of heads. Bird was shaking so bad I could see it in the dark. She gave me a look I'll never forget: *DO SOMETHING, Wallace.* They had a gun, but I didn't give a shit, and I knocked two o' them boys down before they could blink." Something ugly flickered behind his eyes, then was gone. His voice fell, softer.

"Then they hit me with a bat, just below the left knee. While they kept the other guys under the gun, they smashed my leg, man. They broke it in four places. I'd never felt pain like that. I was howlin' at the moon. They brought out rope and threatened to string us up. Till the end, I thought that we'd end up swinging in those trees. But they tied us, and made us watch while they took turns with Bird. Not all of them—two were hurt, and three didn't have a taste for it. Four of those boys kept Bird screaming for an hour solid—one of 'em was from Mercy. All we could do was close our eyes so we wouldn't see her without her clothes."

Chained as I was, I couldn't help empathizing. As for Bird, I couldn't imagine it.

"I passed out and woke up at my grandmama's house, on the swing on her porch. It was dawn 'fore I got to a hospital. I was only half-awake—I'd taken some good thumps on the head—but my friends had decided to tell Coach our car had crashed. Heat looks out for Heat. Emory, Don, and Randy didn't go back to California with the team. They stayed behind.

"Nobody was allowed to see Bird. Her aunt and family were with her, but she didn't want us to lay eyes on her. I wept like a baby every time I thought about what I'd seen. I know for a fact that woman has never been the same. *Never.*"

His voice shook at the lost memory of her.

"Don, Emory, and Randolph came by my hospital room right before dark, everybody tryin' to cheer me up. Said not to worry, I could play again, even though my leg was wrapped up like a mummy's. Without ball, I didn't have a life to go back to."

The machinery outside grated against rocks, then stalled. I heard loud cursing.

Think think think think think think.

"I should have known: They kept sharing these glances back and forth. I was gonna take care of it myself, let them sit it out. Don always had big plans, even back then. I didn't want them dirtied up in it. Revenge works just fine cold. But they had their own ideas, and that night they headed out for Mercy. They figgered you find one, you find the rest. Don got his hands on a pistol, and he brought it with him.

"Don, Emory, and Randolph weren't the first to mistake the Kelly brothers. Five of 'em, all about a year apart. Well, the boy who'd attacked us in the woods was nineteen years old—Eric. But the boy Don, Emory, and Randolph snatched off the street was Lewis, who was seventeen. Lewis had nothing to do with what happened the night of that game, mind you. Probably didn't know anything 'bout it either. But Lewis is the one who took off running and got shot in the back by Don Hankins and his .32."

My heart was beating a river. Senator Hankins had killed an innocent man in 1967! And by sharing that information with me, Rubens had given himself no choice but to kill me. He wasn't bluffing. He never had been.

"Hey, Bear!" a voice shouted from the doorway. The man in the mechanic's uniform stood there. "It's jammed, man. Blue don't know how to work that thing."

"Then get a shovel," Rubens said impatiently.

The mechanic cursed and walked away. I wondered if Rubens had brought the mechanic with him when he went to California to take care of Ebersole, or if he did the tampering himself.

Rubens went on: "Soon as I heard the news that Lewis Kelly had been found dead in the woods, I knew what had happened." The name Kelly seemed vaguely familiar, but I couldn't pinpoint why. My head was clearer, but panic was setting in.

"I broke the bad news to Don, Em, and Randy. We prayed for forgiveness, holding hands. We swore we'd never tell a soul. There's still folks walking around Mercy who know what happened—which boys raped Bird, and which boys killed Lewis Kelly. It's what you call mutual silence. And I've never told nobody 'cept you."

"Does Bird know?"

He looked at me without expression. "She's doin' OK. That's all I care about, all you need to know." Our conversation was about to come to a loud, messy end.

"What about T.D. Jackson?" I said. There had to be another door, a place I could tap on a window, engage his interest, live a little while longer. The only thing that mattered was time. "If you're gonna kill me anyway, tell me what happened."

Rubens only stood up, sighing. He picked up his rifle, hand on the trigger. "I've told enough stories tonight, son," he said.

"Hankins fucked up and killed the wrong guy," I said. "That's how it was, wasn't it? Ebersole started making trouble in Hollywood and Hankins told you to take care of it? And the same thing happened with T.D. Jackson? How exactly did you become Hankins's bitch?"

His hand blurred, and stars exploded behind my eyes. I tasted blood. When my eyes focused again, he was smiling at me. I was lucky: He could have simply pulled the trigger.

"I wasn't nobody's *bitch*," Rubens said. "Didn't you just hear the story I told you? Don saved my ass after my leg got ruined. Sent me money. Helped me get work. Heat looks out for Heat. He flew me out from time to time when he thought my size would make somebody think twice."

Outside, I heard someone turn on music, probably from the truck. This time, two men came into the barn. The taller, thinner one was holding a shovel. "There's all these rocks, Bear," the thin man said. He didn't look at me.

Rubens stood up, beckoning his men. He held his gun by the barrel. I never let Bear's gun out of my sight. I had just run out of time.

"What happened at T.D. Jackson's house?" I called to Rubens.

The stubby one suddenly grabbed Bear's shotgun and jacked a cartridge into the chamber. The CRACK echoed everywhere. When he took aim at me, my skin tried to leap from my frame. At ten yards, his shotgun would take my head off. "Can I shut him the fuck up?" he said.

My mind went blank. I'd run out of words.

Rubens gave me a long look. I'm not sure what he saw in my face—maybe I looked like I finally understood the seriousness of my position—but he shook his head *no*.

"Let's get his bed ready first," Rubens said, walking away. "This is *my* cross."

He sounded so righteous and sad, he could have been about to bury a loved one.

TWENTY-SEVEN

I HAD ONLY ABOUT THIRTY SECONDS to twist the handcuff links behind my back before Janiece appeared with a flashlight and a slow, deliberate walk. For the first time, I noticed that she was wearing heels. Tall ones. I was too mentally confused to remember if she'd been wearing heels all along. I didn't think so.

"Don't make me go run and tell Bear you're not sittin' still." Janiece sat in Bear's chair and crossed her legs. I couldn't read her in the lantern's light. Was there compassion in her?

I panted. I felt as if I had half a cup of thin, greasy fluid sloshing around in my lungs.

"Janiece," I said. "I'm Tennyson Hardwick. Ten, my friends call me. I'm just a guy from L.A. I have a daughter, like I told you. If I die, you're an accessory to murder. Do you know what that means?" I tugged hard against the wall, my brow knitted. The chain clanked loudly.

"*Hey*, cut that out!" she said, rising to her feet. "Do that again, an' I'm tellin' Bear."

"An accessory means that you let it happen," I said. "But if you help me get away, the police won't touch you. Please—do you have the keys to these cuffs?"

Her grin chilled me. "I might. What if they're mine?" she said.

Who *was* this woman? I had to figure Janiece out fast, or she would be the last person I ever met. Janiece wasn't a cop, and I couldn't fathom that Rubens and Janiece were on a kidnap-and-murder spree in Mercy. Why did she have handcuffs? I suddenly thought about every horror movie I'd ever seen set in the country—with an entire family gone feral.

"Your uncle is about to get you sent to the electric chair," I said.

She laughed an earthy laugh. In a crisis, the sound of laughter is sickening. "He calls all his girls his nieces," she said casually. "Or else his angels. An' his crew is his godsons. We're family, but we're not blood."

Janiece was more than a waitress at Pig'n-a-Poke, and the electric chair wasn't on her list of concerns in life. I had to find out who she *was*, and fast.

"What's a honey like you doing in a hole like Mercy?" I said.

My grin knocked her mask askew slightly—she was radiating something, and I couldn't quite place it. Janiece's lips curled. God help me, was that a smile? "I'm savin' up my money to go to Miami," she said. "I got a cousin there. She said she's gonna get me in videos. Say it again, like you did before."

"Say what?"

" 'The future looks bright.' "

I didn't remember saying it. My mouth fell open, then I managed to pull myself back together. "The future looks *bright*!" I said, as brightly as I would on TV.

She clapped her hands. "It is you!"

She had seen my damned commercial? Suddenly placed my face?

I didn't go to church *nearly* often enough. I started improvising, fast. "Girl, forget about Miami! Let me take you to Hollywood. Don't you want to be on TV like me? I'm *hooked up*, Janiece. You want to dance in videos? Be on TV? Shit, girl, you don't wanna be working out of a barbecue joint. My agent can introduce you to movie stars, singers, anybody you want. You get me my phone back, and I'll call him right now. Whatever you want, name it. Just let me go before Bear kills me!"

Her eyes were quiet, watchful, gave nothing.

"What's holding you back, Janiece? You don't think you're ready for Hollywood?" I said. "There's lots of girls out there, lined up around the corner. Afraid you won't measure up? How come Bear's got you waitin' on tables instead of working the room in those fuck-me pumps? Dancin' on that stage? How come he's not showing *you* off?"

Janiece didn't answer right away. Had I hit a nerve? I couldn't keep myself from glancing at the doorway. I expected to see Wallace Rubens and his shotgun at any moment, but my mouth babbled on: "I'll put in a call and say 'Janiece is hot as hell, and she saved my life when I had no one else to turn to.' Girl, you'll go to the *best* parties."

"What kinda parties?"

I had her. My heart thundered. "M.C. Glazer," I said. "Just to name one."

Janiece's lips parted; I could see it even in the semidarkness. Celebrity is magical anywhere, but the magic apparently carried special weight in a backwater like Mercy. I couldn't blame her: M.C. Glazer was an international superstar, after all.

"*Get the fuck out!*" she practically screamed. I winced when she raised her voice.

"*Shhhhh*. . . . .Janiece, please let me go. Let me take you with me. How far are we from the road? Let's both get the fuck out of Mercy."

Me and Janiece against the world.

"Were you at Glaze's party?" Janiece said, twirling her hair on her finger.

I wanted to scream in frustration. Instead, I brought my voice down lower, almost out of Janiece's earshot. As I spoke, I saw her craning her ear closer. "His CD release party for *Plugged* was *sick*. Usher was there. Prince. Cameron Diaz. Diddy. He had it at Club Magique in Hollywood, and those girls were getting paid. Wish you coulda been there. Glaze would go *crazy* for you. Girl, you'd get rich."

Especially if you were fifteen years younger, I thought grimly. I had rescued Chela from M.C. Glazer's house, and his tastes were decidedly younger than Janiece.

"Tell him what my specialty is," Janiece said. We were living in two different conversations. In hers, there was no particular hurry. In hers, it was entertaining to pretend there was a chance in hell she might let me go, just for the sheer animal fun of giving me just enough hope to take it back again.

"What?"

She looked over her shoulder to make sure no one was coming.

"You asked why I'm waitin' tables? I'm a specialty, that's why. I get calls to go all the way to Tallahassee. Jacksonville, even. I got *fans*. I don't have to work the floor at Pig'n-a-Poke."

"Hey, no offense—"

"I'm a mistress," she said, drawing the words out. "Mistress Janiece. You know—S&M? Bondage? That's why I got handcuffs. I've got all kinds of chains. I get paid to tie men up."

Was the S&M thing more than professional? Was she turned on by pain, or death? By the sight of me chained to the wall? Janiece stood just out of my reach, and I couldn't see her face beyond the flashlight beam. If I was going to survive, I needed to climb into her fantasy with her.

"What happens now?" I said. "Give me a little taste to tell Glaze about."

I kept the assured smile on my face, although smiling was the last thing on my mind. Janiece stepped closer, shining her flashlight in my eyes. I squeezed my eyes shut.

"Oh, I get it . . ." she said. "You're about to get your head blown off by a double barrel, and now you want Janiece to blow the other head? You got balls, Telephone Man."

Two more steps brought her well within my reach, practically between my legs. I felt a twisted excitement radiating down from her. She was aroused.

One by one, Janiece stepped out of her black heels. Smiling, she raised her right foot and ran her toes across my upper thigh, toward my crotch. Her breathing was heavy.

"You want me?" she said.

" 'Course I want you, girl," I said, lathering my voice with desire. "Just let me go . . ."

"If you want me, *prove* it," she said. Her toes wiggled across my zipper. The pressure was firm, but I might as well have been numb below the waist.

Her expression soured. She looked like a child denied her candy. "If you want me, then how come you ain't ready for me?"

Shit shit shit shit.

"Wait," I said, my voice urgent, and I closed my eyes.

To this day, I still wonder how I did it. I know I tried to remember the meditation from a yoga class I'd taken with Alice, which she always claimed was her Fountain of Youth. I tried to concentrate on my own heartbeat, which wasn't hard; my heart was shaking my chest.

I tried to forget everything in the room and the armed men outside. And the dog. I focused on imagining a burning white light six inches beneath my navel. The second chakra, Alice had called it. The pathway to the sex drive. I saw April's nakedness in my shower, before she went away.

Janiece's big toe plunged deep between my legs, nudged my testicles, and journeyed back up across my fly. I felt a weak glow, getting stronger, as she stroked me with her foot.

"What are you gonna do for me, girl?" I said to April's vision. "Tell me."

"I'll show you," she said.

In character, her voice was sultry. My anatomy did its part to be free, and Janiece's grin widened, appreciative. Her foot pressed against the growing firmness. I braced, expecting her to dig her heel in hard.

"You're a big boy, huh?" she said.

"See for yourself."

"Call me *Mistress*, bitch," she said. Her foot's pressure grew.

All right, Mistress Bitch. "How far to the road, Mistress? Is this the barn off Route 66?"

She slapped my cheek, hard. My face burned with a flash. She was practiced at hitting. My erection stopped growing.

"You talk when I tell you," she said.

"Yes, Mistress," I said between gritted teeth.

Janiece knelt in front of me, staring me down with a gleam in her eyes. She slid her hand across my fly, massaging. Janiece yanked my jeans open. When she slid her hand beneath the denim, the zipper unfurled. Her fingers knew what they were doing.

I hissed between my teeth as her fingertips glided. All the while, I expected pain.

"Give me the keys, Mistress?" I said to those impenetrable eyes.

I could smell her arousal, so I caressed her with my gaze. Begged her, just the way she liked it. "Please?"

"Can't do that," she whispered, out of character. Her gentle thumb rubbed circles across my sensitive ridges. "But I'm gonna send you out right—give you something worth dying for."

No key was coming; I was just a prop in her fantasy. So much for the easy way out.

Sorry, Janiece. As she leaned over to bring her face closer to my crotch, my right knee caught her under the chin. As she jolted up, I head-butted her directly between the eyes, and she dropped like a sack of rocks.

"Don't flatter yourself, darlin'." Don't get me wrong: A woman's mouth is one of nature's greater creations. But no blow job is worth dying for.

I looked over my shoulder down at the chain. It was thicker steel than the cuffs. No help there. *What*, then . . . ?

The wall. The barn's wood was ancient and worm-eaten. *The weak link.* I braced my left leg and smashed back into the wood with my right heel. The shock ran up my right leg to my twisting hips, then down into my planted left heel, then I switched to the other side, mule-kicking right next to where the bolt fastened into the wall. And again, right-left, back, and forth. With every kick, the barn wall shook, and the cuffs tore at my wrists. I felt something give—the wood, not my wrists, thank God. I shifted angles and set my heel against the wall next to the bolt, and pulled or pushed with damned near every muscle in my body. My shoulders screamed.

Either my bones and tendons were going to give, or that damned wall. I stifled a yell as the wood splintered, but clamped my mouth shut as I fell forward, landing on my shoulder. I was free!

I heard voices outside, dimly. Getting closer. I tried to get to my feet, and the first time I landed on my face, falling nearly headfirst into Bear's chair. A hurricane roared between my ears, and I gasped to breathe. My body felt unfamiliar and new.

GET UP GET UP GET UP.

I tried to stand more carefully, this time with a wider stance. There were five or six pounds of extra weight tugging on my handcuffs from the large metal ring swinging behind me from the broken wall, but I adjusted, staggering to stand up.

Bobbing flashlight beams approached the barn door. I heard barking.

I didn't have time to grab Janiece's flashlight, or hunt for my cell phone or the handcuff keys. The barn's wall planks were like missing teeth, and I ran toward the first open space.

The space *wasn't* open, just dark. I ran nearly headfirst into solid wood, and I was on the floor again. I felt dazed. My name was slipping away from me again.

Barking, someplace close.

I got up somehow. With my shoulder, I broke through a cracking plank. I banged my head, but I was beyond noticing. The old wood gave, and I stumbled through.

I was outside. I saw trees.

It was dark. I heard barking.

I ran for my life toward the night.

I was shoelace deep in the swampy woods, and I was about to get caught. Even while I ran with all my might, I knew I couldn't get away.

Think think think think think.

Running was hard enough without having to think, too. With no flashlight to light my way, and my arms chained behind me, it was a challenge to stay upright. My feet sloshed in soggy ground that sometimes dipped until it was covered by a foot of murky water, making each shoe weigh half a ton. I tripped over the things I couldn't see, bumping my knees and stumbling off-balance. Every step was a triumph. The air felt as thin as if I were climbing Mt. Kilimanjaro again. Still, in the dark I might have been able to evade the men until daylight.

But I couldn't escape the dog. His bark was getting closer. Fast.

I've had more than a few fights with men, but I'd never faced off with a beast. A dog changed everything. No cheap psychology, no bargaining, no bullshit. Just teeth, and my fly was hanging open. If I wasn't very careful, I was about to get mauled. And then shot.

Thinkthinkthinkthinkthink.

In only ten seconds, the dog's barking sounded twice as close. It was running at full speed, and he would catch me in less than a minute. Maybe forty seconds.

I fell to my knees behind a pine tree trunk, an elevated patch. Panting for breath, I lay as flat as I could on the damp forest floor and wriggled my hips and legs through my handcuffs. I expected to feel the hot canine breath on my neck any moment.

Disorientation slowed me down, but I got my bound hands in *front* of me. There was still a rusting metal ring swinging from the handcuffs, but there was nothing I could do about that.

The dog's barking told me I had ten seconds to find a weapon.

I zipped up and searched everything I could see within easy reach—branches, rocks, anything. The ring hanging from my handcuffs was a last-resort weapon. Anyone in the ring's range was too close for comfort. At least I could use the cuffs to strangle someone, or some*thing.*

I tripped and fell again, scraping my knees and palms. I looked to see what I'd stumbled over: a concrete cinder block. I thought I saw other pale blocks nearby, but it was too dark to be certain. I had found the remnants of a construction site.

The block felt like it weighed three or four times its twenty pounds, but I tensed my gut, exhaled hard, and heaved to lift it.

You wanna catch me?

I hid behind a tree trunk and waited. It would be up to my ears. I might not have more than one chance to get it right.

I'd barely taken three breaths before the barking was on top of me.

I quieted, calming the roar of blood, guessing which side of the tree he'd come around. *Quiet. Breathe . . .*

Then . . .

I felt a *POP* in my head, and the dog's barking roared on my *left* side. My bad ear.

I can hear! I thought, just as the blur of the dog's pale muzzle rounded the side of the tree, snapping toward me. The dog growled like he'd found dinner.

My first swing was low. Instead of hitting the dog's head, where I was aiming, the block slammed into its shoulder. The shepherd yelped and skittered sideways, but stayed on its feet. The dog lunged while I staggered, flung off-balance by my own swing.

Teeth pierced my forearm, seeking purchase, tearing but slipping. It hurt like hell.

But I never let go of that concrete block. With its extra weight I was able to yank my arm away from the dog's jaws with another flash of pain. When the gray shepherd lunged at me the second time, my aim was better. A *CHUNK* sound reminded me of my head-butt with Janiece, and the dog was limp on the ground.

I couldn't take any chances that it would wake up and come after me again. I stood over the dog, closed my eyes, and hammered the block down to make sure he'd keep sleeping.

I was in chains, and the men chasing me had guns.

I liked my odds better without the dog.

TWENTY-EIGHT

ONCE, I THOUGHT I HEARD SOMEONE TO THE RIGHT, and was starting at shadows. A flashlight beam probed the woods to my left, and I froze in place for almost a half hour. Twice, I thought I heard a truck engine, off through the woods ahead. A road? Carefully, I set out through the woods, gliding from shadow to shadow, until I reached a glade about thirty feet across. On the other side, more woods. And beyond that . . . I hoped . . . a road.

I could stay in the woods and go around the meadow, wasting time. Or I could cut across, risking exposure. I chose the direct route.

I had only taken a few steps before I knew I'd made a mistake. Only one of my hunters had been smart enough to track me.

The flashlight pinned me like a bug in a blowtorch. I froze, knowing that guns were trained on my head. How many? Where? And was there anything left to do?

"*I hate you killed my dog.*" The voice floated in out of the darkness ahead of me, and its very calm gave the words greater gravity.

Wallace Rubens was breathing in rasps, either from running or rage, or maybe both. His bulk was a mountain rising and falling. I saw moisture glistening on his face. Tears.

"Now you've crossed a line, son. Drop that stick. I'm out of good manners."

I dropped the rebar I had found. There are good reasons guns are more expensive than sticks.

"I'm sorry about your dog," I said gently, "but you would've done the same thing."

"You could've broke his leg," Rubens shot back.

"I didn't think of it."

"Well, you're gonna wish you had."

I already wished I had. "If you wanted to kill me, I would've been dead hours ago," I said. "*You don't want to do it*. You're not a murderer, Bear. Things got out of hand when Hankins sent you after Chad Ebersole, and T.D. Jackson had to be stopped—but don't kill me over a dog."

"Don never told me to kill Ebersole," Rubens said, eyes glimmering. "Just said he had a problem. I came up with the fix. Didn't know Ebersole would die, but truth is I really didn't give a shit. Since '67, there's only one thing I give a shit about: Heat looks out for Heat. You didn't mean no harm, did you? Just wanted to find out what happened to Emory's boy—trying to help Heat. Hell, I wish I could buy you a beer and wish you luck."

"It's not too late," I said. Hope springs eternal.

"Reckon it is," he replied, and he didn't hide the regret in his voice. He sighed massively. "Grayboy didn't mean nothin' to you, but I raised that dog *and* his mama, so we went back some years. And now I'm recalling that question you asked me when you were tied in the barn: You asked if I was man enough to put down my shotgun and take you straight up. I'ma tell you what: Today's Fire Sale day, boy. You're surely about to find out what you wanted to know."

He reached into his front pocket and tossed me a small key ring. I snatched it out of the air. A single key dangled. "Go on, unlock it," he said. "What we got here is a generational difficulty, but I do believe men of goodwill can work things out."

I'd pissed off Wallace Rubens enough that he wanted to kill me with his bare hands. My day had been so bad, that was the *good* news. I was nauseous, half-dizzied, and weak, but I was grateful. He was giving me a chance.

I worked quickly on the cuffs, getting my hands free. Rubens hadn't lowered his shotgun.

"Toss the cuffs and rebar as far as you can," he said. "Then these ugly hands an' that pretty face are gonna talk."

I considered my options and did what he'd asked. The rebar flew about thirty feet, landing near a V-shaped tree trunk. Rubens had size and strength on me. And lack of intoxication. On a good day I had speed, and hopefully training and smarts. I hoped to God this was a good day. It hadn't been so far.

Rubens set his lantern down against a tree, casting a misshapen shadow across the bark. He took off his fishing cap, the gun still raised.

"You set that dog on me, Bear," I said, trying one last appeal. "Only a fool wouldn't have done whatever he could."

"You broke Janiece's jaw."

"You would've killed her," I said.

"Maybe so. But I wouldn't have expected understandin' if I'd been caught."

Wallace Rubens grunted, broke the shotgun and shucked the shells. He set it down behind him almost tenderly, never turning his back on me.

Then, he charged. I spun out of the way, and as he went by I balled my fist and punched him in the right side of his neck. It felt and sounded like hitting a side of beef. *Rocky* sucks.

He grunted and swung around, big meaty hands stretching out for me. I batted his arm up and slid under, too damned close to him, but hooking his rear foot as I went by. He stumbled, and I stomped his knee, driving it into the ground.

You watch WWF wrestlers on television, and marvel at men of such superhuman size and agility. Something in the back of your head screams *He isn't human! He can't be stopped!* And it takes every bit of control you've got to believe you have any chance at all, and look for the opportunity. There's always an opportunity, always a chance.

That's the theory. In practice, it was like trying to fight an avalanche. Bear twisted in midair and caught my left ankle with a grip like a torque wrench, punching me in the left thigh as I kicked him in the belly with my right foot.

I tore my leg free and stumbled back, leg numb, as he sprang to his feet and charged. I had just enough time to shift my weight to the side to avoid his full impact, but he hit me hard enough to send me crashing backward into an upright tree, pinning me. While I was processing the pain, Rubens hit the side of my head with a great sweeping right cross. I rolled with most of it, thank God, but for a timeless instant, the night became day.

I tasted blood, but for the first time that night, my head was clear. Adrenaline is a wonderful thing. I feinted left, and then pivoted right again, moving toward his wounded left leg, where he would be less mobile. I was loosening up finally, finding a rhythm. I jabbed, then hit him with a half fist to the throat, followed by a feinted groin kick that drew a sweeping forearm block—*damn!* There was no way he should have been that fast, but at least now I knew.

I barely evaded another charge, and he hooked my left wrist. He was off-balance, and I should have been able to twist his arm around, skate his entire body on his momentum, but I couldn't. His balance was unnatural. He might have been a fat old man, but under that fat was twice my muscle, and he knew how to control every ounce of it.

He clipped me. I absorbed his second and third punches with peekaboo forearms, but a wrecking ball to the ribs stole my breath and gave Rubens time to ram me against the tree with his shoulder. My right arm was useless beneath him, my rib cage collapsing against my lungs.

I had to get away from that tree. Away from him. Just . . . away. Nothing I hit him with stopped him or slowed him. Every time he hit me, I felt something give. He was killing me.

I tried to stomp his foot, but he shifted his knee, pinning my leg with his mass, too. He grabbed my forehead with one huge palm, vise-like, and smashed the back of my head toward the bark behind me.

GET AWAY FROM THIS MAN, OR YOU'RE DEAD.

Finally, my Evil Voice had some useful advice. I managed to knee him in the crotch, and his moment of weakness let me slip out of his grip. I levered him away from me with my elbows, and slipped from beneath Rubens like an eel.

When he turned, I hit him with a straight right to the left side of his jaw. He barely blinked, but his feet slipped sideways so that they were both on the same line. I kicked his front knee. Bear grunted and thumped down, and I kicked him in the face as hard as I could. Dammit—he got one of those giant hands up to absorb some of the shock, but blood burst from his nose and upper lip. I stepped way back and glanced around me to better weigh my options.

I saw the V of the tree I'd spotted, and I ran for it. My rebar.

"Where you goin'?" Bear panted. "Huh?"

Bear was panting worse than I was, but he pulled me down by the seat of my pants, and pure force brought me to my knees. While we rolled back a few yards, Bear had my right arm and was twisting it like a giant Indian burn, and I jackknifed and kneed him under the chin, breaking away. The kick was solid, but he snapped his hand around my ankle. I lifted myself up with my palms to try to twist my leg free, but he only tightened his grip.

I wrenched my leg away, losing skin in the process.

My best chance would be on my feet, no barriers. Open air. I scrambled up and ran.

If I could keep Bear moving, I could wind him. Fatigue would drain some of that strength. He couldn't afford to let me go, and I couldn't afford to run into the woods and let him recover, gather his allies, and hunt me down. Both of us had to finish it there.

I ran toward the tree marking the place where my rebar had landed. If Rubens wanted honorable hand-to-hand combat, more power to him. I wanted my weapon back.

The adrenaline seemed to be burning off. The drug, the exhaustion, the pain, all combined to turn my legs to spaghetti. He was coming. A quick survey of the grass: no rebar. *SHIT!*

I had to run. Fifty paces, then I slowed and looked back at him, moving like a rhino. Another twenty paces. He was wheezing, but kept coming. He might catch me, I realized. Just like the dog. We were running uphill, and I was already dizzy.

The next time I checked over my shoulder, Rubens had stopped, a slightly quizzical expression on his face, as if he was listening to something. He was panting hard. Was there a godson in sight? I expected to hear gunfire.

Suddenly, Rubens moved from stillness the way he must have exploded off the line that day in '67, a blur of mass that caught me by surprise. I had time to get set, but not to run.

I had a roundhouse waiting for him, slipped to the side and connected dead in the center of his face, snapping his head back. *You might still kill me, but you won't forget me.*

Turned. Ran. *Three more steps up the hill . . .*

Bear spun me around and sank his fist into my stomach. I swear it rattled my spine—I thought he'd punched me all the way through my back. That punch was the hardest I've ever been hit. The hardest I thought anyone could *get* hit.

The ground smashed up against my knees.

Then, I was facedown in the soggy earth. Bear's punch had paralyzed me as surely as the drugs had. I knew he would kill me if I didn't get up, but I couldn't convince my body to move. Not even my fingers.

I was helpless again, forgetting my name. Soon, I might be glad to forget.

Everything was quiet except for Bear's wheezing breaths as he walked to where I lay.

High above me, he laughed. His laughter started so softly at first that I wondered if it was crying. But soon he was laughing so loudly that there was no mistaking it.

He stopped laughing, struggling to catch his breath.

Suddenly he was lowering himself to sit at the base of a wide fallen pine tree, atop a mound of dried needles. He was laughing, but his face was racked with pain. The pain wasn't from the blood staining his nose.

"I've got a daughter in Quincy. Imani," he said. "She's at Quincy Gardens. Don't let her find out from a stranger. Have Jamal, the manager, tell her." Rubens laughed again, suddenly. "Serves my ass right, don't it? I shoulda drowned you in the bucket. That's what Demond said."

My double and triple vision finally converged. Rubens came into focus again.

He was clutching his chest.

"Heart?" I gasped.

"Used to be," Rubens said. He had more trouble speaking. I

didn't think he would be laughing anymore. *It could be a trick*, my Evil Voice warned me. Had he faked a hysterical fear response too?

"Do you have a cell phone?"

Wincing in pain, Rubens patted his front pocket and pulled out a red Palm Pilot. It looked like a toy in his giant hand. He tossed it over to me. "Won't . . . work out here."

He was right. The phone got no signal.

"Don't move," I said. "I'll send someone back for you. The road's that way?"

"There," he said, pointing right. "Northwest. You'll hit the interstate in two miles." His face twisted. "Don't go."

"I'm gonna get the shotgun."

Rubens shook his head. "Don't go."

For the first time, I believed his heart attack was real. No one wants to die alone. "Breathe slowly," I said. "Sit still. I'll be right back."

My walk was a stagger. It felt like hours before I made it back to the lantern, and from there I found the shotgun. I groped the uneven grass until I found both shells.

For the first time all night, I didn't feel naked.

By the time I got back to Rubens, he had aged twenty years. Perspiration slimed his face, and his pale moist lips never fully closed, sucking air thinly. I had seen that look on my father's face, when he nearly died.

But Dad had an emergency room to save him. Rubens didn't.

"Why didn't you kill me when you had the chance?" I asked.

"Why don't you, now?"

That seemed to settle the question for both of us.

"Doctors had to open me up before," Rubens said. "Told me to slow down. Change my ways." He gave a wet laugh. "Shit man, leopard can't change his spots." He closed his eyes. Something titanically painful was happening inside his chest. "Why'd . . . you come here?"

There was no reason not to tell him now.

"Judge Jackson hired me," I said. "Said he wanted the cops out of it. When your name came up, I wondered if he would send someone after you. Hell, I don't know. I wanted to know what happened. The truth."

"Ain't that a bitch?" Rubens gasped. "You came out here to save my ass. Then I kill my own damn ass tryin' to kill you." He laughed again.

I sagged down beside him. A troupe of tap-dancing hippos had used my bones for a xylophone, and I was running on empty. "What happened with that bodyguard and the construction worker out west?"

He panted, and when his eyes opened they didn't immediately focus on me. "Hell of a fight. Ripped a damn good shirt. Bodyguard was good." He grinned. "Not as good as you—you're all right. You know what? I forgive you for Grayboy. That mean old bastard's surely going to hell. Be nice to see a friend."

I didn't want to, but I laughed. But Rubens had stopped smiling. "You're good, but you'll never lay a finger on Donald Hankins," he went on. "No evidence."

"Hankins sent you to kill T.D." I said. I wasn't a question. "What was the second shot?"

"Cleanin' up." Rubens gasped, suddenly looking panicked. His breathing quickened. "My truck. Under the seat. There's a paper bag."

"What about it?" I asked.

"That night in '67 planted a seed in Bird," Bear whispered. "I didn't have a pot to piss in, so I couldn't do nothin' for her—but a friend stepped in to help her keep her honor. They married for all the right reasons, except for love. The only love she'd ever had was for me, and me for her. I tried to put her out of my heart, wish her well. But I never could. And Bird had every comfort, but her home was empty. Raising that boy killed her. She couldn't bear to give him up, couldn't bear to raise him. She tried her best, but she never could love him. She thought it was her duty to do what she did. I have something that belongs to her, and I want you to take it back."

We talked, Bear and I. Some of it was about his life, but mostly about music. He seemed like someone I could have spent a night laughing with. Wallace Rubens was just a terrible old man whose lard-spackled arteries were finally coming apart.

His big hand reached out and took mine. Squeezed. "Never thought I'd live to see it," he said. "Ain't no tellin' what a young man can do in this world today."

He knew what he was doing when he put his gun down. He'd known he was giving me a chance. I looked carefully at Bear's broad, soft, quiet hand. No trace of a thorn.

Before long, he stopped caring whether I came or went. So I went.

SATURDAY, NOVEMBER 1

The barn was empty by the time Bear's shotgun and I made our way back. I scouted carefully, making sure no ambush waited, but no one was in sight. Bear's crew was a bunch of small-time punks held together by the mesmerizing personality of a brutal, charismatic, and oddly honorable man. They would be disappearing into the sticks, assuming I was talking to the sheriff.

I found my cell phone in the barn, and my wallet on the seat of the black GMC truck. My phone's battery was dead. Of course.

Under the truck's seat, I found the brown paper bag Wallace Rubens had sent me for. Wrapped inside was a black jewelry box half the size of my fist. I opened it up.

The contents gleamed.

Well, well, what do you know . . .

A Super Bowl ring.

I finally had a phone signal on Bear's Palm Pilot. I dialed 911.

The EMTs bandaged up my dog bite and gave me ice and Tylenol with codeine for my other aches and pains. I could barely sit upright from Bear's last body blow.

It was nearly dawn before Wallace Rubens was loaded into the back of the ambulance, beneath a heaping blanket. I was the only one who had been foolish enough to wait with the body, and no good deed goes unpunished. I overheard a jurisdictional squabble between Kelly and the sheriff from neighboring Gadsden County, and I rooted for the brother from Gadsden County to win.

But it was Sheriff J. Kelly, the cowboy I'd met at Bear's place, who led me to the back seat of his cruiser. The painkillers seemed to wear off all at once as he drove me to the tiny Stephens County Sheriff's Office in downtown Mercy, which was about the size of a cell back at Hollywood division. It didn't matter that I'd already been through hell: My luck wasn't about to change. The last time I'd been found too close to a dead body, I almost got arrested for murder.

The office was dark and empty, since it was barely dawn. Three desks, a wall clock and a coffee machine. Kelly pointed out the way to his office, where the half-open door was marked SHERIFF JAMES KELLY.

"Please," Sheriff Kelly said, as if I had a choice.

Inside, after I sat in the pine green office chair in front of his desk, Sheriff Kelly read me my Miranda rights. He read from his card slowly and carefully, to make sure I didn't miss anything. "Do you understand these rights?" he asked.

"I want a lawyer."

"What you need a lawyer for?"

Classic cop bullshit, as if asking for a lawyer is an admission of guilt. "Because I'm being detained in a police station, and I have a plane at nine I can't miss."

I have no idea what was going through Sheriff Kelly's head that morning; he kept his thoughts off his face. But for the first time, his eyes burned at me. Anger. "There was a dead man in my county—a dead man who's something like a hero around here—so you'll have to excuse me if I don't give a damn about your plane."

"Am I under arrest?"

"Tell me what happened with Wallace, and you'll be the first to know."

Good sense dictated that I should tread carefully with Kelly. I knew that. His glassy eyes told me that he and Wallace Rubens had been friends. It wasn't smart to piss off a cop who'd just lost a friend. Alone in his office. But I was bone-weary, and my mind wasn't quite mine again.

"Get me a lawyer," I said.

Sheriff Kelly looked at his watch. "It's almost six now, and Meg's in Kissimmee this week. She's our lawyer. They're infested with lawyers in Tallahassee, but you sure as hell won't get anybody before nine. Then you'd miss your flight for sure. Coffee?"

He was more polite than Lieutenant Nelson on his best day. I accepted the coffee, and the caffeine nudged the parts of my brain that were still sleeping.

Flights from Tallahassee had been booked solid, and since none of them was direct, I was already scheduled to arrive at LAX at 5 P.M. I would be pushing it to get home before Chela left. A later flight, and I had no chance. Maybe I should have had other things on my mind, but all I could think about was Chela's homecoming dance.

"Like I told you, Rubens had a heart attack," I said. "Your coroner will confirm that."

"Why'd he beat you half to death, Mr. Hardwick?" Sheriff Kelly said.

"Like I told you, Bear and I went walking, and I fell down a hill. He had a heart attack."

By then, I thought I understood the significance of the sheriff's name, Kelly. I even let him see a glimpse of what I knew in my eyes. I hoped it would get me on my plane.

"Your record's pretty clean," Sheriff Kelly said. "Except for one li'l' blip over in California. You and your dad? I saw that wreck on TV, but I didn't know that was you. Looks like folks who piss you off end up dead."

"Like I told you, I just met Rubens," I said.

"Funny thing about that," Sheriff Kelly said, pulling out a stick of gum he popped into his mouth. "You told me you were a Bobcat. In town for the game? Well, guess what—Tennyson Hardwick's not a name you hear every day . . . and it turns out you've never been registered at Florida. Not even the dropouts. So from the start, I know you're a liar. Then Bear's ticker gives out, and both of you look like you've been in a fight. So . . . you see my dilemma?"

"You got family in town, Sheriff?" I said. My eyes were crystal clear.

Sheriff Kelly sat on his desk like a statue. He stared at the floor. "There's six names on the Mercy town charter from 1855," he said quietly. "One of the names is Kelly. He was an Irish cabin boy. He came here with nothing."

"I understand Wallace Rubens had deep roots here, too."

Sheriff Kelly nodded, blinking. He was working extra hard to keep his emotions battened down. Kelly consulted his notebook. When he spoke again, there was a tremor in his voice. "Looked like there was an altercation of some kind at the old barn," he said. "Lots of footprints. Tire tracks. Some blood."

"My blood," I said. "Nosebleed."

"We found Bear's dog out by the smokehouse. Beat to death."

I shook my head, saddened. "We were looking for the Grayboy. Where was he again?"

"What if we found your footprints, too?"

"Damn. We must have walked right past him."

Sheriff Kelly sighed. "I suppose you have a story about that dog bite, too. Mr. Hardwick, everyone knows Bear had a temper," he said. "And he didn't always keep good company. What I don't know is the magnitude of my dilemma. For instance, if there's gonna be feds sniffing my town's ass."

In some ways, his words reminded me of Lieutenant Nelson's when he walked behind me into his office: *Are you a problem for me?*

"In other words," Sheriff Kelly went on, "I'm mighty curious as to why you came all the way out here from Los Angeles to see Bear. And why you're stirrin' up questions about a football game that happened before either of us were born." His green eyes locked with mine.

The sheriff might not understand everything, but he knew plenty. I got a headache, and suddenly everything about me was in pain.

"I'd like to make a phone call, Sheriff," I said.

"By and by."

"I just want to catch my flight."

Sheriff Kelly stood up. "I'm gonna make a special trip, drive you to the airport myself."

So much for stopping at my hotel to pick up my luggage; my alias at the hotel would make me seem suspicious. *He's not going to drive you to the airport,* my Evil Voice said.

"Your father's retired LAPD," Sheriff Kelly said. "Ain't that right?"

I wondered if he had just begun researching me since the accident, or if he had begun his research the night he met me. As soon as I'd been foolish enough to mention the Sunshine Bowl. I had no idea what Sheriff James Kelly and Wallace Rubens had shared besides family history.

"I want a lawyer, Sheriff," I said.

"Let's just get you on that plane."

"No offense, but I'd like another deputy to ride along with us."

He didn't look offended. His face was nearly blank. "No one's available this early but me, I'm afraid. But I'm a careful driver."

Before Mercy, the last time I'd sat in a police car was when I was arrested for prostitution in 1999. Since Hollywood was my father's command, those guys treated me like I was precious cargo, strict on the protocols. Nobody wanted to be at fault if something went wrong. Once a person is in the legal custody of another, there's room for disaster. Prisoners try to escape. Behave erratically. Get violent.

It happens all the time.

The sheriff drove me in dead silence through the empty streets of early-morning Mercy. I hoped we really were headed toward the interstate and the airport. I even closed my eyes to make it more like a prayer. Didn't work. Sheriff Kelly drove past the green sign pointing the way to the 10, ignoring its arrow.

"Where are we going?" I said.

The sheriff didn't answer.

His car turned on to a bumpier road, hardly paved. I noted a horse ranch, then grass grew high on both sides of the road. Wilderness. Small rocks popped and churned beneath his tires. The car swayed as it drove. Thin pine tree trunks appeared in the windows on all sides of us. He was driving me into the woods.

"I hope you're not about to try something stupid, Sheriff."

"Me, too," Sheriff Kelly said. "Time will tell."

There was a house in the woods, built in an idyllic clearing. The house was large, but it looked like it had been built from the surrounding trees, almost more a cabin. An old man who looked my father's age sat on a crate in the carport, painting birdhouses. The yard was full of birdhouses, all brightly colored. A child-sized all-terrain vehicle was parked off to the side.

It looked like the sheriff's home.

Sheriff Kelly climbed out of the car. His car door slammed shut. "Just be a minute."

Leaving me in the car, Sheriff Kelly walked up to the old man and patted his back. The man grinned up at him as if he hadn't seen him in days. Then the sheriff vanished into the house.

While the sheriff was inside, the old man stood up and walked toward the police car. His hair was a half bale of wilted hay. His walk was unsteady, and his posture was terrible, but once upon a time he was probably a strong, solid man. He peered at me, curious, tapping on the window. His bright green eyes gazed me up and down with childlike fascination.

"Hello?" he called to me.

I nodded, but I didn't answer. If I hadn't just suffered one of the worst nights of my life, I could have smiled. More tapping on my window. "Hey—you want to buy a birdhouse?"

I shook my head. The old man tapped the window again, waving good-bye.

Within about five minutes, the sheriff came back outside, walking down his porch's three whitewashed steps. He was trailed by a boy and a girl who looked eight and ten—both cocoa-colored, with tightly spiraled hair. The children didn't see me in the police car, so they stayed close to the old man. I was struck by how much they reminded me of Maya and Tommy Jackson. I heard one of the children call the man *Grandpa*. A woman's brown-skinned arm waved from the window.

The sheriff's Jeep was suddenly filled with the scent of biscuits and bacon.

"My wife called and said she had breakfast for me," the sheriff said, once he was back in the car. "I brought you a biscuit sandwich for the plane. I hear the airlines don't feed folks for shit anymore."

"What are you up to, Sheriff?" I said.

He looked at me in the rearview mirror. "That man over there is my dad. His name is Eric Kelly. He and Wallace Rubens met a long time ago."

Right again. "Is that so?"

"Did Bear mention my father's brother got killed back in '67?"

I hear a girl also got raped, I thought, but I didn't need to say it aloud. Mercy had made its own accommodations with what happened in 1967, long before I appeared.

"Didn't come up. We talked about music, mostly."

"My father doesn't remember those days, not for a long time now. He's got Alzheimer's. I don't know how much longer I'll have him, so I just try to keep him comfortable. He was a good father. A good man." Sheriff Kelly's voice shook, but I couldn't see his face. "Even if he made mistakes when he was young."

A truth as ugly as Mercy's deserved airing, but neither of us was prepared to bring it to light. The car sat idling for a moment.

Finally, the sheriff drove back to the road. It was just after seven when we got to the interstate. Less than an hour to Tallahassee! Could I dare to hope that I was about to make it home after all?

"Did you ever meet T.D. Jackson?" Sheriff Kelly said, breaking a long silence. The Super Bowl ring was in my back pocket; I could feel it beneath me.

"A couple of times."

"What was he like?" With the sheriff's thick accent, the word "like" came out "lack." But I heard a hunger in his voice that went beyond a fan's admiration. Or a sheriff's curiosity. Maybe he'd been hoping for a little family reunion one day.

"Troubled," I said.

He nodded. "Guess that's no secret now."

"But a hell of a ballplayer."

"Just like Bear," the sheriff said sadly.

That was the last we spoke of it.

I made it to my plane with time to spare.

TWENTY-NINE

I MADE MY CONNECTING FLIGHT and caught tailwinds into LAX, so we touched down ten minutes early. Even with rush-hour traffic, my cab was pulling me on to Gleason by six thirty, a half hour before the kid was scheduled to pick up Chela for the dance. I wanted to kiss the sidewalk. There's no place like home.

A white stretch limo pulled in right after me and parked across the street, in front of Mrs. Katz's house—I would hear about that later, since she grew her rosebushes too close to the road. I tried to peer into the limo's darkened windows. It was empty. I knocked on the driver's door. "Hey, man," I said. "Did you come with . . . Bernard Faison?"

The driver was white-haired. He shook his head. "Waiting for Chela Hardwick. Fifty-four-fifty Gleason."

I had never heard Chela use my surname, even as a joke. And how had Chela been able to afford a limo? Had Dad ordered it? "Whose name is on the bill?" I said.

The driver checked his records and recited a Russian name: Katerina Marmeladova, a character from Dostoyevsky's *Crime and Punishment*. I knew that alias well. *Mother!*

I'd told Mother about Chela's homecoming dance when I visited her in Brentwood, and Mother hadn't forgotten. Maybe there was a heart down inside her somewhere after all. I almost wished I could tell Chela who had sent the limo. Almost.

"What the hell happened to you?" the limo driver said.

"I took a wrong turn on vacation."

"Remind me never to go wherever you were."

Inside my house, everything looked and smelled right. Like always, Sidney's dignified poses greeted me from Alice's wall. I smelled Marcela's food cooking in the kitchen, probably enough for a feast. And the fish were still alive, rioting at the top of the tank for dinner.

I heard rattling as Dad's wheelchair flew across the tiles, and he met me at the end of the foyer. "Damn," Dad said when he saw my face. I'd called Dad earlier to tell him that Rubens was dead, and that we'd had a scuffle, but I hadn't mentioned my loose back tooth, or swollen jaw. I must have looked like I'd been through something. It hurt Dad's eyes to see me that way.

"Glad you went?" Dad said.

I shrugged. "Yeah. Just not glad about the way it turned out." I hadn't killed Rubens, but he had died on my watch. So had Carlyle. I was carrying something new.

"Tell me. Dinner's ready."

He wanted the details, of course. But I wasn't ready to talk about Mercy, even to Dad, so I went to the stairs instead. "Is Chela in her room?"

"I wouldn't . . . go up there!" Dad called behind me.

I knocked on Chela's closed door. "Chela?"

A frantic shriek answered me. "*Oh my GAAAAAWWWWWD. You can't see me until we finish putting on the dress!*" Rehearsing her wedding day.

"Twenty minutes!" Marcela called out next. "Men stay downstairs!"

Dad chuckled when I came back down. "Told you," he said. "Get some food, Ten."

For the next fifteen minutes, while I ate Marcela's famous Cuban *arroz con pollo* and sweet fried plantains called *maduros,* I told my father about Mercy. While I described Bear's story of the Sunshine Bowl, Dad made sure I had water in my glass. Even when his own hand was shaking, he spooned seconds to my plate. It felt good to have someone take care of me.

Dad shook his head, thunderstruck that Donald Hankins was implicated in so many killings, and by the burden he and the members of the Heat carried. He was confounded by the Florida sheriff's attitude. Had Kelly's family kept quiet about the suspects in their son's murder for fear that half the boys in town would be implicated in rape?

I couldn't share the ultimate ironies with him, but he saw his own.

"It's almost like . . . it infected the next generation . . . too," Dad said. "Sins . . . of the fathers."

For a moment, there was sad silence in our house. I thought about T.D. Jackson's Super Bowl ring, and about how even when families move on, their stories follow them. I wondered how many untold stories from my family history were alive and well in me.

A timid knock sounded on the front door at ten to seven.

"Must be him!" Dad said, rolling toward the door. Dad had more energy than I did.

Bernard Faison was tall for his age, although he as was the thinnest wrestler I had ever seen. A strong wind would have turned him into a kite. Wiry strength, maybe. Bernard's tux was smooth. Basic black, down to his shirt and tie. He held a corsage in a plastic container tightly with both hands, as if it might jump free. I couldn't place his ethnicity: His skin was brown, but his eyes looked Asiatic. Like Chela, he was a mixture—and unless bookworms with glasses were more popular now than when I'd been in school, Faison's brains made him an outcast, too.

"Hey, Bernard," I said, reaching for a handshake.

"Mr. Hardwick," he said, and pumped my hand. His hand was broad and firm. He reached for Dad's. "Captain."

A boy with some manners might be a boy with some sense. Dad used to say something like that when I was a kid, and I finally understood what he'd meant.

Bernard was fascinated by the bruises on my face, but he didn't dare ask. He only fidgeted, losing some of his composure. He hadn't learned to stand at his full height yet; I might have to take him aside and teach him to stop worrying about being taller than anyone else.

"You be . . . a gentleman," Dad told Bernard.

"Yessir," Bernard said, glancing down at Dad in his chair, and his face seemed to go waxen. I gave a start when I saw the butt of Dad's gun peeking out from the blanket on his lap. Faison had seen Susie, too. I slapped Dad's shoulder and covered up the gun.

Bernard's shocked expression didn't change after my apologetic shrug. Dad had made the impression he wanted to make. I felt sorry for the kid, even as I tried not to smile.

"Here she comes!" Marcela called from upstairs. "Cameras ready, gentlemen!"

Dad had his old Polaroid hanging around his neck, the same one he'd used at the beach when I was a kid, and I grabbed my digital camera from the television cabinet. "Give me two seconds," I said, turning on the camera and aiming toward the stairs.

"Will you *please* stop making such a big deal?" Chela's voice came from upstairs. "God, you guys are so embarrassing . . ."

Her shadow moved down the stairs first; and then Chela appeared.

Maybe it was the track lighting, or because the day we'd been shopping seemed like a year ago. Mostly, it was Chela's haircut— she'd chopped her hair much shorter while I was gone, a more playful style that reminded me of Janiece's. For an instant, the sick feeling in my stomach came back, as surely as if I were still tied in that tobacco barn. But then I saw the glow on Chela's face as she walked down my stairs in a dress that made her look priceless. I had never seen such a wide smile. Mercy disappeared into its happy depths.

My chest floated.

Bernard needed help popping his eyes back into their sockets. I reminded him to give Chela her corsage, and took a photo while he pinned it. Dad, Marcela, and I filled the room with flashes. For a night anyway, Chela was a superstar, a memory no one could take away.

Chela wasn't going to turn into Janiece. We had gotten to her in time.

"Shit, Ten, what happened to your face?" Chela said, finally noticing me in the flurry.

Dad clucked, and Chela pressed her hand over her mouth. No cussing in the house.

"Long story," I said. "We'll talk about it tomorrow. Go have a good time."

"Are you okay?" The concern in her doelike eyes was exaggerated by her makeup.

"Much better now." I smiled at Chela. "You're beautiful, kid."

I am? Her eyes shone in a way that melted my heart.

"Let me get Chela and Bernard together," Marcela said, waving her camera.

"Hurry, guys," I said. "The limo's waiting."

"That's *our* limo outside?" Bernard said, gazing at me with questions. He looked dazed.

"I told you he's the coolest dad in the world," Chela said.

THIRTY

SUNDAY, NOVEMBER 2

Evangeline Jackson answered the phone when I called first thing in the morning, and she asked me to come to the house at two. "Emory will be at a fund-raiser," she said, her voice hushed. "I want us to be alone."

I felt a twinge of disappointment that I wouldn't see Melanie, but I knew that was best too. Melanie wasn't the woman I was missing; she was just closer, easier to touch. April and I each had one round in phone tag, so I hadn't talked to her since my return from Mercy. It was my turn to try, but her voice was more bittersweet with every call; she was a retreating silhouette.

At her door, T.D. Jackson's mother was dressed in a somber gray sweater and long black skirt, her hair in a perfect bun. Standing so close to her, I realized how tiny her frame was. I hadn't noticed so much when I saw her in the garden, but I towered over her.

"I tried to talk him into canceling his commitments this month, but Emory never can back out," she said, inviting me into her house. "He can't walk away."

We sat in the living room, among the flower arrangements that hadn't yet wilted, well wishes from all over the globe. The room was filled with a sickly-sweet scent. T.D. Jackson's high school photograph stared at us from an easel, poster-sized. I studied T.D.'s facial features—especially his oddly colored eyes. I hadn't noticed before that T.D.'s skin was fairer than either of his parents'.

She sat expectantly, so I pulled out the ring box. I set it on the table in front of Evangeline Jackson. She stared at the box, frozen. She didn't move to open it. Her cheeks quivered as fat tears rolled down. She looked like she wanted to run out of the room. Her face was horrified, confused, broken.

"You had it . . . the whole time?"

I shook my head.

"Then . . . who?"

"Wallace Rubens died the day before yesterday. In Mercy. Heart attack."

Mrs. Jackson's eyes widened with a gasp so deep that it sounded like a death rattle. She hadn't known Bear Rubens was dead. She hadn't expected to hear his name.

"I'm sorry," I said. Open boxes of Kleenex sat everywhere, and I offered her one. She held the tissue to her face, almost as if to hide herself. Her eyes were mad with questions. "He asked me to return it to you."

Evangeline Jackson let out a wail from deep in her belly. It was the deepest pain I'd ever heard from the lips of someone who wasn't dying. It was the sound of lost love, regrets, and more. It was the sound of the swamp.

She took a pained breath, meeting my eyes again.

"He asked me to tell you he loved you." I couldn't remember if

Rubens had said those words, but I knew he felt them. She looked like she needed to hear it.

"Wallace Rubens," she said through her sobs, shaking her head. "That man would do anything for me. *Anything.*"

"Even go to the library," I said gently. "He told me. The five of you were inseparable. You and the Heat."

Bird's eyes surrendered, assumed I knew everything. Almost. I understood the separate bedrooms. Emory and Evangeline Jackson had only married because of duty, not love. Emory Jackson soothed his guilt over a horrible night when he let his friends down—and Bird tried to love the son that reminded her of a night of screaming horror.

"He told you."

I nodded.

More confusion and grief. She crossed her chest with her arms as if she were naked.

"I'm the first he ever told," he said. "He was dying."

Evangeline shook her head. "So . . . he took the ring from T.D.'s study? That's why the police never came?"

A cool wind blew through my chest. The last, missing piece.

"I wondered why nobody found it," Evangeline Jackson said, voice filled with wonder. "I left it on his desk, in plain sight. I never planned to hide. I never planned to deny it. But nobody asked. Not a single person—not even you."

"Why?" I asked, knowing there could be no healing answer.

"It was his eyes," she said in a hoarse whisper that dragged the floor. "Every time I looked in T.D.'s eyes, I saw *them*. I tried so hard not to, but I always did. And then it was like he turned out . . . warped already. Just like *them*. When he killed Chantelle and that poor boy, I knew that history was repeating itself." The words spilled from her mouth now, a torrent. "I had to do it. I was the only one who could make sure he wouldn't hurt Maya and Tommy. I had to be *sure*."

Evangeline Jackson told me how she'd complained about a migraine after Sunday dinner, so no one had disturbed her after she closed her door. She snuck out of her room after her husband retired to his, and she'd left her property through the back garden fence. She had driven away undetected and let herself into T.D.'s house with her key.

"I didn't drive there with an intention to hurt him," she said. "That's not how it happened. I was just desperate to get through to him, not to coddle him like Emory did. To make him understand that he couldn't go on the way he was, that he could be a better man. I called Wallace because he was the only one I could talk to in my worst moments." Her eyes were red-rimmed defiance. "My soul mate. I don't know if a man like you could understand something like that."

"Probably not," I said, voice low and soft.

"I asked him what kind of woman would wish her own son dead." At that, she crumpled where she sat, sobbing. "Wallace never told me he was in town. It was his cell phone. He just told me to lie down. 'Don't lift anything you can't carry, Bird,' he said. But by then I was already parked behind T.D.'s house. I got off the phone and let myself in. T.D. was *so* annoyed when I showed up. Asked me if I knew what time it was. Said he was about to go to bed. When I told him Maya said he'd hit her, he called Maya a liar. We were arguing in his study. I knew he kept his gun in his drawer. The gun ended up in my hands. I was so startled when it went off, I yelled out."

She paused, eyes far away. "I watched myself do it. For the longest time, I just stood there. Then I left the ring T.D. gave me and did what Wallace said. I went home to bed. I thought someone would ask me about the ring from the very first, but no one ever did. I thought Emory had it . . . maybe the police had taken it to protect him. It's been a sword of Damocles, Mr. Hardwick. Hanging over my head, waiting to fall." The edge of a sad, sick little smile twitched at the edges of her mouth.

When Rubens arrived at T.D.'s house and found T.D. dead, he altered the scene to cover up her crime. Took the ring. Fired the gun again, pressing T.D.'s dead finger on the trigger. *That's how T.D. ended up with gunshot residue on his fingers. That's why there's a hole in the wall.*

And that was why Evangeline Jackson sat before me like a person shattered in two. I wondered how she had kept her sanity. Or had she? She looked like a woman who had buried her heart somewhere out in a Florida swamp—but was she a danger to her husband or her grandchildren? How could I turn her in? But how could I let her stay free?

"What happens now?" she said, her eyes glimmering with anxiety.

My eyelids felt grainy and leaden. What could be done for Evangeline Jackson now?

"My father always starts with prayer," I said.

She nodded. She already knew that about my father.

"Professional help?" I went on. "I know people it's worked for. Beyond that, I don't have any answers, Mrs. Jackson. On a good day, I ask the right questions. Best I can do."

"What kind of person am I?" she said, beseeching me; the same question she said she asked Wallace Rubens the night T.D. died. *"What am I?"*

A violent gang rape. A hasty marriage with a guilt-ridden bridegroom. Their honeymoon must have been a riot. A son she couldn't love—who grew up to be a murderer. How much of T.D.'s rage had taken root in the gaps left by his parents' missing love? I wouldn't want to be inside Evangeline Jackson's head when the lights go out at night.

" 'All have sinned and fallen short of the glory of God,' " I said. "I've got no stones to cast. Find a way to heal. You'll never be able to really love those grandkids if you can't heal. Love yourself somehow. I think there's been enough damage, don't you?"

"Please don't tell Emory," she whispered.

"He might understand if you told the truth," I said. "But I'll leave that up to you."

I'll never forget the relief on her face.

I didn't mind the secret. If I could walk away from the secrets in Mercy, I could walk away from Evangeline Jackson's. I doubted that Emory Jackson wanted to know that his wife had killed the man he raised as his own son. Or the grandkids to know that Gramma blew Daddy's brains out. I was sorry I knew the whole sick, sad business myself.

I don't know if it was the codeine or other residual drugs in my system, but my dreams that night were vivid and troubling. They reminded me of the dreams I had when I was a kid, as if time had stood still.

In the dream, I was back in the swamp. It was nearly dark. I saw flashbulbs under the trees. Chela and Bernard Faison were posing for pictures in front of a swarm of paparazzi. Instead of wearing her homecoming dress, Chela was wearing a pink piggy dress from Pig'n-a-Poke. Something large and monstrous began moving toward them through the swarm of photographers.

In a blink, Chela and Bernard were gone. Instead, they had turned into Wallace Rubens and Evangeline Jackson, their faces decades younger. They were dressed for a wedding, holding hands as they fled through the swamp. A pack of dogs pursued them. The swamp they ran through was littered with dead bodies lying facedown in the muck.

I woke up in a cold sweat, practically panting. I expected to find myself in the tobacco barn. I could even *smell* the barn, and Rubens's hand-rolled cigarettes.

But I was in my own bed, without any dogs. I didn't sleep the rest of the night.

Instead, I went down to my screening room and composed a letter on my computer. I'd planned to write the letter in the morning, but I couldn't wait:

To Senator Donald Hankins—

I am sorry for the loss of your friend Wallace Rubens, which you have heard about by now. Before he died, Rubens confessed to me that you were personally or peripherally involved in two killings, Lewis Kelly in 1967 and Chad Ebersole in 1999. Needless to say, this information has convinced me that you are unfit to run for the office of governor in the state of California. Please stop all talk of a campaign in 2010, or I will not hesitate to go public with the information that has been related to me.

You will retire from your current senate seat within thirty days, and you will not seek public office again. I will not contact you further unless you fail to meet these very simple demands.

Prison couldn't be worse than losing your daughter, so I won't turn you in otherwise—but the voters deserve leaders who haven't lost their way.

I didn't sign the letter although I knew he might guess it was from me.

I drove to the post office to put it in the mail that same night.

But I still couldn't go back to sleep.

THIRTY-ONE

Len called before noon, so I knew he had news. I couldn't remember the last time he'd called on a Monday, period. I was at the top of his priority list.

"We're in play with Lynda Jewell," Len said. "I don't know who your lawyer is, but she's a tigress. Jewell wants to settle. Your lawyer found a corroborating witness at the hotel—a housekeeper. Jewell's terrified of bad publicity. Her lawyer's already offering five hundred. I told her to call back when she's up to a million. I say we'll have a settlement by Friday."

I smiled. There's nothing like good news from your agent. A million dollars was a lot of money for a little fondling in a hotel suite. To paraphrase an old joke, I know what I am. Now we were just haggling over the price.

"Great, Len, but it's not about the money," I said. "I'll take it. But I want more. She owes me a copy of that script. Tell her I want an audition. That's what she promised me."

"Ten, that's nuts. You think you'd have *any* shot at getting cast, given your situation with Jewell? Even if the casting director were suicidal enough, you wouldn't want this project now. I say hold out for a mil."

"An audition," I said. "For Troy, or any other part. And tell my lawyer thanks."

"Is she as hot as she sounds on the phone?" Len said, his breathing heavier.

"Engaged."

"Too bad. Where are you? I can barely hear you."

I was in LAX's Tom Bradley International Terminal. The woman's voice announcing the boarding for my flight on the loudspeaker above me was deafening.

"I'm taking a quick trip out of town. I'll be back in about a week." My trip to Mercy had taught me that my family could survive a few days without me, and I'd realized as I lay awake in my bed that I had one more place to go.

"Let's at least wait to see Jewell's final offer . . ." Len said, his final pitch.

"I'm an actor, Len," I said. "I want a chance to show people who I am."

Len sighed. I was ignoring sterling advice yet again, but he was used to it. "You're killing me, Ten," he said. "Have a good trip."

"We'll see."

Whether or not I had a good trip would depend on April.

I'd splurged and bought a business-class ticket to Johannesburg, in hopes that I might get some sleep on the way—without dreams about the swamp, this time. Sometime during the thirty hours of flight time, I hoped I could think of the right thing to say to April.

Len's call had come just in time. Lynda Jewell was part of the reason April didn't think she wanted to be with me anymore, and maybe Jewell's offer would make a difference. Yes, I'd been responsible for my past, and for my own actions—but Jewell's willingness to pay meant she was admitting she'd been wrong.

Dream on. It won't be that simple, my Evil Voice said.

While I sat in my wide seat in the last few minutes before the plane left the gate, I quickly checked my phone for the email that had accumulated while I was in Mercy. I'd missed one, and it caught my eye: A FAVOR FROM AN OLD FRIEND.

I expected the note to be from Mother, about the limo. But it wasn't. I didn't know the user, FIDO26@QUICKMAIL.COM.

There was a chance it wasn't spam. I bit, clicking.

Hey, Ten—

Long time no see.

I'm sorry to pop into your mailbox unannounced, but I seem to have done a bad thing. You should know about it. You may recognize the man in the attached photos. I know it was naughty, but I intercepted them on the way to Chela's secret account, one you don't know about. Don't worry: She hasn't used it in quite a while, he's somewhat frantic about that.

Was it naughty of me to send the pictures to his wife, with an exhaustive history of their "relationship"? I told her to ask about Bomb346@Quickmail.com. You might ask Chela about that account, too. On the other hand, the musician is getting desperate. I suspect Mr. and Mrs. Cradlerobber will be having a heart-to-heart right about now. Your problem is probably over, but let me know.

What do I want in return, you may ask? Only a smile.

Who am I? Wouldn't you like to know . . . ?

—A Friend Indeed

I clicked on the attachment, and the internet went triple-X. The bearded musician was full frontal, aroused, unblessed, just a pudgy predator floating filth to a sixteen-year-old girl. Oh yes, I wanted to be a fly on the wall.

But who had done this? *"A Friend Indeed"*? I didn't know what, but I sensed that some fascinating game was about to begin.

The future was looking bright.

I had to turn off my phone for takeoff, so I didn't have the chance to write a note back to my mystery friend. Someone was watching over me. Or just watching me, period.

My life was never boring. If April wanted boring, she'd been right to leave me behind.

Maybe we were about to learn that April made the right decision. Or maybe we would learn something we didn't expect. It didn't matter. I just wanted to take April out to dinner and look into her eyes. I wasn't going to live the rest of my life like Wallace Rubens and Evangeline Jackson, wishing I'd followed my heart's choice. Dreams deferred explode.

If April and I had a chance, I wanted to know. If we didn't, I wanted to know.

New daylight filled my window. My plane rumbled, gathered its energies, and leaped off the runway, embracing the sky.

ACKNOWLEDGMENTS

TANANARIVE DUE

EVERY NOVEL IS BOTH A SCHOOLHOUSE AND A PLAYGROUND, and this one is no different. First, I want to thank the readers and critics who supported *Casanegra*. I know some folks out there wondered if we were "for real," so thank you for taking a chance on us. Where would I be without readers who were willing to try something new?

Thank you to my husband, Steven Barnes, who opens new universes of possibilities in my life at every conceivable turn. And trust me—book research has never been so much fun. (How can you know if a scene works until you act it out? I encourage you to try out some of the scenes for yourselves. Why should the authors have all the fun?) Somehow, we knew each other almost on sight when we met at that writer's conference in Atlanta in 1997.

Thank you to my family at Atria Books: Malaika Adero, who is an editor, a friend, and an inspiration. Krishan Trotman, for her patience and everlasting good spirits. Christine Saunders, who makes sure our voices are heard. And to Judith Curr, who is not only a terrific publisher, but who invited us to that amazing party at Prince's house. Enough said.

Thanks to my agents, John Hawkins of John Hawkins & Associates and Michael Prevett of The Gotham Group. Thank you to Darryl Miller, a friend, writer, and advance reader who gives us his all every time. Thank you to my favorite mystery writers: Walter Mosley. Michael Connelly. Paula L. Woods. Other writers are always the best teachers, and I know I still have much to learn.

And thanks to Blair Underwood, who is simply a singularity. When the three of us sit together for those long brunches to plan poor Tennyson's fate, we are of one mind and heart. It is an amazing process. I'm so thrilled that Blair's talents are being more fully appreciated each day. Thank you for your friendship.

I have always believed that "a spoonful of sugar helps the medicine go down," as Mary Poppins said. The events depicted in this novel are fictitious, but *In the Night of the Heat* is no different. Some stories are not told often enough, and I feel privileged to have the opportunity to remind readers that some scars take generations to heal.

I am so grateful to my parents, Patricia Stephens Due and John Due, for their example in civil rights and community activism . . . and for the painful stories they repeated so that I would never forget—even in the relative comfort of the world they helped carve for me, my son, and my stepdaughter. Not everyone survived the 1960s . . . sometimes for acts as small as registering others to vote. There are not words enough to thank the foot soldiers, black and white, who died—or sacrificed their hearts—on our domestic battlefields so that all of us might enjoy the promise of our Constitution. (Please vote in November!)

Thanks to my sisters, Johnita and Lydia, for carrying the torch in their own ways.

Thank you to my son, Jason, and my stepdaughter, Nicki, for showing me the face of the future.

Thank you to God, for the wonders that unfold before our eyes each day.

STEVEN BARNES

I CANNOT WRITE ACKNOWLEDGMENTS without thanking P., who trusted me with a truly terrible tale of a hideous injustice that has yet to be set straight. I've carried that truth with me for more than ten years and am grateful for the chance to vent my rage and frustration, even in literary form.

On a happier note, I'd like to thank my Silat instructor and the creator of the WAR system of martial arts, Guru Cliff Stewart, Close Protection Specialist, who opened my eyes about the true nature of the bodyguard profession. Also Jonathan Westover, friend and former agent, who shared stories of Hollywood's seamier side.

Eleanor Wood, my wonderful literary agent, who has had my back for two decades now. And Wesley Snipes for a terrific workout, and critical info on stunt mishaps.

A posthumous shout-out goes to John D. MacDonald, creator of the great Travis McGee adventure novels, who showed everyone how it's really done.

To Blair Underwood, whose casual elegance and charm are the external trappings of a tempered mind and a mighty heart. From day one, it's been an honor.

To my daughter, Nicki, who has tolerated her daddy's physical and emotional absences far too often and, despite my many failings as a father, has matured into a delightful young woman. And my son,

Jason, who every day reminds me that the lessons learned in childhood are with us forever.

My wife, Tananarive Due, the love of my life. I cannot believe how blessed I was to find you. What a tiny window of opportunity we had to make our decision! To this day I'm not sure what miracle gave us both the clarity to see the future open before us, and the courage to act while there was time. You are everything I never knew I wanted.

And you're right, Babe: Some research is definitely more fun than others.

The adventures of Tennyson Hardwick have a special significance for me. While written as novels, in my mind they are meta-movies, stories revolving around the world of Hollywood, but specifically calculated to present images Hollywood will not give us—for the simple reason that non-white males can't have sex in a film without hurting its box office.

Don't believe me? Look at the IMDb database, at every film that has earned more than $100 million. About 12 percent of them star non-white males. About 23 percent of them have love scenes, even if PG-13 in nature. Out of those 350 films that have earned more than $100 million, can you guess how many both star non-white males and have sex?

As of July 1, 2008, just one: *Crouching Tiger, Hidden Dragon*.

Not one single black man can be an erotic human being, and be fully accepted by the American audience. Will Smith can't do it. Neither can Denzel, or Eddie, or anyone else. Black *women* can . . . but only if they bed down with white men. It's one of the big, open, nasty secrets of this industry. Anyone who thinks this a statistical fluke hasn't been paying attention. It will change one day, I have no doubt. But until then, Tananarive, Blair, and I are creating the movies Hollywood won't make. Getting it done, in other words, By Any Means Necessary.

BLAIR UNDERWOOD

TENNYSON LIVES TO FIGHT, live, breathe, and love another day only because the first installment of the life and times of Tennyson Hardwick, officially *Casanegra*, was embraced by so many of you now reading these words.

When Steven Barnes, Tananarive Due, and I embarked upon this journey of creation and exploration, we were acutely aware that if the initial story did not leap from the pages, then the subsequent adventures that we only dreamed of would never come to pass. This sequel, *In the Night of the Heat*, represents the launch of an exciting and new detective series unique in its specificity of character and the emotional odyssey traversed by its central figure, Tennyson Hardwick.

It continues to be inspiring and humbling to work with such gifted novelists as Steven and Tananarive. Their genius of craft is surpassed only by their depth of spirit and profound sense of humanity. I am truly honored to know you both, and I thank you for allowing me to become more proficient in the "literary" art of storytelling while looking through your refined prism.

To Krishan Trotman, Christine Saunders, and everyone at Atria Books/Simon and Schuster, I believe you have completely spoiled me because you have been absolutely supportive and enthusiastic about this series from the very beginning. Judith Curr, when I grow up, I want to be just like you—calm, collected, and brilliant while quietly moving mountains and making a difference in the lives of many. You've certainly done that for me. Thank you for believing in me and for being my publisher again and again.

Malaika Adero, thank you so much for your patience and encouragement each step of the way. Every author should have an editor as amazing and receptive as you. I'll never forget your comments after reading the first "steamy" draft of *In Night the of the Heat*. Suffice it to say, "I don't smoke either."

Desiree, I honor you as my bride and the life force that keeps our family and household perpetually flowing smoothly. No small feat. I love you and am eternally grateful that our paths crossed so many years ago because, "I sho like havin' you around, girl."

Mom and Dad, Col. (Ret.) Frank and Marilyn Underwood, I'll never be able to repay you for instilling in us the ability to dream. Such a simplistic concept but often abandoned when adulthood and responsibility inevitably engulf us. This book and everything in the creative arts, as well as life, begins with a dream. A dream propelled by action and cultivated by faith gives birth to new realities and new beginnings. This book, as well as our country (in the year of our Lord 2008), represent new beginnings. Thank you both for living lives that personify the "audacity of hope."

Cousin Lynne Andrews, your exuberant spirit is always a ray of sunshine in our home. So much of what you do enables me to have the freedom to create and do what I do. I thank you for that.

My Seeds, Paris, Brielle, and Blake, I thank God for you every day. Though you won't and shouldn't read this book for years to come, I hope that witnessing this novel coming to fruition resonates as evidence that dreams DO come true. Never forget, "imagination is intelligence . . . having fun!"

Frank, Marlo, Jackson, Mellisa, Tammy, Kelly, Khloe, Kamden, Owen, Carter, Austin, friends and family too many to name, you influence and inspire me more than you know. Thank you for being such a critical part of my life and who I am.

Ron West, my manager, who would have thought that we'd be releasing yet another novel? Go figure. When others, I'm sure, laughed and didn't take me seriously, you never faltered. Thanks for always believing in a brotha.

Lydia Wills, yes, you are still the personification of "cool" and the rest of us are just taking notes. You constantly amaze me with your business savvy and discerning intuition. Thank you for taking this journey with me.

To everyone at the Paradigm Talent agency as well as Patti Felker, Mark Wetzstein, and Bruce Gellman, many thanks for being a constant source of support and motivation.

Lee Wallman, you can open your eyes now that you've read the last chapter! I feel absolutely blessed to have you as such an integral part of my life and career. I am immensely grateful for all of the hard work that you do on my behalf.

Here's to New Beginnings and the audacity to believe that we can all be better and do better!